THE
COLDWATER HAUNTING

MICHAEL RICHAN

THE COLDWATER HAUNTING

DANTULL

THE COLDWATER HAUNTING

ISBN-13: 978-1-09023-814-6

Published by Dantull (150919149)

First printing: April 2019

By The Author

THE RIVER SERIES

The Bank of the River

Residual

A Haunting in Oregon

Ghosts of Our Fathers

Eximere

The Suicide Forest

Devil's Throat

The Diablo Horror

The Haunting at
Grays Harbor

It Walks at Night

The Cycle of the Shen

A Christmas Haunting
at Point No Point

The Port of Missing Souls

The Haunting of
Johansen House

Evocation

THE DARK RIVER SERIES

The Dark River: A

The Blood Gardener

Capricorn

THE DOWNWINDERS SERIES

Blood Oath, Blood River

The Impossible Coin

The Graves of
Plague Canyon

The Blackham
Mansion Haunting

The Massacre Mechanism

The Nightmares
of Quiet Grove

Descent Into Hell Street

———————

The Haunting of
Pitmon House

The Haunting of
Waverly Hall

A Haunting in Wisconsin

———————

The School of Revenge

———————

Slaughter, Idaho

———————

The Coldwater Haunting

All three series share characters and there is some plot crossover.
They can be read in order within each series, or, for a
Suggested Reading Order, see the back of the book.

For Kristina,
who knew it was haunted

Chapter One

"Ohhh…that's not good," said the man wearing overalls.

Ron stepped back from the round opening in the ground, its plastic green cover removed and pulled to the side. He wasn't sure what he expected to see, but this wasn't it: rising from the hole was a domed pillow, streaked brown and white. It was speckled with bubbles.

"It's marshmallowing," another man in overalls diagnosed. He stood up straight as he said it, stretching his back, compensating for the time he'd spent removing screws from the cover.

Ron looked up, waiting for more. "Yup," the man finally offered. "Not supposed to look like that."

Ron was frustrated. He was a city dweller most of his life; septic systems were completely foreign to him. He understood how they worked in theory, but not in real life. Nothing he read on the internet mentioned anything about marshmallowing.

The other man from McLean Septic Pumping slid the green cover back into place.

"Look, I've never had a septic system before," Ron said to the first, "so I need you to educate me a little. Exactly how bad is it?"

"No poopy," the man replied, as his co-worker inserted long silver screws into the cover.

"No poopy?" Ron repeated. "I've been living here a week."

"And you've been using it?"

Ron shrugged. "Yeah."

"I'm surprised it's not backed up."

"Nope. Every toilet flushes fine."

"Huh," the man grunted. "Well, I'd be careful about that until we can get it pumped."

"When will that be?"

"Not today."

Ron felt anxious again. He wasn't going to drive into town every time he needed to shit. He looked up at the woods surrounding the house, and knew exploring the thick blackberry bushes for a spot to dig a hole wasn't an option, either.

"Why not today?" Ron asked.

"Booked," the man replied. He picked up a long metal rod and began sticking it into the bramble, poking the ground beyond the thorny bushes. "You've got a 2630; that means there's two more covers, just like that one. They gotta be in here somewhere."

The rod struck something other than ground, making a scraping noise. "There's one of 'em," the man said. "Other one's probably behind it, deeper in." He turned to face Ron. "I'll have to bring a chainsaw and clear a path to them. And of course we got to bring up the truck. It's busy today. I'll get you on the schedule."

The two men left the side of the house, returning to the pickup truck they arrived in. Ron wondered how he might convince them to bring the pumping truck earlier rather than later. "I've got a chainsaw," he offered. "I'll make sure it's clear within the hour."

"You've got some issues with the electronics, too," the man said as he slipped into the truck. "You've got an alarm going. We don't do electronics, but I know someone who does. I could give them a call if you want."

"What do the electronics do?" Ron asked. "I thought the...stuff...just moved on out to the leach field."

"You've got at least two pumps," the man replied. "And probably a sand pit, somewhere out that way." He extended a piece of paper to Ron through the truck's window. Ron took it and oriented it; it was a hand-drawn map of his yard.

"That's your entire system," the man replied. "We just opened the tanks by the house. See them?"

Ron studied the crudely drawn map. "Yeah."

"We'll come back and pump out those tanks," he replied, starting up the vehicle. "I'll get you on the schedule."

"Do I need to be here when you do it?"

"Nah. Usually no one's here. Usually we pump them while the house is on the market. But this was a foreclosure, you said?"

"Yeah," Ron replied.

"Banks don't do shit."

Ron smiled at the pun; he felt his frustration ease a little as he decided he liked the guy. Although Ron had bought several houses in his lifetime, he'd never purchased a foreclosure, so he was unprepared for the take-it-or-leave-it approach that a bank employed. Every vendor he'd spoken with in the past few days, however, seemed well versed in how banks behaved. "They sure don't," he agreed.

"I'll get you on the schedule," the man repeated, placing the truck in gear. "And I'll have the electronics guy give you a call."

"Any way you could pump it this week?"

"It'll be this week. Not sure what day yet."

"Thanks," Ron replied, and watched as the man backed the truck out into the turnaround and disappeared up the tiny dirt road of his driveway, quickly becoming blocked from sight by the trees.

Ron loved that tiny dirt road, and for a moment he stopped to appreciate it. It was one of the main reasons he bought the property. He remembered the first time he drove down it, trying to find the house; it seemed to go on forever, with overgrown weeds jutting out into the path, scraping against the side of his car. The road finally came to an end, and a small clearing appeared with the majestic house smack in the middle. It seemed like a jewel hidden in a carved-out alcove, surrounded by a small yard, ringed by thick blackberry bushes and trees, hiding in the woods – waiting for him.

Perfect, he thought. *Just what I want. Quiet. Seclusion. That road is a dead end; no one will come up it. I'll put up a sign to that effect, back where it splits off from the small lane at the next closest house.*

Twenty-eight acres between me and them, he thought, feeling lucky. Turning around, he saw nothing but green, and now that the septic guy's truck was far enough away, not a single sound, either.

Heaven.

He looked at the house. Its tall, two-story facade rose grandly, dark grey paint peeling from its siding, its white trim weathered and darker than it should be. The bay windows on the second floor looked dim; in fact, as he scanned its surface, he liked that he couldn't see into the house through any of them. The realtor mentioned that there had been a break-in during the time the house sat vacant, so he wasn't interested in advertising anything. Wherever he had lived he always tried to make his home look respectable and inhabited, but not enticing.

I should come out here at night and see how things look when it's dark, with the lights on inside, he thought.

Then he reconsidered. The sounds he heard the past few nights made him wonder exactly what was in the forest that surrounded his home.

Gun first, he thought, remembering his resolution to buy a weapon, made the night before at 3 AM.

- - -

"No, Ron, I can't," came Elenore's voice through the phone. "This Europe thing isn't an option. Ira was very clear about who was going and who wasn't."

Ron sighed. "It's just..." He stopped himself, knowing that pleading with her was a bad move.

It had been hard enough to convince Elenore to buy the house; things between them had been rough the past year, and pressuring her about her work wasn't going to make her any happier about it.

After months of fighting, the new house had become an awkward focal point for their differences. The way each of them responded to the property couldn't have been more opposite. Ron remembered being excited when they found it, on a hunting expedition without their realtor. Elenore asked him to turn the car around as they navigated the long, tiny road Ron found, but Ron protested that there was nowhere to perform the turn, and he was right; they were a quarter mile in, and only the two skinny ruts ahead of them were an option, given he had no intention of backing out that far. He kept going, and she kept suggesting they stop.

"It's got to be up ahead," Ron said. "I'll turn around once we find it."

"We don't know what's ahead," she replied. "This road might go on for miles."

"The blue dot is right there," he nodded at the phone she held.

"It took us to the wrong place ten minutes ago! It might not be here at all!"

"It has to be. Look at the pictures on the listing. It's *some*where. Just gotta…"

And with that, the road descended slightly and made a left turn…and the clearing appeared.

"Oh!" Elenore exclaimed. "It's…huge."

Ron smiled. He knew he liked it even before he brought the car to a standstill on the cement driveway in front of the garage. He was out of the car well before her, walking up to its large front door.

"We shouldn't poke around without the realtor," Elenore called, stepping out of the car.

"No one's here," Ron said, peering through the engraved glass in the door.

"Does it have a lockbox?"

Ron checked the handle, but it had been removed, leaving a large round hole. Above it was a combination lock that had been roughly attached where the deadbolt belonged. "No, some other kind of lock," he called back.

He stepped away from the door until he was out from under the porch. Bay windows to his left offered a view inside. He placed his hands against the side of his head to shield the sunlight and glanced in.

It was a small square room. Windowed double doors led out of it to the right, and a hexagonal window was perched high on the left. The floor looked like old hardwood, but was difficult to make out.

The next bay window to his left offered the same view, but when he reached the third, he could see through the room's windowed doors to a grand staircase beyond. It was immediately intriguing.

He continued walking, reaching the north side of the house. Before he turned the corner, he glanced back at the car; Elenore was still there, standing by the door.

"Aren't you going to check it out?" he called.

"I'm fine," she replied.

"I'm going around back." He turned, irritated. She was either done with house hunting for the day, or not impressed enough with the mansion in front of her to even give it a walk-around. It wasn't the first house where their expectations and reactions didn't sync, but it chapped him nonetheless.

Things with Elenore had reached a peak recently. He suspected she was resentful of their move, even though she insisted she wasn't. He knew she liked living in Portland more than he did. When he first presented the idea of taking advantage of the equity in their suburban home to move out into the country, she wasn't receptive, but he wore her down over time. Wearing her down had come with costs.

He'd been raised in the country, and felt a yearning to return to it the older he became. He explored properties online after they adopted Robbie, and a local shooting turned his yearning into a sharply focused goal. He hated the school Robbie attended in Portland, and was determined to find one more like the one he experienced when he was young; small and able to spend time on learning and fun and innocent pastimes instead of active shooter drills.

And while Robbie had been the galvanizing force that made him start hunting, it wasn't as though he didn't have a list of things he wanted changed about his living situation. Neighbors were his biggest complaint. He didn't want any. He wanted to be as far away from a next-door house as he could get. No more dogs left to bark all day, music and screams from drunken pool parties, or acrid smoke from a neighbor who invested in every loud outdoor gadget, running their goddamn new fire pit on every hot night that required open windows.

What I want is fifty acres, he remembered thinking, *with a house right in the middle of it. Maximum buffer. Keep all the people away.*

Elenore didn't share his passion. Whereas he was happy with the idea of a long drive into town for groceries, she wanted to be in a neighborhood where they would deliver. He had spent almost three decades in the city and was ready for a change; she said she'd be happy living the rest of her life where they were. When they first started discussing options, he showed her properties in the middle of nowhere; she'd suggest condos on the waterfront, even closer to the heart of downtown than they already were.

To keep her happy, he agreed to tour some of the condos if she'd look at country homes. The house they were living in sold as their search continued. Now they were cash-rich, living in a short term apartment still in the city. He was anxious to find a place, but every time they scheduled an excursion, she seemed to lose enthusiasm just before they left, and he felt like he had to drag her along.

He rounded the corner and looked out over the back yard. It was a large oval of dried grass, ringed by the blackberry bushes they had seen while driving in.

To his surprise, a solitary deer stood in the middle of the grass. It was frozen in place, and for a moment he thought it was made of plastic, an odd, leftover statue from the previous owners. *Looks very lifelike,* he thought, slightly disturbed by how real its glassy eyes appeared in the sunlight, and how close he was to it – not more than ten feet away.

Then its ear twitched slightly, and he realized it was alive.

This is what I'm talking about, he thought, wishing Elenore had come with him so she could see it.

Movement in the bramble caught his eye, and he saw a fawn, half the size of the deer in the center of his yard. It was paused at the entrance to a bear run, looking ready to bolt, awaiting a sign.

He stood still, not wanting to spook them, hoping the moment would last.

The deer slowly lowered its head to a long, thin wildflower, its eyes still on him. It snatched it off and began to chew.

Wow, he thought. In his three decades of city living, he'd never been this close to wildlife.

He continued his walk around the outside of the house. His movement spooked the fawn; it disappeared into the blackberries. The mother moved away, but didn't run; she positioned herself at the back of the yard, continuing to snack on weeds, watching him as he moved.

A giant chimney rose ten or fifteen feet above the steeply angled roofline. The paint on the chimney seemed patchy in spots, as though it hadn't been properly painted in the first place. He knew chimneys had to be built in a certain way to produce draw, but this one seemed strangely tall, beyond what was needed.

Windows lined the back of the house, and he peered into them. A kitchen was there; it looked huge. He was too low to be able to make out the exact layout and the appliances, but the size of it immediately appealed to him; he did most of the cooking, and the kitchen they had in Portland was less than half the size of the one he was looking at now.

Those fixtures gotta go, he thought, observing dated wrought iron pendant lights over a counter.

Around the south side of the house was a door, securely locked, with a small pet door at the bottom. He pushed on the plastic; it swung inward, unhindered. "Not good," he muttered to himself, wondering what animals might have used it.

Looking up, he could see weeds growing out of the rain gutters that surrounded the roofline. *Easy to fix,* he thought. Ahead was a huge, white, twenty-five hundred gallon water tank, sitting next to a six-inch thick metal pipe jutting up from the ground.

Elenore was to his right, still standing next to the car.

"I like it," he said. He turned to her; she was staring at her phone. "You should at least look at it."

"It's too...quiet," she replied, glancing up briefly, then back to the phone.

"That's what I like about it."

"And that road."

"I like that too. People won't want to come down it. No traffic."

"Will it even be passable in the winter?"

"They get very little snow here. And we have a four wheel drive."

"What's with the paint? It's all patchy."

Ron joined her and looked up at the structure. What he saw was a grand facade, a home that someone had designed to look interesting, not flat and boxy like their home in Portland. It was only after looking harder that he saw what she was talking about, a slight variation – almost like a gradient – in the paint along one section of the front. "Paint is easy; we just give it a fresh coat. Look in the windows, at least. We drove all the way out here, you might as well see it."

She walked tentatively to a double set of windows between the front door and the garage and looked inside. He joined her. Ron calculated it to be the room on the other side of the staircase. Through an exit in the back, he could see the cabinets of the kitchen he observed earlier.

"A dining room?" he guessed.

"Maybe."

"Look through these windows on the porch," he suggested. "There's an amazing staircase."

She followed him and pressed her hands against the panes. "Huh," she said.

"Makes me want to see inside. We could give Susan a call."

"I don't know, Ron. This is farther out than I wanted."

"We can at least look at it. I like it enough to want to see the interior. I get a good vibe. A really good vibe."

"I do not."

"Want to see it? Or get a good vibe?"

"Neither," she sighed. "But if you really want to come back with Susan on Wednesday, that's fine."

"You don't like it?"

"Not yet."

He stepped back from the porch, trying to take in the large facade once again. "I do. I think it's great. Ticks a lot of my boxes."

"Well, we'll have to agree to disagree," she replied, returning to the car.

"Looking inside might change your mind."

"Maybe."

Ron took out his phone to snap pictures, circling the house in reverse. He heard the car door close as Elenore sealed herself inside.

He took his time walking back around the property. At first he found himself wanting to delay his return to the car to spite her, to emphasize how serious he was about the house in the face of her lack of enthusiasm. As he took photos and looked in every window, he found his attraction to the building increasing, and he forgot about Elenore completely, losing track of time. He felt himself developing a connection to the house, just like he experienced when he bought their home in Portland years ago. It was the thing that every financial advisor advised against and every realtor fostered – making a purchase based on emotion.

As he rounded the final corner, he saw Elenore in the front seat of the car, waiting. She didn't look happy. He snapped a few more pictures of the front of the house, then joined her.

"What was the point of that?" she asked, frustration in her voice.

"What?"

"I've been sitting here for twenty minutes!"

"I wanted to get a few more photos."

"From every possible fucking angle? What are you doing to do, build a 3D model?"

"I was just checking things out. Looking into each window, trying to get an idea of the layout."

"Which we'll see when we come back with Susan."

"Right."

"It's 2:30," she said. "I have work I need to do."

"I thought you had the day off."

"No, there are a few things I have to finish up tonight. I didn't think this was going to take all day."

"Alright," he replied. "We'll head back."

He started the car, and they returned down the tiny dirt road, the trees and blackberries so dense it almost felt like passing through a tunnel.

Chapter Two

His arm slid under the cold sheet, expecting to land on her soft flesh. Instead it stretched out unimpeded. *Elenore?*

He sat up, at first thinking something was wrong. She wasn't there.

His head felt fuzzy and he raised his hands to it, rubbing against the skin of his face. *Of course she's not here, you idiot,* he thought. *Just like last night, and the night before. She won't be here for weeks still.* He turned to his nightstand; the clock read 3:07.

Lie back down. It's the middle of the night. Don't think about anything, you'll just keep yourself up. Shut down and sleep.

His head hit the pillow. He was about to close his eyes, but a new feeling of unease washed over him, leaving a residue of panic, a sense that he must do something to defend himself.

He turned his head to the right. Large windows near the bed, not yet covered by blinds or drapes – blinds were number one hundred and twenty-three on the to-do list – offered a view to the east. From the master bedroom on the second floor he could see stars out the window, the tops of the trees that surrounded the property, and, if he raised himself from his prone position, through a small notch in those trees, a view of the lights of McLean in the distance. Immediately outside the window was an uncovered deck, still in need of a power wash. A crack in the outer pane of the double-pane windows interrupted and altered the view; *item number one hundred and seventy*, he thought, feeling that the consideration of tasks, normally counterproductive to sleep, might now be a good idea, a way to distract him from the anxiousness itching over his body.

He looked out the window, waiting. It was still and dark, but he kept watching, refusing to close his eyes. *Something's outside. There's something – or someone – out there.* It wasn't because of what he'd seen or heard, or thought he heard – it was merely an impression that wouldn't shake.

He waited for something to appear, to make its presence known. The longer he waited, the more afraid he became, sure he would see a shift in the shadows and his fear would be confirmed. As the minutes ticked by, he convinced himself he was being stupid. Nothing appeared. Only the dark outline of the side of the house was there, the starry sky, and slightly shifting trees in the distance.

He closed his eyes, trying to force himself back to sleep. Turning over in bed, he situated himself in a cold spot and breathed slowly, wanting to calm down and find a way back to slumber.

Thump.

He sat up. It sounded as though someone directly above him had dropped something on the floor. He looked up, unsure what he might see; the pale, textured ceiling was silent above him, offering no clue. *What's up there?* he wondered. *The attic? Is someone in the attic? Maybe an animal?*

Tap.

Sccccccratch.

The sound came from his right. He slowly turned his head to face the window once again, terrified, expecting to see someone outside, staring in.

Nothing was there.

He kept watching the window like before, waiting, aware that his eyes wanted to blink, but holding them open to let in as much light as possible, not wanting to miss any telltale sign.

I heard that, he thought. *I didn't imagine it. Something scratched the window.*

Then it came again, confirming itself. The first tap drew his attention to the top pane of the window, where the tip of a finger was touching the glass. It produced a long scratching sound as its nail ran along the outside.

It quickly retracted and was gone.

An electric bolt of terror raced down his spine. He could feel his heart racing in his chest, and wondered if it might fail him, if he might have a heart attack right there in bed and be found dead in the morning. He was alone in the dark house, miles from town, isolated...

Not alone any more. Someone's out there. I can't see them, but they just let me know they're there. Outside my window.

It can't be, it's the second story, there's no way up to it...

What do I do?

He thought about calling the cops. In Portland, when his alarm system had errantly gone off, the police arrived within minutes. Here, out in the sticks, he guessed it would take them at least fifteen or twenty minutes to navigate through the woods.

That's plenty of time for someone to break in, he thought. *Plenty of time to do god knows what.*

Now he imagined people finding him the next morning, not dead in bed from a heart attack, but spread all over the room, blood everywhere, cut into pieces by a madman. His rational mind told him to get a grip, but the horror of it, the idea that whatever was outside could result in such an ending, kept his hair standing on end.

As he'd explained to friends that he and Elenore were moving to the country, some of them had joked about needing a gun, and he joked back about getting one.

Now he wished it wasn't just a joke; he wished he'd stopped in McLean and bought one.

Too late now, he thought. *They're outside.*

He stared out the window, feeling adrenaline surge through his body. His phone was on the nightstand; it would only take a moment to dial 911 and test the local authorities.

And tell them what? he wondered, looking at an empty porch on the second level, knowing it would have been hard – maybe impossible – for anyone to climb up. The moonlight allowed him to quickly confirm that no one – or thing – was on the porch right now; it was small and still empty of furniture; he could see practically every square inch of it from the window. Nothing was there.

What is the explanation for what I saw, what I heard? Was it an animal? It was high on the window, maybe a bird?

It didn't look like a bird, it looked like a finger…

He placed his feet on the floor and stood up. He normally slept naked, and with the house being so remote, he hadn't worried much about modesty when he prepared for bed or rose in the morning. Now, with the window four feet in front of him, he felt exposed and vulnerable.

The new position gave him a different angle of the small porch. Still, nothing had changed; it was empty.

Unless it's under the window, he thought, and stepped forward, looking down.

He felt cold resonating from the glass as he approached. Within seconds it was obvious that nothing was under the window, either. He glanced to the left, to check under another window, and at the double glass doors that led from the bedroom out onto the balcony.

Nothing. Completely empty. The adrenaline was still flowing, but he knew he had to regain some calm if he was ever going to get back to sleep.

Tap!

He stepped back, any calm that he'd achieved suddenly gone. It was the same sound, the same tap he'd heard before.

Now standing, facing the window, he saw the disembodied fingertip appear more distinctly; the white skin of its first knuckle clear and vivid in the moonlight, striking the glass and remaining there, the tip pressing against the pane, flattening a little.

It tilted up slightly so that its dark-edged fingernail pressed more firmly against the glass, then slid downward, producing an eerie, teeth-grating squeal. As it finished the screech, it retracted and disappeared.

"Fuck!" he shouted, the expletive exploding from his body as though he'd popped, stabbed by something sharp. Stepping back, he felt the cold metal of the bedframe at the rear of his calves. *Impossible! There's no way! No one's there!*

He stared out into the darkness, waiting for more to appear; a body, a face. Something. Anything that would explain the eerie finger.

Nothing appeared. The porch sat quiet, empty.

He felt like a statue. He didn't want to look away and miss seeing who or what was outside. Yet, inside him, every iota of survival DNA was demanding action, insisting that he run and hide.

It'll tap again, he thought. *Just wait.*

All of his senses were on high alert; he felt like he suddenly had super-hearing, able to pick out the smallest sound, and his eyes, even though he'd just woke up, were clear and open wide, taking in everything, vision sharpened by fear.

Just like the deer in the yard, he thought, seeing the black eyes of the creature in his mind as it stood frozen, monitoring for threats. *I'm like the deer.*

Tap!

The finger appeared again. This time he approached the glass, wanting to see it close up.

Sccccratch. It slid downward. He knew it would disappear, just like before.

Fuck it! he thought, suddenly opting for action. He grabbed his robe and tossed it over his shoulders, pulling it closed and tying it as he walked to the glass doors. He unlocked them and pulled them open, now seeing the two bedroom windows from the outside. Cold rushed in, hitting his bare legs and feet. He stepped onto the planks of the porch, turning quickly to catch what might be lurking on the roof above, expecting something to be there, readying his body for the shock of an attack.

Nothing. There was no sign of anyone or anything.

He glanced down at the porch, checking for footprints, but could see none.

A breeze blew, rustling the trees around the house. He turned, looking out into the back yard, momentarily expecting to see some-one running away. The yard was empty and silent.

He stepped forward, reminding himself that the railing around the deck had been identified by the house inspector as defective. He stopped a foot from it, trying to see to the left around the corner of the house. Moonlight didn't reach that area, and it was too dark to make out anything.

Well fuck it, I'm up now, he thought, and decided to check out everything. He turned on all the lights as he went downstairs, where he searched for a flashlight. As he flipped on switches, he noticed that floodlights on the south and west sides of the house came on, brightly illuminating those parts of the yard. "Ah ha!" he said aloud to no one; "I was wondering what those switches did!" After checking each of the rooms and double checking the locks on every window and door, he went outside with the flashlight and pointed it in all directions, concentrating on the north and east sides, where, without the aid of floodlights, things were much darker.

There was nothing. No deer, no possum scampering into the blackberries, no signs of disembodied fingers or body parts or persons of any kind. Nothing at all but the trees and the bramble.

The breeze returned, and he shivered in the cold. *I didn't imagine it. I heard it, I saw it.*

He thought again about calling the cops, but decided not to. *What would I tell them? I saw a finger? Not a person, but just a finger? They'd label me a crackpot and be slow to come out sometime when I really need them.*

He walked back inside, turned off the lights, and carried the flashlight to the master bedroom, where he ditched the robe and tried to go back to sleep, despite the nagging fear that the tap and scratch at the window would return. He opted to leave the bed stand light on, and he stared up at the ceiling, wondering about the noise he'd heard overhead, the thump that had preceded it all.

Chapter Three

Sure, buddy," Jake said. "You've probably screwed the place up already. I'll come unfuck it."

Ron immediately felt relief. Jake didn't exactly live close by, but he was graced with handyman skills and didn't keep an aggressive work schedule. And with Robbie and Elenore still weeks away from joining him, he could use another human around. Jake would be able to give advice on how to deal with some of the issues he was running into with the house.

And maybe help tamp down my paranoia, he thought. "You're sure Freedom won't mind?"

Jake's voice lowered to a whisper. "I think she'd prefer it." He coughed, and raised his voice to a louder volume. "What's that? You're gonna need tools, too? How big a job?"

"She can hear you, right?"

"That might take a while, a couple of weeks maybe. It'll cost you more if I have to get a motel, you got a room I can use?"

"Why do you make up shit? She'll hate me even more when she finds out."

"OK, I'll have to arrange things, but yeah, I can be there tomorrow. OK...see you then." The line went dead.

Ron slipped his phone into his pocket. Over the course of his long friendship with the man, Jake had dated several women. Ron liked most of them, and tried to get along with all of them, but it didn't take long for each to eventually dislike him. At first he thought it was something he was doing, alienating them in some way. A couple of relationships back, Elenore pointed out that the reason the women disliked him was because of how *Jake* treated them, not him, and ever since she shared that observation, he paid more attention to how his friend behaved. Elenore was right: Jake lied a lot for some reason, and his girlfriends initially blamed the lying on Jake's friends, thinking if they could isolate him from them, he'd straighten up. Eventually they realized it wasn't his friends that were the problem but Jake himself, and they left him. Freedom was Jake's fifth live-in partner since he'd known him, and she was mid-way through the Jake discovery cycle; in a couple more years, she'd reach the end of her patience and, just like the others, leave Jake for greener, more honest pastures.

Although this was Jake's Achilles heel, in all other matters he was a pretty stand-up guy. He had always been quick to help when asked, and was reliable when it came to being a decent godfather for Robbie. He was someone Ron enjoyed being around; a fairly reliable friend and a good drinking buddy. After trying unsuccessfully to exorcise Jake's one flaw out of him, Ron decided long ago he would just have to accept it and move on.

Thinking of Elenore and knowing the problems they were going through, Ron knew he had no standing to pass judgment – not that he ever did. He and Elenore had been together much longer than any of Jake's relationships, but that didn't mean he was some kind of expert. Ron knew there were large cracks forming between himself and Elenore, cracks he wasn't sure how to mend. He had no business criticizing Jake's relationships.

Great, he'll be here tomorrow, he thought. *Gotta get that guest room in order.*

He looked around the kitchen. Bright sunlight streaked in through eastern-facing windows, but despite the sun, the room still seemed dark. He walked to the switch and turned on the lights, but even with them on, the corners still seemed murky, the walls a little dingy.

It's the color of the paint. Going to have to brighten up this room somehow.

Looking out the windows and into the yard, things looked quiet and peaceful. The giant trees beyond the bramble looked beautiful and calming – a world away from the terror he felt six hours earlier, in the dark of night.

Gun. Gotta go into town and get one, along with thirty other things to pick up at the hardware store.

At least Jake will be here tomorrow. Having someone else around will help.

He realized he meant not only to help with the work, but with the loneliness, too; approaching nightfall had begun to come with a sense of terror, and Jake being in the house with him would help ease that. Then it occurred to him: *Jake has an arsenal of firearms, and a rack on the window of his truck. Why buy one?*

He pulled out his phone and texted his friend, asking him to bring along a rifle and a shotgun.

Little bubbles appeared as Jake formulated a reply, but Ron knew what it would be before it arrived:

"Fuckin A."

- - -

"I hate to be the grim reaper here," the man said, looking at the thin metal bob he just reeled up from a six-inch-wide pipe in the ground. "This hill is notorious for it, though."

"I would have thought four hundred feet was plenty," Ron replied.

"You can never tell. I could drill over there and hit at two hundred, or over there and not hit at five. It's not an exact science."

"What about making it deeper?"

"Sure, we could try. Probably your best bet. Runs about forty a foot. Our driller could get you on the schedule in the spring." He stopped to look around, eyeing the driveway. "Maneuvering that road might be tough, though. It's a big rig."

"Is there anything else you could do to increase the flow? Some kind of fracking, maybe?"

"There's outfits that'll try," he replied, loading gear back onto his truck. "They'll charge you thousands, but I've never known it to work. No, sorry, you're producing a half-gallon a minute here, and in my book, that's dry. A bank won't loan on less than ten gallons a minute sustained over two hours."

"So, I'm screwed."

"Basically."

Shit, Ron thought. Selling the property – or getting a loan against it – just became much more problematic. Not that he had any plans to sell, or need for a loan, but still…it didn't feel good to have options lopped off.

The man handed him a card. "Here's a water delivery guy. He does a lot of jobs this time of year, and usually needs a day or two lead time, but if you tell him you're completely out of water, he may be able to speed things up. Have him fill these two reservoirs. The above ground tank looks a little nasty inside, I'd pour in some bleach while he's filling it." He got inside his truck and started it up. "I'll have my driller call you."

"So, water deliveries until then?"

"And maybe even after. There's a reason this huge tank is here: this hill is mostly rock. Some drillers won't even return your call when they hear you live on Mt. Soltis. We drilled this one sixteen years ago, that's the only reason I'm out here today."

"Great."

"Sorry, buddy. Like I said, hate to be the grim reaper." He started up his truck and backed out.

Ron walked into the house. He'd been drinking bottled water since he moved in, as he didn't trust the cleanliness of the reservoirs either, and hadn't yet been able to schedule a water test. *At least I can keep making coffee,* he thought, digging out his phone to place a call to have water delivered.

He was relieved to learn they would try to fit him in later that evening. *So, I got a single flush in all the toilets until then,* he thought, sinking into a chair in the living room.

He looked around. The bare floor and walls still seemed foreign. Most of their furniture was in storage; his plan was to move it in about two weeks, after he finished a few projects. With Elenore out of town and Robbie still in school in Portland, he could push back the furniture move to get more things done with Jake.

The half-empty room seemed even more spartan as he raised his head to look up; two stories open, it was massive. He could see cobwebs in the corners, twenty feet up, and higher still, recessed flood lights that were burned out. *I need one of those long, extension things to change those bulbs,* he thought.

Suddenly the news of the well sunk in, demoralizing him. *Forty dollars a foot to drill deeper,* he thought. *What is that, four thousand to go another hundred feet? And no guarantee it'll improve anything?*

And now my options are limited. No one could get a bank loan to buy this place, even if I did want to sell it.

Which I don't, but still…

For as demoralized as he felt, and as dark and in need of a cleaning as the giant space above him still demanded, he knew he didn't want to bail. Two huge setbacks, the sewer and the well, were going to cost him…but it was all money he knew he would have spent to acquire the place, even if he'd known they were going to be so expensive.

But I'll never buy a bank repo again, he thought.

He walked out onto the front porch, resuming the work that had been underway when the well guy arrived. He brushed at the dozens of spider webs, slowly removing them from corners as the deck wrapped around bay windows. Every now and again a large spider, upset by his cleaning, would drop from above in a mindless attempt to escape; he had to keep an eye out for ones directly overhead.

And I've still got to deal with the furnace, he thought, feeling another wave of desperation and depression pass over him, making him feel like shit. He jabbed the broom deeper into the corners, taking his anger out on the arachnids.

Elenore will rub this in my face, he thought. *She was already pissed about the septic system. I promised her move-in ready, and she suspected it wasn't, even though the inspection seemed to suggest most of the fixes were cosmetic.*

Goddamn it, he thought, stabbing the broom.

He rounded the corner of the house, continuing to clean until the porch came to a stop ten feet down the side, where an opening lead to the crawlspace. *I wonder if the raccoon is still down there? The inspector said it was in the farthest spot, where he saw two red eyes in the distance, cutting his crawlspace inspection short. Apparently house inspectors don't deal with raccoons. Or inspect wells. Or septic systems.*

The hatch is still in place, he thought. *If it's still under there, the raccoon hasn't been coming and going through here. Maybe it left already; I've made enough noise in the house that it probably moved on. That's how websites said to get rid of one; light and noise.*

He looked up at the underside of the porch's ceiling. It was in need of paint, as was most of the exterior. *That's something Jake can help with,* he thought. *He's a great painter.*

Suddenly his feelings changed; he felt better. Knowing that help was on the way was part of it, but most of it was a turn of perspective, accepting the new, financially burdensome facts of the day, and not blaming an inanimate structure for them. *I could have had the well inspected separately,* he thought. *But I didn't. This is on me, not on the house.* He swept at another corner, this time more gently. *It's been poorly treated for years; what do you expect? A house can't keep itself maintained; it expects its owners to do that.*

He thought of the claw marks under each window sill inside, the smell of pet urine in the tile grout of the back bathroom and the carpeting of the stairs. Looking up, he saw the shell of the heat pump ten feet farther down the side of the house, inoperative, and knew they hadn't maintained that, either.

Of course. You abuse a house, it's going to be like this. I may not have known about the well or the septic, but I knew it was going to need some care.

How long has it been neglected? Years? Probably. It'll take some time to reverse that, for the house to realize it's loved again, and to become warm and welcoming, not the cold, sterile money pit it seems to be at the moment. You knew that going in. It needed some work, even though you told Elenore it was move-in ready. Time to suck it up and deliver.

He kept sweeping, knowing that with the news of the well, he had little choice.

Chapter Four

As the afternoon drifted toward evening, Ron broke out the box that contained his security system, intent upon setting it up.

He intended to go into town earlier in the day, but various chores kept him from that goal. Now, as he mounted each of the system's entry sensors on doors and windows, he talked himself out of the trip.

Jake is bringing a gun, he thought. *Hell, probably two, or maybe even an arsenal. You don't need to buy one. They'll be here tomorrow.*

Somehow the sunlight streaming through the windows bolstered his confidence in what he was telling himself, distancing his thinking from what he'd experienced the night before. *If I can get all these sensors set up, that'll help. That can get me through one night, at least.*

In the back of his mind he knew he was kidding himself; the best the alarm system could do was alert him to someone breaking in, and, if he didn't respond to the alarm, call for police. All his rationale for not calling the cops the night before still applied. As he stuck the small sensor at the top of the kitchen door and aligned it to a magnet on the door frame, he tried to ignore all that, realizing he wasn't going to make it into town before dark, anyway.

He recalled walking past the gun counter at Walmart several days before. Various rifles and shotguns were inside a plastic display that you could rotate, allowing visual inspection of the firearm from all angles. He quickly felt overwhelmed by the choices and options, and decided not to buy anything until he could talk to someone with expertise about which one would be the right choice for his situation. Since they varied in price from ninety-nine to nearly five hundred dollars, he figured he needed to do some research before he plunked down the money.

I'm not going to buy the nail gun and compressor until I do some research, too, he told himself, placing a motion sensor on the shelf of a bookcase. *I need one to reattach all that molding, but there's no sense spending the bucks until I know I'm buying the right one.*

He unspiraled the cord from the base of a small camera and looked for a spot to stick it. So far, he'd unpacked twenty or thirty boxes, but was quickly becoming sick of the process of trying to decide where to put things that came out of them. He had a sinking feeling Elenore would wind up moving half of what he'd already placed, so the entire thing felt like a waste of time. He selected the top of a set of Ikea shelves that had a wide view of the living room and kitchen, figuring that when the camera panned, it could capture the entry and stairs as well. As he threaded the cord behind the shelving unit, he grumbled to himself, irritated that she wasn't there helping him, relieving him of some of the work. He plugged the camera in, watching as it reset itself and turned to center on his face.

She's gone to Europe, he thought. *With Ira.*

He started an app on his phone and tested out the camera, moving it from side to side to confirm the coverage area.

She says she's up for this move, but she's not being honest with me, he thought as he watched himself in the image on his phone. *She said she'd find a way to work from home, so we could live out here. She says she agrees, but secretly she doesn't, she wants to find a way to stay in the city. Ira will pressure her to not move. He'll make it hard, and she won't fight for it, she'll cave to whatever he asks.*

He lowered the phone and stared at the camera, frustrated not only at the lack of Elenore, but his fatalistic thinking. *You're being a putz. She's working, for Christ's sake. Someone needs to bring in money while you pull off this house caper. Ease up.*

He sighed, his irritation still growing. There was so much to do, so many little tasks as well as huge projects, he knew he was making things worse by entertaining paranoid thoughts about Elenore. *Don't go down the rabbit hole,* he thought. *You'll just get worse and worse, and spend the night drinking instead of working. Beyond here there be monsters.*

He turned, leaving the camera, and walked out to the garage to find another box to unpack.

He always trusted Elenore, determined not to let the failures of his first marriage impact the second. It wasn't easy. He never imagined it would happen to him, but betrayal became an infection that wasn't isolated by the imaginary lines of a new relationship. Logically he reminded himself that just because he'd been abused and lied to and treated like a stupid, naïve boy scout by his first wife didn't mean everyone on the planet would treat him the same way.

Easier in principle than in practice, he thought as he carried in a new box, remembering what his therapist had told him.

He placed it on the counter and opened it. At first he couldn't tell what was inside; it was full of bundles of bubble wrap, multiple layers concealing small objects, sealed over with packing tape. It took several careful minutes with scissors to free one from its cocoon. A small ceramic replica of the Empire State Building emerged.

Elenore's souvenir collection, he thought, looking at the dozen other bundles in the box, all similarly ensconced in thick wrapping. Looking at the six-inch ceramic replica, his first thought was of *An Affair to Remember*, and he smiled.

Then he remembered visiting the observation deck with Elenore several years ago, when she picked up the souvenir. Unlike the movie, all they had done during that excursion was fight. Their experience was the exact opposite of Cary Grant and Deborah Kerr's.

He knew what else was in the other bundles: more towers. The CN, Sears, Eiffel. The Chrysler Building. The Space Needle.

Fuck no, he thought, closing the box. *She can unwrap them herself.*

He thought of calling her, but knew it was the middle of the night in London. He wanted to call Robbie, but knew Elenore's mother would bristle at the change of routine – the calls were always at night, just before bed – and decided against angering his in-law.

Outside, the last of the day's light was fading. He checked the time; it was 7:30. *I'll call in an hour,* he thought. *Soon enough, and it won't piss off Henrietta.*

Henrietta wasn't her real name; he just thought of her as the woman in the cellar from *The Evil Dead.*

For a moment he felt another pang of irritation, upset that he couldn't call his own son whenever he damn well pleased. *She's doing us a favor watching him,* he reminded himself. *It keeps him in the same school until we're ready to finalize the move.*

I miss him, though.

Ron walked to the kitchen windows that looked out over the back yard. Through the notch in the trees he could only see sky; the best view of the town was from upstairs, looking down. He listened, appreciating the lack of any sound. *This is what you wanted,* he thought. *Isolation. Quiet. Now you've got it.*

As dusk turned to evening, the trees in the distance became darker, and he had a sense of things closing in, the darkness providing cover for whatever was out there, moving in the shadows: animals waking up, preparing for nocturnal hunting, or people with nefarious designs, wondering if the house up the hill in the woods was still vacant and worth prowling through, or...

Or what else?

He turned on the lights, which caused reflections in the windows. Now he couldn't see out, but he knew whatever might be out there could see in.

There's no one there. That was the whole point of moving here. Maybe a raccoon, or a deer, but not a single human being. You don't need curtains or blinds, because there's nobody to see in. You could run around the house naked and it wouldn't matter. You're just used to the city, where there are plenty of people who could look through your windows if you didn't cover them at night, people who used telescopes and considered it a hobby to spy into other people's homes.

Here, there's no one for at least twenty acres of dense woods. The nearest neighbor is down the twisty road at least a quarter mile.

He stared out the window, not entirely convinced, wondering if, by standing there, he was daring whatever might be out in the woods to come take a closer look.

I'm not afraid, he thought. *Let them see that.*

- - -

Thump.

He sat up in bed, looking out the windows, even though the sound came from above him. Stars shone in the distance, no clouds. Light from the moon was minimal; things looked dark.

He reached for the light on the bed stand, sliding the dimmer just enough to illuminate the room. Immediately the window was filled with the reflection, making it hard to see out.

He sat still, listening. After a few moments, he heard another noise…

Steps.

Someone coming up the stairs?

He listened hard, straining his ears. The steps continued. At first he felt frozen by panic, but then his subconscious opted for fight instead of flight and he bolted out of bed, grabbing his robe and throwing it on. He walked to the locked double doors at the other end of the room and cocked his head, listening.

The sound stopped.

Whoever it was heard me, he thought. *They stopped when I began moving around inside the bedroom.*

He waited, expecting to hear the steps resume. When they didn't, he reached for the doorknob and quickly pulled the doors open, exposing the long hallway that ran the length of the house.

No one was there, and for a moment he wondered what exactly he would have done had someone been. *You need something to protect yourself,* he thought, feeling adrenaline surging. *And now you'll never get back to sleep unless you check the entire house.*

Office on the left, laundry room on the right. Each was empty. He walked the hallway, the living room opening up to the right; glancing over the railing, he could see down into the sparsely furnished area and the dark windows inside.

Two more bedrooms ahead at the end of the hall, before the stairs began. He checked each quickly, his heart rate increasing as he went, knowing he was moments from the stairwell.

Turning a corner he glanced down, expecting to see a figure frozen still on the steps. He knew he was being unrealistic, that any intruder would likely have fled once they heard him up and about, but his mind was racing with possibilities, keeping the fear alive, unstoppable.

The stairs were empty. He descended, stopping at the landing where they branched, one leading to the kitchen, the other to the front foyer.

He took the kitchen route, and turned on lights as he went. Slowly the entire house lit up as he made his way through each room. When he finally reached the front door, he paused, knowing the entire exercise had been futile; no one was there.

Behind him he heard a faint noise, a small whirring that caused a shiver to slide down his spine. He turned and walked into the living room, looking for its source.

It was the camera, sitting on top of the Ikea shelves, tracking him as he went. He stopped in front of it, watching as it centered on him. Then the whirring noise resumed, and the lens slowly rotated away, panning to the left and aiming slightly downward. It had turned to the foyer.

I'm the only movement, he thought. *It should be tracking me.*

He looked to the left. At the end of the foyer sat the large front door of the house, wood with an oval inlay of glass cut into patterns to provide privacy. He felt his legs moving, taking him down the hallway toward the door as his mind raced. *I might have dreamt the footsteps on the stairs,* he thought, *but I'm not dreaming now. The camera moved. It doesn't do that on its own. Something caused it to move.*

As he neared the door, he scanned the surface of the glass, wondering if he might see movement beyond. Like the other windows, light from inside the house was reflecting in the cut patterns, making it difficult to see beyond.

Maybe all the lights attracted something, he thought. *Maybe one of the deer came up onto the porch, drawn by the light. The camera would respond to that, wouldn't it?*

Frustrated that he couldn't detect anything through the glass, he flipped on the porch switch, realizing he was holding his breath. Light from the fixtures outside streamed in through the oval.

He reached for the deadbolt and threw it, then pulled on the handle. The door opened, and his alarm system began to beep, wanting a code. The keypad was next to the door, so he stopped to punch it in, and then looked out.

He wasn't surprised to see the porch empty. Slowly he exhaled. *Of course it's empty, you dolt.*

Light from the porch illuminated part of the front yard, which seemed still and quiet. His car sat in the driveway to the left, and he could just make out the road that led into the woods. Beyond that, it was too dark to see a thing.

He shut the door, deadbolted it, and reactivated the alarm. Behind him was a faint buzzing sound; it was the camera, moving once again. He turned to look at it; its domed lens was slowly panning, swiveling to point into the living room.

He expected to see the camera track back to focus on him as he walked toward it, but it didn't move; it was pointed past the fireplace, to a set of windows that faced the back yard.

With his eyes he followed the angle of its lens, looking at the particular window it had settled on. The hairs on his neck stood straight up.

There was a face in the window, looking in at him.

Gooseflesh rapidly spread across his body as the face quickly withdrew, swallowed up by the darkness.

For a moment he wasn't sure exactly what to do next. Finally his body kicked into gear, and he ran for the switch that would turn on the flood lights. When he flipped it, the entire yard lit up, looking exactly as it had the night before when he first discovered the switch; quiet, dark, and entirely empty.

The side of the house! he thought, feeling unprotected in a robe, but wanting to catch whoever he'd seen.

As he passed the base of the stairs in the foyer, he grabbed a hammer that he'd been using earlier in the day to remove tack strips. He turned off the alarm and unlocked the front door, stepping out, his bare feet coming into contact with the cold decking. First to the right, then the left, he watched, hoping to see whoever had been in the window, running away to the road. He waited, but no one appeared.

They could be hiding on the side of the house, he thought, and went back inside. Near the door was a muddy pair of shoes; he slipped them on over his bare feet and walked back out, feeling the laces slap his bare ankles as he moved quickly through the front yard to the north side.

Things were darker here, but there was enough light spilling over from the back yard to see if anyone was hiding. He walked as far as the derelict heat pump to make sure no one was crouched behind it, then continued around to the back of the house.

Bugs were already congregating around the flood light, set high at the roofline. He glanced into the bramble, not detecting any movement. Quickly he ran to the south side, knowing that if anyone was there, this was the only place left.

A pile of abandoned wood sat in the shadows, too short to hide anything. He checked the side door to the garage, the spot where vandals had broken in before he bought the place; it was secure.

Rounding the edge of the house, he came back to the front yard and scanned it again. He'd circled the entire place, but found nothing. Stepping onto the porch, he saw the front door wide open, as he'd left it.

Unless they circled the house ahead of me, and have now gone inside.

He was aware that paranoia was getting the best of him. He intended to double-check every single room and corner of the house again before making his way back to bed – there was no way he would be able to sleep if he didn't – but he knew the outcome was going to be the same. No one would be there.

Could it have been an animal in the window? he wondered as he secured the house, moving through the ground floor, turning off lights, mentally clearing each area. *No – it was a face. You're trying to rationalize it, to find a way to make it OK in your head.*

It was a face.

Ascending the stairs, he tried to remember features, but those details were fleeting and becoming more indistinct by the moment. His rational mind was busy, forcing what he'd seen to comport with his perception of the world, the things he believed were true and not true. By the time he finally reached the master bedroom, the pale image he thought was a face had become more of a blur, a quick retraction from the window that could have been most anything.

Still carrying the hammer, he placed it on the bed stand and slipped off the robe, tossing it at the foot of the bed. As he slid between the sheets, he wondered if leaving the hammer in that particular spot was a good idea. *If someone does break in,* he thought, *and they somehow silently make their way into my bedroom, they might see it there, and use it to smash in my skull.*

A gruesome image of his body lying in the bed – red splashed across the white pillow, his head a pulpy mess – suddenly filled his mind. He hated when he thought this way, when he entertained horrific possibilities, knowing it would only make things worse.

Jake will find my body lying here tomorrow when he arrives, my head a flattened cantaloupe, blood everywhere, my brain pulverized, the hammer discarded on the floor, pieces of my skin still attached to its claws. All because I stupidly left it right there, easy pickings for an invader to use.

He sat up and grabbed the hammer, choosing instead to hide it under the bed where he could still reach it if needed, but not sitting there like an advertisement, begging an intruder to commit a crime of opportunity.

As he closed his eyes, he heard a scream in the distance. It wasn't anywhere nearby; it sounded far, far away, as though it was travelling over the hill from a property miles in the distance. He listened carefully, wondering if perhaps it was just another emanation of his imagination, another in a growing list of self-produced horrors. He strained and heard it again, fading in and out due to the wind, too weak to remain sustained, too far away to be distinct. It was a woman's scream; it sounded full of horror and pain, and he wondered if it was someone living in a house nearby, someone who had endured night after night of imagined terrors just as he was experiencing, and was relieving herself in the only way she was able.

He closed his eyes. *None of it is real,* he thought, repeating it over and over in his mind until it became a calming mantra, meaningless, just repetition, and he finally drifted off into uneasy slumber.

Chapter Five

Ron walked through the house in his robe, padding over the kitchen tile on his way to the coffee maker. Through the windows he could see patches of fog still clinging to the trees outside. Sunlight was rapidly burning it off.

The previous night's events haunted him as he scooped coffee into the machine, but the concern was burning off, too, just like the fog. In the daylight, the very palpable fear he experienced just hours earlier seemed silly and remote. *Of course everything is fine,* he thought. *Nothing to be frightened of here. In fact, there's no one around for acres in any direction. It's what you wanted. It's stupid to be afraid of something you worked so hard to achieve.*

Once the machine finished, he poured a mug and walked into the living room, intending to sit in an oversized chair and browse on his phone while enjoying the caffeine.

Halfway to his destination, he stopped.

A door to a storage space under the stairs was ajar, exposing an inch-wide crack of darkness. Having carefully scoured the house multiple times the night before, he knew he hadn't left it that way.

Last night's fear returned. As he walked to the open door, a pricking sensation danced along his spine.

Inside, near the back, was a piece of black wood mounted under silver metal ducting. He'd noticed it before, but thought it was the back of the closet.

He placed his coffee on the ground and walked in. *It's not the back*, he thought. *It's something that has been pushed under the duct work.* He reached for it, grabbed, and pulled. It slid toward him. To his surprise, it was the side of a short dresser, abandoned furniture from previous tenants. The way it had been placed under the ducting, it almost looked like it belonged there.

He kept sliding until the entire unit had been pulled from the closet and into the hallway. The empty space behind it was dark, so he went for a flashlight and shone it inside. Aside from a few cobwebs, he could now see all the way to the underside of the bottom stair. It was empty.

Turning his attention to the dresser, he noticed a missing handle on one of its drawers. He tried the others, finding ephemera; tiny screws and washers, double-stick tape, and a couple of electrical wire connectors. In one of the larger drawers there was a stack of old catalogs for seeds and essential oils.

When he tried the drawer with the missing handle, he found it stuck. He dug the tips of his fingers around the edge of it, trying to gain a spot to pull, but it was wedged tight.

Resuming his coffee, he considered the dresser's shape. Its appearance was poor; he could see why it was abandoned. However, it was made of solid material, and didn't have the look of pressboard or laminate. While the front, sides, and drawers had been painted black, its back was unfinished wood which appeared thick and substantial.

I don't like it, he thought. *And Elenore will hate it, having belonged to someone else.*

But it is a big house, and we do need to fill it.

He lifted one side and found it to be heavy. His back was already in agony from the boxes he'd moved, so he decided to wait until Jake showed up and ask him to help haul it upstairs. The master bedroom was so large, it could go against a wall in the sitting area there and the room would still feel sparse. In the meantime, in order to get it out of the hallway, he slid it into the guest room.

Ah, the cleaner, he reminded himself as he parked it in a corner. *Gotta get that stuff soaking right away.*

He walked to a small bathroom adjacent to the kitchen, opened a gallon jug of enzymatic cleaner, and poured it slowly over the room's tile, watching as it pooled and ran into the grout. Then he set a timer for an hour, to remind him to return and add more.

I don't care how much of this shit I have to sink into that flooring, he thought. *I'm gonna get that cat piss smell out if it's the last thing I do.*

- - -

"Dad!"

The sound of his child's voice on the line was happy and enthusiastic – an immediate balm, reversing any guilt he felt for calling in the morning instead of at night, when his mother-in-law preferred. He felt his worries about the house suddenly drift away, and he realized how much he missed his son, how painful the short few weeks they would be separated were beginning to feel.

They chatted about school. Robbie asked about his mom, and Ron told him what he knew. The kid lost track of why she was gone, but he did remember she was in England, and was excited at the prospect of what souvenir might be his when she returned.

"Can't I come now?" Robbie asked.

"No, the house isn't ready," Ron replied, trying to sound comforting. "Soon."

"But I really want to. I could help you work on it."

"School is more important than that. Tell you what, when you do finally get here, I'll let you help on projects. There's a lot to do."

"Like what?"

"You name it. There's wood work, plumbing, painting. I'll put you to work."

"OK," Robbie agreed. "Do you have a TV there? Will I be able to set up my PlayStation?"

"As soon as everything gets moved in," Ron replied. "That's part of the process. I gotta get all this work done before we move things in, because it's harder to do the work if the house if full of stuff. Get it?"

"Yeah."

Once I don't need to hide a hammer under my bed, he thought. *Then it'll be OK.*

They chatted for a while longer, Robbie telling him that his grandmother was too strict about certain things, but that she let him watch any TV show he wanted. Ron reminded Robbie of the favor she was doing them, letting him stay there so he could keep going to school, and that just because Grace might say it was OK to watch something violent on TV, didn't mean he should watch it.

By the time the call ended and he hung up, he was feeling more like a regular dad again, and not just the caretaker of a house. It made him resolve to get the work done, and ensure that by the time Elenore returned, they could both move in and sleep soundly throughout the night. No septic problems. No cat piss smell on the stairs.

No faces in the window.

- - -

What are the odds? Ron thought, standing at the counter in the McLean Post Office.

"Yeah, we bid 347," the postal worker said. "Didn't get it. You're the 351 bid, huh?"

"Yeah, that's me," Ron replied, feeling sheepish.

The bank sold the house using an online auction site. The entire time Ron had been bidding, there was another bidder he'd battled against. It was blowing his mind that the other bidder was now standing across the counter from him, wearing a postal worker uniform. His name badge read "Randy."

"My wife wanted a view," Randy said. "We liked the view of town you could see over the trees. And Mount St. Helens."

"Yeah, the view is nice," Ron replied, still shocked and feeling very awkward.

"You got assholes for neighbors," Randy continued. "We got lost trying to find it, and they called the sheriff on us. The guy actually put me in cuffs, if you can believe that. My little girl was in tears. But, I'm kind of glad we didn't get it. Everything about Mt. Soltis seems to be a problem. You know the city considered annexing it once, but the people were such pricks about it the town just threw up their hands."

Sour grapes, Ron thought, looking down at the form Randy had slid across the counter. He began to fill it out while the man kept talking.

"And even though the view was nice, my wife didn't like the vibe of the place, she didn't like the history. Some places just make you feel depressed, you know?"

"I noticed there was a set of mailboxes by the highway, where the road turns off into the hill," Ron said. "Is that where we get our mail?"

"It's all private, so you'll have to talk to the locals. There's an HOA that maintains the roads; they probably run the mailboxes, too. We don't have any say in that, we don't have any of the keys." Randy had a sort of *and good luck with that!* tone that made it obvious dealing with the HOA was going to be problematic.

Well, they did call the cops on him, Ron thought. *More sour grapes maybe.*

"You know that address is always going to be a problem, right?" Randy continued. "That road is completely inaccessible; it's why we got lost trying to find it. A fire truck would never reach you. Cops might have trouble, too. You should go to the county and have them assign a new number, maybe something off that dirt road where the driveway starts."

Ron slid the completed form back to him, wanting to leave. "I'll consider that."

"Yeah, sure glad I didn't get it," Randy replied, looking over the form. "Woulda been an albatross around my neck. I don't care how good the view was."

"Thanks for your time," Ron said. He forced a smile, and turned to leave.

Randy didn't reply, just motioned for the next person in line to come to his window.

How many people have I met in McLean? he thought as he walked to his car. *Ten? Twenty? There's fifteen thousand people in this town, and I run into the* one *guy who bid against me for that house?*

As he drove back to his home, he considered the man's suggestion to have the address changed. *How does one go about that? He mentioned the county, some office of theirs, I imagine.*

Would the fire department really not be able to find me in an emergency?

If my alarm company were to call the cops when an alarm went off, would the cops not be able to locate me, either?

As he followed the twisting roads on Mt. Soltis, he remembered how he found the place the first time, when Google Maps had sent him to the wrong area. Eventually he managed to sort it out and find the property, but he completely understood why Randy had become lost. Difficulty in finding the place had been part of the reason, he suspected, that there were so few bidders.

Most of them gave up, like I almost did.

Ahead on the one lane road, a rare occurrence: an approaching vehicle. He recognized it as the brown van usually parked by one of the houses on the route. The road was narrow, so they'd both have to move over for each other. He selected a spot that looked safe, hoping his right tire didn't slip into an unseen ditch.

As the van slowly passed, it came to a stop mid-way. He gave a friendly wave, as was the custom between drivers on the hill, but noticed that their window was down.

He lowered his own window and saw an older woman in the van. At first he thought it was Patricia Neal; her hair set firmly in shape, looking stern yet slightly worn-out. She glared at him, and he noticed little differences in her face that confirmed she wasn't the long-deceased film star.

"Hello," he offered.

"You up on Pinedo Road?" Her voice was as deep as Neal's, and just as raspy; he imagined she was a heavy smoker.

"Yeah, just bought it."

Her eyebrow went up as though she was intrigued, then Ron got the impression that she changed her mind about what to say, and instead, her arm came out of the window, swinging wildly to point at the road. "You're the one kicking up dirt!"

"Oh?"

"Speed limit is 20 on the mountain! You should do 10 on these dirt roads, be considerate of all the mess you're making!"

"I'll be sure to slow down."

She eyed him. "Sometimes I have grandchildren over. I don't want you running into them, creating a hazard like it's the city. You're from the city, I expect."

"Yes, you're right."

"And now you're here, in the country."

"Yes."

"Well, I'm Jane Hughes, and I live in the blue triple-wide up around the corner."

"I'm Ron Costa. Nice to meet you."

"Well, I'm pleased to meet you too, because I've been wanting to talk to you about how fast you're driving."

"I will slow down, I promise."

"You move from the city for a change of pace, I imagine, so there's no sense in racing around these roads like a house a'fire."

He stared back at her; having apologized and agreed to her point several times, he was unsure that agreeing again would satisfy her. He looked in his rear-view mirror, worried they might be blocking the road, but quickly realized they could stay there chatting for another ten minutes and likely not encounter another car. He decided to change the subject. "You've lived here long?"

"My entire life," she replied, rolling up her window, ready to move on now that the subject wasn't his driving. She pulled a gearshift near the wheel and slid away from him, leaving him on the side of the road.

He raised his window and continued on. *Geez, I thought I was going pretty slow already. Don't want to antagonize the locals, though...guess I need to lighten up, at least when I pass her place.*

As he turned onto his property, snaking through the overgrowth, he appreciated that the driveway had been part of the reason he'd won the bid, too. When the property was for sale, the road was overrun with blackberry branches. He remembered how they scraped against the side of his car the first time he drove Elenore to look at the place. *Most people wouldn't have bothered,* he thought. *They took one look at that road and thought, "I'm not going down that!"*

Just exactly why I wanted it, he reminded himself. A place so remote, so tricky to enter, people would give up before driving to it. Of course he'd trimmed back the worst blackberries once he closed on the property, but the road was still small and had the feeling of being rarely used. He tried to imagine a fire truck maneuvering down it, and had to admit it seemed like a tight fit.

When he finally reached the house, he was surprised to see Jake's truck parked in front. He pulled up next to it and got out, searching for his friend. Jake was in the back yard.

"You're early!" he said, walking up to him.

"Nice house!" Jake replied, smiling. "Went for the mansion in the woods, huh?"

As long as Ron had known him, Jake always smiled. He stood six foot two and was stocky but not fat, wearing a worn cap with the logo of a metal bearings company. They shook hands.

"No problem finding the place?" Ron asked.

"Your directions were spot on. And you're right, Google was no help. I'll bet you like having a place no one can locate, eh?"

Ron thought about his conversation with the postal worker. Up until that morning, he definitely considered it an asset; now he wasn't so sure. "I do like how quiet it is."

"That brown house a quarter mile before the turn off, that your closest neighbor?"

"As far as I know. You saw the gated-off road at the other end?"

"Yeah," Jake replied, as they walked around to the front of the house. "You know where that leads?"

"Well, I assume it was the original road to the house, the one the address is based on. That gate looks like it's been chained up for a long time, though."

They walked to the driveway. Opposite the small road that led out, a metal gate was chained to a post. Beyond were the faint makings of a path tucked into the side of a slope.

"The realtor thought they used it to haul in everything," Ron said. "Maybe a temporary arrangement with the land owner. Once it was built, they switched to using this other driveway for some reason."

"That's why your address don't work," Jake observed. "It's based on this old road."

"I'm guessing. I wish a property came with something like a Carfax, the way cars do, so you could see what exactly happened to it over time."

Jake turned to look at the building's facade. "Housefax? Yeah, that'd be somethin'. Take all the fun out of it, though."

"Not fun finding out the well's dry."

"Dry?"

"Well, low producing. The guy from the drilling company considered it dry. I got a water delivery coming tonight."

Jake walked to the side of the driveway, where a huge 2,500 gallon storage tank sat next to the well. "Low producing isn't uncommon. That's why you have the tank. What's the flow?"

"Under a gallon a minute."

"How much under?"

"I think he said a half gallon."

"OK, so, all day long, and overnight too, this well pumps what it's got into this holding tank. That's thirty gallons an hour, so overnight you've got two, three hundred gallons right there. Why's this tank empty?" He bent down, looking at the well and the various pipes and wires that came from it.

"The well was turned off at the power breaker," Ron said. "I tried turning it on, but no water came into the house, so I turned it back off."

"Go turn it on," Jake ordered, his attention drawn to a broken piece of PVC pipe that rose an inch from the ground near the tank.

Ron walked into the garage and threw the circuit breaker marked for the well, then walked back out to where Jake was on his haunches.

"Hmm, nothing," Jake said, pointing to the broken piece of PVC. "Maybe that's not it. Well, one thing's for sure," he rose and walked to a black domed cover on the ground, lifting it to expose the tank underneath, "this here's your reservoir, and the equipment that pumps water into your house."

Ron joined him. The tank was empty. "It was full of water when I bought the place."

"They might have filled it just so water would run while people looked at the property," Jake replied, lowering the cover. "I think the setup here is, the huge tank feeds this underground reservoir when needed. Not sure how the well plays into it. Maybe it never did."

"Seems complicated."

"For someone who's only used municipal water, sure, but out here in the sticks there's all kinds of setups. We get this plumbing fixed, we can find out exactly how much water you've got, and set up a system that works a bit better."

"So, I'm not screwed?"

"Well, you might not get ten gallons a minute, but I'll bet you'll be fine most of the time if you can build it up. The water table probably drops during the dry months, so you might need to augment it with a delivery or two, but we should be able to get this thing operational to some degree. I think."

Ron felt like a huge weight had been taken off his shoulders. "I'm glad you're here," he said, patting Jake on the shoulder.

"City boy like you trying to live out here in the woods," Jake replied. "Kinda funny."

"If I've got a well that will keep me in water, that'll be enough."

"We'll see how Elenore feels about it after she smells it."

"Smells it?"

"Well water isn't always pretty," Jake said, kneeling again to examine the broken pipe.

Chapter Six

"Why's it so dark in here?" Jake asked, taking a swig of beer.

It had been a long day of tasks. They made a mid-day trip into town for hardware, and Jake spent the afternoon fixing pipe, cutting wood to replace exterior trim, and tearing out the bad handrail on the upstairs deck. They both worked well into the night. Now, they were sitting in the living room, drinking, shooting the shit.

Ron looked up at the recessed lighting two stories above. "I gotta get one of those long poles to change the light bulbs. You know, one of the telescoping ones."

"Like they use at banks."

"Yeah."

"Sure is quiet," Jake said, taking another mouthful. "If quiet's what you wanted, I think you got it."

"Listen," Ron replied, holding his hand to his ear. "No sirens. No dogs barking. Nothing."

"I heard a train earlier."

"Far in the distance."

"You lived twenty-five years in the city…"

"Twenty-eight," Ron corrected.

"...I think all this silence is going to drive you crazy. You're not used to it. Any little noise will wake you up."

Ron thought of the previous two nights he'd spent in the house and wondered if he should tell Jake about them. *No,* he thought. *I'd just sound stupid.*

"I'll admit I had to turn on a fan the first night," Ron replied, "to make some white noise."

"Defeating the whole purpose. You can run a fan anywhere and drown out sounds."

"I'll adjust, trust me. Just gotta ease into it."

"And Elenore?"

"When she comes back from Europe, she'll ease into it."

"I've never known her to ease into anything. I can't imagine she likes this place."

"Why do you say that?" Ron asked, knowing that Jake had hit upon the truth, but pretending otherwise.

"Come on, the problems!" Jake answered. "The well, the septic, half the molding, the cat piss in the tile grout, you name it."

"I like to think of them as opportunities."

"Beer bottle half full kinda thing?"

"You know me."

"I'm surprised she agreed to it. Hard to picture. Every time she comes out to our place, she always comments on how rural it is, and she's got that *tone.* This is far more rural than my place."

"You have a well and a septic system," Ron countered.

"Half of America has a well and septic," Jake answered. "Doesn't mean shit, just means you got enough room for a leach field."

Ron looked up again at the dark ceiling. He was a little uncomfortable, as though the house might be listening to the criticism; he had the strongest feeling that he needed to defend it from Jake's comments, as well as justify his decision to buy it. "I think Elenore's fine with the place as long as I solve all the problems. The foundation, the structure is sound. It's little things. I mean, come on, it's obvious that the people who lived here before basically abused the place. It needs some TLC."

"Well, we might get all the mechanics taken care of, but solving the vibe, hell, that's gonna be a tough one."

Ron paused, surprised that Jake used the same word the postal worker had said. "Vibe?"

"You know, how it feels."

"No, what do you mean?"

"The creepy vibe, man. I assume that's why you bought it. Hard to ignore."

"You think it's creepy?"

"This place is fucking haunted as hell, I'll bet."

"Really? You think so?"

"Sure feels like it."

"I don't feel anything like that. I loved this place the minute I saw it."

"Doesn't mean it ain't haunted."

"What makes you think that? Just a weird vibe that I don't feel?"

"Well, it's so fucking big, for one thing. That's always a sign of trouble. Huge houses have lots of opportunity to have weird shit going on in some corner somewhere."

"Interesting," Ron replied, smirking a little. "I assume you have more reasons than just that."

"OK, so then there's the entryway. You come in, and there's those stairs, going all which ways."

"I thought it was a feature, not a problem. Kinda convenient."

"It ain't normal. Never seen a staircase like that."

"So, stairs, gotcha. What else?"

"You gotta admit, that back bathroom is creepy as hell. Seems really dark, too."

"I just don't have the right fixtures in there yet. They made some really strange decisions I'm still trying to figure out. In the office upstairs there's a forty watt bulb in a single outlet fixture on the ceiling, but in the closet there's two seventy-five watt bulbs in a double. Closet is nice and bright, the room is dark as hell. Makes no sense. Once that kinda stuff is fixed, the mood will be better."

"I haven't been into the crawlspace yet, or up in the attic, but I'll bet there's plenty of problems there, too."

"Problems? The inspector didn't mention any problems in either."

"I mean weird shit. It's always the crawlspaces and the attics that have the creepy stuff."

"You're joking, right?"

"Don't tell me you don't think this place is a little whack. I've known you for twenty years, I know you don't like normal, boring stuff, that you're drawn to this kinda thing, stuff with character and that kind of shit. I just don't understand you leaving the city. I always thought of you as an urbanite."

"It's always been the retirement plan. There's no way I could retire with a mortgage."

"You lived in that Portland house the entire time I've known you. It must have been close to paid off."

"It wasn't close; I refi'd it a couple of times," Ron replied, getting up to grab more beers from the kitchen. "What pushed me to do it was the price of things. I made enough money selling it to pay cash for this place, so I've got no mortgage here. I own it all, free and clear. That's why."

"You coulda bought a condo on the river," Jake called.

Ron brought him another bottle. "Like you wouldn't take a bullet to the head before you'd ever buy a condo."

Jake twisted the cap. "You're right about that. But I bet it's what Elenore would have preferred."

"Couldn't get the kind of deal on a river condo like I got here. I had to move out of the city to make it work financially. The prices were crazy, that's why I could cash out like that."

"Did you make enough to buy this place *and* fix all the shit we're gonna have to fix? These are big ticket items. It won't be cheap."

"I hope so. There was a good chunk left over." He paused for a moment, feeling as though he'd defended the place pretty well. "So…what do you think is first to do? Of the major stuff?"

"Well, the plumbing," Jake replied, drinking. "Have you noticed the water pressure is weird? When I run a tap, or a toilet refills, the pressure isn't constant. Goes back and forth."

"Yeah, it's almost rhythmic. At first it bugged me a little, but now I don't mind it at all. When it pulses like that, the house is…I don't know, it's like it's alive. Breathing. Almost a heartbeat, like the pipes are its veins. I decided I kinda like it."

"Well, thanks a fuckin' lot for putting that idea into my head. Now I'm gonna be creeped out by that, too, like every time I wash my hands I'm rinsing them in blood."

"You're welcome."

"Even though you might like it, it's a problem. We need to replace your pump regulator, which is probably the culprit. All that stuff looks rusted and corroded as hell, and needs to be changed out and redone before it craps out completely."

"It'll make the pulsing stop?"

"It better. Ain't *supposed* to pulse like that. Probably putting stress on the pipes."

Like it has high blood pressure, Ron thought, aware that he was continuing to ascribe human traits to the place, but unable to stop. He liked the idea that the house had life; it gave it charm. He was a little disappointed that the pulsing would stop once Jake corrected the regulator. *He's right, you're a glass-half-full kind of person, and you're inventing stupid reasons to like the house that balance out the problems of the past few days. Compensating. Stop it.*

While Jake continued to explain the plumbing, Ron found himself wondering if there was some way to keep the regulator, despite knowing it had to go.

- - -

Ron's eyes opened, sure he'd heard a noise overhead, a single thump – something dropped onto the attic floor.

He listened.

Steps. Someone was on the stairs, like the night before.

Then he remembered: Jake was downstairs, sleeping in the guest room off the main hallway.

It's probably just him, moving around.

He listened, straining. The steps resumed, sounding for all the world as if someone was slowly marching up the stairs.

Maybe he's coming up to see me about something.

Then the sound stopped.

Despite his best effort to remain calm, fear began surging through his veins, nagging at him to do something. He threw off the cover and swung his feet to the floor, feeling the softness of the rug under them. He stood, naked, and looked out the window.

In the moonlight, he could see something moving on the ground outside. It was indistinct and he could only make out part of it beyond the edge of the porch.

What is that? he wondered, then walked to the set of bay windows in the sitting area adjacent to the bedroom. Away from the porch, it would offer an unrestricted view of the back yard.

He looked down through them, suddenly alarmed, frozen in place. People were outside. They were facing the house, looking into the windows on the ground floor. As he watched, a half-dozen moved around each other, changing position to gain new vantage points.

Burglars! he thought. *I need to warn Jake!* He wanted to break free of his paralysis, but found his feet glued solidly to the floor. Something was off; the people outside didn't look right. What at first he thought must be men in dark clothing, casing the house, he now realized were both men and women moving strangely, not walking normally. He tried to observe their legs and their feet as they shifted positions, but everything below their knees seemed shrouded in shadow.

Their legs aren't moving, he thought, still watching carefully. *Their bodies move, but I can see their upper legs, their thighs, and they aren't shifting, aren't going back and forth like a normal person walks.*

Then he realized they were disappearing into the darkness, fading as a group, as though their image had been made by a projector with a bulb that was going out. Slowly they became more and more indistinct, until only the outline of their bodies remained. Then the image suddenly intensified and the entire shape of their forms returned, becoming visible as though power had been restored to the projector.

Now there were more; a dozen figures all staring at the house, peering into the ground floor windows, dissatisfied with what they saw, shifting to gain alternative perspectives through different windows. It wasn't a group of teens looking for a way in to rob the place; it was a mixture of men and women of different ages, dressed in a variety of clothing from various eras, some looking recent, while others looked from the latter decades of the last century.

What are they doing? he wondered, still in shock, still frozen in place, unsure that he wasn't dreaming. Their appearance seemed unreal, and his mind churned as it tried to calculate an explanation; someone was playing an elaborate trick on him. That had to be it.

Jake, he thought. *He's projecting this into the back yard, trying to scare me. They're just images on his phone...he's got one of those tiny projectors, and he's fucking with me.*

One of the figures slowly raised its head, scanning the second story. Ron suddenly felt the need to hide so he wouldn't be seen in the window, but it was too late. The eyes of an older man dressed in a suit locked on him, and he saw the ghostly figure begin to rise from the ground, levitating away from the others.

This isn't Jake's doing, his brain tried to communicate through the fog of fear that kept him locked in place. Standing naked he felt completely exposed, but for some reason he couldn't move his arms to cover himself, or step back from the window. The image of the levitating figure was so fantastically unreal, so bizarre and frightening and intriguing at the same time, his brain wouldn't let go, wouldn't allow him to move other than to stare at the image and try to figure out what it was…how it could possibly be there, doing what it was doing…floating.

Outside, the man's feet rose above the heads of the others, while they continued looking into the house from the ground floor. His feet were bare; the skin looked pale white and translucent, almost as though he could see through it. The figure continued to ascend, his arms slowly rising out in a crucifixion pose. Ron looked at his face, confirming that the man's eyes were still fixed on him, that he knew he was in the window, just inside the house.

They're looking for people, Ron realized. *This one found me.*

The edges of the man's mouth slowly curled up, showing emotion for the first time. The figure began to drift toward the window, and as it got closer, the man moved his arms from his side, now reaching forward as though he wanted to grasp something.

When the image was just feet from the window, Ron's brain suddenly released the hold it had over his body. His skin contracted, giving him the shivers. The figure continued to drift toward him until its outstretched fingers were inches from the glass.

Ron backed up rapidly, unable to break his gaze from the apparition. He slammed into a wall behind him, fully expecting to see the figure's hands pass through the window and into the room.

Instead, the man's face came right up to the panes and stopped.

He's so close, his breath should be fogging the window, Ron thought. *But there's no fog. He doesn't have any breath.*

He's dead.

The man's eyes were locked on him at first, but then drifted, searching inside the room. Ron could feel adrenaline surging through his body, a reaction to the sensation of being targeted. He felt singled out for the kill.

"Jake!" Ron yelled at the top of his lungs, unsure if anything had come out. It felt like a scream in a dream, trying to mouth words and force them out, but just uttering nonsense.

"Jake!" he yelled again, raising his right hand until he felt it slide across a switch faceplate. He groped at it awkwardly until his fingers flicked it upward; light filled the room, making him wince.

The image of the man in the window disappeared.

Ron paused for a moment. His heart was racing. His mind immediately formed an explanation, a bullshit reason for what he'd just seen. He hoped he hadn't actually yelled, that he hadn't accidentally woken Jake and that his friend wasn't currently coming up to see what was wrong. *This was all some kind of dream,* he thought. *I'm just waking up now. I turned on the light, and I'm finally waking up.*

But the story his mind was inventing irritated and frightened him, making him feel as though he was deluding himself, making himself crazy. He flipped off the light and looked at the window, wanting confirmation that he really had seen what he thought he saw.

The window was empty.

He slowly walked to it, this time covering himself with his hands, wishing he had grabbed his robe. As he looked down into the back yard, he saw the figures once again. The levitating man was gone, but a few others that were close to the ground floor windows were still there, still looking at the house as though they wanted desperately to come inside.

Tap, tap…

Ron turned his head to look back into the master bedroom. In a window that faced the other side of the house, he was shocked to see a face staring in at him. It raised a finger to the glass and slid a fingernail against the pane, making a nerve-shattering screech. Ron recognized the face as the levitating man, and when it registered that Ron had seen him, it smiled.

Ron ran for the light in the master bedroom and flipped the switch. The brightness seemed to banish the image from the window.

He stopped for a moment, catching his breath, trying to think.

Is it still out there? he wondered. *I can't see it in the window, but is it still there?*

He grabbed his robe, tossing it around his shoulders and tying it up. It was impossible to see anything outside with the light on in the room.

He placed his hands against the glass, and bracing himself for a shock, moved his head between his cupped fingers, shielding the light. He expected to see the man's face just inches away, staring at him.

Instead he saw the south side of the house, empty except for the blackberry bramble a few feet away, and a ravine beyond from which trees grew at haphazard angles, slowly waving in the wind.

Fuck this! he thought, and walked out of the room and into the upper hallway, turning on lights as he went. When he reached the ground floor, he walked through the kitchen and to the living room, illuminating everything. He approached one of the ground floor windows, one of the ones he knew the figures had been looking in, expecting to see them still outside, staring in.

Once again, light from inside made looking out impossible without the aid of a flashlight, or placing his hands against the glass to shield his eyes. He stepped up to the window and raised his hands, looking out quickly.

The backyard seemed empty.

"Wha...?" Jake mumbled behind him, emerging from the guest bedroom.

"Sorry," Ron said, still staring out the window. "Thought I saw something."

"Should I get my shotgun?"

"No, not yet," Ron answered, not turning from the window.

Jake paused for a moment, then padded off. "I gotta piss."

Ron kept staring out, remembering what Jake had said about the place being haunted. *If I tell Jake what I saw, he'll use it to confirm his stupid idea. I'll tell him it was just a deer. Lame, but better than listening to his "haunted" bullshit.*

"Anything?" Jake asked, returning from the bathroom.

"Nah, just deer."

"Deer woke you up?"

"Yeah."

"Huh. I'm back to bed then."

"Yeah. Sorry for waking you."

Ron waited until Jake had returned to the guest room and shut the door, then made his way back through the house, turning off lights as he went. When he reached the master bedroom, he walked to the bed and slipped off his robe. He glanced quickly at the window where he'd seen the levitating man's face, fully expecting it to return, bracing himself for the jarring image – but nothing was there.

As he slipped under the covers, he knew, once again, it was going to be hard to go back to sleep. *I'll get up in a few minutes and check out the window again. Leave the lights off, so I can see out easily.*

Slowly he drifted off, forgetting his idea to check on things, and didn't rouse again until he heard Jake moving around downstairs with the light of day streaming through the windows.

Chapter Seven

When Ron came down the stairs the next morning, Jake was already up, drinking coffee, staring out the windows into the back yard.

"Morning," Ron said, walking past him to grab a mug.

"Morning," Jake replied.

"How'd you sleep?"

"Not good."

"Sorry I woke you up."

"Nah, wasn't that," Jake replied, still staring out the windows. "Whatever was in the back yard last night kept waking me up. And I don't think it was deer."

Ron reconsidered telling him what he'd seen, but still hated the idea of encouraging Jake's irrational thinking. Worse, he knew if he did, he'd be crossing a personal line: *the craaazy line,* he thought. *What does it say about me if I claim I saw a bunch of ghosts in the yard, floating around like ducks in a pond? No going back from that, I'm in loony tunes land from that point on.*

Is that what they were? Ghosts?

He hadn't thought of the term the night before, but in the light of day he wasn't sure what word would better describe them. *What else drifts over the ground without moving? Floats in the air? Disappears when you turn on the light?*

Vampires?

Werewolves?

Some other kind of fucked up entity?

Entity? Is that what I saw? Entities in the back yard, looking in?

Goddamn it, there's so much to do here, so much work that needs to get done, I don't need to be focused on shit like entities and vampires and werewolves, I need to...

"Ron?" Jake asked.

"Huh?"

"You're pouring coffee on the counter."

Ron snapped to awareness, righting the carafe and looking down at the mess he'd made. "Fuck! Clumsy. Sorry, not quite awake yet."

"It's your counter, don't gotta apologize to me."

Ron reached for a roll of paper towels and began soaking up the spill.

"At first I thought it was a tree or the branch of a brush," Jake continued. "Now I see there's no plants anywhere near the windows, so it wasn't that."

"A tree or branch?" Ron asked.

"Tapping at my window."

Ron froze. *Like the tapping I heard – saw? The ghostly finger that briefly emerged from the dark and disappeared again?*

"And there was this scraping sound. A tap, and a scrape, like someone was at the window, wanting in."

It wasn't my imagination! Ron thought. *Jake heard it too.* "Interesting that you should mention that," he said, finally pouring a proper mug and deciding – since Jake had brought it up first – to take a small incursion into Crazytown.

"Interesting? Why?"

"I heard the exact same thing night before last, at my window upstairs."

"An animal maybe? Has to be, right? Maybe a bat?"

"Did you see it? Whatever made the noise?"

"No. I was trying to ignore it. Kept waking me up."

"Well, whatever was at my window wasn't a bat."

"So, you saw it?"

"Yeah."

"What was it?"

Do I tell him the truth? Ron wondered. *Here's another line to cross; once I step over it, it'll be hard to come back.*

"There was a finger," Ron finally replied. "And a face."

He intended to gauge Jake's thoughts by watching his reaction, but he didn't have to bother – he could feel Jake's stare without looking.

"A finger?"

"Yeah."

"Like, a person's finger?"

"Yeah."

"On the deck outside the windows up there?"

"Yup. I got up to look at it, and I saw a finger on the other side of the pane. It tapped the window, and scraped down the glass with the fingernail. Then it disappeared."

Jake looked a little confused. "Disappeared?"

"It was like it came out of a fog, then pulled back into it."

"So, it was foggy?"

"No, not really. I just mean something was concealing it."

"And you saw a face?"

"Very faint. Disappeared, too."

"Was there a body attached to this finger and face?"

"No."

Jake sat still for a moment, staring from across the room, before a wave of the willies passed over him, briefly making his entire body shake. "Fuck! I hate that kind of shit! You want me to just pack up and head home? Keep up with that shit and I'll be outta here!"

"You were the one who said you thought the place was haunted."

Jake smiled as his features relaxed. "Oh. So, you made it up to teach me a lesson."

"No, I'm not making it up. It scared me to death. It's one of the reasons I asked you to bring a gun."

Jake looked at him again, trying to decide if his friend was lying or not. "You're fucking with me."

"No, I'm not," Ron replied, walking into the living room and sitting on the couch. "That's what I saw, night before last. If you think that's creepy, you don't want to know what I saw last night, in the back yard."

Jake seemed skeptical. "You *are* fucking with me."

"No, it's why I got up."

"You said it was a deer."

"You heard it too. You know it wasn't deer." Ron wasn't entirely sure if Jake would swallow what he was about to tell him. *If he doesn't, he's already set it up as bullshit designed to scare him, so I can go with that if I need to backtrack.* "I saw figures moving outside. They were drifting over the lawn, coming toward the house, looking in the windows. When I turned on the light in my bedroom, they were gone."

"Looking in the windows?" Jake asked, his voice expressing a new concern that hadn't been there before.

He's buying it, Ron thought. "Yes. Before I turned on the light, I watched them for a while. They were…geez, how do I put this? It's like they weren't all there."

"What's that mean?"

"There were times when you could see through parts of them."

"Like, transparent?"

"Exactly. They all seemed interested in the ground floor windows, but one of them noticed me watching from my room upstairs. It…" He wasn't sure how to relate the levitation to Jake.

"What?" his friend asked, hanging on what he was saying.

"It…floated up. To my window."

"Fuck it!" Jake spat, and marched out of the room.

Ron watched as his friend left, headed for the guest bedroom. He could hear the man moving things inside, and the sound of a luggage zipper. *He's packing!* Ron thought. *Damnit, I've pissed him off!*

Ron rose from the chair and carried his coffee to where Jake was busy tossing things into an open bag on the bed.

"What are you doing?" Ron asked.

"If you think I'm staying here with that kind of shit going on in your back yard, forget it." He pulled the plug on an electronic device by the bed and began wrapping the cord around it.

"You're not leaving," Ron said. "Stop."

"I'm not into all the weird woowoo shit, like Freedom," Jake said, tossing the device into the open bag.

"What's that?" Ron asked.

"What?"

"What you just put in your bag? What is that thing?"

"This?" Jake replied, lifting it back out. "It's a noise machine."

"You give me shit about using a fan for white noise, while you're using that damn thing?"

"It helps me sleep."

"Jake, stop. Come on. I need your help here."

Jake kept loading his bag, looking determined.

"I made it all up, alright?" Ron said, realizing he needed to change gears. "I was just yanking your chain. You said all that stuff about the house being haunted last night, and I wanted to get back at you."

Jake stopped and looked at him, examining him, evaluating. Finally he said, "No, you didn't. You're just saying that so I won't go."

"Geez, Jake, seriously? You're gonna let a little ghost story spook you into leaving me high and dry? Come on, buddy. You're surprising the hell out of me; I wouldn't have brought it up if I thought you couldn't handle it."

That seemed to stop the man. He had a toothbrush in his hand, but instead of packing it, he sat on the edge of the bed and looked at its bristles. "This kinda shit gives me the willies. Big time."

"I didn't mean to upset you," Ron replied. "I seriously need your help."

"I don't know how much you know about Freedom," Jake said, still staring at the toothbrush he turned in his hand. "I know you two don't get along all that well, so I expect she's never opened up to you about what she's into."

"Into?" Ron replied, wondering for a moment if something weirdly sexual was about to be admitted.

Jake looked up at him, saw his reaction, and smirked. "Not like that, you pervert."

"What?"

"She's into all kinds of spiritual crap," Jake replied, returning his gaze to the toothbrush. "Shamans, that kind of thing. The house is covered in dreamcatchers. She's got an altar in the closet of our bedroom; you should see it. Man, it looks like something right out of a voodoo movie. Creeps me the fuck out."

Nothing Jake was telling him about Freedom was a surprise; she had always been a little odd. What was unusual was how Jake was talking about it; he seemed irritated, but under the irritation Ron could detect legitimate fright. It was something he'd never seen his friend express before.

"So, I'm not a fan of that stuff. She knows I'm not, so she usually doesn't involve me in any of it. She lets me watch football on the weekends without interrupting, I let her do her weird spiritual shit without interrupting. As long as the lines don't cross."

"Sure."

"You know, compromise."

"You don't gotta tell me about compromise."

"Well, although she might say otherwise, my football has never bled into her life the way her stuff has sometimes bled into mine."

Ron found himself becoming more intrigued the more Jake talked. "What do you mean?"

"Like," Jake said, pausing for a moment, "like sometimes whatever she's doing seems to…I don't know, like…invite things. Bring things into the house. Fucked up things."

"Things? Like what?"

"Spirits, demons, I don't know what you'd call them, bad shit, alright? It's happened a couple of times. Things start to go weird in the house; stuff moves, drawers open when no one's in the room, lights flicker – there's nothing wrong with our electrical, believe me…I did it all, it's perfect. One morning I found knives on the floor in the kitchen, all arranged in a pattern. Every knife had been removed from every drawer and laid out like some kind of ritual. One was stuck into the laminate, a good two inches buried into the floor."

Ron was uncomfortable with Jake's story. It seemed too improbable, something he would never personally believe, but he didn't want to derail his friend; he needed him to stay, to help. Finally he said, "That would be freaky."

"Every time weird shit like that happens, I talk to her about it, tell her I'm pissed that something's going on. She argues with me, but I know she knows exactly what I'm talking about. I can see it on her face, it's like, 'oh, it's happening because of *that*,' something she's done with her woowoo shit, and sure enough, a day later things are back to normal, like she went and fixed it. It's always something she's been causing."

He's taking this seriously, Ron thought, no longer worried that Jake might consider him crazy.

"So, I don't like this shit, Ron," Jake said, looking up again. "I've hated it since I was young. And I get enough of it at home, from her. I could use a break."

"I promise you, I'm not causing it," Ron replied. "Whatever is going on here, it's not because of anything I'm doing."

"Well, that's even worse!" Jake said. "At least Freedom knows how to stop it when I bitch about it!"

Ron knew he needed to move the conversation toward normality if he had any hope of convincing his friend to stay. "Look, let's just concentrate on the stuff that has to get done. The plumbing, replacing the trim, getting this place ready to survive a winter. There's no way I'm going to finish it all without your help, you know that."

"Yeah," Jake admitted, returning the toothbrush to the adjacent bathroom. "I guess." He seemed a little sheepish, as though he'd overreacted to what Ron had told him. "But if things get too fucked up, I reserve the right to leave." He returned to his bag and removed the noise machine, unwrapping the cord.

"Let me ask you a question," Ron said. "I mean this seriously: do you really believe in any of this? What I described in the back yard, the tapping at the window…the stuff Freedom does?"

"I do." He continued to unpack.

Ron nodded, then returned to the living room, sipping at his coffee.

Maybe I should take my own advice, he thought, *and just try to ignore things. Concentrate on the tasks. Forget all the weird shit, don't give it any mind.*

Maybe it'll go away.

- - -

Funny how daylight makes things seem normal, Ron thought as he carried another handful of boards to where Jake had set up his saw. Although wisps of fog still hung in the trees, most of it had burned off quickly and the afternoon was sunny and warm. They worked to replace exterior trim, removing pieces that were too far gone to be worth painting, nailing in freshly cut sections. It made the house look even stranger, its partial paint job now interrupted with bright bare wood.

As evening approached, the two exhausted men retired inside, sharing more beers. Ron was careful to avoid any discussion of the previous night's events. Old times, politics, and catching up on mutual acquaintances seemed more in order, and by the time Ron's eyelids felt heavy they'd managed to skirt around the unspoken subject of woowoo successfully. Ron wished Jake a good night and headed up the stairs.

He was halfway up when Jake called to him. "I'm keeping a shotgun loaded by my bed, just so you know."

"Good," Ron replied and kept walking. *Subject not forgotten,* he thought as he ascended. *Still right there, under the surface, easily acknowledged by both of us.*

Ron brushed his teeth and got into bed, wondering what the night had in store, hoping there might be a reprieve.

"You idiot!" Ron said to himself. "It'll never make it. They'll find out before it even arrives! You have totally fucked yourself!"

A crushing wave of guilt descended, making him feel as if all was lost, that it was only a matter of time before he'd be caught and his life would be over.

"Sending a head through the mail!" he muttered to himself. "Why wouldn't you just leave it in the box and cart it in the U-Haul, like everything else? It's like you *want* to get caught!"

Panic began to set in as he realized his options were few. At some point, someone in the postal system would wonder what the smell was, why strange liquid was leaking from the package – for god's sake, why the package itself was wrapped like a bowling ball, obviously round, obviously the size of…

"They'll hunt me down for sure. It's only a matter of time. So stupid!"

He'd kept the dismembered body locked away in a box in the cellar successfully for many years. It had been so long, he almost couldn't remember why it was there in the first place, although he was sure he'd been the one responsible. There was no question that he murdered a man and hid the remains, tucked it back in the far corners of the cellar and surrounded it with other boxes. There it sat for years, somehow avoiding detection by bugs and critters, and especially other people – Elenore, Robbie, neighbors, the authorities. Hell, even the dog that had been part of the family for a few years never found it.

"So, now it's time to move everything, and you fuck up the most important part!" Ron said to no one in particular, pacing in the new house, shocked at his own incompetence. He remembered taking the package to the post office and applying a number of stamps until it had enough postage to make it; he remembered handwriting the destination on the wrapping, the letters and numbers rising over the ridge that covered the head's nose. Placing it into the mail chute. Walking away like he'd done the right thing.

"Stupid!"

Somehow, he had the wherewithal to transport the rest of the corpse without involving the federal government's postal system, but for some damned reason, he thought it would be best to *mail* the fucking head to his new home.

"You *want* to get caught!" he said, still pacing, feeling anxious and sick to his stomach. "It's a cry for help. You murdered that person years ago, kept the chopped-up body in the cellar for all those years, just to fuck it all up and mail the goddamn head instead of simply moving it!"

Maybe they'll lose it, he thought. *The post office loses stuff all the time, right?*

Maybe the address will rub off and they won't be able to track me down. Maybe it'll get damaged in transit, pulverized between two other packages, somehow turned to dust.

He pictured the head, bouncing inside a mail bag on the back of a truck, barreling down I-5 on its way to a processing center, where someone would try to load it into a machine that would automatically read its address and bar code. Its unusual shape would never survive the system, he was sure – it would gum up the works, trip an alarm, halt processing. The nose would get caught on a metal gate as packages stacked up behind it, building pressure. Blood would seep from between the layers of wrapping, streaking the conveyor belts, staining other packages and eventually triggering something that required human interaction. A worker would remove the oddly shaped package from the gate, lifting it quickly so the other packages could continue along the conveyor. They'd march the package over to a special machine, the one they used to check suspicious packages for bombs. They'd place it on a small platform so that a giant x-ray could expose the package's contents.

They'd see the eyes, the tongue…the goddamn nose that got caught on the metal gate. The rough severing of the neck.

Maybe they'll think it's just a souvenir, like those shrunken heads you can buy on the wharf. Maybe the worker won't give a shit. There's a chance he might put it back on the conveyor and let it go through. Maybe it'll show up here at the house in a few days, just like I planned.

No. They're not stupid. It'll smell, it'll be leaking blood. They'll alert someone, and that someone will determine a murder was committed. They'll read the address, and they'll come for me.

He sat up in bed, feeling cold and clammy. A hand went to his forehead where he felt moisture; for a moment he wondered if the roof was leaking. Realizing it was only sweat, he forced himself to lay back down. The pillow was squishy and soft, soaked.

Fucking dream, he thought as he glanced at the alarm clock, seeing 2:38. *Go back to sleep.*

He tossed and turned for another ten minutes, until he decided he'd never drift off unless he switched out his pillow for something drier. Tossing the covers back, he let his legs fall to the floor and he stood up.

Through the dark windows he could see McLean in the distance, its lights faintly obscured through the trees. Everything seemed quiet and still, and he resisted looking down, afraid he'd see something disturbing in the back yard.

A thump from above caused him to jump. Like the thump he'd heard previous nights, it was muffled, as though something heavy had fallen on carpet. He waited, listening. After a few moments of silence, the familiar sound of steps returned; steps on the staircase, someone climbing them. He grabbed his robe and went for the door. When he reached the upper hallway, he stopped to look over the side, down into the living room.

Something was definitely wrong.

The room was dark, but what little light came through the windows made the flooring look white, and in motion: it was a dim layer of fog near the ground, hanging in the air above the floor like a pillowy carpet. He made his way downstairs, and as he reached for the light, he was startled by the shadow of a figure.

Someone – or something – was sitting in the recliner of the living room.

He flicked the switch and squinted. Jake sat in the recliner, a gun lying across his lap. Surrounding him, on the ground around the chair, were mounds of white. At first Ron was confused, but spying the empty shell of a pillow from the couch, lying on the floor amongst the scattered batting, he realized that, for some reason, the pillow had been gutted, its contents spread all over the floor.

"Jake?"

His friend snapped awake, quickly raising the shotgun and pointing it at him.

Ron's hands went into the air. "Jake! It's me! Don't shoot!"

His friend had one eye closed and the other squinting down the sight. Ron felt a moment of terror. *This is how it happens. An accident. A simple mistake.* He readied himself for a blast from the firearm, unsure if his friend was really awake or just moving on instinct.

Time seemed to freeze as Ron awaited his fate. Jake's face remained the same for a long time, until finally he seemed to become aware of what was happening. Ron watched as recognition appeared in his friend's eyes, and the barrel dipped. "Ron?"

"It's me, buddy," Ron replied, his hands still in the air above his head as though he was being robbed. "Can you lower the gun?"

Jake seemed unaware he was holding one. He looked at his hands, and suddenly seemed shocked that he had the firearm pointed at his friend. The barrel swung to the side and down.

"You OK?" Ron asked, looking around the room at the contents of the gutted pillow.

Jake seemed to sense how odd things looked. "Uh, yeah. I'm OK."

Ron walked to the sofa across from where Jake was sitting. "Kind of a mess in here."

"Yeah," Jake acknowledged. "I..." He fumbled with what to say. "I...well, fuck it all, Ron. I'm sorry."

"Sorry?" Ron asked, settling into the sofa.

"I...I thought the stuff inside the pillow would...Jesus Christ, I'm a little fucked up, buddy."

"It's OK," Ron replied. "Just keep the shotgun pointed away from me, and tell me what's going on."

Jake checked the safety and placed the gun on the floor, the barrel pointing behind him. "I...I thought I heard something, so I got up to see what it was."

"OK."

"There were these...creatures. Small, like the size of rats. They were running around in here. It was so weird; they'd rise up out of the flooring, then dip back down into it. I got the gun, but then I realized if I shot at them, it'd ruin your furniture, and the floors. We'd have a mess I'd have to fix. So... they kind of cornered me in this chair, and for some reason, I decided that...god, this is totally insane, but for some stupid reason I thought that if I spread the stuffing from that pillow around me, it would keep them away. Like a buffer they wouldn't cross."

"So, you tore up a pillow?"

"Yeah, that one that was on the chair," Jake replied, looking down until he found the pillow's carcass lying amongst the batting.

"That one there, the blue one. Christ, I'm sorry buddy, I don't know what I was thinking, I tore your pillow to shreds. Elenore will be pissed."

"It's no biggie. I hated that pillow anyway."

"They were all over the floor, scampering back and forth, appearing and disappearing. Why I thought the stuffing would keep them away I don't know, I just did."

"No rats here now, Jake."

"They weren't rats, they had little domes on their backs, like turtles, but they moved really fast."

"You were dreaming."

"Right…right. Of course."

"I'm glad you didn't shoot. We'd have buckshot everywhere."

"Yeah…"

"Did it work?"

"What?"

"The stuffing? It kept them away?"

"I…" Jake looked confused, as though part of his mind was still there, replaying earlier events. "I…think so. I remember spreading it around, and I put the gun in my lap, across the arms of the chair, and…I guess I fell asleep."

Ron rose from the couch and walked to the windows, stepping on the batting as he went. When he reached them, he cupped his hands and looked out, wondering if he might see Jake's creatures outside, scampering over the lawn. The back yard seemed empty and quiet, the light from the windows casting just enough to illuminate the blackberry bramble.

"Are they out there?" Jake asked.

"What? Your turtles? Nah, there's nothing out there." Ron turned from the window to look at his friend. "I guess we should go back to sleep. It's 3 AM."

"This is fucked up, Ron," Jake said, looking at the mess. "I'm sorry."

"Don't worry about it, we'll clean it up in the morning."

"No, I mean everything. The ghosts, the creatures. All of it. It's all fucked up."

"I had a bad dream, too. It's that pizza we ate just before bed. I've still got heartburn from the sausage."

Jake rose from the chair. He still seemed dulled; shell-shocked by something. He moved to the door of the guest room as though he was sleepwalking. "Good night," he said.

"Good night," Ron replied, looking at the mess on the floor. In all the years he'd known Jake, he'd never seen him behave so strangely. *We've never spent nights together, though...I wonder if he's a sleepwalker, if this is something he's done before. I could ask Freedom...*

Nah, don't want to know bad enough to deal with her.

He turned off the lights and went back upstairs, hoping, with one less pillow in the house, he might still find a dry one to sleep on.

Chapter Eight

"What's she doing here?" Ron said, looking up from the table saw. A white Volkswagen Beetle came to a stop behind Jake's truck, and Freedom emerged from it, her hair piled high on her head, her makeup achieving a half-Amy Winehouse.

Immediately Ron felt defensive. Freedom was carrying a small bag over her shoulder. She chewed gum with her mouth slightly open as she approached Jake.

"Baby!" she said.

"Thanks for coming," Jake replied, smiling at her, showing her the paint that covered his hands.

Ron walked up to her, offering a fake smile. "Freedom."

"Hi."

Ron turned to Jake. His friend looked away, not returning his gaze.

"Nice place," Freedom said, studying the facade. "Why he couldn't tell me he was working on your new house I don't know. Boys' time, I guess. Everything's got to be a secret from the old lady, like I'm gonna throw a fit or somethin'."

"He didn't tell you?" Ron said, feigning innocence, doubting Freedom bought it. He turned to Jake. "I can't believe you didn't tell her. I guess you haven't been communicating properly."

Jake offered a weak smile as a reply.

"You want the tour?" Ron asked.

"Sure, why not," she answered, walking to the front door. "Can I use the potty first?"

"Let me show you," Ron said, leading her to the guest room. "Just drop your stuff there; the bathroom is inside."

Freedom went in and closed the door, the sound of her smacking gum quickly fading.

Ron looked at Jake, and this time Jake sheepishly returned the stare.

"All this weird shit freaked me out, dude," Jake said. "Especially that stuff last night. I couldn't get back to sleep. I kept thinking I needed to do something, but I didn't want to bail on you, so, at like 4 AM I had this wild idea that maybe she could help, so I texted her, asked her to come. I felt better when she texted back saying she would drive up."

"You could have told me."

"Then when I woke up, I felt a little stupid about it. Seemed kinda chicken shit on my part, so I didn't want to tell you. Didn't want to ruin your morning."

"I appreciate you letting me have a nice morning," Ron replied sarcastically.

"It might work out OK, buddy. You never know, she might be able to help."

"Help?"

"With what's going on here."

"Going on?"

"You know, all the weird shit."

"What's she gonna do? Put crystals everywhere?"

"Maybe. Wouldn't hurt. She might help in other ways, too."

"She gonna help us with the work?"

"No, I meant she might...detect some things. Figure out why all the weirdness. Couldn't hurt, right?"

"No, I suppose it couldn't hurt," Ron replied, realizing that as much as he wasn't going to enjoy Freedom being around, it was a done deal now, and he'd have to tolerate her if he wanted Jake's continued help. They stood outside the guest room door awkwardly for a few moments, waiting for her to return.

"I shoulda told you."

"Yeah, well."

"Sorry."

Another pause.

Freedom emerged. "Well, Ron! Jake tells me you need a cleaning."

"Yeah, the house is filthy."

She began to walk around, inspecting. "It does need some Spic and Span, that's for sure, but from what he tells me, you need a very *different* kind of cleaning."

"What exactly did he tell you?"

"I just told her that things seemed a little weird here," Jake offered, his voice carefully balanced to sound neutral. "You know, that things didn't feel quite right."

"There's no question the place is energetically skewed," Freedom replied, walking into the kitchen, looking high and low, scanning everything. She paused and closed her eyes as though she was sensing something. Ron watched as her hand reached out to the kitchen counter, and she gently glided her fingers over the granite.

"You're gonna need to reseal that," she said, opening her eyes and continuing her self-led tour.

"Lots to do here," Ron replied. "That's why I was so grateful Jake was willing to help."

She made her way around the rest of the ground floor, spouting observations as though she was house shopping, commenting on various features and things she liked and didn't like.

"I can only stay the night," she said as she made her way through the dining room. "I gotta be in Portland tomorrow for a seminar. Man the table."

"The table?" Ron asked.

"She sells stuff," Jake offered. "At these little get-togethers they throw."

"It's not a get-together," Freedom corrected, turning the corner and making her way to the stairs. "It's a seminar. There are speakers and stuff." Ron thought she was going to go up, but she changed direction at the last minute and came to a stop at the door under the stairs. "Is there a basement?"

"No," Ron replied. "That's just a closet."

She reached for the doorknob, but pulled her hand away quickly before touching it, as though her fingers had been shocked. "Nuh uh!" she said dramatically. "No way!" She turned and went back to the stairs, her eyes rolling as she walked past.

"No way?" Ron asked.

"Not going in there!" she said. "Nuh uh." She started up the staircase. Ron and Jake followed.

"Why not?" Ron asked.

"When you become attuned to things like I am, you know how to avoid the bad juju."

"Under the stairs is bad juju?"

"Most definitely," she replied, her gum smacking as she climbed.

"Why? What's in there?"

"Don't know, don't wanna know," she replied, cresting the top of the stairs and continuing her inspection.

"I thought by walking around you were trying to get rid of bad juju," Ron said. "How can you do that if you avoid it?"

"Who said I was trying to get rid of it?" she replied. "I thought you offered a tour! Besides, I cannot have any of that kind of negative energy for tomorrow. I won't sell a damn thing if I do. Oh, look, a Jack and Jill bathroom!"

The tour continued until Freedom had seen every room and corner of the house. They came to a stop near the bay windows in the master bedroom. "OK," she said, looking down into the back yard. "I'll clean what I can while you two work."

"You think that'll fix things?" Jake asked nervously.

"Depends," she replied.

"Sounds iffy," Ron said.

"I can clean the place," she continued, "but that doesn't guarantee anything."

"Huh," Ron replied. "Why doesn't that surprise me?"

"It's worth a shot, though," Jake said, jumping in. "Right, Freedom? Can't hurt?"

"Like I said, it depends," she answered, turning to look at them. "You don't expect a doctor to cure you if you're not willing to tell her what your symptoms are, do you?"

"What's that supposed to mean?" Ron asked.

"Well, Jake has told me what he saw. I have some idea of what he's experienced, but I suspect you've seen some things too, Ron. Am I right?"

It was one thing to let Freedom run around his new house, checking out the place; it seemed an altogether different thing to confess to her all the strange things he'd seen the past few nights. He didn't care for the idea of explaining to her how terrified he felt when he saw the weird figures in the yard, or how paranoid his dreams had become. It wasn't just that he disliked the idea of subjecting himself to Freedom's perspective or analysis; he didn't want to admit to *anyone* the fear he experienced. It made him feel vulnerable; his brain was telling him he needed to remain stalwart. Looking at Freedom's face, the smirk just under her smile as she readied to hear him relate something that she would use to validate her irrational and ridiculous interests and passions – something she knew he was dismissive of – made him decide to play things down.

"It felt like something was here," he wound up saying, knowing it was vague.

"Something? Like what?"

"Hard to say. A creepy feeling."

"Jake made it sound like a lot more than that."

"What exactly did you tell her?" Ron asked Jake.

"Never mind that," she said, "why don't you just tell me, Ron?"

Now she's looking to see if I'm lying, he thought. *Comparing what Jake might have already said to whatever I might say.* He resolved to not give her the satisfaction. "Like I said, a creepy feeling."

"Tell her about the ghosts," Jake said.

Ron feigned ignorance, looking at Jake as though he'd made it up.

"You know, the ones you saw in the back yard," Jake continued, "looking into the house." Jake was clearly not taking his cue that he didn't want to spill everything to Freedom.

That's because he actually thinks she's here to help, while I think she's here to show me up, to rub my nose in things, to make me look like an idiot.

"I think that was a dream," Ron replied, giving Jake a half smile, hoping he'd take the hint.

"Tell me about it," Freedom insisted. "I need to know."

Ron sighed. In light of her insistence, he decided to cave a little. "I thought I saw figures outside, down there on the lawn."

"Looking into the house?"

"Yeah."

"How many?"

"A dozen or so."

"What did they look like?"

"I don't know, kind of fuzzy."

"What did they do?"

"Just stared into the downstairs windows."

"Were they moving?"

"Yeah, a little. More like drifting."

"Tell her about the one!" Jake interjected. "The one who floated up!"

Ron cringed. "It was a dream."

"One floated up?" she asked.

"Yes. It saw me and rose up from the ground until it was hanging in the air, right out there." Ron pointed to the window.

"Just hanging?"

"Yeah. Kinda crucifixion like."

"What did it do after that?"

"I don't know; I turned on the light. Couldn't see out anymore."

"So, that's it? Nothing else?"

Ron was still unsure of how much Jake had told her, but since she seemed ready for a conclusion, he didn't feel the need to offer any more. "Yeah, they were gone."

"So the light from the room cast out through these windows," she speculated, looking back into the yard, "and it dispelled them?"

"I guess you could say that. When I woke up, I..."

"Was it a dream, or not?" she asked, cutting him off. "I need to know. There's a big difference."

"In retrospect, it felt like a dream."

"But not at the time?"

"The next morning."

"Because your rational mind needed an explanation?"

"I suppose."

"But it seemed real, when it happened?"

Ron sighed again. She seemed so insistent that it was real, and he hated the idea of agreeing with her, of acknowledging that it had really happened and in some way validating her perspective. "I suppose," he repeated, trying his best to sound skeptical.

She peered down into the yard, thinking. "Working outside is more involved, but the weather seems OK. There's a few things I can try. I'm gonna need some quiet in the house for a little while; can you two work out in the garage? Stay out for, say, an hour or so?"

"You're gonna sage the place?" Jake asked.

"Definitely. More, if required."

"More, like what?" Ron asked.

"Come on, Ron," Jake said, pulling his friend by the shoulder. "Let's just go outside and let her do her thing." Ron allowed himself to be turned by his friend, following him downstairs.

"And I don't guarantee anything about that room under the stairs!" she called after them.

Just what I need, Ron thought. *She's gonna enjoy inspecting every little nook and cranny of the house, looking for flaws. Stuff she can use to tell Elenore the house is defective.*

When they got outside, Ron walked to the table saw and picked up the board he'd been working on. Before he turned on the blade, Jake stopped him.

"I'm sorry, buddy," Jake said. "I can tell you're pissed."

"Not pissed."

"Yeah, you are."

"Well, I hope *she* doesn't think I'm pissed."

"What she's gonna do might really help!" Jake offered, almost pleading, trying to diffuse and right things at the same time. He returned to a piece of trim he'd been working on before Freedom's arrival. "Can't hurt, right?"

Can it? Ron wondered, starting up the table saw so he didn't have to answer his friend. *Is there something she can do that would make things worse, aside from making Elenore hate the place even more? Whatever she's about to do, could it stir things up? Cause more things to happen? Piss off whatever is here?*

Maybe she'll irritate them to the point they leave. God knows she irritates me.

- - -

They worked on trim for a while, then turned their attention to the plumbing for the well. After several hours outside, Ron realized that he hadn't heard a single peep from the house.

"Do you think she's done?" Ron asked. "I need to go in and use the bathroom."

"I have no idea how long her stuff takes to do," Jake replied.

Ron considered peeing into the bramble, but decided he'd rather disrupt Freedom. He walked through the garage and entered the house, intending to slip in and use the back bathroom. Everything was quiet as he entered, and he couldn't help glancing toward the living room as he went through the kitchen, ready to explain himself if he should encounter her.

He stopped; something on the ground in the living room caught his eye.

It's a shoe...

Concerned, he changed direction. As he rounded the corner from the kitchen, Freedom's body came into view; she was lying on her back, her head facing up.

His first instinct was to call for Jake, worried that she was in trouble. Catching himself before he hollered, he wondered if Freedom was still performing her cleansing, and if he might be interrupting if he were to yell.

He approached her. She looked stiff; her arms were extended rigidly at her sides. When he saw her face, he knew something was definitely wrong; her eyes were open but white, rolled back into her head. *She's having a seizure,* he thought, checking her breathing. Her chest rose and fell steadily, her nostrils parting slightly with each breath.

He decided to check her pulse, anticipating that she would awake when he touched her wrist. *She might be pissed at me for disrupting whatever she's doing,* he thought, reaching for her arm, feeling between the tendons.

Steady pulse. Breathing fine. Maybe it's all part of her ritual.

He left the room, headed for the garage. He found Jake sawing through a PVC tube, and waved for him to stop. The man lowered the saw.

"Freedom is lying on the floor in the living room," Ron said. "Staring up at the ceiling."

Jake looked confused. "On the floor?"

"I felt like I should check her…she's breathing and her pulse is fine. Is this part of her cleansing thing?"

Jake's confusion turned to concern. He placed the pipe on the ground and walked inside, Ron following. They came to a stop near Freedom's feet and stared down at her.

"So, is this normal?" Ron whispered.

"I don't know," Jake whispered back.

"I didn't want to wake her, if it was part of her thing she was doing…"

"Yeah."

"But she didn't wake up when I checked her pulse."

Jake moved to her side. "What's wrong with her eyes?"

"They're rolled back in her head. So, you've never seen her do this before?"

"I usually don't hang around when she's doing her woowoo," Jake replied, then turned. "What's this?"

Lying on the ground a few feet away was a curved shell, about the size of a hand. Next to it was a bundle of small, thin twigs that had been tied tightly together with red thread. Jake lifted them from the ground and sniffed at it.

"Sage?" Ron asked.

"Looks like she dropped it," Jake replied, observing the charred end of the bundle. He glanced at his girlfriend again, then back at Ron. "Maybe something is really wrong."

"I was thinking a seizure. She ever had them before? Seizures?"

"No," Jake answered, looking down at Freedom, "not as far as I know. I think we should try to wake her. If we're interfering with her work, she'll be pissed, but if something's wrong I may need to get her to a hospital. Only way to know is to do it." He knelt next to her and reached for her arm, giving it a light tug.

Freedom didn't respond, so he tried her shoulders, shaking her gently. When that didn't work, he looked at Ron. "What now?"

"I don't know."

"Wish we had some of that shit they use on TV, stuff they hold under people's noses when they faint. They smell it and wake up."

"Smelling salts."

"Yeah, got some?"

"What, you think it's 1850? No, I don't have smelling salts."

"Something else that smells strong? Garlic, maybe?"

"Yeah," Ron replied, walking to the kitchen as Jake continued to shake Freedom's shoulders, trying to rouse her. He returned with a clove and handed it to him.

Jake pinched the clove and raised it closer to his face, taking a sniff. "Oh, yeah, that's strong." He held it under Freedom's nose, moving it from nostril to nostril, but her eyes still remained in the back of her head, the lack of pupils becoming more disturbing by the second, making it appear that she was under some kind of trance, or possession.

"Well, fuck," Jake said, growing inpatient. "What now?"

"You could slap her," Ron offered.

Jake looked up at him. "Really?"

"You know, like in the movies."

"Fuck, she'll be pissed."

"Well, try patting her cheeks. See if that does it."

Jake leaned over her again and lightly slapped at her face. "Free? Come on, Free, wake up." He increased the force of the pats. "You passed out, babe, you need to wake up. Come on, come on!"

Ron noticed Freedom's cheeks began to flush; however, her eyes didn't change.

Jake continued patting, calling, trying to revive her. After a couple of minutes with no response, he became frustrated. "This isn't working, either," he said to Ron.

"Give her a good slap," Ron said.

"Fuck, I ain't gonna hit her!"

"Then the next step is loading her into the car for a trip to the emergency room," Ron said.

Jake looked up at him. "We don't have any insurance."

"No insurance?" Ron replied, exasperated.

"It's fucking expensive!"

"I know how expensive it is!" Ron dropped to Freedom's side to check her pulse again. "Heartbeat's good. She's breathing fine. A little flush with all the slapping you've been doing already. She just seems…asleep. We've got to…"

Jake brought his hand back and landed a loud smack on Freedom's cheek, causing her head to flip to the right. "Wake up!" he yelled.

Freedom's eyes blinked and closed. As her head turned back, they opened again, this time with her pupils centered. She seemed to be staring at the ceiling for a few seconds, but then drifted to look at Ron and Jake. Ron could see the exact moment when she returned to her senses, and she resumed chewing her gum. Slowly her face began to contort with emotion; Ron stood up and took a step back, sure she was about to freak out at Jake for the slap.

"You OK, babe?" Jake asked meekly.

"Help me up!" she demanded, reaching for him. Jake grabbed her arms and pulled until she was upright, then placed a hand on her back to steady her.

Freedom looked at both of them. Ron thought she looked angry, assuming the slap was the reason. "I'm outta here!" she said, and pushed them both aside as she walked between them, headed for the guest room.

Ron glanced up at Jake. He looked as though he, too, had steeled himself for an angry response from Freedom. As she stormed off, their defense changed to concern. Jake went after her, and Ron followed.

"I'm sorry, babe, we were worried! I thought you had passed out or something! I didn't mean to interfere with your..."

She suddenly stopped and whirled around. "Interfere? You didn't interfere!" She turned to look at Ron, and as she did, he realized the look on her face wasn't anger, it was fear. "My advice to you is to sell this place and move." She grabbed her bag from the bed in the guest room and turned, headed for the front door. When she reached it, she grabbed the handle, opened it, and marched out.

"What the fuck?" Ron asked Jake.

Jake shrugged, and ran after her. "Where are you going?" he called, following her across the front yard.

"I'm not spending another moment in that house!" she yelled over her shoulder as she stormed to her car. "I can't be anywhere near this place!"

Jake caught up to her as she reached the Volkswagen and stepped between her and the door. "Wait a sec! Calm down! What happened?"

Ron came up behind her. Freedom turned to face him. "There's something extremely evil in there," she said, raising her arm to point at the house behind him. "I've never seen anything like it, never felt anything so...so..."

"Evil?" Ron repeated, his skepticism showing.

"E-vil!" she emphasized each syllable, and turned back to Jake. "I have an event tomorrow! I won't sell a damn thing if I'm coated in this...this..."

"Evil?" Ron repeated.

She turned back to face him. "Don't patronize me! I don't give a fuck what you believe, and I sure as shit don't have to put myself at risk!" She pushed her way past Jake and reached for the door handle, opening the car. "And you!" she said to Jake, "you better not spend another night in this place, you hear me?"

"Where are you going?" Jake asked.

"I'll spend the night in Portland," she replied, getting into the car.

"You left some stuff inside," Ron offered.

"Stuff?"

"Your shell, the bundle of weeds I presume is sage."

"I don't want it, it's tainted now."

"Tainted?" Ron repeated.

She slammed the door closed. Ron and Jake watched as she took several deep breaths, calming herself. Finally, she rolled down the window. "You can be as dismissive and skeptical as you want.

Doesn't change anything. That house is fucked up." She started the car.

"Wait!" Jake protested.

"At least tell me what happened," Ron asked. "I mean, you came all the way out here. 'Fucked up' isn't much to go on. Did something happen to you? Why were you passed out?"

She paused for a moment, then turned the engine off and looked at Ron. "There's something inside there. It's been there for a long time. It's evil. I sensed a kind of determination…" She shook her head, as though the move would jar loose more information. "You know, most spirits aren't good or bad, they just hang around for some reason or another. This is different. What you've got in there, it has an agenda."

"What?" Ron asked.

"Don't know. I backed away…tried to, at least. I kept hitting a wall, couldn't move where I wanted to. What I could sense was an overwhelming desire to pursue something, willing to do anything to get what it wanted. A kind of overwhelming determination."

"Determination? To do what?"

"I can't tell you, I don't know, and I don't want to know. I have to make sales tomorrow, Ron! The people at my event can feel things, they'll pick up on this, and they'll steer clear of my table! It cost me three hundred dollars to register, and I've got to make that back!" She started up the car again.

"Don't go, babe!" Jake said. "Please stay! We need the help. Ron needs it."

"I don't work the dark!" she replied. "You of all people should know that." She put the car into reverse. "Don't spend another night in that house, Jake. Do what I say! Go back home. I'll see you the day after tomorrow."

"I can't just abandon him!" Jake protested. "He's hired me to work! I'm making bank here, babe. We need the money. And he doesn't know what he's doing with a lot of this stuff."

She stared back at him, unmoved.

"His damn well doesn't work!" Jake continued. "He's got no water! He needs help!"

"Yeah," Ron added. "I can't do this alone."

"Nothing you make working here is worth the risk," she said to Jake. "Don't stay! You go home *tonight*, you hear me? I'm warning you!" She suddenly became disgusted at the gum in her mouth, and spat it out the window. The car backed up, and within seconds she had completed a turn and headed up the driveway, disappearing into the trees.

Ron glanced at Jake. He expected his friend to look a little sheepish, but instead Jake seemed perturbed.

"What was all that?" Ron asked.

"Hell if I know. Not like her."

"I'm guessing this wasn't her normal woowoo result."

"No. It's usually all light and wonderful and crystals and shit. I don't think I've ever heard her say the word 'evil' before."

"What do you think happened to her, in there?"

"I have no idea."

"Do you think she made it up?"

"Why?"

"To get you to go back home? It's no secret we don't get along."

"So, you think she'd make shit up just to get me to leave?"

"Wouldn't put it past her. I've known some possessive women in my time. You know she doesn't like me."

"She was knocked out in there, Ron!" Jake replied. "No, I don't think she made that up. And you have to admit, there's some really weird shit going on here. That's why I texted her in the first place."

"Yeah, I suppose that's true."

There was a pause. Ron was afraid of how Jake might answer the next question, but he knew he needed to ask it. "You gonna stay?"

"Of course," Jake replied. "She can't order me around like that."

Chapter Nine

"There are times when my stomach sounds like a dog howling at the moon!" Jake said, looking down at his body.

"Christ!" Ron replied, listening. "It sounds like a zoo in there!"

"Sorry, it might go on for a while."

"You can't be hungry, we ate an hour ago."

"It's digesting," Jake replied, leaning back in a chair in the living room and placing his feet on a box that served as an ottoman.

"It's like it's screaming in agony," Ron observed, sitting across from him with a piece of pie on a plate. "You sure you don't want one?"

"Had two already. Might be why the tank is rebelling." He glanced down at his stomach. "Shut up down there!"

"I'm sure another shot of bourbon will help," Ron replied, nodding to the bottle next to Jake.

His friend took the hint and poured himself another glass, immediately downing it. "I'll drown the little fuckers!" he said, wiping his mouth with the back of his hand.

"I gotta say, we did some good work today. I'm grateful you stayed."

"Yeah, a lot of work. More than I thought we'd do. You happy with what we did on the reservoir? I thought it was a clever solution, if I do say so myself."

"Might have to redo some things after they deepen the well, but this'll get me by until then."

"Christ, you really gonna do that? I thought it was going to cost an arm and a leg."

"Forty dollars a foot, plus a lot of other charges."

"Oh, phaw!" Jake said, waving his hand. "Four hundred isn't so bad! Just have 'em do it."

"Forty times a hundred is four thousand, not four hundred."

"Oh, yeah...got my zeros wrong. Christ, that's a lot."

Ron could hear Jake's phone buzzing in his pocket, but his friend wasn't making any moves to retrieve it. "Not gonna check that?"

"Already know. She's been texting me every half hour with threats."

"Threats?"

"If you stay there, you'll...You come home before midnight, or else...that kind of shit. I responded to the first couple but I've been ignoring her for a while."

"Damn, I'm sorry, I feel like I created a problem between the two of you."

"Forget it. It was my decision to come, my decision to ask her to stop by, my decision to stay. You've got nothing to apologize for." Jake poured himself another shot.

Outside, dusk had become darkness, and the lights inside the house caused reflections in the windows. Ron tried to look out from where he sat, but was unable to see anything through them. He felt a growing sense of dread. *Maybe Freedom was right, and we shouldn't stay here.*

Don't be stupid, he corrected himself. *You own this house. You have to live in it. What are you going to do, stay in a motel? You wanted to be out of the city, alone, with solitude. Now you have it. You're going to have to learn to enjoy it.*

"Dark out already," Jake observed, when he saw Ron looking out the windows. "What is it, 8?"

"After 9," Ron replied, feeling sleepy. "Long day."

"Yeah," Jake answered, lifting the glass to his lips. Instead of tossing this one back, he sipped at it. "I'm already feeling it in my back. Although this booze is helping me forget it's there."

Ron rose from his chair. "I realize it's still a little early, but I'm beat. I'm gonna turn in." He started for the stairs.

Jake stopped him. "Ron?"

"Yeah?"

"I'd like you to promise me something."

"What?"

"If you see anything weird tonight, wake me up so I can see it too. I don't want to spend the night lying in there, thinking something might be going on, when it isn't. I'm gonna assume you'll cut me in if shit starts up, otherwise I intend to sleep."

"If it's weird shit, I would have thought you'd prefer to be left out."

"No, I'm the one with the gun. I'll have it by my bed, ready to use. You call down and wake me up, and I'll do the same if I see anything weird."

"OK, buddy," Ron replied, and started up the stairs. "It's a deal."

He made his way to the master bedroom and cleaned up before stripping down and getting into bed. The long, physical day took its toll, and Ron found his eyes closing before his head even hit the pillow.

- - -

He awoke to the feeling of cold metal against his nose. In the dim light of the bedroom, he could make out a shadow by the side of the bed. As he became more conscious, he realized it was a man looking down at him, shoving something toward his face.

In horror he realized it was the barrel of a gun.

"Jake?"

"I can't let you do it!" the figure replied, sobbing. "All those innocent people!"

"Jake? Jake? It's me, Ron." His heart was beating so fast, he could hear it pounding in his ears like a drumbeat. He felt like yelling, but didn't want to shock or stir up emotion in his friend, not with the cold metal of the barrel right under his nose. "Move the gun away from my face."

"You promise you won't do it?" Jake pleaded, wrapped up in some kind of dream. He'd never heard Jake cry before, and it made his voice sound higher than normal. He wanted to reach up and grab the barrel to push it away from his face, but was afraid the movement might startle him.

"I promise," Ron replied, not knowing what he was agreeing to, but trying his best to sound sincere. "Just move the gun. I promise I won't."

"OK," Jake said, and the barrel shifted to the left. Ron grabbed it, pointing it into the mattress by his side in case Jake pulled the trigger. He slipped out of bed, his fingers still wrapped around the barrel. "Give me the gun."

Jake released the firearm, and Ron took hold of it. His friend stumbled back, away from the bed.

"You OK?" Ron asked.

Jake didn't speak, just kept retreating until he came to a wall, where he stopped and slid down until he was sitting on the floor.

Ron placed the gun on the bed and reached for his robe, throwing it around his shoulders and switching the light on his night stand.

Jake had his head in his hands, still gently crying.

"Buddy?" Ron asked, walking toward him. "You OK?"

"You were setting bombs," Jake said through his hands, not looking up. "You placed all these bombs all over the house, like in a movie, and you were going to set them off. All the people were going to be killed. Innocent people."

"People in the house?"

"Yeah, it was full of people. It was this house...but it wasn't, too, you know, how things aren't quite right in a dream."

"Yeah."

He looked up. "I can't believe I pulled the gun on you."

"Me either. I about shit myself."

"I don't know why…I mean, I've never sleepwalked or anything like that. It's just…it seemed so real. Like you were really going to do it, and I had to stop you, I couldn't be part of murdering all those people." He looked up. "I…I might have killed you."

"Maybe having the gun around wasn't the best idea," Ron offered, looking over to the bed where the firearm still lay on the covers.

"Yeah," Jake agreed, lowering his head again. "What if I had pulled the trigger? Freedom was right; I should have left. Maybe you should, too."

He sat next to his friend. "Don't sweat it, buddy. It's over. It was just a dream."

"Nearly killed you."

"But you didn't."

"How do I go back to sleep? How do either of us? I might try it again."

"We'll lock up the guns."

"You don't understand," Jake replied. "It was overwhelming…I *had* to stop you. If I hadn't found a gun, I would have used a knife from the kitchen. My bare hands. I was convinced you were going to blow the place up."

"Like a movie."

"Just like that. Sticks of dynamite all bundled up, wires and timers and shit…"

"Why? Do you know why I was doing it?"

"No. Just that you were determined. I had been helping you, but at the last minute I realized how many people you were going to kill, and I realized I had to stop you."

"I think all the spooky shit going on – and your girlfriend's visit – might have sent our imaginations into overdrive." Ron rose from the floor. "I've had some weird dreams lately, too. Very bizarre. They seemed real, but of course dreams always do."

"Like what?"

"Just bizarre shit. Paranoid stuff."

"Like someone is going to blow the place up?"

"Well, not that exactly, but paranoid, yeah."

Jake rose. "Listen, I want to stay here and help you, I really do, but I thought it'd just be two buds hanging out, working, drinking, you know. A nice getaway from my old lady for a while."

"Don't tell me you're going to ditch me. Listen, we'll keep the guns in your truck."

"Wouldn't have made any difference. I'd have gone to the truck for them before coming up here."

"Then I'll go into town and get locks. We'll secure them. Just don't bail on me."

"We've got to do something about this shit, Ron!" Jake replied. "It's not just plumbing and the siding. If you want me to stay and help, you need to…" He paused.

"What?"

"I don't know, clean this shit out, have the place exorcised or something, so we can actually work here."

"Exorcised? Don't be crazy."

"Freedom was gonna clean it out before she got scared and ran off. Something is here, and it needs to go. If you want my help, it's gotta happen. I can't stay here and take this shit. We clean out the weirdness, then I'll stay and we do the rest. But fuck, we're not getting any sleep, we're starting to go crazy ourselves."

Ron felt that Jake's demand was ridiculous, but there was no question he needed the help, and if indulging Jake's idea bought him more time with his friend, he decided the best thing was to go along with it. "OK, so say I agree...then what? Freedom ran out. She's the only person I know who's into this type of stuff."

"There's someone else," Jake replied. "I can try calling him in the morning."

"Who?"

"A guy in Port Angeles."

"Christ, way up there?"

"I'm sure Freedom could refer me to people, but there's no way she would; she's pissed enough at me as it is. This guy might be able to help. I'll call him and see."

Ron sighed. "What's he gonna do?" he muttered.

"I don't know, sage the place? Banish stuff? I mean, Freedom didn't even finish sageing, so we know the house still hasn't been cleaned."

"Do you hear yourself?" Ron asked. "Cleaned...it sounds ridiculous."

"I am trying to be upfront with you. Do you seriously think you can live in this house, like this? How about Elenore? Robbie? What happens when you wake up one morning, holding a knife to Robbie's throat? What then?"

Suddenly things switched in Ron's thinking. Jake was right; if weird stuff kept happening after Elenore or Robbie arrived, it would be terrible. It was already hard enough to win Elenore over to the idea of the place; she had a long list of legitimate, physical problems that needed to be addressed – that he had *agreed* to address – and adding ghosts and night terrors and paranoia to that list would topple any chance he had of convincing her that the house was really where they belonged.

And he couldn't imagine subjecting his son to any of it; the idea of his boy waking suddenly to find his life in danger was unacceptable. Despair washed over him in waves, making him feel ill. Now he wanted to throw in the towel, put the place up for sale, and never let Robbie anywhere near it, despite the way he'd played it up to his son, all the wonderful aspects of the house that he'd described to Robbie in detail, hoping to win him over, too.

You can't sell, he thought. *The well. No water. No one will be able to get a loan to buy the place. You're stuck.*

You need Jake not only to fix the place up to a point where it could go on the market, but to get it clean of all this weird shit as well. You need his help on both fronts.

"Alright," Ron replied, feeling as though he was betraying common sense, but at a loss for alternatives. "I agree. We'll try whatever; this Port Angeles guy, anything else you think we need." He looked at the clock on the bed stand. "It's almost 5. I'm not going back to sleep, are you?"

"I don't think so."

"I'll start some coffee, then."

- - -

Jake had been gone about an hour. Ron continued to work on the exterior, replacing worn trim, cutting each piece to fit, using tricks he'd picked up from his friend. He saved the pieces for Jake to nail up when he got back, knowing he would do a better job of it.

He was about to take a break when he heard Jake's truck in the distance; soon it appeared on the road. He watched as it pulled in, and Jake got out.

Ron was momentarily confused when a kid emerged from the passenger side; the boy looked like a teenager. *This is who Jake thought could help?*

"Ron, this is Terrell," Jake said, as the kid pulled a backpack out of the truck and slung it over his shoulder.

Ron extended a hand and they shook. "Nice to meet you."

"Same here," Terrell replied, and turned to look at the house. "This it?"

"Yeah. Want a tour?"

"Do you mind if I just explore a little on my own?"

Ron looked at Jake. "Did my friend here tell you what happened to the last person who worked alone in there?"

"Yeah," Terrell answered, "she passed out or something?"

"Might have lit the house on fire with that burning sage she dropped," Ron replied.

"No sage here," Terrell said, slapping his backpack.

"Yeah, sure," Ron replied. "Go ahead, explore. Door's open. We'll be checking on you in a bit, though, just to be safe."

Terrell nodded and walked to the house, disappearing inside.

"What is he, twelve?" Ron asked.

"Older than that. He owns a business. He's gotta be eighteen at least."

"And why him? What did you say his qualifications were?" *As though this type of thing has qualifications.*

"He owns a ghost tour business in Port Angeles. Freedom and I went on it last summer when we were up there for one of her gigs. She thought he was impressive."

"Impressive? In what way?"

"She said he has the gift."

Ron rolled his eyes. "That just sounds so...stupid, like a flattering word these people made up for themselves. 'The gift'...what the hell does that even mean?"

"Freedom thinks she has the gift, too. But she said this guy had more."

"More, like it's something you can quantify? Like they all have little gas gauges?

"She seemed to think so. Not the gas gauges, of course."

"And this is gonna cost me two hundred bucks?"

"Plus room and board, for at least a couple of nights."

"Well, it's not like there aren't enough bedrooms. I can unfold that futon thing, I guess." He walked back to the saw.

"Oh, hey, look at that!" Jake said. "You cut some trim!"

"I can't guarantee they're all correct. You'll just have to see."

"I'll let you know how many I have to redo."

After giving Terrell some time in the house, Ron decided to check on him. He found him at the top of the stairs. "Things OK?" he asked.

"If by OK you mean dead, yeah."

"Dead?"

"Oh, sorry, I don't mean dead-dead, just, 'dead'… it's what I say when I mean there's nothing here."

"Nothing…weird? Is that the right word for it?"

"It's as good as any. I'll keep looking." Terrell turned and continued down a hallway, while Ron walked into the kitchen to find something to drink. He removed a bottle of water from the fridge and sat in a chair in the living room, relishing the chance to get off his feet for a few minutes. He heard the thumping of Jake's nail gun as pieces of trim were attached to the side of the house.

After a couple of minutes had gone by, he heard Terrell coming down the stairs.

"Nice house!" Terrell said, walking into the living room.

"Thank you."

"Mind if I sit?"

"Sure. Want some water?"

"That'd be great."

As Terrell walked to a chair, Ron rose and retrieved a bottle from the kitchen. "So?"

"So, I don't sense a lot."

"Really?" Ron asked, handing the bottle to Terrell.

"Not really."

"How about under the stairs?"

"No, didn't notice anything special there."

Ron sat in his chair. "How do you sense these things, exactly?"

Terrell smiled. "Jake said you were skeptical. It certainly comes through in your voice."

"Sorry. I don't mean to be condescending or disrespectful."

"It's all good. I'm used to it. Lots of skeptics on my ghost tour. I take it in stride, doesn't bother me."

"So, your ghost tour is in Port Angeles?"

"Yup. Been doing real well ever since I got new flyers. The old ones I had were so lame, people didn't take it seriously. The new flyers are really slick, very professional looking."

"And that made you more serious?"

"Ah, more cynicism! Like I said, doesn't bother me."

"I'm just trying to understand what you do. Did Jake tell you about the things we've seen here?"

"He did."

"Did he tell you everything? Mind repeating what he said?"

"He said you've seen some ghosts – or, what he thought might be ghosts – at night. That you were having weird dreams. That his girlfriend tried to clean the house but it went badly."

Hmm...no mention of the gun incident, Ron thought. *Probably didn't want to scare the kid away.* "Anything else?"

"No. Maybe you could tell me exactly what you saw?"

For a moment Ron considered playing things down, but then figured, *I'm paying this putz two hundred dollars. Might as well go for broke.* "There were figures on the back lawn, looking into the house. At first I thought it might be real people; there was a break-in when the house was on the market. It didn't take long to realize they weren't normal people, the way they moved over the ground...I guess 'drifted' is a better word. One of them saw me looking at them from the upstairs window, and floated up to me."

Ron took a look at Terrell. The kid seemed calm but fidgety, as though he was secretly terrified and trying to hide it with a veneer of professionalism – or what he considered to be professionalism.

"When I turned on the light in my room," Ron continued, "they were gone. Well, that's not true. I turned the light off again, and *most* of them had gone."

"Light banished them?"

"Banished? I suppose. There were less of them."

"Hmm."

Ron could see Terrell's eyes going back and forth as he thought, mulling something. "What?"

"Well, that's interesting. The light thing isn't uncommon."

There was something about the way the kid replied, his tone, how he adjusted himself in the chair, which sent up a red flag in Ron's mind. It wasn't that he was dislikable; Terrell seemed personable and friendly, not overly dramatic like Freedom, much more down to earth. It was Ron's sense that the veneer was still there, that the kid was trying to cover over something, maybe some secret, or inadequacy. *Might be nerves, he might just be uncomfortable with meeting new people. Lack of confidence.* "What's next? Do you have a game plan?"

"Sounds like night is when the action will be," Terrell replied. "It's a few hours until sunset. I'd like to get ready by placing a few things around the house and out in the yard. If you don't mind."

"No, go ahead, whatever you need to do. Jake's staying in that room, over there. I'll put you in a room upstairs, the one to the right at the top of the stairs. It's just a futon, sorry. Don't have a lot of the furniture here yet."

Terrell smiled and rose from his chair. "A futon is great. That's what I have at home." He walked out of the room, into the kitchen, and opened a door that led to the back yard.

Ron went to one of the windows and watched as Terrell inspected the area. The kid walked up to the blackberry bramble and looked carefully into it, as though he was searching for something. After making his way around the entire thing, he came back to the center, walking carefully over the grass until he reached a spot where the grass thinned, exposing bare dirt. He stopped for a moment, then swung his bag from his shoulder and removed something. Kneeling, he placed a small object on the spot, then went back to the bramble and repeated the process, removing items from his pack and placing them on the ground in carefully selected locations.

Wonder what that is, Ron thought. *I'll ask him later.*

Eventually Terrell wandered around the side of the house, and Ron lost sight of him. He decided to go back to the garage and work with Jake.

- - -

As dusk approached, Ron and Jake called it a day and put away the tools. When they came inside, Ron found Terrell in the living room, his ear against a wall.

"We're gonna make some dinner," Ron said. "I presume you're hungry."

"Shhh," Terrell replied, raising his hand. He listened intently, then whispered to Ron, "Do you have mice? Rats?"

"Wouldn't surprise me," Ron whispered back. "Haven't seen any, but the inspector said there were a lot of mouse turds in the attic. Which is a little weird, since this house obviously had cats."

Terrell removed his head from the wall. "I swear I heard something in there."

"It makes a lot of different noises," Ron replied, returning to the kitchen, where Jake had already removed beers from the fridge. "I'm slowly getting used to them."

"How about a scratching?" Terrell asked, following him. "Like something with claws, inside the walls, wanting out?"

"Christ, that sounds sinister," Jake said.

"No," Ron replied to Terrell, "but there was a face in my bedroom window one night. He scratched at the glass with a fingernail. Does that count?"

"Really?" Terrell asked, as Jake handed him a beer. "It made a sound, like it was really there?"

Jake shivered. "Gives me the willies just thinking about it."

Ron continued, "He'd scratch at the window a couple of times, then pull back, disappearing into the night."

"It was a man?" Terrell asked.

"Take that back," Ron answered. "Just saw the finger the first couple of times. The man part came later."

"That's like a creepy fucking campfire story," Jake said. "Gives me the willies. Was this before I arrived?"

"Yes."

"And you conveniently didn't mention it when you asked me to come help?"

"No."

Jake handed him the other beer. "Some friend you are."

Ron started making dinner. "To be honest, I thought there was a good chance it was all a dream, or that I was hallucinating. I wasn't going to bring it up and sound like a total crackpot. It wasn't until you saw stuff here, too, Jake, that I realized it wasn't just me."

"Some entities can move things," Terrell said, "but it's rare. Tapping or scratching on glass is unusual. They tend to pass through the physical."

"That would make sense," Jake offered, "being ghosts and all. Just like the movies, right? They're translucent and shit, right?"

"Yes," Terrell answered. "So normally they can't interact with physical things. But sometimes they expend energy that traverses the veil and interacts with a real, physical thing, like knocking over a vase, or tossing a book. It's something they build up, kind of like a really intense exhale. You see it with entities that are a nine or ten on the trauma scale, filled with emotions so strong that instead of dissipating upon death, the emotion spins them up into a non-dead state, making them worse than in real life."

"Like *Poltergeist*?" Jake asked.

"Well, that was Hollywood," Terrell answered, "but yes, kind of like that. I've never heard of them doing anything as elaborate as stacking chairs, but I do know of a case where knives were animated. They slid out of a block, one by one, and flew across the room."

Jake looked as though he was about to comment, but raised the beer to his lips instead, glancing down at the ground after he swallowed.

"Christ!" Ron replied to Terrell. "Was anyone hurt?"

"No. The knives landed against a wall and fell to the floor. Someone could have been seriously injured, though, obviously, had they been in the way."

"Where did this happen?" Ron asked, skepticism in his voice as he stuck a foil-covered pan into the oven.

"Freeville, New York, to the daughter of a professor who taught at Ithaca." Terrell replied, looking pleased with his answer. "From March 1981 to July of the same year. It's referred to as the Cassavant Incident."

Ron nodded in acknowledgement, impressed that the kid had all the details at the ready. "OK."

"Imagine how much effort it took a non-corporeal entity to perform such an act; removing each knife, positioning it, and hurtling it through the air."

"I guess you could ask, what was the point?" Ron replied. "If it's that demanding upon the entity, why expend the energy?"

"Well, in the Cassavant case," Terrell said, "the entity seemed to be intent upon terrorizing an old man who came to live with the family at the house. There had been no activity while the family lived there from 1976 to 1981, but in March of that year, the eighty-year-old father of the woman of the household became ill, and rather than put him in a care facility in Rochester, they invited him to live with them. Shortly after he moved in, the incidents began. They ended when he died in July."

"So people assumed he was the cause of whatever happened?" Ron asked, setting a timer.

"They did," Terrell replied. "Somehow, he was the focal point of the manifestations."

"So…" Ron continued, "instead of believing the old man performed those actions himself – he threw the knives and whatever else – the family turned it into a ghost thing?"

"He wasn't in the room when the knives flew, or the other incidents happened."

"Who was?"

"Usually the woman's daughter, age ten."

"Let me guess, it was the girl who discovered all the weird shit that happened, reported it to the family."

"You're suggesting the girl made it up, that she was upset about her grandfather coming to live with them."

"Seems logical."

"That's what the father suspected. He went so far as to accuse the grandfather of molestation, thinking that his daughter was acting out in response to trauma. Authorities became involved. The old man claimed innocence. The girl was interviewed by police and examined by doctors. There was no evidence of abuse; the girl said she loved her grandfather, and that nothing inappropriate had ever happened between them."

"Doesn't mean she wasn't secretly unhappy about things, that she didn't stage stuff like the knives."

"And there are many cases of entities reacting to children of that age," Terrell replied. "Something about all the pre-pubescent emotions and hormones seems to bring them out of the woodwork."

"Or make the kids even better at inventing shit. They're old enough to know how to construct fabrications. They don't want to get caught, so they try to lie their way out of things."

"The knives flying through the air was witnessed by the mother, the father, and the girl's older brother. The three of them were in the kitchen when it happened."

"Huh," Ron replied, surprised, not quite sure how to respond to keep his line of argument going. "I guess it's too much to suggest collusion."

"To what end?"

"Notoriety. Wasn't *The Amityville Horror* right around that time, in New York? You said the incident even had a name. Someone wanted to make some money from a haunted house story, perhaps."

"Well, I can't really speak to that. Obviously it was before my time, and I wasn't there. As far as I know, the situation was never reported in the press, nor was there any attempt to capitalize on it. The only records of it were made by an organization I trust."

"Organization?"

"Yes."

"What, like a ghost writer's club?"

"Not exactly. But their record for documentation is solid."

"Who are they?"

"You wouldn't know them. They don't publish for notoriety, just enthusiasts."

"Like you."

"Yes."

"What, like books? You bought their books?"

"Christ, the third degree!" Jake interjected. "Give the kid a break, Ron!"

"They don't make money selling books," Terrell offered. "Trust me. They're more photocopies than books. What I paid for the information barely covered the cost of the paper, I'm sure."

"Whatever," Ron replied, noting the scowl Jake was still giving him. He tipped his beer and took a long swig of the cold beverage, feeling the subject dissipate as the alcohol entered his system.

"I told you he was skeptical," Jake said to Terrell.

"What I don't get," Terrell replied, turning again to Ron, "is that you yourself told me you saw ghosts in your back yard. Yet you discredit this story I'm telling you about the knives."

Good point, Ron thought. "My rational brain struggles with this kind of shit, almost constantly. My first inclination is to search for an answer that has some basis in normal, cogent thought. History is full of mystical justifications for things that were later given concrete, scientific explanations, making the supernatural explanations look stupid. I'd hate to think I'm jumping to an irrational idea just because the real answer isn't immediately apparent." He grabbed his beer and walked to the living room to sit down. "I remember a TV show, years ago, where this guy would walk around a group of people and claim to be receiving messages from the dead. He'd say things like, 'Someone seated in this area is thinking of the color orange, or has a family member who died in an accident,' and someone would raise their hand, and then he'd tell them more about a message he was receiving from their dead uncle, or mother, or whatever. And it really came off as creepy, like he really was channeling something. The people would be in shock at what he told them because it was all so accurate. He'd have them in tears, telling them their father wanted them to know this or that, or that their sister who died of some disease was happy in some better place, and for them not to worry. I remember watching it with Elenore, and she actually told me she thought he was some kind of miracle, that he had 'the gift' and was the real deal. I remember reading that this guy charged astronomical rates for private readings, and the waiting list to see him was years long."

"I remember that guy!" Jake said enthusiastically, sitting on the sofa. "John something or other. Freedom loved him! She has some of his books. He hasn't been on TV for a while, though. At least, I haven't seen him."

"So, I did some research," Ron continued, "and the guy uses common techniques most people don't know about. I found out the show was heavily edited, a three or four hour taping cut down to a half hour, showing only the parts he happened to get right, cutting out all the things he got wrong."

"I know who you're talking about," Terrell said. "He's a grand-stander. Not what I do, not what I study."

"My point is," Ron continued, "if you didn't know about the tricks, the techniques, the editing, it was so easy to just default to 'the guy really has a connection to the dead!' like Elenore and Freedom."

"And me!" Jake added. "I was convinced."

"And then you study up on it," Ron continued, "even just a little – it took me all of five minutes on the internet – and you find out the whole thing is sleight of hand. *Skilled* sleight of hand, like a magician, but with words."

"Agreed," Terrell said.

"So, you can see my reticence to buy into the things you're saying without some research into more plausible explanations. Human beings are complex, and the world is complex, and because of that, people like simple answers that make them feel good. I don't like being naïve or a fool because I bought some charlatan's line that appealed to the human need for simplicity."

"Hey, wait a minute, are you saying I'm naïve?" Jake asked.

"If you thought that guy was for real, yeah, you're a sucker," Ron replied. "You're the kind of person that's easy pickings for hucksters."

"Thankfully, I have you to rain all over the parade and take all the fun out of things," Jake said, toasting him with his bottle.

"I understand exactly what you're saying," Terrell added, "and, please believe me, I completely agree with you. The world is full of opportunists. What I study, though, is different. I'm not an opportunist. I'm more of a student. Since I was little, I was drawn to these kinds of subjects. My friends would buy comic books, but I was buying paranormal studies, building a collection. I would devour them as quickly as I could get them, always wanting more. After a while, it became easy to differentiate between the fake, sensational stuff like Amityville and the real, usually unreported events that were truly bizarre. I went so far as to contact some of the people who were involved, just to assure myself that what I was reading actually happened."

"My girlfriend said you were gifted," Jake replied. "That's why I called you. Do you consider yourself gifted?"

"There are all kinds of gifts," Terrell started, interrupted by Ron scoffing. "You're thinking of the TV medium when you hear that word, I get it. What I'm talking about is different. Most of the people I know who are gifted don't put out a shingle, don't try to make money off it. They keep it to themselves."

"But you run a ghost tour," Ron said.

"It's really more of a historical tour of the town, with a few local legends thrown in," Terrell replied. "I'm not reading fortunes, or trying to communicate with the dead for a price."

"It was a good tour," Jake interjected. "Both Freedom and I liked it a lot. You tell a good story."

"Thanks."

"So, your gift is being a storyteller," Ron replied.

"Well, no, not really. That's not the aspect of 'gift' that I'd describe for myself."

"What is it, then, since we're being so open about things?"

"Well, as I studied, I realized that most genuinely gifted people had ways of sensing things, things that aren't always visible or apparent."

"Ghosts?" Jake asked.

"Yes, that's one, but there's far more than that. Some people described it as a kind of...of..."

"Dimension?" Jake offered enthusiastically.

"No, not quite that. More like a flow of information. Kind of like the internet. You know how there's thousands of sites and services on the web, but none of them really, physically, exist? Everyone knows Amazon's storefront, for example. But it's not really there. It's just a bunch of zeroes and ones stored in computers – something you or I would consider baffling if it were to be made physical in some way, like printed out on paper. But in our minds it's really real, we can picture it. And it certainly has made billions of dollars. It's a real thing."

"But can't be seen," Jake said, stirred by the metaphor Terrell was weaving.

"It has a headquarters and warehouses and all that," Ron countered.

"Yes, but the storefront, the place where you shop, browse, search, place orders...that's all ephemeral. What I'm referring to is kind of like that. Things exist that aren't physical, but are made real by observation. There are people with gifts that allow them to see those things, or parts of them, even though most people can't, or won't. It's like they have their own private internet browsers that let them tune into this ephemeral flow of information that surrounds us."

"Bullshit," Ron replied. "Sorry to be so blunt about it, but come on."

"Do you know how much stuff is flying through the air around us right now?" Jake said, coming to Terrell's defense. "Stuff none of us can see? Wi-Fi and radio and television signals, microwave? Just because you can't see it doesn't mean it isn't there!"

"I have yet to meet someone who can detect Wi-Fi networks without using their phone or a laptop," Ron replied.

"It's internal," Terrell replied. "Like an organ, almost. Some people are born with the ability; most are not. Of those who have it, some have a lot, some less. Most people have a little, and most of them ignore what they have. There are people, I promise you, who have a ton of it and know how to use it. The more I studied and dug into the obscure cases, the more I learned that they are there. I think I have a little of it, and I've been trying to cultivate it, to make it grow, like exercising a muscle. And I found someone in Port Angeles who I'm pretty convinced is loaded with it, almost like a master of it, and I've been trying to meet him, to see if he'd mentor me. So, yes, they're out there. They really are. You just have to get to a real one. A good sign that someone is for real is that they don't sell their services."

"Like the two hundred dollars I'm paying you?"

"The two hundred is approximately what I'm going to lose from my tour business by coming here," Terrell replied. "And *you* called *me.*"

"*I* called you," Jake interjected.

"I didn't advertise anything," Terrell finished.

Ron was about to reply when a timer went off in the kitchen. Instead, he rose and walked out of the room to check on dinner.

"He's really a nice guy," Jake said. "Sometimes an asshole, but most of the time nice."

"No biggie," Terrell replied. "At least half the husbands on my ghost tour were dragged into it by their wives and don't believe a word I speak. So, I'm used to it."

Chapter Ten

Ron put the call on speakerphone. He figured, the house being so large and locked in his bedroom, it was unlikely the others would be disturbed. "Hope it's not too early," he said.

"No, it's fine." Elenore sounded sleepy. "Sun's just coming up. There's really no better time to call."

"How's it going?"

"Half and half. Some things smoothed out yesterday, but Ira thinks it's going to drag on. He's probably right."

"Drag on? How long?"

"Don't know yet. We have to see how negotiations go over the next few days."

"Does this mean you're not coming back next week?"

"Like I said, Ron, I don't know. Plans are still for then but they could change."

Ron was disappointed. "Well, shoot," he finally said in response.

"Don't lay some kind of guilt trip on me. It's business. Has to be done."

"No, I know. Can't I be sad a little, though? I miss you."

"You have that house to work on. You'll be fine."

"You can't talk to Ira? Maybe he'd let you take a weekend off, fly back?"

"No way I'm going to approach Ira with that! No one else on the team is asking for that kind of thing; it would make me look less committed. Plus, I'd lose the whole weekend to flying, I'd be spending all my time in the air! No, I'm staying here until it's done and the group goes home. You know how important this is to me, Ron. They finally consider me part of the group, and I'm not going to ruin it with a bunch of demands that the others don't require. It'll just single me out as a problem."

"Alright, I get it."

"Talked to Robbie?"

"Yeah. He seems fine."

"And Mom?"

"She says he's behaving himself. Have you talked to him?"

"It's been a couple of days. I've missed a couple of calls."

"I'm sure he'd love to hear from you. I know he misses you too."

"He's been calling early, and it's still during the work day when I can't stop and take it. By the time I can return it, he's in school. We keep missing each other."

"Maybe I should ask Grace to have him call you at night, like I try to do."

"As long as it's not too early here. If I have to wake up at 4 AM for the call, I'll be a mess the next day."

"Gotcha."

There was a pause as Ron considered how he might reconnect his son with his wife. Before he could suggest alternatives, Elenore replied.

"I've got to start getting ready. We've got an early meeting, and it's quite a ways from the hotel."

"Alright, I'll let you go. Love you."

"Me too. Bye."

The line went dead.

Ron placed his phone on the nightstand and looked at the large king bed. One side was ruffled and disturbed where he'd been sleeping; the other side still maintained some order, emphasizing the fact that Elenore hadn't slept it in for a while.

A long while, he thought. *She hasn't yet even slept in this house.*

Given everything still to do, and all the weird shit, maybe that's a good thing. If she has to stay longer, that gives me more time to get things fixed.

He felt a little better.

Still…not one question about the house, how things here were coming along.

She's focusing on work, he argued with himself. *She's not thinking about the house, she's got a ton of things to do where she is.*

But…when it comes right down to it, she doesn't really like the house, and isn't excited by it.

He stripped down and slipped into the sheets, enjoying the crisp coolness of them, waiting for the bed to warm a little.

It would have been nice if she'd at least asked about it, though. Face it; you love this place, and she doesn't. She never did.

I wonder what Robbie will think of it. There's so much more space here, compared to our cramped home in the city. He'll be able to explore and play and enjoy himself, without cars constantly screaming down the street, or the vagrants or drunks or criminals that constantly case our neighborhood, looking for opportunities, always looking for ways to steal things or break and vandalize things. Pissing on the sidewalk. Leaving syringes on the curbs. Here, he'll have this huge yard with no one around. We won't have to monitor him every second of the day.

He closed his eyes, thinking about how long it would be before Robbie could make the move. He was grateful to Grace for allowing their son to stay in town and keep him at his school, until the house was ready and Elenore was back, and a proper move-in could occur. *Two weeks more?* he wondered. *Three? A month?*

God, I hope not that long.

Terrell was in a room at the end of the upstairs hall that had a view of the back yard. Jake was still in the guest room downstairs, his guns now unloaded, secured with trigger locks, stored in his truck. Terrell had advised them to not become concerned if he moved about the house during the night, and also asked to be woken if either of them experienced anything unusual.

The evenings were getting colder. Ron turned his head to look out the window. It was clear, and stars were out. He wondered what constellations he was seeing; he knew the Big Dipper when he saw it, but all the others he'd never successfully memorized. *Maybe I should learn them. There's probably an app that would tell me which stars I'm seeing.*

He wondered if the face he'd seen at the window several nights before would return tonight. In his mind, he replayed how it scratched at the window, how it pulled back so quickly into the darkness. He tried to remember features, but the whole incident seemed fuzzy and unreal. It was easy to pretend it never happened, that it was all just part of a waking nightmare.

It made him think of the way he'd argued with Terrell and Jake earlier.

What if I take Terrell at his word, and accept that the paranormal is real? Are there really things out there, on my property? Creatures of some kind? Are they normal, run of the mill entities? Or are they unusual creatures, things not seen before, things that just exist here, on the one piece of land I happened to buy? Maybe there are real animals that are unique, that exist nowhere else but here. Maybe this is some weird little ecosystem, still completely natural, just unusual because it's isolated. Like Galapagos. Things have evolved differently on this patch of land, and over time, it produced unique things that seem strange when compared to normal areas. Things like...

Ghosts?

The word seemed silly, and it made him throw the brakes on his speculation. Ghosts were something children were frightened of, not adults. Adults knew it was all make believe.

Suddenly he shivered under the covers, a full-body convulsion of the willies.

He closed his eyes, irritated that he'd managed to scare himself just before trying to sleep.

- - -

Smoke!

Why aren't the detectors going off? Ron wondered as he awoke, reaching for his robe, wrapping it around him. He ran for the door.

The hallway was dark; he switched on a light, looking for the source of the smell. The air appeared clear; no smoke anywhere. The smoke detectors were all silent; he looked up at one directly above him on the ceiling. Its little green light blinked once, a signal that it was working and everything was fine.

But he could smell it.

He heard movement downstairs, and looked over the banister, into the living room. Jake had come out of his bedroom.

"You smell that?" Ron called down.

"Yeah," Jake replied. "Something's burning."

"Think it's outside? A neighbor?"

"I don't know. It's strong. I'll check."

As Jake walked to the front door, Ron crossed the hallway toward Terrell's bedroom. He reached for the handle and felt warmth. Suddenly he was confused; something he'd once heard or seen about the danger of providing oxygen to a fire stopped him from opening the door.

"Not outside," Jake called up. "Things smell fine out there."

"I think it's up here," Ron replied, and heard Jake climbing the stairs. He knocked on the door. "Terrell?"

"What's he doing in there?" Jake asked, as he arrived at his side. "Burning incense or something?"

"Smells like wood," Ron replied, and knocked again. "The door handle is warm."

"That's not good. Want me to open it?"

"I don't know, could that feed the fire, if there is one?"

Jake stepped to the door and pounded on it with his fist. "Terrell? You in there?"

They waited a few seconds more, hearing nothing.

"Fuck it," Ron said, and grabbed the handle, turning it and pushing the door open. "Terrell?"

The room was empty. The futon had been slept on, and Terrell's backpack was on the floor next to it, but the kid was gone.

"Where is he?" Jake wondered.

"He said he might wander," Ron replied. "The smell is stronger; it's definitely coming from here. Where's..." He walked to his right, where a shadow formed an odd patch on the wall. "Turn on the light, would you, Jake?"

When the light came on, Ron could see the discoloration distinctly. Small wisps of smoke emerged from it, like steam. "It's inside the walls," he said, trying to understand what he was seeing. "Something's burning in..."

"Fuck!" Jake shouted, cutting him off. Ron turned to his friend, who was frozen, staring at the ceiling over the door.

Terrell was there, fully dressed, tucked against the corner of the ceiling and the wall, stretched out with his eyes closed as though he was sleeping.

Upside down.

At first Ron was angry, wondering why the kid would pull such a stunt, assuming that whatever was burning inside the walls was his doing, something he'd cooked up as part of his ghost hunt.

"How the fuck is he up there?" Jake asked, fear in his voice.

"I have no idea," Ron replied, looking around the room, seeing more discolorations in the other walls; it appeared to be spreading. "We need to get him out of this room, though. There's a fire behind the walls. We've got to call the fire department and get out of the house."

"Terrell!" Jake yelled, walking under the kid, trying to wake him. "Terrell! What the fuck are you doing up there? Come down!"

Terrell remained frozen, his eyes closed, his body still and stiff against the ceiling.

"We've got to get him down," Ron said, and went for the futon frame, sliding it across the floor until it was next to the door. He climbed on top of it; it gave him the couple of extra feet he needed to reach Terrell. He grabbed at the kid's jacket and tugged, expecting the body to fall, but it didn't; Terrell remained attached to the ceiling. "Terrell!" he called again, slapping at the kid, trying to wake him up.

Terrell's eyes finally opened. He seemed disoriented and confused. Within seconds the look changed to fear, as he realized where he was. Ron grabbed again at his jacket and pulled. Suddenly Terrell dislodged completely, falling onto Ron as if some kind of switch had turned gravity back on. The two of them collapsed onto the futon frame, breaking it in half.

Jake rushed to help them up.

"Come on," Ron said, gaining his feet. "We need to get out of here."

They stumbled out of the room, Ron leading, Jake pushing Terrell ahead of him. They made their way down the stairs and out the front door, into the cold of the night.

Terrell was slowly regaining his senses. "Why are we out here?" he asked, finally able to assess where he was.

"Do you have your phone?" Ron asked Jake. "Mine's inside."

"Yeah," Jake replied.

"Call 9-1-1," Ron said.

"Wait," Terrell replied, holding up his hand between Ron and Jake. "Why?"

"There's some kind of fire," Ron said. "We smelled it. It's what woke us up."

"Where? Exactly?"

"In your room," Ron answered. "It's burning inside the walls, spreading. We need a fire truck and while they're coming, we should…"

"Don't call," Terrell said to Jake.

Jake looked at Ron, phone in hand, wondering what he should do.

"Listen, Terrell," Ron said, "there's a fire in your room. It's behind the walls. It's going to…"

"No," Terrell replied. "If you call the fire department, you'll just be embarrassed. Don't call them."

Jake lowered the phone. "Embarrassed?"

"Let's go back to the room," Terrell replied, looking at Ron. "Please."

"There's no time to waste, Terrell," Ron said. "I can't afford to have the house burn down. I…"

Terrell cut him off again. "Come with me," he said, and marched back inside.

Ron looked at Jake, who gave a big shrug, still holding the phone. "Do I call, or not?" Jake asked.

"No!" Terrell shouted over his shoulder.

Ron ran to catch up with him, and Jake followed. When they got inside, Terrell was already at the top of the stairs. He waited for them to catch up, and the three of them walked to Terrell's room.

"Door's closed," Terrell observed. "Did you shut it behind you, when we left?"

"I don't think so," Jake answered. "We just ran out."

"And the lights are out in this hall," Ron added. "I had turned them on."

"Smell anything?" Terrell asked.

Ron sniffed at the air; he couldn't detect any smoke, but that didn't assure him. *Olfactory fatigue,* he thought. "I can't smell anything, but that doesn't mean…"

Terrell reached for the door handle, turned it, and pushed it open. The room was dark. The other two looked into the room from behind him.

"I know we left the light on," Jake said.

"Do you see it?" Terrell asked quietly.

At first Ron thought Terrell meant the light switch, but felt a shiver of horror as he realized it wasn't the switch Terrell was referring to. Something else was in the room. He strained his eyes, trying to take in the shadows.

Then he saw it; a tall, thin figure in the exact center of the room, slowly twisting to face them. It was darker than everything else around it, and the longer Ron stared, the more he was able to clearly distinguish its edges.

"I see it now," Ron whispered.

"What?" Jake asked.

"In the middle of the room," Terrell said, stepping forward until his hand slipped past the doorframe, searching for the light switch. A few moments later, it clicked.

For a split second it remained as light filled the room, even though the shadows had gone. In that fraction of time, Ron saw its eyes, saw that it wasn't staring directly at him, but at Terrell. A look of irritation passed over its features. Every instinct in Ron's primordial brain told him that the dark creature standing before him was a threat.

Then it evaporated quickly, disappearing from sight.

"What *the fuck* was that?" Jake asked, his voice breaking with fear.

"Very, very..." Terrell said, walking into the room, looking down at the broken futon, "...troubling."

"Troubling?" Ron asked.

"The fucking devil!" Jake said, turning to Ron, his eyes wide with horror. "Did you see it? Did you see that fucking thing?"

"I did," Ron replied, turning his attention to the walls, looking for the discoloration he'd noticed earlier. He couldn't find any, and couldn't smell anything, either.

"That fucking thing is in your goddamn house!" Jake said, his voice rising with intensity. "The devil's inside this fucking house!"

"That wasn't the devil," Terrell replied.

"It looked like the fuckin' devil!" Jake replied loudly, working his way into hysterics. "It was right there! We all saw it!" Not receiving the confirmation he wanted from Terrell, he turned to Ron. "Goddamn it, Ron, it was standing right the fuck there!" He emphasized each word, pointing to the center of the room.

"Calm down," Ron said. "You're shouting."

"You're right I'm shouting! Did you *see* that? That wasn't no ghost, man. That thing looked just like the fucking devil!"

"It wasn't the devil," Ron replied, still inspecting the walls. "There's no such thing as the devil."

"I just fucking *saw it!*" Jake replied with an angry growl. "Don't tell me I didn't see it!"

Terrell suddenly looked concerned. "My traps. I need to check them." He grabbed his backpack and walked out, headed downstairs.

"He was right about the fire," Ron said, placing his hand in several spots on the wall, checking for heat. "They're cold. Whatever we were seeing before, it's not here now. No sign of anything burning, or burnt."

"Jesus Christ, Ron, tell me you saw it!"

"Yes, I saw it!" Ron replied, turning to his friend. "I already told you I saw it. Calm the fuck down, you're giving me the jitters."

"I'm waaay past the jitters, man."

"Where'd he go?" Ron asked, looking out the door after Terrell.

"He said something about traps."

They left the room and went downstairs, finding Terrell by the kitchen door. He was flicking light switches, causing overhead lights to turn on and off. "Do you have one that will light up the yard?"

Ron went to a different plate on the wall and threw the switch.

Terrell, standing in front of the glass door that led to the back deck, reached for the handle, but stepped back once he saw what was outside.

Coming out of nowhere, thick billows of fog now swirled against the glass, making it impossible to see the deck chairs a few feet away.

Ron walked to the windows that looked out over the back yard and pulled up the blinds. The entire back yard was gone, immersed in a thick, greyish fog that blew and billowed against the panes, reflecting the light of the flood, making it impossible to see anything but the mist.

"Where the fuck did that come from?" Jake asked.

Ron walked through the house to the front door, leaving Jake and Terrell in the kitchen. He flicked on the front lights and reached for the door, but by virtue of its large oval decorative glass, he knew before he had it cracked that the weather phenomena he'd seen in the back yard wasn't duplicated here; the front yard looked as clear as when they'd ran out into it, just moments before.

He stepped onto the porch, looking into the distance. The lights by the garage were not as powerful as the floods on the side and back of the house, but he could see all the way to the bramble and the beginning of the driveway that led into the woods. It was completely clear – no fog at all.

As he stepped down from the porch, Jake came up behind him. "What the fuck, Ron? How..."

"I don't know," Ron replied. "Doesn't make any sense."

They stared out into the darkness, stumped for the next thing to say. To Ron the illogic of the events was piling up, reaching a point where it was easier to simply go numb than to try and formulate explanations.

They heard Terrell behind them, and as the sound of his footsteps changed from the decking to the soft crackle of dirt, Ron saw a wall of fog suddenly form out of thin air, at the farthest spot down the driveway. It billowed and churned over itself, widening out, moving rapidly toward them.

"Jesus Christ!" Jake said, his eyes glued to the approaching mist.

As the fog reached the end of the driveway and entered the yard, Ron watched in horror as a solid dense wave rose several feet into the air behind the blackberry bramble that surrounded the house, curling over the brush and falling down to the ground where it crashed like water, roiling for a moment, then hurling toward them. The hair on the back of his neck rose from the sheer magnitude of the spectacle.

It felt as though they were under siege.

"Back!" Ron said. "Back in the house!"

The fog obliterated any view behind it, rapidly erasing the yard as it tumbled forward, covering fifty feet in a matter of seconds. Jake turned to run, but Terrell appeared frozen, watching the phenomenon with fascination. Ron grabbed him and pulled him back, snapping him into action. They raced behind Jake, running through the open door. Jake slammed it shut just as the fog spilled in behind them, hitting the house. Some made it through the crack of the door before it had completely closed; Ron watched as it quickly dissipated in the warmth. Through the oval window of the door they could see it churning, twisting against the door as though it had sealed them inside and intended to keep them there.

"I need to get to my traps," Terrell muttered, turning to go back to the kitchen. Ron and Jake followed him.

"Are you crazy?" Jake asked as they approached the rear windows. The fog in the back yard was still there, pressed so tightly against the house it almost looked like a film of grey had been painted on the panes of glass; only the occasional twist and turn of the mist gave any hint that there was still motion there, a force pressing it against the house.

"Those traps..." Terrell started.

"...can wait," Ron cut him off. "You can't go out in that."

"It's just..." Terrell started again. They all knew he was about to say "fog," but he stopped himself.

"Fog doesn't do that," Jake said.

"He's right," Ron added, remembering the feeling of threat he felt in the front yard. "Something's wrong with it. You step out into that stuff, I'm not sure you'll come back."

Terrell's head tilted a little to one side as he considered what Ron was saying. "You may be right."

"What do we do now?" Jake asked.

Ron checked his watch. "It's 3 AM. We make some coffee, and we sit in the living room and wait until morning. Unless either of you think you can get back to sleep?"

Both Jake and Terrell nodded in agreement.

Chapter Eleven

Ron felt a hand at his shoulder. He opened his eyes.

Although the adrenaline and coffee had managed to keep them up for a couple of hours, the conversation eventually halted, and both Jake and Terrell drifted off, sitting in the living room. Ron found himself with heavy eyelids too, and fell asleep in an uncomfortable position in a recliner.

Now, waking up, he had been in the middle of a confusing dream and found himself trying to make sense of it; lots of intersecting lines and angles, geometric forms that extended out into the distance, making streets and walkways. A voice in the distance…no, not a voice, more of a sense of presence, something that was watching him as he moved through the patterns. The lines converged to form a hallway; doors passed on the sides as he walked, not sure where he was headed, but knowing he had to keep moving or the presence would manifest. There were screams…the sound of slicing, of cutting…a dull thump. All the while, the presence was watching, taking in every move he made, calculating.

He felt his body revolt at being revived; an ache brought on by lack of sleep. Jake was shaking him gently.

"Sun's up, fog is gone. Kid wants to go out."

Ron reached for the recliner's lever and lowered the foot rest, forcing himself to stand.

Terrell was by the kitchen door. "Everything looks fine now," he said, staring through the glass of the door to the back porch and the yard beyond.

"I told him to wait until you gave an OK," Jake said to Ron.

"Why would that matter?" Ron asked.

"Well, as the homeowner, I assume you're the one with the liability insurance."

Ron turned to the window where he'd raised the blind in the middle of the night. Sun, filtered through clouds, lit every square inch of the previously impenetrable yard, making things look like any ordinary day. "If you want to go out, go out," Ron said. "We'll come along."

Terrell opened the kitchen door and stepped onto the deck, Jake and Ron following closely. They moved as a group, making their way down the deck's steps and into the yard. Terrell crossed to the spot in the bramble where he'd placed one of his items. He knelt down to look at it.

"That's odd," he said, reaching to retrieve it. "I covered it with soil. Now it's completely exposed." He pulled it from the ground and raised another small device to his eye; it looked like a small kaleidoscope, or magnifying glass inside a tube.

To Ron, the small stone Terrell was examining through the tube looked like any common rock.

"Huh," Terrell muttered.

"What?" Jake asked.

Terrell didn't reply. Instead, he slipped the rock inside his pocket and moved to another spot, retrieving another of his traps. "This one's exposed, too. Something uncovered them. Very odd." He held it to the kaleidoscope, turning it over. "Hmm."

"What?" Jake demanded, more insistently.

"There's data, but I can't read it," Terrell replied. "Normally I can. Read it."

"Data?" Ron asked.

"Hard to explain," Terrell replied, leaving them to hunt for another at the back of the yard.

"He doesn't explain much, does he?" Jake whispered to Ron, once Terrell was far enough away.

"I'm beginning to think he doesn't really have anything to explain," Ron replied.

"Huh?"

"I don't think he has the faintest idea what's going on here."

"Oh."

They watched as Terrell moved around the yard at the edge of the bramble, picking up his rocks and examining each of them.

"In fact," Ron continued, "if we hadn't experienced what we did last night, I'd say this kid is a complete charlatan. I mean, seriously, Jake…rocks?"

"Guys?" Terrell called. "Guys? You should see this."

Ron and Jake walked to the other side of the yard, where Terrell was standing next to the blackberries. "What?" Jake asked as they approached.

Terrell pointed to the ground. "I don't recall seeing this yesterday, when I placed these traps."

A hole in the ground behind Terrell was about two feet wide and rectangular; three feet of it exposed up to the bramble, the rest of it disappearing under. Ron stepped up to it and looked down; it was deep, at least five or six feet. The edges were squared off, as though it had been created with a shovel.

"It wasn't," Ron confirmed. "I guarantee that wasn't there."

"Maybe it was under the blackberries?" Jake offered. "And somehow the fog exposed it?"

"I don't think so," Ron replied.

"It looks like a..." Terrell said, but stopped.

"Yeah, I know," Ron said. "We need to cut these back. I'll get the chainsaw." He left for the garage.

"Bring gloves, too," Jake called to him, then turned back to Terrell. "The thorns on those blackberries'll tear your hands up."

Ron returned with the tools and gloves, and cranked up the chainsaw. He cut into the bramble, slicing through the thick stems. Jake and Terrell stepped back to avoid the thorny branches as they unpredictably flew like shrapnel from Ron's blade. Ron deepened the recess that exposed the hole, slowly revealing more of it, confirming what they suspected it to be.

As he cleared the top edge, the chainsaw hit something hard and bounced back in protest. At first he thought it was a rock, but as he used the tip of the saw to more precisely cut around it, the shape of the stony form also became evident.

Ron turned off the chainsaw, and everything became quiet.

"A headstone," Jake said.

"There are carvings in it," Ron replied, kneeling, taking care to avoid the sharp thorns. Using his gloves, he wiped at the dirty surface of the stone, exposing shallow engravings that looked as though they had been made hundreds of years ago. "It's initials. T.S." He stood up, looking at Jake and Terrell, who both had their eyes locked on the pale grey stone.

"Sullivan," Terrell said. "My last name is Sullivan."

Ron saw the blood drain from both Terrell and Jake's faces at the same time.

Jake looked back at him. "Don't try to tell me it's a coincidence, Ron."

"It's not," Terrell replied, also looking up at Ron.

It was as though they were waiting for Ron to pronounce something, as though his confirmation would be official. "I don't know what to think," he finally replied.

For the first time since he arrived, Terrell looked really shaken. "Can you take me back to the bus station?" Terrell asked Jake, his voice wavering. "I need to go home."

"I don't blame you," Jake said, looking back at him. "If one of those shows up with my initials on it, I'm gone too. Hell, I'm not sure why I'm still here."

"I need to go back to Port Orchard to talk to someone about the traps," Terrell replied. "I think there's data in them, but I just can't read it. I know somebody who probably can, though. He'll help me. If he can make out what's in them, it might give us some place to start."

"Right," Ron replied. *If I just found my initials above an open grave, I'd be looking for an excuse to leave, too.*

"Come on," Jake said. "Pack up and I'll run you into town."

As they walked back inside, Terrell seemed to be apologizing. "I just can't see them the way I normally can. Usually I can interact, but you guys tell me about these things that happen, and I don't have any recollection of it."

"You don't remember being on the ceiling last night?" Jake asked.

"No. Everything feels hidden. I'm not..." he paused, considering his words. "There are other people who are more gifted than I am. Abe might...that's the guy I want to show these traps to, Abe is much more powerful. He might..."

"Listen," Ron replied, cutting him off. "I appreciate you coming all the way here. I don't have any explanation for that grave in the back yard. I don't blame you for leaving. It's OK."

"No, I'm not scared of the grave," Terrell said. "Really. This whole thing, it's totally fascinating. I'm just completely stuck, I can't figure out any of it. When I get back home, and convince Abe to help me, I'll call you and let you know what he thinks."

"You do that," Ron replied as they entered the house, and Terrell gathered his things.

"I'll be back in a few," Jake said to Ron, walking Terrell to the door.

As Ron heard Jake's truck start, he sank into the recliner and tried to let the events of the morning slip away. He knew he had to figure out how that hole appeared in the ground and work his way back, rationalize all the other weird things that happened over the course of the evening. He settled in, intending to think it out, but realized he was too tired.

The room, now quiet and calm, conspired with his aching body to demand sleep. His mind wanted nothing more than to drift off, despite knowing he needed to try and analyze things, to figure out why a six foot deep grave suddenly appeared in the back yard. He decided to go with the path of least resistance, listen to his body, and see if an hour of additional shut-eye would clear his mind enough that he could come up with the rationalizations he needed.

- - -

How come you can never program your dreams the way you really want them? he wondered, as a sense of tumbling forward crested over him, making him roll like an inner tube dropped down a set of stairs. He felt as though he was going to crash into something, but after a while, when he didn't, he decided to try and enjoy the sensation rather than fight it. It was like when he flew in dreams; terrifying at first, but kinda amazing once he bought into it.

He had a compelling desire to call out, to warn someone about something dangerous, but there was no one there to call to. It was just him, rolling, twisting forward and coming back up, descending, as though he was a graceful acrobat performing an endless series of spins above a trampoline or a circus net.

At first the point in the distance didn't look sharp, it just seemed like something he'd roll right past. Each time he turned, it grew and became closer, until it was obvious that he was headed toward it. It was a long, sharp spike, like a piece of rebar sticking out of cement, tapered at the end to a fine point. He kept tumbling toward it, trying to shift to the side, fearful that he might hit it. No matter how he attempted to influence the dream, he kept falling toward the protrusion, and he realized with horror that he was going to land directly on it. Panic rose in his throat, and he reached out in frustration, hoping to alter the course of his trajectory, but it was no use. He completed another turn and the tip of the spike ripped into his outstretched hand, piercing through it. He expected it to hurt, but it didn't; it simply slipped through his flesh and came out the top of his hand as he continued to fall. As his hand slid down the spike, he felt bumps of resistance, and he wondered if it really was rebar. The sharp tip moved closer to his face, and for a second he thought it was headed for his eye, preparing to impale him and achieve one of his worst nightmares. As he neared the spike, he tried to avoid it by raising his head as far back as it would go, hoping the sharp point would miss his chin. Instead, he felt it plunge into the underside of his neck, just below the jaw, and effortlessly slide upward into him, passing through his brain and hitting his skull.

The recliner physically shook in reaction to his spasming body. He awoke to find himself gripping the upholstered arms, his chin thrust forward into the air, lifting his head from the chair's back. He shook for a moment until he realized that he was awake; there was no impalement, just his reaction to the horror of the dream. Slowly his body relaxed until he was resting fully against the recliner. He felt each muscle give into the realization that everything was OK, that he wasn't dying.

The house was still quiet. He checked his watch; it had been an hour. Jake would be back soon.

If he comes back at all, he thought. *Given last night, it wouldn't surprise me if he bails. I've never seen the guy so freaked out.*

He rose from the recliner and walked to the nearest bathroom, adjacent to the guest bedroom where Jake had been sleeping. Before he managed the turn into the bathroom, his eyes caught the dresser against the far wall.

It was the dresser that he found under the stairs days before, and had slid into this room to get it out of the way.

Ignoring the bathroom, he walked to it and examined its top. It was made of wood; nicks and scratches pockmarked its surface. Someone had painted it black, probably in an attempt to lessen the appearance of the imperfections. He wouldn't have given it the time of day if it was in a used furniture store; not his style, and not in good enough shape. Still, there was something about it he liked, though he couldn't identify what it was, exactly. Before the sale of the house was completed, the bank was supposed to clean all items out of the property, but for some reason, they hadn't removed this dresser. *Maybe they just missed it,* he thought. *I did, the first time I looked into the closet. I didn't realize what it was until I pulled it out.*

He'd already checked the drawers, but he found himself wanting to inspect them again. Although all of the pulls were intact except for one, he went for the one that was missing. In the pull's spot was an inch of metal screw that formerly held the pull in place, jutting out dangerously. It was enough to grip between his fingers so he could slide the drawer open. For a second he worried it might have sharp edges and cut him, but wood that had accumulated inside its ridges made it feel smooth, and the drawer slid out easily.

Like all the other drawers he'd inspected when he first found the dresser, it was empty.

Oh, no, they weren't all empty, he remembered. *There were those old catalogs.*

He was about to slide it back in when he saw something small fall into the back of the drawer, something that had been attached to the underside of the dresser's top. At first he thought it might be a spider, and expected to see it move. Instead, it sat inert in the back.

He pulled the drawer out completely, and sat it on top of the dresser.

He was sure it wasn't a spider, but wasn't exactly sure what it was, either. It was black in the center, about the size of a nickel, with wiry coils looping out from underneath, giving it the vague appearance of a dead arachnoid with many thin legs curled under itself.

He reached for it, stopping before the tip of his finger touched its edge.

I don't know what the hell that is, he thought. *What if it really is some kind of insect, and comes alive?*

Pulling his hand back, he looked in the room for something he could prod it with, a pen or a short piece of wood. He found a long receipt inside a plastic bag next to the bed Jake had been sleeping in, and folded it several times until he made a rigid six-inch paper stick that would at least allow him to poke at the thing and see if it reacted.

He eased the paper into the drawer and lowered his face closer to better observe. He slowly edged the probe toward it, and getting no response, gently nudged it. It slid a little, the thin coils at its edge firm and unmoving. As he pushed it around the bottom of the drawer, his confidence that it wasn't an insect grew. He'd seen spiders that he thought were dead suddenly come to life after being jostled awake, but this thing was heavier than a spider, and although difficult to make out exactly what it might be, appeared more mechanical than animal.

He reached in with his other hand and picked it up. He expected the coils to feel like metal, but they were soft, like hair, almost tickling his skin. He flipped it over, for a split second expecting to see the armored underbelly of an arachnid; instead the surface was smooth and black, with a small whitish discoloration in the center that looked vaguely like a face, or a portrait.

A cameo? he wondered. If it was, it was severely deteriorated to the point where the likeness was indistinguishable. It looked more like a flaw in the stone, like a cloudy vein running through the black.

He turned it over several times, his brain trying to assess what it might be. He felt a headache coming on. Here was another baffling thing, a mystery without explanation, another to add to the list of irrational things in the house.

He heard the front door open, and Jake came inside. He left the bedroom, slipping the object into his shirt pocket. "Success?"

"Yeah, he's on the bus," Jake replied, placing a bag on the coffee table. "I stopped at McDonald's. There's two Egg McMuffins in there. Figured you might want some. I ate mine already."

"Thanks," Ron replied, realizing how hungry he was, and going for the bag.

"Listen, Ron," Jake said, "that was some pretty heavy shit last night."

"You gonna bail on me?" Ron replied, taking a bite of the sandwich.

"I don't wanna. But, Christ, Ron, that kid floating on the ceiling, the fog, that grave...is it still out there?"

"I don't know, haven't checked."

Jake walked to the window and looked out. "Yeah, it's gone, of course. Like it was all just a fucked up dream. That's the problem. All this shit happens at night, then you wake up the next day, and things seem normal again, and you write it all off as a friggin' nightmare. Except people don't share nightmares, Ron. And then the shit happens again, the next night. Freedom said to leave, and frankly I'm thinking maybe she was right."

"Well, I can't make you stay, but I would appreciate it. There's still a lot of work to do."

"Do you remember that dark thing in the room upstairs? The thing we both saw before you turned on the light?"

"I do."

"That's in your fucking house, Ron! I think it's been here the whole time. We just happened to *see it* for the first time last night."

Ron finished the sandwich and ran a hand down the back of his neck, wincing. "That's where I don't know, Jake."

"Here it comes."

"What?"

"Your bullshit rationalization. You're gonna tell me it was a shadow, or we hallucinated it because of dinner, or some other kinda horseshit."

"Not horseshit, it just…"

"Yes, horseshit!" Jake replied, cutting him off. "I know what I saw, and I know you saw it too. You've got the fucking devil in your house, Ron. You can spin it anyway you like, but I saw it with my own goddamn eyes, buddy."

"Will you listen to yourself?" Ron replied, going for the second sandwich. "Like, Satan? Like, the lord of darkness or some such bullshit, camping out in my house, of all the houses in the world? Are you hearing yourself? It's crazy."

"What's crazy is staying here," Jake replied. "It's like a horror movie where the people are all stupid, too dumb to just pack up and move."

"I can't just pack up and move!" Ron said. "You know that! All my money is in this house. I can't sell it until that well gets deepened. No one will get a bank loan to buy it until there's enough water."

"In the meantime, if it were me, I'd live in a fucking motel. Hell, you can move in with me and Freedom."

"Did you run that past her?" Ron replied. "'Cause I highly doubt that idea will fly."

"There's no way Elenore will accept any of this. And if you move Robbie in here, that's, that's..."

"What?"

"Well, it's goddamn child abuse, that's what it is! Subjecting a little kid to this kind of scary shit? You can't do that to him. It'll traumatize him for the rest of his life! Hell, I feel like I'm traumatized, and I'm 38 goddamn years old!"

"I need your help, Jake, you know that."

"I can't stay here, Ron. I'm sorry, I can't."

"How about this...the weird shit happens only at night, right?"

Jake thought for a moment, then nodded in agreement.

"Well, how about you work with me on the house during the day, and I'll put you up in a motel in McLean. You can spend the night there, and we can keep working on the house during the day-time."

"And you'll stay here? At night?"

"Yes."

"And I'll just drive back and forth, show up in in the morning, leave before nightfall?"

"Yes."

"And you'll pay for the motel?"

"And the gas to go back and forth. Listen, you're my best bet at getting this work done before Elenore comes back. Yes, I'll pay for all that."

"You're crazy. I'll arrive one morning and find you in a grave, just like the one we saw out there."

"I'll chance it. It'll give me some comfort knowing you're going to arrive every morning."

Jake took a moment to consider Ron's offer. "A motel's not go-ing to be cheap."

"Well, I'm not gonna put you up in the Ritz. It'll still be cheaper and faster than trying to land a contractor."

"True...OK. I'll stay."

"Good."

"But if that thing shows up during the day, I can't guarantee I won't cancel this arrangement and head home. I don't want to see any more of this devil crap."

The idea that Jake considered what they'd seen to be the devil stuck in his craw as ridiculous, and for a second he was about to continue arguing with him, but decided instead to accept the win of having convinced him to stay. "Alright. Terms accepted. Shall we get back to work?"

Chapter Twelve

It was early afternoon when the truck from McLean Drilling appeared, slowly ambling down the driveway. Ron and Jake were working in front of the garage, and Ron stopped to slip off his gloves as the vehicle parked and a tall, thin man emerged.

Younger than I expected, Ron thought. "You must be Stewart," he said, extending his hand.

"That's me," the man replied, shaking. "Got a note from Gary that you wanted to see me."

"Gary? Was that his name?" Ron replied. "If he told me his name, I forgot. He kept calling himself the grim reaper."

"Yeah, that's Gary," Stewart said, returning to his truck to retrieve some gear.

"He said we'd have to extend the well," Ron replied, following him.

"Well, before we get to any of that, let me make a few assessments of my own," Stewart said, hauling his gear to the well. "Give me a half hour, would you? I'll know more then."

"Sure," Ron answered. "We're just working on the exterior. Let me know if you need anything."

Stewart began to drop a line down the well, similar to what he'd seen the grim reaper do days earlier. He left the man to his work, returning to Jake.

"That the driller?" Jake asked, as he finished a cut on a fresh piece of trim.

"Yup. He wants to figure things out on his own."

"Maybe it won't be as bad as the other guy thought."

"I'm hoping. Maybe it'll be worse."

"I'm half full, you're half empty."

"Like always."

They continued their work, stripping and replacing trim on the side of the house. The late autumn sun provided some warmth, but each day seemed to be cooler than the last, and unlike the previous days of labor, Ron found himself keeping his jacket on.

He had almost forgotten about the driller when the tall man appeared next to him, paperwork in hand. "So, I've looked it over," he said.

Ron removed safety goggles from his head and placed them onto the table saw. "What do you think?"

"Gary was right, it's low-flow. Not enough to live on, for sure."

"Great. What do you suggest? Extend it?"

"We could try that. By the way, do you know this is the second well?"

"Second?"

"There's another on your property, according to the records."

"No, I didn't."

Well, somewhere around here there's a well we started for you, and stopped at a hundred and ten feet. It's capped off. Then this well," he pointed to the metal tube protruding from the ground behind him, "we did that one too. Four hundred and thirty feet."

"Why would there be two?"

"Hard to say. Before my time. Lots of rock on this hill; it's not easy."

"Yeah, that's what the grim reaper said."

"Well, he was right about that. This is a notoriously hard area to work."

"What do you think about deepening it?"

He walked to it. "We could give it a shot. Another house a half mile down the road has pretty good flow at six hundred feet, so maybe we go another two hundred and see if things improve. We could also look into the other well, see if it's at all viable, figure out why they stopped when they did."

"What's that gonna cost me?"

The man grimaced and turned away. "Don't like to give verbals. There's a lot that goes into making a clean estimate." He stared down at the well.

"How about something ballpark, so I know what I'm in for?"

"Well, to start, the drilling itself is forty dollars a foot, but don't settle on that. There's extra charges for bringing in the rig, and your road is gonna be a real challenge. There's a charge to reopen the well, and to perfect the drill, and…" He stopped, looking up. "I can see the blood draining from your face. See, this is why I like to do a proper paper estimate."

Ron had quickly done the math and knew the eight thousand for the drilling alone was going to take a huge chunk out of their move-in funds. *With all the other fees, it'll probably top ten thousand. Fuck.* "Well, I would appreciate the written estimate when you can complete it," he managed to say, "so I can do some evaluating."

"Sure," Stewart answered.

"Gary mentioned something about no guarantees."

"That's true," Steward replied, stowing his gear. "Two hundred feet is a target. If we hit a good flow sooner than that, well, great. If we have to go deeper, we go deeper. Might go eight hundred feet and still be dry. That's rare, mind you, but the contract will spell out that we get paid no matter how it ends up."

"Great business model," Ron muttered, and noticed that Stewart stiffened. "No offense. I get that you put in the work, regardless."

"That's the sum of it."

"How soon do you think this can happen?"

"At least six weeks out," Stewart said, getting into his truck. "I'll take a look at the calendar and send along some potential dates when I email you the estimate. It'll take a day or two to work it all up."

"Alright."

The truck started up and backed out, turning to head down the small road. Ron returned to Jake.

"Is it bad?" Jake asked.

"Kinda what I expected. I drop ten thousand, they may or may not hit water."

"Christ. Nature of the business, I suppose."

Ron nodded.

"Hell, if I knew how to do it, I'd do it for you for half that."

"You're doing enough already," Ron replied, reaching for his goggles and starting up the table saw.

- - -

It was while they were finishing up the afternoon's work that Ron felt the object in his shirt pocket move. He had forgotten he'd placed it there, but when he noticed the sensation of something crawling next to his skin, he thought a bug had managed its way under his jacket and shirt. Shaking with the willies, he pulled off his gloves and reached under his collar, finding nothing. While his hand was over his chest, he felt it move again inside the pocket, shifting a little against the back of his hand.

He reached for it and pulled it out. The object he found inside the dresser was still there, inanimate, looking like a tiny craft project gone awry. He waited for it to move again, but nothing happened, and the longer he stood there, staring at it, the more he felt stupid. Jake was around the other side of the house, but would return to the workbench at any moment to use a saw. He slipped it back into his pocket, put his gloves on, and resumed work.

It was as Jake was saying goodbye for the evening that he felt it move again; a wiggle, as though the tiny hairs or threads he'd seen around its edge had come to life and it was looking for a way out of his pocket. He placed his hand over his jacket to keep it still just as Jake turned to walk to his truck, grateful that his friend hadn't noticed the gesture.

Jake called out the window of his truck, saying not to worry, he'd be back early in the morning, bringing breakfast with him.

Dusk was beginning to settle in as Ron walked inside the house, crossing the threshold and feeling the object jump again. He quickly shed his jacket and pulled the pocket open, waiting to see it move.

It sat still.

Of course it's still, he thought. *It's an inanimate object.*

He reached inside and pulled it out, turning a little so light from the entry would illuminate its face. Then he flipped it over.

The small smear of whitish color that he originally thought similar to a cameo had changed. Instead of being centered, surrounded by black, it had swirled out and become iridescent, looking like pearl.

Huh, he thought. *Maybe it reacted to my body heat, like a mood ring.*

As he was about to slip it back into his pocket, he thought he saw the swirls inside the black surface shift and twist, and it stopped him. He walked into the kitchen where the light was brighter and looked more carefully at its underside, waiting to see if he was mistaken, or if it might move again. He felt a tickle against his fingertips, coming from the other side of the object. Instinct made him drop it; the sensation was too much like the feeling of insect legs. It fell to the granite counter and bounced, coming to a stop on the edge of the sink.

Get a grip on yourself! he thought, feeling stupid. *It's not alive. That was some kind of phantom sensation. Be a fucking grown up and...*

As he watched, one of the hairs extended from its side and pressed down onto the granite, causing it to rise slightly. Liquid began to ooze out, black with streaks of pearly white, slowly seeping across the countertop.

It was alive! he thought. *I killed it when I dropped it!*

He moved closer to the small object, watching as the thin streak of liquid continued to extend from the raised edge. One inch, then two, then three...more body fluid than he thought it could contain. It came to a stop after a couple more inches, and the trail of liquid began to pool until it had formed a circle about the size of a quarter.

Ron blinked, and in that split second, the object disappeared from the side of the sink, reappearing where the pool had formed. All of the liquid had gone; Ron presumed it had all been sucked back up into it.

"What the fuck?" he muttered, taking a step back.

He wasn't sure how long he spent looking at the counter watching it, waiting for it to do something else. He began to feel that time was getting away from him; all of the other weird occurrences in the house notwithstanding, this tiny object seemed to make him a little confused about whether a minute had passed, or an hour. When he broke free from what had begun to feel like a trance, he felt his muscles ache, as though he'd been holding a position for far too long.

I need to sit down, he thought, deciding to leave the object on the counter. He stopped to grab a beer from the fridge on his way to the living room, where he popped it open and fell into a recliner, taking a long swig, enjoying its coolness.

Should I show that thing to Jake? he wondered.

No. He's already freaked out as it is. It'll just make things worse.

Ron thought about the figure they'd seen in the bedroom upstairs. There was no question that it had been frightening. He couldn't blame Jake for the reaction. *Not the devil, though,* he thought. *There's no such thing.*

He closed his eyes, knowing he wouldn't fall asleep, just wanting to make everything disappear for a few moments while he relaxed. His grip over time seemed to return, and soon he felt the long list of to-do tasks poking at his brain, making him feel guilty for resting. He forced himself out of the chair, carrying his beer back into the kitchen.

The object was still there, but it had moved. It was another foot from the edge of the sink.

Fuck, he thought. *What am I going to do with this thing? Put it back in the dresser?*

He reached for it, picked it up, and began walking to the bedroom, turning on lights as he went. When he approached the dresser, he felt the object react, shifting a little in his palm. The sensation of insect legs returned, and for a moment he wanted to drop it – but he held tight, keeping his fingers wrapped securely around it, intent upon replacing it in the drawer.

He reached for the tip of the screw that acted as a pull, but when he touched it, he felt a sharp pain from his other hand, as though it had bit him. He stopped and open his fist. The object was gone. Dozens of tiny red dots, arranged in a circle, appeared in his palm, as though he'd been pricked by a round pincushion. He turned his hand over, wondering if it might have crawled out of his grip, then he checked the floor below him to see if it had fallen.

Looking at his palm again, the dots were fading; a few seconds more and they were gone.

Where the fuck did it go? he wondered.

He opened the drawer and searched inside. Nothing. He opened all the other drawers of the dresser, reaching in to feel every corner; it wasn't there.

Scouring the floor around the dresser and coming up empty, he pulled it from the wall, searching behind it. It wasn't there, either.

Some sliver of his mind briefly entertained the idea that it had somehow slipped *inside* him. The balance of rational mass in his brain overrode the idea immediately. He looked at his palm again. There were no marks of any kind. His hand looked as it always had; a little banged up from the work they'd been performing on the house, but other than that, completely normal.

Where's that beer? he wondered, remembering he'd left it on the counter by the sink. Returning to the kitchen, he reminded himself of how absurd this whole episode was, how his lack of sleep and the stress of the new house – the problems with the well, the septic, the interruptions at night – all of it was to blame for losing the strange object. His mind wasn't working at a hundred percent. He must have misplaced it and not even realized it.

Not by a long shot, he thought, retrieving the beer and returning to the recliner. *I'm fried. I'm seeing things. What is it they say about spots in front of your eyes? I'm seeing dots in my hand. I'm imagining that a button I found in a dresser has little legs. The damn thing probably fell down the sink and is sitting in the drain trap right now, surrounded by water, and I dreamt the whole goddamn thing while I was resting my eyes in this chair.*

He didn't believe most of the story he was telling himself, but it did give him a moment's peace, just long enough to let the alcohol from the beer dull his senses a little and allow him to drift off. Exhaustion won out over the guilt from the task list, and he felt himself falling asleep, grateful for the opportunity to stop thinking and just zone off into oblivion.

Chapter Thirteen

Thump!

It was 3:37, and he was in bed. He remembered dragging himself out of the recliner at some point and making his way upstairs, stripping off clothes, and falling asleep the moment his face hit the pillow.

Now, his eyes were open, staring at the ceiling, wondering what the sudden noise had been.

A series of pops reached his ears. They were coming from downstairs.

Feeling exhausted, he threw off the covers and donned his robe. Passing the windows, he glanced down into the yard. While the grassy area was empty, he thought he saw two shiny eyes, low to the ground at the edge of the bramble, reflecting the light of the moon. As he moved, they retreated, pulling back to hide under the cover.

A raccoon, he thought.

Once clothed, he walked downstairs, searching for the source of the sounds. The lights came on, and the living room was illuminated, looking still and quiet. The kitchen was the same, as was the dining room and the hallways.

He walked to the front door, but stopped as something odd caught his eye. He lowered himself to look at a power outlet near the ground. The white vinyl of the outlet plate was smeared with black, a singe that looked like residue from a spark or short. He ran his finger through it; the black film easily wiped away, darkening his skin. He wondered if it had always been there and he was just noticing it for the first time, or if it was the source of the sound he heard.

To answer his question, another loud pop came from behind him. He turned and saw another outlet, similarly coated. He could smell the bitter electric odor the spark had produced.

Returning to the living room, he searched for outlets hidden from view behind couches and chairs. He found more singe marks. Panic began to rise in his chest, as he wondered if some type of surge was hitting the house, frying the wiring. Intending to shut down the circuit breakers, he walked to the garage, but accidentally set off the home alarm when he opened the door. He ran back through the house to the front door, where the keypad was located, and entered the code to silence the alarm.

I'm gonna get a call, he thought, *and if I don't answer, the alarm company will send the police. And my damn phone is upstairs, set to vibrate.*

He ran up the flight of stairs, reaching his bedside just as the screen on his phone lit up. Disconnecting the phone from its recharger cable, he carried it as he spoke to the agent on the other end, providing his pass phrase and telling them it was a false alarm. By the time he ended the call, he was back at the garage door, and worked his way through piles of boxes until he found the panel. He threw the master switch, and the light in the garage went out.

Activating the flashlight on his phone, he made his way back through the garage and into the house, looking for more outlets that had been damaged.

He couldn't find any.

Returning to the living room, he pulled the couch away from the wall and examined the outlet he'd seen earlier. Whereas its lower half had been covered in a black film when he first inspected it, it now looked fine; clean and white, no discoloration.

He pushed the couch back into position and walked to the hallway, to the outlet where he first noticed the singe.

It, too, looked fine.

Raising his finger, he held it under the light of the phone. There, on the tip, was the black smudge he'd wiped from the outlet's plate just moments before.

Standing in his robe in the middle of the dark house, anxiety pumping through his system, he felt confused and angry. It was the middle of the night. He was exhausted. He'd just shut off all the power to the house, fearing some kind of electrical problem, or fire.

He didn't know how to respond, what to do next. He felt himself begin to lose it.

He sat on the second step of stairs and clicked off his phone, set it beside him, then lowered his head into his hands. He wasn't a crier, but his exhausted body wanted to scream out in frustration, to heave a huge sob and just give in to the nightmare that had become his life since he entered the house weeks ago.

Things were supposed to be improving, but nothing was getting better. He was working hard to keep going in the right direction, but it wasn't paying off. The initial gut punches of the septic system and the well seemed ages ago, but they were still there, mostly unresolved. The pile of exterior work still to accomplish, the roof, the heater – none of it seemed on the right track. On top of it all, there was the weirdness: the ghosts – or whatever they were – in the yard, the noises at night, the bizarre things in Terrell's room. It was all combining to wipe him out, to keep him exhausted and unable to focus.

And now, if the electrical system is bad, too…another thing wrong, another thing to fix!

But is it? What I saw isn't there anymore. Maybe it never was there in the first place.

It's fucking with me. This house is fucking with me.

He felt like crying, but he knew he wasn't going to give in and actually let loose. The house had been a test of his determination, his ability to prove to himself and to Elenore that he wasn't wrong about the place. It was really a great house. It was the perfect house. It just needed more care and attention than a normal one.

He stood, walked to the garage, and threw the circuit breakers back on. Returning to the living room, he checked the outlets; they were still clean, bearing no evidence of a short.

He walked to the front door and reactivated the alarm, then went upstairs and crawled back into bed.

"You can fuck with me all you want," he said out loud, staring up at the ceiling. "It won't matter. I am going to live here, and my family is going to live here. So, fuck you."

He waited, wondering if the house would reply.

- - -

It was difficult for the sound of knocking at the front door to make its way through the large house and into the master bedroom upstairs, but Ron slowly came awake, unsure if he'd heard someone pounding on the door or if he had dreamt it. Now conscious and listening, things seemed quiet, and he was about to convince himself that he'd dreamt the sound when the pounding returned. He swung his legs out of bed.

Christ, he thought, looking at the clock. *7 AM? What the fuck is Jake thinking?*

He donned his robe and went downstairs. Dawn had just settled in; it was cloudy outside, and weak, grey light was filtering in through the windows. As he approached the door, he could tell it wasn't Jake on the other side, and he immediately became suspicious. Instead of opening the door, he called through it. "What?"

"Just wanted to return this to you," came the muffled reply.

Ron punched in the alarm code and threw the deadbolt on the door. He opened it a crack.

Standing on the porch was a man holding a sign. He extended it. "This blew into my yard. I think it's yours."

Ron opened the door more. "It's kinda early."

"Sorry, I'm on my way to work, and I thought I'd drop it off."

Ron took the sign; it was, indeed, the small sign that advertised his use of an alarm company. He looked out the door and to the left, where it was normally planted in the ground. Not there.

"Blew into your yard?" Ron asked, finding it hard to believe.

"Those winds last night," the man replied. "Incredible. Hi, I'm Tom. Your neighbor past the ravine." He nodded to the left and extended his hand.

Ron studied him for a moment. The man was about his height and weight, with a pale complexion and glasses that seemed a size too small for his head. Not wanting to be rude, he shook the man's hand and then opened the door, inviting him in. "You want some coffee?"

"No, I gotta get to work," Tom replied, stepping inside. "Just thought I'd drop it by. I wasn't sure it belonged to you, but I saw the sticker on your window, and the name matched, so I figured it must be."

"Right," Ron replied. "Well, thank you. I can't believe it could travel that far."

"Not the first time. Crazy winds around here; I've had stuff from miles away land in my yard. The worst is when they get caught in the pines and you have to figure out how to get them down from thirty feet in the air."

"Yeah," Ron replied, wanting coffee himself. "Well, I appreciate it."

Despite mentioning work, Tom didn't seem in a hurry to leave. "So, all moved in?"

"Not really. Fixing up a few things first."

"Oh, of course. You married?"

"Yes. And we have a son who will be joining me when all the work gets done."

"Oh. Where you moving from?"

"That's a lot of questions for early in the morning," Ron replied, wiping at his face with his hand.

"Of course, I'm sorry, I've woken you up. I've been up for an hour, already caffeinated."

"So, you're a neighbor?"

"The parcel past the ravine," Tom replied. "Little white house. Live there with my wife and daughter."

"To be honest with you, I hadn't noticed it. Next time I keep driving up the main road, I'll look for it."

"You have to take the Crestview branch at the top of the hill," Tom replied. "Our property lines touch, but access is from the other direction."

"Oh, gotcha. I guess that explains the other road, the one that's blocked off."

He wondered if Tom might shed some light on the abandoned road, but instead the man just walked into the living room.

"You liking the house?" Tom asked.

"Yeah, sure. It's great."

"So crazy, this place. Such a lot of history for a new house."

"History?"

Tom's eyes danced around the room, as though he was inventorying the place. "You know, the renters. The deaths. All that."

"Deaths?"

Tom looked at him, and Ron saw a wave of regret pass over his face. "The previous owner?"

Ron stared back at him blankly. "No," he replied.

"Maybe I shouldn't have said anything."

"There were deaths here?"

"Well, I don't mean to say the wrong thing. Perhaps I have already."

"No, tell me, what?"

"Well, I guess it's a matter of public record, it's not like I'm telling you anything you can't read in the papers. The whole mountain knew Mr. Lucero. We were all kinda of shocked."

Ron closed his eyes for a moment, feeling impatient. "At what?"

"The way he...well, his wife, Alice, had been sick for a long time. He was her caregiver, of course. He was old, too, so he was set in his ways, followed routines like we all do. Still..."

"Yes?"

"She passed away, and he kept caring for her, you know, like she hadn't really died. Didn't report it. Whenever we'd see him, we'd ask about her, and he'd say she was still fine, he was still looking after her. But, really, she had died. She'd been dead a long time when he finally passed and the police found them both. Four months, they estimated."

"Christ," Ron muttered, feeling some of the anxiety from the middle of the previous night return.

"I heard the bank had to hire a special company to get rid of the smell," Tom said, taking a deep breath. "Seems like they got it, though. Can't smell a thing." He smiled.

Ron remembered the odd smells in the house when he first moved in; he had assumed they were all from pets. The memory of the rank odors, in light of this new information, was making him feel nauseous.

"You look a little white," Tom said. "Shit, I'm sorry, maybe I shouldn't have told you."

"How long have you lived next door?"

Tom's eyes looked up. "Let's see, almost fifteen years. Maybe sixteen, seventeen. Something like that."

"So you were here when they built this house," Ron replied. "It's only twelve years old."

"Oh, yeah," Tom answered, then checked his watch. "Shit, I gotta run. Gonna be late. Sorry to have woken you up." He turned, heading for the door.

"Hey, listen," Ron said, catching up with him, "I wouldn't mind picking your brain sometime about the history of this place, as well as the mountain. Seems like there's some kind of animosity between McLean and here. Maybe it's just my imagination, but when people in town talk about it, they…"

Tom cut him off. "You're right about that. There's plenty of bad blood around here. Lots of history, lots of entanglements, if you know what I mean. I'd be happy to fill you in, but I have to get to work. Already late."

"Of course," Ron replied. "Maybe you know something about that road, too. The one that…"

"Tell you what," Tom said, cutting him off again. "I can stop by later tonight if you'd like, after work. Bring some beers."

"Sure."

"Sometimes I work late, might be 8 or 9. That too late for you?"

"No, should be fine."

"Alright," Tom replied, extending his hand again. "See you then. I didn't get your name?"

"Ron," he replied, shaking.

"Ron," Tom repeated. "Ron. Short for Ronald?"

"Nope, just Ron."

"Ron. Right. Just committing it to memory! See you later then." He opened the door.

"Tonight."

"Right. 8 or 9."

"Bye."

"Bye."

The door closed, and Ron looked at the alarm company sign in his hand. He placed it in the corner, intending to replant it later, more interested, at the moment, in the kitchen and coffee.

- - -

A couple of hours later, Jake arrived bearing a bag of fast food breakfast sandwiches. Ron poured him some coffee as the two ate.

"Anything weird last night?" Jake asked.

"What, like the devil manifesting at a demonic ritual?" Ron replied sarcastically. "Walking the halls, breathing fire, dragging a tail?"

"You know what I mean, don't pretend you don't."

Anticipating that Jake would ask, Ron had resolved earlier to skip telling him about the electrical burns on the outlets, as well as the revelations from the neighbor; there would be nothing gained by feeding Jake's paranoia, and plenty to lose.

"Nope, nothing. Quiet night."

Jake chewed for a moment on his sandwich, then swallowed. "I don't know if I believe you."

"Believe what you want, but nothing happened."

"You have that look when you're lying. I think you're telling me what I want to hear, so I don't bug out on you."

"Really?" Ron replied, his hand over his heart. "Me? Do that?"

Jake's phone went off, and he pulled it out of his trousers. "Hello?...Oh, hi, Terrell...yeah...uh huh...wait, hold on, I wanna put you on speakerphone so Ron can hear you too, alright? OK? Hang on a second." He lowered the phone from his ear, pushed a few buttons, and placed the phone on the counter. "Can you hear me?"

"Yes," Terrell's voice crackled over the connection.

"Morning, Terrell," Ron said.

"Hi, Ron," Terrell replied.

"So, start over, tell Ron what you were saying," Jake instructed.

"Alright," Terrell sighed, taking a big breath. "I made contact with my friend, the one I was telling you about."

"The guy you were hoping would mentor you," Jake added.

"Yeah. His name is Abe. He's old, really old, and he knows a lot. He's a local authority on these kinds of things. He's also totally paranoid, so it required some real work on my part to get him to see me, but last night he finally let me in and took a look at my traps."

Terrell paused.

"And?" Jake urged.

"Well, it's not good news."

Jake looked up at him; he shrugged in response. "What do you mean?" Ron asked Terrell.

"So, listen, some people have the gift, and some don't. Some people have it in different quantities. I have some. Abe has a ton, he's super gifted, so I have to trust him even though he incinerated my traps! He took a look at what was in them, and said it was...I don't remember, it was some German word, started with a 'v'. Verbatim?"

"Verboten?" Ron offered.

"Yeah, that was it. What does it mean?"

"Forbidden," Ron replied.

"Oh, OK, that makes sense, that fits in with all the other things he said. Anyway, he completely fried my traps, they're useless now. Said he had to kill it."

"Kill what?" Jake asked.

"What was inside them," Terrell replied. "What they had trapped."

"Which was what, exactly?" Ron asked.

"He wasn't very precise about that..." Terrell replied slowly. "He just went on and on about how I was not to have anything more to do with it. He'd be pissed I'm even calling you, but I figured you needed to know."

"Know what?" Ron asked, irritated. "You haven't told us anything!"

"Yeah, why does Abe feel this way?" Jake asked Terrell. "Did he say why you couldn't contact us?"

"He said verboten, he said it was dangerous, that I had to steer clear. He said there are some things that those of us with the gift can help a lot with, and other things that we can help a little. But he said this thing we can't help at all, and that it was too dangerous to get involved with. He made me promise I wouldn't go back."

"Dangerous? Ron asked. "How?"

"So, I did a little reading about it after I met with Abe," Terrell replied. "There's a strain of phenomena that is highly toxic to those with the gift. It's like something that has soured, or become infected. Instead of being a normal haunting that we can deal with, this strain contains things that can be lethal."

"Lethal?" Ron asked, looking at Jake, whose face had gone white.

"Lethal to those with the gift," Terrell added. "I'm not saying it's lethal to you. Might not be; might seem like a normal haunting to you. But it's potentially deadly to Abe and myself. I told him the things that occurred while I was there. He was especially freaked out about me floating on the ceiling, and that I couldn't remember it happening. He said it was all an attack on me, personally, and that if I had stayed, I might have been killed."

There was a long pause. Ron wasn't sure what to say, and Jake looked baffled as well.

"So," Terrell continued, "I guess what it comes down to, is, I'm sorry, I can't really do much for you, at least, not in person, not there. I'm happy to research anything I can, but Abe made me promise I wouldn't go back down to your place, and I kind of have to keep that promise if I ever want him to teach me more things. Which I do. Want him to teach me."

"Well, great," Jake muttered. "That's just great."

"So that's it?" Ron asked. "Nothing more about what was in the traps?"

"I'm gonna keep researching stuff for you guys from up here," Terrell offered.

Ron could hear the regret in Terrell's voice, and it sounded sincere, as though he really wanted to help, but couldn't.

"I will try to get more from Abe about what was in the traps," Terrell continued. "Of course, they're fried now, useless, but I think he knows more about what was in them than he's telling me. He just wants to protect me, I think, and that's a good thing, of course. Maybe if I word it right, and he doesn't think I'm becoming more involved, he'll tell me. And I might discover something in my books. I have a big library, and I'll go through it, look for anything I can find about verbatim…"

"Verboten," Ron corrected, rolling his eyes.

"Right, verboten stuff. If I find out anything, I will call you. I promise."

"How much can you realistically do long distance?" Jake asked. "How are you gonna exorcise the place? Do I need to get my girlfriend involved, ask her to try and cleanse it again?"

"No!" Terrell replied. "I don't know if your girlfriend is really gifted or not, but if she is, and she interacts with the things in your house, it could kill her! I believe Abe's warning. Don't involve her."

"Well, fuck," Jake muttered, turning from the phone. "How do we solve this, then?"

"I don't have answers for you just yet," Terrell replied. "Like I said, if I find out anything more, I'll call. Sorry, guys. That's the best I've got at this moment. Just don't involve any gifted people. You'll be putting their lives at risk."

"We won't," Jake said. "Thanks, I guess."

"Bye for now."

Jake tapped the phone, ending the call.

"So, he can't do anything," Ron said dismissively, "which doesn't surprise me. I wasn't really expecting much from him, anyway. Or from Freedom, for that matter."

"Do you think this Abe guy is right? About it being lethal?"

"Who knows? He might be some random old man who wants to keep Terrell close so he can bring him tea and do chores."

"I was gonna say it seemed like a little progress, at least, finding out about the traps, but you just negated all that."

"That's *my* gift," Ron replied, smiling.

"Well, nothing happened last night, so maybe things will quiet down. You wanna move on to sealing up the siding today?"

"Nothing would give me more pleasure."

- - -

It was late afternoon. Clouds had begun to form, and Ron was worried it might start to rain. His fifth tube of caulk was nearly used up when his phone buzzed. He pulled the tube from the gun and tossed it into the trash, set down the gun, and retrieved the phone from his pocket.

"Oh, got the bid."

"The bid?" Jake asked, midway up the side of the house on a ladder.

"For the well," Ron replied, scrolling. "Jesus Christ."

"That bad?"

"Yeah. I don't know what I was expecting. Several thousand in flat fees, plus the per foot charges."

"What's the total?"

"To go another two hundred feet, almost fifteen thousand."

"Fuck me."

"Huh...he's included a bid to reopen the first well."

"First well?"

"If they go two hundred feet on the existing well but don't hit anything, he's proposing extending the first well. No extra fees, just the per foot charges."

"Why would you do that? Wouldn't that cost more?"

Ron put the phone away and went for another tube of caulk. "Hell, I don't know. He doesn't explain it. I'll have to give him a call."

He heard a yell, and looked up. The ladder Jake stood on was tipping to the right. Jake was about fifteen feet off the ground, and as the ladder continued to slide along the side of the house, he clung to it, riding it as it scraped against the siding.

Ron ran to the ladder, hoping to right it before it could tilt any farther, but it was already half fallen by the time he reached its base. Jake kept yelling, and Ron watched in horror as it fell the rest of the way. Jake held tight, and when it was just feet from the ground, he leapt backward, pushing himself away from it. He landed on his legs but fell back onto the ground as the aluminum crashed against rocks that surrounded the foundation.

Ron ran to him. "Are you OK? What the fuck happened?"

"It just slid," Jake replied, still on the ground. He rolled to one side and moaned.

"Did you break anything?" Ron asked, kneeling next to him. "Ribs?"

"I think it's just the air knocked out of me," Jake gasped, rolling over. "Help me up."

Ron grabbed his friend by the shoulders and lifted.

Jake struggled to his feet. "I didn't shift my weight or anything," he said. "Goddamn thing just started to slide."

"You OK?" Ron asked again, now that Jake was standing.

"I think so. Gonna have a bruise or two." He walked back to the ladder, and Ron followed. "I thought I had it set pretty well, it...wait..."

Jake stood next to the feet of the ladder, looking down. One of the legs was bent near the bottom, the aluminum crunched in upon itself as though it had been twisted under a vice. "Oh, would you look at that. It buckled!"

Ron knelt next to the damaged ladder. "That's crazy. This ladder is brand new...they don't just..." He stopped, not sure he wanted to vocalize the rest of his thought.

Jake's eyes went wide as he suddenly hit upon an idea. "Lethal! Like Terrell said!"

Ron was immediately dismissive. "There must have been a flaw in it that I didn't see when I bought it."

"What if I'd been up near the roof line?" Jake asked. "I might not have survived that fall!"

"I know, we're lucky."

"Or dumb as shit!" Jake knelt down next to the ladder, running his fingers over the twisted metal. "Christ, Ron, I've never seen a ladder do this! This ain't normal. Not by a long shot!"

"Let's not overreact," Ron replied. "You're not the first person to fall off a ladder. This one had a defect, that's all. I'll return it and get another one with..."

"It won't matter, don't you see that?" Jake said. "They'll just crush that one, too."

"They'll?"

"Maybe you'll be at the top of it when they do, and you'll..."

"Who's they?" Ron asked, cutting him off.

"You know."

"No, who exactly are you talking about?"

"The...things in your house, Ron! The ghosts. Whatever the fuck you want to call them!"

Ron paused, considering his options. Continuing to argue with Jake didn't seem like the best way to proceed; the man was clearly convinced that the accident had been caused by something supernatural, and the more he argued with him about rational things, the more Jake seemed to dig in.

Ignore it, he thought, wanting to move on and act as though none of it had happened, but remembering how he'd taken the same approach to the singed outlets. He stuffed both ideas deep, but knew they'd resurface. "Why don't we take a break?" he offered. "Go inside, maybe relax for a while, make sure you're OK. Did you hit your head at all?"

Jake reached to the back of his skull and felt there, searching for a bump. "No, I don't think so. Just my back."

"Might be a good idea to get some painkillers into you."

Ron headed for the garage, and Jake followed. Once they were inside, Jake went for the refrigerator and a beer, and was lying down on the couch in the living room when Ron found him and passed him the bottle of pills.

"The ground was solid," Jake said, after Ron sat down with another beer. "I had the ladder in the same spot yesterday when I nailed up trim. Nothing soft. Nice and hard."

"Like I said, a flaw in the aluminum," Ron replied. "That's all."

"Your problem is you don't believe the obvious," Jake said.

"Twisted metal, Jake. Plain to see."

"You know what I mean. That ladder was perfectly fine. Legs don't twist like that."

"The one out in the yard proves you wrong."

"Terrell said that whatever is here, it's lethal. Then this happens. Not a coincidence, my friend."

"You ever heard of a thing called confirmation bias?"

"No."

"You're interpreting every new thing that happens in support of your original theory. It's flawed, but you don't see that because you force everything to fit."

"Just because you have a bunch of fancy words doesn't mean my theory is flawed!"

"The ladder might have been nothing more than an accident, but it doesn't matter what happens around here, you're gonna say it's because of ghosts or Terrell or the devil, all because you've got some kind of disposition to believe this nonsense."

Jake closed his eyes. "You're a good friend, Ron, but honestly, sometimes you're so full of bullshit."

"Am I?"

"There are good reasons why I think the way I do. You don't know everything about me. We've known each other for a long time, but that doesn't mean you've gone through what I've gone through."

"Never claimed to."

"Yes, you do. You think everyone should have your perspective. Well, a person's perspective is based on what they've experienced in life." Jake turned his head to look at him. "Have you ever seen anything like what's happening here? In your house? All the weird shit we've seen? Be honest."

"No."

"Well, I have. I've seen really weird, scary shit in my life, when I was younger. I have some basis for my thinking, some history I can fall back on, whereas you don't. So, it's not just confirmation bias, my friend. I know what I'm talking about."

Ron paused. When Jake didn't continue, he said, "Are you going to tell me what?"

"You'll just be dismissive; you'll do your big scoffing thing you do and not take it seriously."

"No, I won't. I promise I'll be respectful. We're just sitting here, relaxing, anyway. Go ahead and tell me."

Jake turned his head back, looking up at the ceiling. He took another swig of beer. "I haven't told anyone about this since college, because it creeps me the hell out to even think about. But that thing I saw upstairs…it's just too familiar."

He took another breath and began.

Chapter Fourteen

Jake stared at the tiny balls of fur swinging slowly in the wind.

By the base of the wooden pole was a roll of string with several inches free, lying in an S shape like one of the garter snakes they frequently found in the yard.

No sign of what she cut the string with, he thought, looking around. *Probably those safety scissors she used on her dolls.*

He returned his attention to the small corpses dangling from the clothes line. A towel hanging behind him flapped in the wind, hitting him in the back of the head. He was grateful the towels were out drying; it hid the sight of the bodies from his mother, who would freak out if she saw them.

Marty had used a clothespin to attach each string to the line. He pinched it, freeing the ball of fur, and caught it as it fell. It felt cold and stiff.

Mom might come out to collect the laundry any second, he thought, and decided he should hurry. He removed the remaining six, letting them collect in a pocket he formed by lifting the bottom of his shirt. When he finished, he turned to look through the space between the towels, checking to see if his mother had left the kitchen door, not wanting her to catch him when he transported the bodies to the side of the house.

If she sees them, he thought, *she will lose her mind.*

Determining that the coast was clear, he hurried across the yard to a narrow patch of ground between the bricks of the house and the wooden fence that separated their property from the neighbor's. He fell to his knees and lowered the front of his shirt, allowing the bodies to gently fall to the ground.

No one will notice here, behind the chimney, he thought. *I can get the spade from the garage, dig a hole, and bury them before anyone notices. And if Mom comes out, I can leave them here and come back, finish later.*

He looked down at the pile of tiny kittens and felt pity and sadness. While he really wasn't a cat person, he had played with the reddish one a little bit, and had become fond of it. He watched Marty play with all of them over the past few weeks, seeming to enjoy them; not a single hint that this horrible act was coming.

Now, he looked down at the red one and felt his anger rise. His first inclination had been to protect his younger sister by making sure their mother didn't find the horrific display, but as he hid her terrible misdeed, he made a few resolutions.

She has to stop, he thought. *She thinks she can keep doing things like this to get her way. I will have to convince her it won't work.*

Even as he thought it, he knew it was going to be a challenge he may not win.

Although he was tempted to run to the garage, he walked, not wanting to draw any attention to himself in case his mother appeared. The spade was sitting in a stack of clay pots just inside the door, and as he grabbed it, he considered how it would look if he was carrying it through the yard and she happened to come out. Only his parents performed yard work, and he knew she'd be suspicious if she saw him with it, unlikely to believe any story he might construct.

He also knew she used a timer that sat next to the refrigerator to remind her to take down the laundry.

He dropped the spade and walked to the kitchen door, hoping his mother was somewhere else in the house. *I wonder if Marty is watching me do this from her upstairs window.* He closed the door behind him and went to the fridge. The small black timer was on the counter; three minutes remained.

Not enough time, he thought.

He pressed the "+" button a few times until the display read 6:14. It continued its countdown: 6:13, 6:12.

That's better, he thought, and went back outside, grabbed the spade, and headed for the side of the house.

The ground wasn't soft. His mother planted flowers all over the yard, but not in this area, as it didn't receive much sun, and there were no windows that looked out upon it. A couple of evergreen shrubs were there, recently trimmed back.

This might be a good place, he thought, *since she never works over here, but with the hard soil, it's going to take longer to dig a hole deep enough for all of them. And the dirt will be disturbed, too; it'll be obvious something is buried here. I'm going to have to camouflage it somehow.*

Again his anger bubbled up. He wouldn't have to be doing any of this if he didn't feel the damned need to protect his sister. It was instinctual; he'd felt protective ever since she was born, and he knew it wasn't something he could shed now, now that she had become so...so...

Unpredictable.

Protecting her, yes, that's something older brothers do; Dad had said as much, had reinforced it many times. He felt justified as he dug the hole deeper. But – she didn't need to kill innocent creatures. That was unnecessary. She was becoming cruel. It had to stop.

Satisfied that the hole was deep enough, he gently placed the kittens into it, trying to arrange them with some dignity but knowing he didn't have the luxury of time or space. In the end, they were huddled closely next to each other, and before he began to cover them with dirt, he noted that their positions reminded him of when they would sleep together, usually after feeding.

Slowly the animals were concealed, and with each spadeful he became more incensed at his sister's boldness. *I have to find her and sit her down, explain to her that this was unacceptable, that now she's really gone too far, that…*

He knew she wouldn't listen. She had already gone too far, long before this.

He returned the spade to the garage as his mother emerged from the kitchen, carrying a laundry basket. "Come help me with these," she said, walking to the clothesline. She commonly recruited anyone who happened to be in the backyard whenever she was hanging or taking down laundry, so he knew it would be useless to resist.

"What are you doing out here?" she asked, as the towels began to come down.

"Looking for something in the garage," he replied, dropping towels into the basket.

"What?

He thought for a moment. His mother was very good at detecting lies; whatever he chose to tell her, it had to be plausible. "I was looking for my old…"

"Jake Mathias Andrews!" she said, angry. "Show me your hands!"

He turned his palms to her; they were dirty.

"Now look, you've soiled these clean towels! Why didn't you tell me your hands were filthy?"

He gave her his best shrug, the one that told her he didn't know exactly what to say, and somehow charmed her even when she was really irritated. It had worked many times in the past.

"Take these two back to the hamper, wash those hands, and come back out and help me finish!" She handed him the ruined ones.

He took them, giving her another apologetic smile. "Sorry, Mom."

"Don't 'sorry' me, just get back out here before I'm done."

He ran inside, doing as he was told.

- - -

Jake stepped into Marty's room and shut the door behind him.

Marty was on the floor, playing with a row of Barbies that had been arranged against the wall, firing-squad style. The hair on most of them had been cut off, leaving short stubs growing out of the plastic holes in their skulls. Jake noticed that several of them were missing heads altogether. Marty had arranged the heads on a series of blocks stacked next to the wall. They looked like spectators in stands, attending an execution.

She looked up at him. "Did she find them?"

"I took them down."

A slow frown crept over his sister's face. It seemed to Jake that the temperature in the room changed as his sister's countenance shifted, becoming colder.

Time to set her straight, he thought, sitting down on the floor across from her. "Listen to me. First, you're going about this all wrong. I guarantee you that kind of thing won't work with them, it will absolutely backfire. Second...what a horrible thing to do, Marty! What's wrong with you?"

It was something he'd begun to wonder the past few months, as he watched his sister become more demanding and sinister when she didn't get her way.

"I want a Sega Genesis," she hissed at him. "I don't care about cats."

"You should be ashamed. They were living things, Marty. They're not like your dolls. That was cruel."

"Sonja plays Sonic," Marty said slowly, emphasizing each word. "I want to play it, too."

"If you think killing kittens will convince Mom and Dad to change their minds..." Jake said, feeling exasperation, not sure how to convince her, "...well, it won't. It will make them dig in and you'll never get a Genesis. You'll just get grounded, or worse."

She stared at him blankly; his appeal seemed to be falling on deaf ears.

"Why are you being this way?" he asked. "You're acting so crazy lately. What's wrong?"

Her eyes focused more intently on him. "You don't realize that I deserve it," she said. "I can make it very bad for you. For them."

"They can make things bad for you, too. If you think a two-week grounding is bad, you can't imagine what would have happened if Mom had found those kittens hanging out there. What they'd do to you would make a two-week grounding feel like a trip to Disneyland."

"What did you do with them?"

"What?"

"The cats."

"I buried them."

"Where?"

"None of your business. You're not listening to me."

"I've heard every goddamn word."

"Marty! You can't talk like that! If you slip up and say something like that around Mom, she'll wash your mouth out with soap!"

"I'd like to see her try."

Jake looked at her, frustrated and annoyed, not knowing what to do or say next. In the back of his mind he could hear his brain reminding him that this conversation wasn't going to work in the first place, that – *told you so!* – she wasn't going to listen. Whatever strange track his sister was on, he didn't possess the key to stopping it, or changing it.

Marty turned her attention back to the dolls. "His fish are next."

Jake thought of the forty-gallon tank in his father's study. "Marty, don't. He's raised some of those fish for years. He'll be…"

"He'll be devastated," she finished.

"I was going to say 'pissed', but, yeah, he'll be really upset."

"Devastated," she repeated, positioning the severed doll heads to better view the execution wall. "He'll be heartbroken." She launched a small plastic truck against the wall, hitting the dolls, sending them flying. "That's what he gets for caring about them more than me."

"He doesn't care about the fish more than you," Jake said. "You know that."

Something moved under him, a faint rumble that made the carpet he was sitting on vibrate just a little, as though the floorboard underneath had been jostled. For a moment he thought it was an earthquake, and he reached to the floor, bracing, wondering if he should find a doorway and advise Marty to do the same.

"Get out of my room, Jake," Marty said, not looking up from her scene of doll mayhem.

Some talk, he thought. *You really convinced her...of nothing!* He felt compelled to stay, to try and achieve his goal. Maybe with a few more sentences, some carefully chosen words, he could...

The carpet slid slightly, pulling him a couple of inches away from her. She looked up at him, glaring, her eyes reiterating the command she'd uttered seconds before, overriding whatever sense of duty or obligation he felt to try and convince her to stand down, to stop making demands of their parents, demands that were never going to be met.

Before he could push himself up, he felt pressure against his chest, forcing him back, causing him to slide across the carpet. He reached down to stop the movement, but unable to grab anything, used his hands to steady himself so he didn't fall. His back hit the door with a thud and the pressure continued to build, painfully pinning him against the wood.

"When I tell you to get out," she said from across the room, still glaring at him from the same position, "I mean, get out!"

Finding it hard to take a breath, Jake reached up to the handle, just as he heard the wood crack behind him and he sunk another inch backward. The handle was hard to turn with the pressure on the door. He twisted until the mechanism cleared the frame, but the door didn't pop open into the hallway; it was designed to open in, and was blocked by the jamb.

"I'm leaving," Jake said, trying to stand. "I'm leaving, OK?"

The pressure suddenly disappeared, and he pulled on the handle, swinging the door into the room. He stepped out into the hall. Before he closed the door, he looked down to see a crack in the door's wood.

"Dad's gonna be pissed about that," he said, looking again at her.

"Couldn't give a fuck," she replied.

Her response chilled Jake to the bone. *This isn't her,* he thought. *My sister doesn't talk this way.*

As he closed the door, the light in the room seemed to disappear, becoming darker as he shut it. He watched the final inch closely, the room beyond almost completely dark; no illumination from the windows, even though it was the middle of the day. No light from the overhead fixture. The room was completely enveloped in black.

He pulled the handle until the door latched, having the feeling that he'd just sealed his sister inside her room with something else, something sinister. *She didn't evict me from her room,* he thought. *She's never done that before. I was evicted by whatever else is in there with her.*

His instinct to protect his sister was still strong, but he felt confused, unsure what he should do. Was he dealing with his real sister, the one he had known from the moment she was brought home from the hospital? Or was he dealing with something evil and dark that had taken over her room?

Something that had taken over her?

- - -

The next day after dinner, Jake walked into his father's study to find his dad hovered over the tank, sweeping a net through the water. It appeared that far fewer fish were swimming inside.

"Everything OK, Dad?" Jake asked.

"OK?" his father repeated, turning quickly to look at him. "No, things are not OK!" He turned back to the net, sliding it until he caught something that he lifted from the tank. "Look."

"Oh, no, the tiger pleco," Jake said, looking at the five-inch bottom feeder in his father's net. "We had that one since it was really small."

"I just can't figure out what's happening to them all," his father replied, dumping the fish into a garbage can that Jake noticed was holding several other casualties. "I've treated the water for everything I can think of – fungus, parasites, you name it."

"What about a water change?"

"I change a little every week. A massive change can kill them just as quickly as whatever is killing them now. I don't know…fish going belly up comes with the territory, I guess." He sunk the net back into the water and scooped up another, not bothering to show it to Jake before he dumped it into the can. "Damnit, I think I'm gonna lose the whole tank. Just doesn't seem right."

No, it doesn't, Jake thought, torn between his desire to protect his sister and his sense of honor and honesty with his father. *Telling him that Marty's to blame won't bring the fish back, but…*

He stopped, knowing it was getting out of control. Marty had been sabotaging things around the house for weeks now, somehow imagining that her actions would force Mom and Dad to reverse their decision on her video game. His parents hadn't connected any of the strange occurrences to Marty; so far, they had just written them off, like his father was doing now with the fish. *They can't im-*

agine their daughter would do things like this, Jake thought. *It doesn't even occur to them. And they may never piece it together, until something really bad happens, something that might hurt someone.*

Would Marty go that far?

A month ago Jake would have said no, not a chance. Now, he wasn't so sure. These weren't impulsive acts of a pouting child; these were planned, premeditated acts of cruelty, designed to hurt. *Devastated,* Jake remembered his sister saying. *He'll be devastated. Heartbroken.* She *wanted* her father to feel pain.

"Oh, not the swordtails!" his father moaned, scooping out more fish. He seemed disappointed, but not heartbroken. In fact, he appeared more mystified than anything; confused as to why all his hard work over the past few years had suddenly resulted in a forty-gallon graveyard.

Marty wanted him to be heartbroken, Jake thought. *But he's not. He's not devastated, not like she thought he'd be. She would be heartbroken if this happened to her, but he's much more circumspect about it, reacting more maturely. If she wanted him in tears, this isn't going to cause it.*

She's going to be disappointed. And when she realizes she didn't go far enough, what then? What will she do next?

Kill the dog? Set the house on fire?

How far would she go?

Poison their mother or father?

Kill them?

Kill me?

"Marty did it," Jake said. "She killed your fish."

His father paused. Jake saw the net sink a little into the tank as he turned to look at him. "What did you say?"

"The kittens didn't crawl off," Jake said, "and they weren't moved by their momma. Marty killed them. I found them and buried them. When I asked her why she did it, she told me she intended to kill all the fish, too."

His father's brow wrinkled. "Why?"

Jake sighed. "She wants a Sega Genesis. She's mad that you told her no." He felt a huge relief that the secret was out, that he wasn't the only one who knew the truth.

His father's face began to change, from disbelief to confusion, and from confusion to anger. "If she killed the kittens, why didn't you say something? Why didn't you tell me or your mother?"

"I was protecting her," Jake said, offering a slight shrug. "You always said to look out for her."

"Not cover up crimes!" his father retorted, walking past him out the door and into the house. "Karen! Karen!" he called, trying to find Jake's mother.

At first Jake didn't want to follow him, but when he heard his parents discussing the matter in the kitchen, he decided he'd better make an appearance in case they got details wrong, or in case he needed to defend himself before irrevocable judgments and punishment decisions were made.

His mother stopped talking with his father when he walked in. "Is this true?"

"Yes," he replied, trying his best to signal regret, not wanting to come off as a snitch.

"Why didn't you tell me?" she asked.

"Dad always said to protect her!" he replied.

"Oh, come on, Jake! You're smarter than that." She marched past him to the base of the stairs and called up to Marty, insisting that she come down, then returned to the kitchen, avoiding looking at him, choosing to share concerned glances with his father instead.

"What?" Marty asked, walking into the kitchen.

"Jake tells us you killed my fish," his father said. "And the kittens."

Marty turned to look at him, not angry, but as though she could care less. Jake instantly felt like crawling out of the room, embarrassed, but knew he had to stay and face the music.

"Is this true?" his mother asked his sister.

"What if it is?" Marty replied, in a tone that Jake knew would infuriate them.

"Answer the question!" his father demanded.

"Why would Jake fabricate such a thing?" Marty answered. "Jake never lies. He's perfect." She turned to him, her voice lowering drastically. "Did you dig them up and show them the little rotten carcasses?"

Jake took a step back, alarmed at the sudden change in his sister's countenance. Her tone was foreign, her voice too deep. She was using words beyond her age, displaying a corruptness he'd never seen in her before. She was always his cute – if irritating – younger sister, not the little monster currently on display.

He noticed a similar reaction in his parents, his mother raising a hand to her mouth, shocked by her daughter's language and tone. Her reaction confirmed Jake's feelings, doubling them, making things seem even worse. His father appeared ready to release his anger, which usually meant the pronunciation of sentence. A grounding was coming. Or worse.

"What's wrong with you?" his father asked, furious. "All this for some damn video game?"

"You don't seem to understand," Marty replied condescendingly, turning to look at him with a defiance Jake had never seen – certainly something he had never tried, and knew would stoke the flames, invite more wrath. "I...deserve...it!" Marty yelled, her pitch rising with each word.

She's going to throw a tantrum, Jake thought, *just like when she was little. She hasn't done something like this in years, but the signs are all there, just like when she was two.*

Somehow my nine-year-old sister has become a full-fledged brat.

Marty turned to face him, as though she heard what he thought. Her face was contorted in anger, twisted in a way he hadn't seen since she was a toddler, having a meltdown.

Suddenly he was pushed again, a huge, unstoppable force pressing on his chest, making him slide across the floor as though he was skating backwards. Within seconds he hit the wall, and china plates on a shelf above him fell, crashing to the floor and shattering into pieces at his feet. The pressure held him tightly in place, unable to move, pressing him upward until he felt his heels leave the ground, his toes pointing down, still touching, as though he was standing on them. He looked down, recognizing the tourist designs on a couple of the decorative plates that were now in pieces: the stone faces of Mt. Rushmore, El Capitan from Yosemite, the Golden Gate Bridge.

His father was on the move, and Jake looked up to see him reaching for Marty, inches from her arm. She pulled back and ran, disappearing into the dining room. His father followed her, but before he could leave the kitchen, the refrigerator next to the doorway pulled away from the wall, stretching its cord from the outlet. It tipped and fell over, twisting the plug in the socket and sending a large volley of sparks into the room as it shorted out. It landed with a heavy crash, blocking the path to the dining room, its door opening and its contents spreading across the linoleum floor. His mother, shocked at the sudden movement of the heavy appliance, walked backward until she was against the opposite wall, her hand still at her mouth, frightened.

His father stood next to the fridge, milk beginning to pool around his feet. He turned to look at Jake's mother, then at Jake, as though he was double checking that he hadn't just imagined what had occurred.

"Paul?" his mother said, reaching out and walking to his father. "Are you alright?"

"Yeah," his father replied, turning to her.

Jake felt the pressure against his chest release, and his feet fell flat on the floor. He stumbled over the broken china and toward his parents, where his mother grabbed him. "What happened?" his mother asked.

"She's done it before," Jake said. "When she's mad."

"You're saying your sister did that to you?" she asked.

"And that," Jake replied, pointing to the refrigerator.

- - -

Jake walked into his sister's room.

Toys had been stored away long ago. The made bed still seemed odd; Marty never made her bed when she was home. His mother had straightened everything up after the second time she was sent away, and it remained in a state of suspended animation.

He hated it. He hated the sterility and order, the fact that his sister wasn't at home, the changes that had come over the family.

But most of all, he hated this room.

He walked to the bed and sat on it, looking at the walls. Pictures Marty had colored were tacked up, next to a poster of a sloth in a tree, "Hang In There!" emblazoned in an ugly yellow font along its bottom.

Something's still here, he thought. *She's gone, but it's still in here. Mom and Dad refuse to believe it, but I know it's true.*

Whatever is in here is why Marty is at Southbrook.

His sister had been taken to Southbrook two days after the incident in the kitchen. The three of them recovered from the shock of the events; Jake had helped his father right the fridge, and while his mother attempted to clean the floor of the spilled food and destroyed china, Jake listened as his father tried to talk to Marty through her bedroom door. His sister screamed obscenities from inside, and when his dad grabbed the door's handle to open it and confront his daughter, he yelled and pulled back his hand. He claimed to receive some kind of electric shock.

The mood of the house changed dramatically after that. His mother and father spent a lot of time huddled in conversation. Occasionally they'd quiz him about Marty's behavior, things he'd observed, and Jake answered them as best he could, his guilt over ratting her out now gone. Marty stayed in her room and didn't come down for meals. His mother began leaving plates of food by the door, which Jake noticed were polished off when no one was looking.

The next night, Jake had been asleep for about an hour when his father shook him gently. "We're taking your sister to a hospital," he whispered. "Get dressed quietly and come with us. Quick."

Five minutes later he was in the back seat of the car, watching as his father carried his sister from the house and through the darkness, placing her into his mother's arms in the front seat. Marty was completely passed out, and didn't rouse as the car bumped along the surface streets to a facility a half hour away. Jake sat in the car as a nurse and orderly appeared from the front entrance to the building, and helped take Marty from his mother. He watched as his parents talked with the nurse and the orderly, and disappeared inside with his sister.

When they returned to the car, Jake asked, "What is this place?"

"It's a special hospital that can help your sister," his father replied, driving them home.

"You drugged her," Jake said.

His mother turned to look at him. "I don't know what's happening to Marty, but something is very wrong. We were afraid if we didn't get professional help, something horrible might happen."

"Something worse than what's already happened?" Jake asked.

"Yes," his father confirmed. "You saw what was going on. I don't need to explain it to you."

He paused, watching as houses along the dark street went by in the car's windows. Finally he asked, "How do they treat her? What do they do to her?"

"Therapy," his mother replied. "She may need medication. They figure all that out."

"How long will she be there?"

"Enough with the questions!" his father replied. "She'll be there until she's cured. We're all exhausted. Now we just go home and try to get back to normal. We'll call the hospital and check on her every day."

"Can we go in? Visit her?"

"Not until they say we can," his mother answered. "She's very agitated. The nurse thought it best that they limit her stimuli for a while, and that includes us. We'll visit her as soon as the staff says she's better."

They rode home the rest of the way in silence.

It was two days later that Marty was back home. The doctors said there was nothing wrong with her, physically or mentally.

When they went to visit her, Marty seemed her normal self, happy and playful, wondering when she could leave. Jake saw the confusion and anxiety that her sudden change produced in his parents; they began second guessing themselves, wondering if the steps they'd taken were an overreaction. They checked Marty out of the facility.

Things were fine for a couple of days, but it didn't take long before Marty changed again, speaking coarsely, slamming doors as she went through the house. Renewing her demands for the video game system she wanted.

One day, Marty wouldn't come out of her room. They all tried to talk to her through the door, urging her to come out, but she refused. Jake received a nasty burn on his hand when he tried to use the door handle to go inside. His mother began leaving plates of food once again, and the hopeful mood of the house reverted to the dark, somber tone of the previous week.

That night, a man arrived at the house and spent some time talking with his parents in the living room. Jake left his bedroom, trying to overhear the conversation. Eventually they came upstairs, and his parents introduced Dr. Furness to him, who asked him a few questions about Marty's behavior. He answered them as best he could, then watched as the doctor and his parents moved down the hall to Marty's room, and tried to communicate with her through the door. The doctor yelped when he touched the door handle, despite having been warned by Jake's father.

"Did you get the glove?" the doctor asked.

My father produced a shiny black glove, and handed it to the doctor.

Dr. Furness slipped it on; it was thick, and looked like it was made of rubber. He reached for the handle once again, and was able to turn it and push it open before the glove melted away, burning into his hand. He screamed as he pulled it from his arm, dropping it to the ground. Smoke was rising from his fingers as he held them up to examine the damage.

The door was still open, and Jake was curious to know if his sister was OK inside. He ran down the hall until he was standing next to his father, with a clear view into the room.

Marty was in the center. She was floating in the air a couple of feet off the ground, facing away, her body leaning weirdly to the left. Her hair should have been hanging down, but it wasn't. In the blink of an eye she spun around to face them. Her features were twisted, making her look like someone else.

Terror raced down Jake's spine as he heard his mother gasp in horror. "Marty!" she cried, but before she could enter the room, the door slammed closed.

He could smell the bitter odor of the melted glove. He watched as his father turned to the doctor, who was still holding his hand in the air.

"Well?" his father demanded.

The doctor's mouth was open, frozen by the spectacle he'd witnessed. Slowly he closed it and turned to Jake's parents. "Bring her in again."

That night his parents drugged her food like before, and moved her back to the facility. Marty seemed completely normal once she was there, just like the previous visit, but the doctor kept her longer this time, saying he wanted to observe her reaction to different types of medication. His parents seemed happy to let the doctor experiment, desperate to find a solution.

Jake had come into his sister's empty bedroom several times since then. The first time was the morning after she left. Her room was still a mess, but later that day his mother cleaned it up, putting things away and straightening everything. Since then, the room hadn't changed.

They're medicating her, Jake thought, *but it won't matter. Nothing's wrong with Marty. What's wrong is in this room. It's still here, waiting.*

Even as he sat on the bed, he could feel impressions entering his mind, a sense that things weren't fair, that what he wanted was paramount and should be paramount for others. Injustice felt like the tip of a chisel cracking its way into his body, wanting him to become more assertive and stand up for himself, to learn how to insist upon his own way, and make sure he got what he wanted, no matter what.

It felt manipulative and foreign, and he knew it was exactly what had happened to his sister. She was fine at Southbrook, but if his parents brought her back to this room, she wouldn't be. He wouldn't be either, if he spent more time there.

He stood up. "Whatever you are, you need to leave. My sister isn't coming back, and if she does, I'll make sure she doesn't stay in this room. There's no one here for you to infect."

He waited silently, wondering if he'd receive some reply. Aside from a shiver that passed over his arms, causing his skin to form goose bumps, no reply came.

Chapter Fifteen

"What happened to her?" Ron asked.

"She stayed in Southbrook for a year," Jake replied, still lying on the couch. "I hate to think how much crap they pumped into her during that time."

"And after the year?"

"She came home. Now she's a lawyer in Virginia. Has two kids."

"What about that room?"

"Don't know. We moved to a new house while she was in Southbrook. Whatever was in the room stayed there. I presume it's haunting whoever lives there now. Or, maybe not. I don't know. I was happy to leave it behind."

"And your sister was fine in the new house?"

"Yes. So, fast forward a few years. I told this story to a woman I met in college. She seemed to know what it was. She said there are these dark things that live in some houses."

"Ghosts?"

"Eh, kinda. More like vagrant squatters…ghosts that came there from somewhere else. You know, a normal ghost is the spirit of someone who died there, or used to live there, that kind of thing. These dark ones are from some other place."

"Where?"

"She didn't say. But she did say that what I described seemed like them. I told her I thought it might be the devil, and she said I might be right...which is why, I suppose, I called that thing you've got upstairs the devil."

"How would she know? Did she have experience with them?"

"She sounded like she knew what she was talking about."

Ron scoffed.

"You're missing the point!" Jake continued.

"You're saying what you saw upstairs looked like what you saw in your sister's room?"

"I never exactly saw anything in my sister's room except for the weird darkness. It was more like...a vibe."

"A vibe," Ron repeated skeptically.

"And my college friend said it can infect people in different ways. The one in my sister's room turned her into a monster; a monster who could do terrible things to get what she wanted. My college friend knew one who infected someone and drove them mad about money; made them obsess about it. She said it fucked up their life. And Terrell...it stuck him on the ceiling, Ron. And he didn't even realize it was happening. Normal ghosts might make noises and knock things off shelves and scare the shit out of you, but they can't *infect* you. Not like these dark things. They're different."

Ron paused, considering what Jake was saying.

"I'm telling you," Jake continued, "you've got something like that upstairs. It may not be the devil, I may not be right about that, but it's bad. Way bad."

"Suppose I lose my senses and say you're right. What am I supposed to do about it? Freedom and Terrell ran away from it. According to Terrell, no one with the gift can even help, not without putting themselves at risk."

"I don't know, man. We solved it by moving."

Ron's first reaction was to reiterate to his friend that moving wasn't an option. There was no money to buy another place; everything was tied up here. The only realistic way forward was to find a way to fix everything first. *That's all the house needs,* he reminded himself. *It's been mistreated; it just needs attention, and it'll be fine.*

But with all the mounting problems, a nagging corner of his mind agreed that the idea of abandoning it all did sound appealing. For a moment he allowed the idea sink in, accepting it, letting all else fall away. He wondered what would happen if he just packed up everything and left. He'd have to sell the house somehow, of course, down the road...and he couldn't sell it in its current condition, so he'd have to...

"I think I'm gonna head to the motel," Jake said, rising from the couch. "It's dark out. Day's over."

Ron looked out the window. Jake was right; dusk was ending. He abandoned his line of thinking, knowing that he couldn't just throw in the towel; his pocketbook couldn't withstand it. He felt a little ashamed for even considering it.

"Alright," he replied. "You good enough to drive?"

"I'm fine," Jake answered, headed to the door. "You sure you're gonna be alright alone, again?"

"Have been so far."

"Alright. See you tomorrow, then."

Ron watched him leave, grateful that he was still willing to return the next day.

Particularly in light of what he went through with his sister.

- - -

Ron was in the middle of microwaving a meal when he heard knocking at the front door. He left the kitchen and walked through the house. More knocking came, reverberating through the front hallway.

"Hi, Ron!" Tom said, smiling as the door opened. He raised his hand to show the six pack of beer that he'd brought.

I completely forgot about him, Ron thought, remembering the man's promise earlier that day. "Come in!"

"Can't stay long, the wife said an hour tops," Tom replied, entering. He handed the six pack to Ron, who carried it into the kitchen.

"Have a seat," Ron said, removing two bottles and leaving the rest in the fridge. He handed one to Tom, and the two sat down in the living room, Ron in the same chair where he'd sat during Jake's story, and Tom in the same spot where Jake had been.

Tom twisted the bottle's cap and took a swig. "You settling in?"

"Still a lot of work to do," Ron replied, taking a drink.

"Looks like it. House has needed work on the outside for years now. It'll be nice to drive by and see it all fixed up."

Drive by? Ron wondered. *It's a dead end.*

"Where is your house, again?" Ron asked, feeling a little light-headed. "Past the ravine?"

"Yes."

"You must come at it from a different road," Ron said. "My driveway is the end of the road from the east."

"Yes," Tom replied. "I use the road from the west. It was an old logging road; there are a lot of them, all over the mountain."

"Hey, let me ask you a question," Ron said, the lightheadedness growing, making it a little hard to think straight. "Do you have a well?"

"Sure."

"How deep is it?"

"I don't know, four or five hundred feet, I think."

"Huh. Lots of water flow?"

"Never been a problem."

Ron remembered taking mushrooms in his twenties, long before he met Elenore. They caused all kinds of hallucinations and produced a buzz that floated through his system, making him feel alternatively euphoric and sick. The sensations passing through his body as he watched and listened to Tom felt almost the same; at times, things seemed heightened and sharpened. Seconds later, he wondered if he needed to find a bathroom. Then things sharpened again.

Tom chuckled. "In some ways I envy you. A new house, all this possibility. So much ahead of you."

Ron thought about replying, but his thoughts became convoluted as he tried to form a response. He hoped that Tom didn't notice what was happening. *If I can get him to leave, I can sleep off whatever this is,* he thought. "You know, I'm not feeling well. I wonder if I could take a rain check on tonight."

"I know what you mean," Tom replied, smiling. "It's a lot to take in, the enormity of the place, the scope of all the work. You've got acres of history here. It's overwhelming, I'm sure."

Maybe if I insist, Ron thought, feeling the sudden need to vomit. The urge passed, and he swallowed, tasting something vaguely like copper. *Maybe he didn't hear what I said. Maybe I didn't actually say it.*

"Despite all that," Tom continued, "you're really quite lucky. Most of the time, he doesn't ask to see them. You must be special."

"He?" Ron managed to squeak out.

"Upstairs," Tom replied. "A couple more minutes, and I'm going to take you to him."

Ron watched as Tom leaned forward and raised his arm, holding it to the side of his head. Tom's hand was missing; in its place was a twisting ball with filaments trailing from its sides, like a bundle of string coming undone.

"What do you see?" Tom asked, as though he was having a vision exam.

Ron wasn't sure how to reply. He knew something was very wrong; whatever Tom was doing in his house, it wasn't why he'd allowed him in. They weren't going to chat about McLean and the history of the mountain. Yet he couldn't bring himself to object, to ask the man what was going on. The sensations he felt soothed him and made his concerns seem inconsequential, that he should play along and not resist. *Just go with it,* he thought. *It's OK.* He stared at the strange object at the end of Tom's appendage, a little confused by the bizarre image, but unable to do more than answer Tom's question.

"String?" Ron offered.

Tom lowered his arm. "A couple more minutes."

Ron concentrated, hoping he could regain control, but it was like when he tried to force a dream; thoughts were going in too many directions. He attempted to focus on one specific thing so he could ask Tom a question that still seemed important.

"You don't live beyond the ravine, do you?" Each word was an effort. He wasn't sure what he verbalized made any sense.

"No," Tom replied.

"Where do you live?"

"Here," Tom answered, smiling.

"Why...why..." Ron tried, the words not coming.

Tom raised his arm again. "How about now?"

Ron saw a spinning orb at the end of Tom's wrist. It was shiny, reflecting the light from the room, and looked like it was made of silver.

"Metal," Ron answered, surprised that he was able to say the word. "Ball."

"Very good," Tom replied, lowering his arm and standing up. "Let's go."

In the back of his brain, Ron knew he should be resisting, should be refusing to answer or to follow Tom's commands, but all of his senses seemed to think things were OK, that following along was perfectly fine. He felt himself rise from the chair, unable to override the buzz that was guiding his movements. Tom turned and walked to the stairs, and he followed.

"So glad you ripped out the carpet here," Tom said as they ascended. "The color was horrible."

"They smelled," Ron replied, again surprised that the thought successfully emerged as spoken words. It was almost as though he was using a different voice, employing an entirely different route to speak than he normally would.

"The smell never bothered me," Tom said, leading him up. "But then, I can't smell like I used to. One of the first things to go, I'm afraid."

As they reached the landing, it suddenly occurred to Ron that he was being led to *that* room, the one Terrell slept in; the one with the dark entity that Jake said was the devil. He knew he should be feeling some kind of defense, some sense of danger triggered by the need for self-preservation, but the sensations running through him neutralized his fight or flight reaction, making him feel perfectly fine.

"Do you intend to put in new?" Tom asked.

"New what?"

"New carpet?"

"Yeah," Ron replied, taking step after step, following Tom. "Can't leave them wood, like this."

"No, I suppose not, not with a wife and child coming. What color?"

"Color?"

"The carpet? I think red would be stunning, myself. Would really set things off."

"I don't know yet," Ron replied. "I thought I'd let Elenore decide."

"Be careful giving your family too much leeway," Tom replied, reaching the top and heading for the bedroom. "It's best that you make the decisions, and that they know who's in charge." He came to a stop in front of the door. "Ah, here we are." He opened it and stood aside. "Please, go in."

The room was completely black, and it made Ron remember the story Jake had told earlier in the evening. His legs seemed to move on their own, unafraid, carrying him into the darkness. Once he was inside, the door shut behind him, eliminating all light.

His eyes began to adjust. There was movement in front of him, something darker than the darkness that filled the room. It shifted and approached him.

"I am Ezra." A rancid warmth accompanied the words.

Ron felt the fuzziness of the mushroom effect dissipate a little; clarity returned, but without fear.

"Ron," he replied. "Ron Costa."

"You're in terrible danger, Mr. Costa."

The stench from Ezra was overwhelming. Ron turned to look around him. The room was pitch black; no illumination came in under the door or from the windows. He stretched his eyes wide, hoping to let in maximum light. His ears picked up a slight shift in Ezra's location; he was moving as he spoke.

"You've heard it at night, I expect," Ezra continued. "Walking up the stairs. You can hear the thump of its steps as your head is on the pillow, trying to sleep."

Ron knew exactly what the voice in the darkness was talking about. He heard it almost every night when he was lying down; the faint sound of feet ascending on the wooden steps. "That's you, coming up the stairs?" he asked.

"Not me. Them. They walk it every night, searching for you. It will get worse. You won't be able to sleep. You won't be able to stand it."

"I don't know, I'm a pretty good sleeper. I've managed to sleep through all the other crap."

"But eventually they will find you. When they enter your room, they will surround your bed while you sleep. They are horrible, and their presence, so close to your body, will cause nightmares. Maybe you've already felt their influence, and dreamt terrible things. It will eat into you. You will sense it, but be unable to stop it. You'll be terrified. Every time you hear those steps on the stairs, know that they are getting closer."

"You're trying to get me to leave. I'm not leaving."

"They will destroy you. If you bring your family here, they will destroy them. If you value your life, or theirs, you *must* leave. This house, this land…it's…gone. Lost. You can't hope to understand it or combat it; it's beyond your ability. Forces far greater than you have tried and failed. There's a sickness here, an infection. It's in the ground, and it cannot be removed."

"What sickness?"

Ron felt a chill go up his spine; it felt as though an icy finger had been placed at the base of his back, and slowly slid upwards. When it reached his neck, more fingers solidified, wrapping around his throat, freezing his skin, pressing inward. Breath suddenly stopped; he struggled to inhale.

"Do you feel that? Death as cold as the frozen snow, an end to everything you've ever planned. Your wife, a widow…your son, an orphan. The extinguishment of all hope."

He gulped, moving, shifting, hoping to dislodge whatever was holding him, reaching to his throat in an attempt to grab at the fingers cutting off his air. Nothing was there; there were no fingers to grasp, and when he moved to the side, the asphyxiation moved with him, undeterred.

"Inevitable as the sunset, snuffed out like a waning candle. It's hard to imagine not existing. Yet, it's just moments away. And there's worse."

He felt cold fingers at his mouth, prying it open. He resisted, but the muscles in his jaw were uncontrollable. As his lips parted, something wide and slimy entered, sliding quickly into him past his throat. He choked as it moved inside, twisting, spreading an icy numbness throughout his torso, making him feel as though his lungs were freezing solid. Trying to gasp, he grabbed at his chest, sensing his heart slowing.

"Imagine how this will feel to your little boy…"

The thing inside him suddenly energized, tearing him up, slicing at him like a motorized blade, ripping up his organs and causing his entire frame to shake. Holes were cut open through his flesh and warm blood poured out, coating his body. It went deeper, causing excruciating pain, churning up his liver and kidneys, his intestines, and finally landing at the bottom of his torso where it spun like the blades of a blender, slicing him until he had nothing left inside but a soup of gore.

Why am I not dying? he thought. *I should be dead.*

At that moment he saw the faint eyes of Ezra, just feet from him, small grey orbs dimly floating in the air. They moved and shifted, but seemed lifeless, like doll eyes. Desperate, Ron tried to reach out toward them, hoping he might grab onto something and find some means of defense, but his arms were unresponsive; they hung at his sides like tubes of meat, swinging as he shook, unable to execute the commands his brain was sending.

Then, just as quickly as it had entered him, the invader retreated, pulling out through his mouth. The icy fingers around his neck released, and he took in a breath, grateful that he still had lungs with which to breathe.

Light fell in from behind, illuminating the scant furniture in the room. Fading in front of him was Ezra; the grey eyes were inside a head that was translucent, looking as though it was made of dark glass, reflecting small patches of light from the door. Another second, and the figure was gone.

A hand at the back of his shirt tugged on him, pulling him out until he was standing in the hallway.

Tom reached for the door and shut it, then grabbed him by the shoulders, spinning him around until he could stare him in the eyes.

"I do hope you'll reconsider the red. I really think it would make things pop." He smiled and let go.

Ron turned to look over the railing into the living room below. The house seemed peaceful and silent, a jarring contrast to the bizarre horror he'd just experienced in the bedroom.

When he turned back, Tom was gone.

"Fuck me," Ron muttered, making his way to the stairs. The buzz of whatever had drugged him still coursed through his system, but now he felt functional, able to think and move.

Exhausted, he checked the time and saw it was past ten. What had seemed like a twenty minute visit from Tom had actually lasted several hours.

As he checked the doors, preparing for bed, he thought about Ezra, wondering what the night might have in store. He knew he should be afraid; it was clear that fear was what Tom and Ezra wanted. Yet, the same part of his personality that prioritized rational thought – the stubborn part that refused to let go of normality despite the obviously non-normal things around him – that same part resisted giving in to the fear. Just knowing that they wanted him to be afraid was enough to make him reject it.

He made his way upstairs. As he passed the closed door to the bedroom where he met Ezra, he stopped. "Sorry, but I normally leave this room open," he said aloud, as though he was informing the ghosts. He reached for the door handle and pushed it inward.

Faint moonlight appeared on the floor, falling in through the windows. He turned on the overhead fixture for a moment, looking over the room, seeing nothing unusual, nothing that would hint at the painful, frightening encounter he'd participated in just minutes before. Satisfied, he turned off the light and left the door open, then walked down the hallway toward the master bedroom, looking over the banister into the living room below as he went.

Ten minutes later, after his nightly routines, he was under the covers with the lights out, looking up at the ceiling. The house was insanely quiet, and he could hear little pops and creaks as it cooled down.

When will it start? he wondered, straining his ears, waiting.

He rolled to his side. Now, with one ear pressed into the pillow and the other perched upward, he heard it – faint, almost not really there.

Thump.

Overhead, something in the attic. How it always seemed to start.

Then, almost so imperceptible as to not even be there, the slow plod of steps on wood.

They're coming up the stairs, he thought. *Like Ezra said.*

He sat up, and the sound stopped. Waiting, he realized the loudest thing he could hear was his breathing. He held his breath for a moment, straining to listen, looking at the locked doors at the other end of the bedroom, wondering if they had any chance of keeping them out once they – whatever they were – reached the top.

Nothing. No sound.

He reclined, his head back on the pillow. He closed his eyes, hoping he might fall asleep.

Thump. Thump.

He's fucking with me, Ron thought. *The steps on the stairs will go on, but nothing will ever arrive. He wants me to be scared, to throw in the towel on this place and leave.*

Thump...thump. It was rhythmic, perfectly timed to mimic a slow ascension. Perfectly designed to scare.

He realized his heart was beating rapidly. *It* does *work,* he thought. *It* does *scare.*

He reached for his earplugs and gave them a squeeze until they were thin enough to slip into his ears. As they sealed shut, the sound from the stairs faded away.

Then, as he tried to fall asleep, he came to a decision.

Chapter Sixteen

"You're gonna what?" Jake asked, almost choking on his coffee.

"I'm gonna fight it," Ron replied. "I'm spinning in circles, pretending it isn't happening, spending all my time rationalizing something irrational. Meanwhile things are getting more and more fucked up. I'm tired of it. Insanity is doing the same thing over and over, expecting a different result. I have to take a different approach. It's clear to me now that their goal is to scare me off my property, and that's not going to happen."

"Well," Jake replied, sipping more coffee. "I don't know what to say. I've been trying to convince you for days now, so I guess I'm glad. Whatever happened to you last night, I'm happy it finally made you see the light."

"It put a face to it," Ron replied. "Vague ghosts, fleeting images of things, all that seemed too unreal to take seriously. But actually meeting the person behind it, realizing his agenda...that's something I can seize on. I can fight this fucker."

"Right, fight..." Jake said. "So, as you'll recall, you've had two experts here already. Neither of them had any success."

"Experts?" Ron replied. "Don't take this personally, Jake, but what is Freedom an expert at? Selling crystals and dreamcatchers at psychic fairs? And Terrell, he seems barely able to function at life. I can't imagine his ghost tour business does very well, he doesn't seem like the type who would make a success of something like that."

"Freedom does OK selling crystals," Jake replied. "But, come to think of it, there were only a couple of other people on that ghost tour with us, so you might be right about Terrell." He paused. "Then again, it was Port Angeles. Not going to draw a crowd."

"And by his own admission, he didn't have much of 'the gift'. He seemed more a student of it than someone who could command it. If it even exists."

"His mentor seemed to think something is definitely going on here."

"The same mentor who warned him not to become involved. Damned convenient. You don't help, you can't fail. How do we know his mentor knows jack shit? He might only be good at knowing a bad bet."

"OK, so you don't like the people I involved. You have a better plan? You gonna round up better experts?"

Ron checked the time. "The county building is open in fifteen minutes," he said, grabbing his jacket. "I'm going to start there."

"The county?"

"I'm gonna start with the assessor. I want every bit of info I can get about the history of this property, every little piece of paper, every scribbled note, every sideways thought. And after them, I'll hit the recorder, the treasurer, and any other department that might have information. Then I'll go to the utilities people, and..."

"OK, geez, I get it."

"You coming?"

Jake grabbed his coffee. "Yeah. I'm not staying here alone, that's for sure."

They left the house and drove along the small, overgrown driveway until they came to the dirt road that snaked down the mountain.

"So, you really think the assessor is gonna know something that will solve things?" Jake asked, trying to sip coffee as the car bounced over potholes.

"I'm gonna start there."

"Maybe I should try Terrell again. He said he was gonna keep researching. I could see if he's uncovered anything new."

"Feel free, but that's not my approach. There's no sense in pursuing something I don't really believe in. I'm going to start with facts, the facts that are public record. Whatever these things are, these entities in my house, around the property...for all the irrationality of their existence, there has to be a set of facts at the core of it that explains things."

Jake paused for a moment, thinking. Then he smiled as though he'd had some kind of a breakthrough. "You know, that's absolutely true! Like *Poltergeist*!"

"*Poltergeist*?"

"You know, the movie. There's all kinds of weird, scary ghost shit going on, but when you get to the base of it, the fact is that asshole moved the headstones but not the bodies. That caused everything."

"Which, presumably, you fix by correcting the facts," Ron replied. "You move the bodies the way they were supposed to be moved in the first place, and the problem is solved. Right?"

"Presumably. I don't remember if the sequel dealt with that or not."

"So, if my approach works, I just need to find a set of facts that needs correcting. I don't need a bunch of mumbo jumbo. Facts are something I can deal with."

"Yeah. Now that you mention it, all the ghost experts they brought in didn't help anything! It took the dad digging up the tidbit about the housing development and what that asshole had done."

"Exactly."

"Then again, in *The Exorcist*, the fact at the base of it was that the little girl really was possessed. The priest died."

"Yeah, but Ellen Burstyn and Linda Blair survived just fine."

"Doesn't that make Terrell's point, though? Trying to solve it, to help them, the priest became possessed, jumped through a window, and broke his neck. It's dangerous for someone with the gift to become involved."

"I'm not sure *The Exorcist* is entirely analogous to what's happening in my house."

"I don't know. That thing upstairs sure seems like the devil to me."

"I don't intend to involve anyone with a gift, so you don't need to worry. No broken necks in my house."

"I don't know, man. They really needed that old lady in *Insidious* to figure shit out, and those people weren't stupid. Without her, they were fucked."

"I'm not going to use Hollywood as a guide, Jake. Just because things happened in a movie doesn't mean it has anything remotely to do with what's happening here. That's fiction."

"Huh," Jake replied, sliding down a little in his seat, and taking another sip of coffee. "I guess."

- - -

The bear of a man dwarfed the counter he stood behind. He had a dark complexion and a series of tattoos that ran down his right forearm. He swung a monitor around so that Ron and Jake could see what he was looking at.

"Here's your property lines," he said, using thick fingers to move a small mouse, highlighting green boundaries that defined Ron's acreage. "If we go back in history, you can see that nothing changes much as we move back...1950 survey, things are still the same...1946...1939..."

"I'm impressed that all this is on the computer," Ron said. "I was expecting big books we'd have to browse through."

The man lowered his voice. "We got a grant from the state to digitize three years ago." The screen stopped on 1934. "Yeah. That's it. Same plot lines."

"Is that as far back as it goes?" Jake asked. "1934?"

"We've got records older than that, but they've been scanning in the data starting with more recent years, since that's most of the demand."

"Wouldn't matter anyhow," a short, rotund woman said as she walked behind the man, returning to a desk. "The fire."

"The fire?" Ron asked.

"The records prior to 1934 are all hammajang," the man answered, spinning the monitor back around.

Ron and Jake looked confused.

"Sorry, 'hammajang' means screwed up."

"He's from Hawaii," the woman offered. "I've learned a few new words since he started working here. There was a fire in the courthouse storage in 1933. What wasn't destroyed in the fire got ruined by the water they used to put it out. They saved boxes of bits and pieces, but no one's very anxious to try and stitch it all together, and then figure out how to input it into the doom beast."

"Doom beast?" Ron repeated.

"That's what she calls the computer system," the man answered. "Doesn't like it."

"The books worked fine," the woman piped up. "Worked fine for fifty years. No one complained. But that thing…" she pointed at the monitor. "Bah!"

"What else do you have on my property?" Ron asked. "Anything other than just the boundaries?"

"Yeah, there'll be a file in the system with all the documents. Twenty-five dollars gets you a print up."

"Great, I'd like the full set. Can you do that for me now?"

"No," the man replied, pulling a sheet of paper from under the counter and placing it in front of Ron. "You fill this out and pay the fee, then we mail it to you. Takes about ten days."

"That long?" Ron asked, filling in the form using a pen with a large plastic flower glued to the top. "I thought it was all digitized?"

"Yes, you'd think it'd be faster," the woman said, "what with a newfangled system and all. We used to provide it in three days before. Now it takes ten days. Progress."

"Might be less than that," the man offered. "I've seen them go out in a week, but we're supposed to say ten days."

"Gotcha," Ron replied, finishing the form and sliding his credit card to the man.

"There's an extra fee for credit cards."

"Of course there is. I'll pay the fee."

"Gotta take this in the back to run it," he replied. "Be right back."

"Everything's digitized, but he has to go somewhere else to process the card?" Jake asked Ron, under his breath.

"Tell me about it," the woman piped up, clearly able to hear the whispering. "We have to run back to that machine fifty times a day." She rose from her desk and approached the counter, where she reached under it and produced a metal and black plastic contraption. She laid it on the counter in front of them and smiled as though she had produced a diamond. "Remember these little beauties?"

"A credit card slider," Ron said, smiling back at her. "I do."

"So now I know how old you are!" she replied, her demeanor becoming more conversational. "I could process a card right here, have the little form filled out in less than a minute. Now he has to run it into the back. Takes three times as long; longer if it's down. Which it is, half the time." She slipped the machine back under the counter.

"I'm surprised you still have that," Ron offered. "I haven't seen one of those in ages. They never went down, though, did they? They always worked."

She seemed pleased to have found a sympathetic ear. "They wanted to throw it out, but I insisted it stay as a backup. They wanted to get rid of the typewriter, too!" She pointed to a corner, where a lonely IBM Selectric sat on a small table. "But I put my foot down. You have to be able to do your job, you know."

"Absolutely true," Ron replied.

"I still have to use that thing sometimes!" she protested. "Not every form has an electronic version yet, you know. There are still some forms that are on paper. How are you going to fill them out without a typewriter? Professionally, I mean."

"You couldn't be more right."

His response made her beam; she smiled up at him. "You know, sometimes when we need information about Mount Soltis prior to 1934, I go to Mrs. Hughes. Her family has lived there since the area was settled."

"Really?"

"We have a department policy against operating off hearsay or memory, but her mind is like a steel trap. I hope I'm that sharp when I reach seventy-eight."

"She provides you with information? About the mountain?"

The man returned with papers, and the woman raised her hand to her mouth, twisting her fingers at her lips as through she was turning a lock, her eyes rolling upward and to the side. She stepped away so the man could deal with Ron at the counter, where he placed a credit card receipt and asked him to sign.

"So, a week or so," Ron asked, completing the slip.

"Ten days," the man corrected, handing him more paper. "Here's a copy of the form. There's a number on it if you want to call in and ask about the status. Reference the number in the corner, that's your request number."

"Thank you both," Ron said, smiling, gathering the papers.

"Good luck to you!" the woman offered, giving him a wink.

They left the office, walking back to the central lobby of the county building. Jake looked up at the old, ornate ceiling and the row of second-story offices above them. "Do we have to hit all the departments in here?"

"Nope," Ron replied, heading for the doors. "I think I got exactly what I needed. I want to find this Mrs. Hughes."

- - -

"Aw, shit," Ron said, pulling into the short driveway. Two dogs came bounding out from behind a shed, chains stopping them just feet from the car.

"They're chained up," Jake offered. "We can get around them."

"Not the dogs," Ron replied. "That van. I recognize it. I talked to her before, passed each other on the road. She yelled at me."

"For what?"

"She thought I was going too fast. She seemed really crabby."

"Were you?"

"What? Going too fast? I don't remember."

The dogs were barking continuously, straining at their chains. Ron looked at the one nearest his door; he wasn't much for detecting breeds, but its wide face made him think he was looking at a pit bull, or a mix that contained a lot of it. Its large mouth, rapidly opening and closing, exposing wide rows of sharp teeth, made him wonder if tracking down this woman was really such a good idea.

Jake got out of the car and the dogs reacted, focusing on him as he walked to the front of the vehicle. As Ron got out, one of the dogs lunged against its chain, stopped three feet from him, straining so hard it rose up on its hind legs.

"Jesus Christ," Ron said, looking up at Jake as he hugged the side of the car until he joined his friend. When they turned around to face the house, an old woman was already on the wooden porch built onto the side of a blue, triple-wide trailer. Her brunette hair was perfectly coifed around her head without a spec of grey; again he had the impression she was Patricia Neal. He half expected to see a gun in her hands, but instead her arms were folded, watching them avoid the dogs.

"Mrs. Hughes?" Ron called.

"That's me," she called back, her voice raspy. "And that's Harry and Sally," she added, nodding toward the dogs.

"Beautiful animals," Jake said.

"What do you want?" she called, unimpressed by Jake's observation.

Ron stepped forward. "I just bought the property at..."

"I know who you are," she said, cutting him off. "Pinedo Road. We talked already. You drive like a lunatic."

"Yes, well, I'd like to think I took your suggestion and have slowed down."

"Good, I don't need my grandkids run over by city slickers. What do you want?"

"We were just down at the county building. I was trying to dig up some information on my property."

"So?"

"So, well, I found most of the information back to the '30s. I mean, they're sending me the information, but I understand you're an authority on the history of the mountain. Before that."

"Who told you that?"

"I...I don't remember her name."

"So what if I am?"

"I was wondering if I could pick your brain a little. I have...questions."

"What kinds of questions?"

"Well, everything really. I'd like to know the history of the place. Of this mountain, specifically."

"You mean you want to know the history of your property. Your house."

"Yes, that's part of it."

She turned, her arms still folded, looking into the forest that began not more than twenty feet from her trailer. Ron got the impression that she was considering whether or not she really wanted to deal with him, weighing something, trying to decide.

"I don't mean to take up your time," he added. "I was just hoping you might be able to share a few things. I could really use your help."

Finally she turned back, dropping her arms to her side. "Well, you better come in, then."

They walked to the trailer, the dogs still barking furiously. She held the door open for them as they stepped inside.

The trailer seemed much larger on the inside than it looked from the outside. The furnishings were modest, but clean and orderly. It exuded a sense of routine cleaning and obsessive straightening.

"You like some coffee?" she offered, motioning them to a small kitchen table, covered with a tan plastic tablecloth containing faded images of utensils and pans.

"That'd be nice," Ron said.

"Not for me," Jake replied.

The table was arranged against a wall. One of the seats appeared to be the one most used, with a small stack of mail and other papers arranged around it; Ron chose one of the other seats, as did Jake. She placed coffee in front of him and sat with her own, steam rising from the mug, and then returned with the entire pot, which she sat on a cork trivet in the center of the table.

"Sorry, I don't have any cream or sugar, I drink it black," she said, sitting in the chair and running her hands over the apron that covered her dress, straightening any wrinkles.

"Black is fine," Ron replied.

"So, Mr. Costa. What do you want to know?"

"You remembered my name."

"I remember everything," she replied, smiling a little. "Although if you expect anything I say to hold up in a court of law, I'll tell you right now, you're barking up the wrong tree."

"Why is that?"

"Courts of law can't always deal with some of the facts of life. They like to think they can, but they can't. Not always."

"I suppose that's true," Ron replied. "Not everything is purely black and white."

"Not exactly what I meant, but never mind."

Ron took a sip from the mug. "Excellent coffee."

"Go ahead, asked me whatever it is you came here for."

Ron cleared his throat. "Well, for starters, I was wondering if you could tell me about the history of the mountain. Generally, I mean."

She smiled at him. "Working your way up to it?"

Ron was surprised by her directness, but before he could reply, she continued.

"The Hughes family has lived on this mountain since it was settled. My great-grandfather owned three quarters of it, but before he died, he sold off everything but the plot we're sitting on right now. He needed the proceeds to pay off debts he ran up with bad investments in lumber. How anyone could go wrong with lumber in those days is beyond me, but according to my grandfather, Josiah had a knack for believing any old song and dance."

She stopped, taking a sip of her coffee. Ron found the raspiness of her voice to be oddly soothing, and when it stopped, he found himself wishing she would start again, just so he could hear more of it.

"Anyway, half of what he sold was bought by the Coldwater family. Most of their lots were sold off over the years, bought by people who thought they owned it once they paid for it." She smirked a little.

"Thought?" Ron asked. "They didn't? Own it?"

"They thought they did. They moved into whatever house was there, thinking it was theirs." She stared down into her coffee.

Ron waited, hoping she'd explain, but she seemed to have come to a stop. "Was there some problem with the deed?" he asked, prodding her to continue.

"Oh, no, no problem with deeds. Or anything legal. Nothing like that. If you went to the county, they'd say it had been sold, fair and square. But...well, it was really still the Coldwaters'. Even to this day."

Ron shifted uncomfortably in his seat as she looked up at him.

"If I asked you if you believed in Bigfoot, what would you say?" she asked.

Ron looked at Jake, unsure how to respond.

"I believe in Bigfoot," Jake offered, smiling.

"Of course you do," she answered, turning back to Ron. "But what about you?"

It felt like some kind of test. The last thing Ron wanted was to fail it, to cause the woman to shut down and not share more information. Still, he didn't want to lie...perhaps that was the test, to see if he'd be truthful.

"Well," he finally answered, clearing his throat again, "this is Bigfoot country, that's for sure. Lots of speculation."

"Lots of sightings," she added.

"Yes, there seems to be," Ron replied. "And I hate to claim that someone is a liar, that they'd just make something up when I suppose there's a chance they actually saw something, maybe not a Bigfoot per se, but something else that..."

She reached forward and patted his hand. "Let me spare you the gymnastics. I was just asking if you believed in it or not. You obviously don't, which is fine. I don't either. But that doesn't explain why the market at the junction is named Bigfoot Gas and Go. Or why half a dozen businesses in McLean have Bigfoot in their name."

"Marketing?" Ron offered. "Bigfoot sells. It attracts tourists."

"That's part of it. But why does it attract tourists? There's more to it than that. Beliefs are powerful things. If they are powerful enough, they can cause things to happen. Make things that aren't real become real."

Ron didn't reply.

"You look skeptical. I guess my Bigfoot analogy didn't really work for you, eh?"

"I should have just told you I don't believe in it."

"That's fine, but what I'm getting at is that your disbelief in it doesn't mean that other people's belief in it doesn't have consequences. Real, physical consequences. There are people in McLean for whom their livelihood is dependent upon this completely bogus belief."

"You could say that about religion," Jake added.

"So you are not a believer?" she turned to him.

"I don't know if I'd say that or not," Jake answered. "It's just that there's a lot of business built up around it. All the televangelists and all. Tons of money."

"I see what you're getting at," Ron said. "People create physical manifestations of things based on beliefs. I can agree with that, even if it's something they do unaware, or subconsciously."

"Alright," she replied, and rose from the table. She walked out of the room and returned a moment later, carrying two old books.

"This one belonged to my grandmother, Margot. She married my grandfather, Hal, in 1928, at the age of seventeen. It's her diary."

She sat at the table and opened the book.

"I don't think I can explain it any better than her."

Chapter Seventeen

Hal has been gone for over an hour, and I'm frightened. What if he doesn't come back? They might fight, something bad could happen. He was certainly angry when he left.

I can't blame him. Our goats looked as though they had been mercilessly slaughtered with a machete, hacked apart in a most gruesome way. We know it was them, on account of their complaints last week. The fact is, their property is too far away to ever hear them, and the wind blows from their side to ours, so they can't smell them, either. They just like to complain, to push their nose into other people's business.

I wish my father hadn't sold to them. The mountain was such a peaceful place before that. I remember the day I first saw people moving onto the hill; I told my father we had squatters. He informed me that they had a right to it, because they had bought those parcels from him. I remember feeling confused; the mountain had always been ours. I could wander anywhere over it and never encounter another soul, other than the deer and possum. And the occasional bear, which father would run off with his shotgun.

I know it's the memories of a silly child. I know the Indians had the land before we ran them off. Now I find myself feeling a little like they must have felt – as though others are infringing, ruining our lives and our privacy, trying to…I don't know, intimidate or force us to do things against our will. We've had goats as long as I can remember. They keep the undergrowth down and provide milk, as well as an occasional slaughter. People can't just force you to give them up, can they? Can people invent reasons why they don't want them around, and force you to get rid of them, even though they're really of no consequence to them at all?

I was proud of Hal for standing up to him. Mr. Coldwater has a way of speaking that makes it sound like he will bring holy hell down if his demands aren't granted, but Hal remained patient and repeated over and over that the goats had been with us for years, they weren't bothering anyone or anything, and that, no, we would not be getting rid of them.

Apparently Coldwater decided to do it himself. Or, I'll bet he hired men to do it, those workers he uses on the other houses. The savagery of it still makes me see red, and the indifference shown by leaving the butchered carcasses, meat that could have been used, speaks to his morals. I'd rather he'd stolen them than just ruined them as he has; the waste of it makes my blood boil.

It's not the first time he's thrown his weight around to get what he wants, he and that entire family. He's encroached on our land with his buildings, costing us the wages of a surveyor to correct. His wife, pretending aristocracy she doesn't possess by doting on her stable of expensive horses, instructed her stable boys to dump their muck on our property. And the man's nephew, Larry, caught red handed by Arlo years ago, playing with matches behind our shed. It was the middle of summer, and everything was dry! He would have burned it down had he not stumbled upon the kid. I know most young children do not understand the idea of property boundaries but a fish rots from the head, and his disregard for our rights is a direct result of his uncle's attitudes and instruction. Now that he is older, he is no better.

What bothers me even more is how they subdivided and leased to other families that now live here, all of them loyal to the Coldwaters in one way or another. Before my father died, he warned me of what would happen, sorry that he had sold so much land. He never would have sold it all to one person. He thought the other individuals who bought, as he continued to whittle away at the mountain to address his insolvencies, would retain their properties. When he learned that the Coldwaters had bought out a number of them, he realized a coup was underway, a coup to take over the entire mountain. My father told us we'd need to be strong to withstand them, to maintain our way of life and what we've built here.

His concerns bore out. Now it seems the Coldwaters own most of the land that surrounds us. He's tried to cut us off, blocking the roads in various ways, claiming they're on his property, but county law is clear on that, and his efforts have failed. He doesn't have the sheriff yet, although he donates a lot of money in the elections, and is bound to wind up with a sympathetic one at some point.

If Hal isn't back in a half hour, I will have to go check on him myself. I pray to God he isn't already dead, or lying bleeding somewhere between here and that man's house.

\- - -

Mrs. Hughes stopped and flipped to pages deeper in the book. Then she continued.

\- - -

I found a couple of odd things today, in the woods just behind the house. If it had just been one, I would have thought it strange, but the fact that I found three of them makes me think something is underway, some kind of attack from Candace, their eldest daughter.

I assume this because of the things Amy has said. She lives a mile to the west, and works up at the Coldwaters' as a maid, cleaning most of the time. Amy and I go way back; I do not think the Coldwaters would have hired her were they aware of our long friendship. She and I have met for tea and cribbage twice a week for many years.

Amy told me that Candace has become much worse. The teenager has not appeared to the staff for weeks, remaining locked away in her rooms at the west end of the Coldwater mansion. Amy has been forbidden to clean those rooms, and instructed to not speak of them outside of the house, but she has always told me of the comings and goings of the place as we peg our way down the streets. She told me all about the odd change in Candace's demeanor and how, after several weeks of increased hysteria, the parents decided to sequester their daughter.

Amy gave me the most queer look when she explained the frequency with which Mr. Coldwater enters Candace's rooms, remaining inside for long stretches of time. Disturbingly, he often looked disheveled when leaving, tucking his shirt into his pants.

With the mystery of what has happened to Candace deepening within the ranks of the staff, speculation has run rampant, and several of them have tried to learn more.

Amy said she recently placed an ear to one of the doors to Candace's room, and heard low, guttural grunts and laughs, then the rapid recitation of a strange language, a phrase repeated over and over with varying intensity. "Very strange rantings," Amy said, her left eyebrow cocking when she told me.

I replied that it sounded like Candace had gone mad. I was half joking, but to my surprise Amy quickly agreed, saying that what she heard through the door did, indeed, sound like the ravings of insanity, and that upon hearing the sounds, she had the most evil and ominous feeling, as though she was hearing words concocted in hell.

That was when she came over last Thursday, and I presume the events she witnessed were in the days just prior to that.

Anyway, I mentioned the items I found today to Hal, and my suspicion that Candace might be behind it. He seemed skeptical, but he was not aware of what I had seen the other night, something I hadn't told him.

The night before last, I woke around 3 AM, thinking I had heard a sound. Hal remained asleep, quietly snoring; a parade could be marching through the bedroom and he'd never wake up. I rose and investigated, coming finally to the kitchen window that looks over the back yard.

There, her white skin reflecting the moonlight, was a woman who I thought was Candace – naked as the day she was born. Although I hadn't seen her since she was ten or eleven, her face was still the same, even though her hair was much longer and her breasts and hips had grown as they do during the teenaged years. She appeared to be in a trance, walking gently through the trees at the far end of our clearing, unaffected by the cold. She stopped once to squat, almost disappearing from view, but then stood again and continued on. I remember standing there at the sink, wondering if I should wake up Hal or not. The girl seemed to wander aimlessly; she didn't appear up to any type of mischief, she was just meandering, giving the trees a kind of bewildered stare. Eventually she continued on and made her way beyond my line of sight.

I wrote it off to sleepwalking. It was odd, yes, and I considered mentioning it to Hal. I even thought of bringing it up with the Coldwaters, but with things so acrimonious between us, it seemed easier to just ignore what I'd seen. They were not a family I felt any sense of obligation to help; in fact, just the opposite. Had the girl seemed in distress, I might have reacted differently, but, given how she behaved, I felt no compunction to inject myself into whatever malady accounted for her behavior, instead blaming poor oversight of her habits upon the Coldwaters themselves, which is the truth. The blame, as it usually does, lies with the parents.

There is a part of me that believes this choice was uncharitable. However, it doesn't take long for the memory of the many uncharitable and downright wicked acts of the Coldwaters against my family to remind me that they are owed no favors.

So, when I found these items in the yard earlier today, I put two and two together, and deduced that they were placed there by Candace, perhaps when she bent down and disappeared briefly from my sight. I did find them in a spot close to where I had seen her walking.

A potential fallacy of my deduction is that she was naked; if she had been carrying them, it would have been obvious. I have given this some thought, though, and I believe that, seeing her through the kitchen window from a distance, I might not have noticed them in her hands. Or, she might have placed them before I detected her.

Anyway, how else can I explain it?

They are round, about five inches in diameter, with soft hair that curls out from their edges, disappearing back inside their shape. Quite odd, and of a material that I cannot discern.

The hair, however, looks exactly like Candace's, and I wonder if it is hers.

- - -

I had the most unusual dream last night, and wanted to write it down before it left my memory.

A woman, dressed in some kind of animal skin – like an Indian – was moving through the woods, trying to find her home. She had a basket of fish in one hand; I remember seeing perch and trout. She was climbing through a trail in the brush, anxious to get away from something following her. At times during the dream I was behind her, watching as she hurried, and at other times I could see through her eyes, scanning the trail ahead.

She came to a clearing where people were standing; dozens of people, all frozen in place, all staring in the same direction. They frightened me, looking exactly as I imagine ghosts might appear. She kept running as though she didn't see them, and I watched as she continued to hurry, passing through them with her basket, causing their forms to come apart and dissolve a little. As she made her way to the other side of the clearing, entering a trail that continued on, I remember turning to look back at the figures. They were still there, reformed, facing me, looking angry at the disruption. I had the feeling they might attack me in some way, and it scared me to the extent that I forced myself awake from the dream, sitting up in bed, gasping.

I always keep a glass of water on my nightstand, and was grateful for it, sipping at it until I felt myself calm down.

Hal, of course, remained unstirred, sawing logs as if he were a lumberjack.

- - -

Amy said that today all hell broke loose.

She was cleaning on a side of the Coldwater mansion near Candace's rooms, when the entire house shook as though it had been hit by something. Paintings fell from the walls, and several vases toppled, falling and breaking on the floor.

At first she thought it was an earthquake, but she said it began and ended so quickly it didn't remind her of any of the earthquakes we've had before. It was one sudden, massive bombshell, knocking the house nearly from its foundation.

Two others on the staff found her, and the three of them began to speculate on what the massive jolt could have been.

It was then that the smell appeared. Amy said all three of them detected it at the same time, a horrible odor that smelled worse than rotten eggs. They held their noses, wondering what might cause such a stench.

Then they heard yelling in the distance. Mrs. Coldwater was shouting, yelling, screaming about something. As they heard her approach, the other two left Amy to return to their assignments, not wanting to appear idle to the matron, as she was known to be highly critical of their work.

Mrs. Coldwater's voice grew louder, and the stench grew more intense. Amy was moments from leaving, wanting to go outside to get fresh air, when the matron rounded the corner from the hallway. Her hair, normally a dark brown, now looked a light grey, and spilled from her head, disheveled. She was wearing her nightgown, which was torn in a couple of places; her hands alternated from wild gesticulations in the air, to grabbing at her own clothes and rending, giving Amy the impression that the tears were caused by the woman herself rather than some other person.

But, as odd as the entire scene was, Amy said the most chilling part was the words coming from Mrs. Coldwater's mouth: her lips seemed to move rapidly, and a strange, guttural language came from her, phrases Amy couldn't understand, which the woman shouted and screamed, looking up at the walls and the ceiling as she yelled, as though she was cursing the building with a bizarre, heathen tongue.

Amy found herself glued to the spot, even though she wanted to run. The matron walked right past her, screaming and ranting, her arms flying about rapidly, tearing at her clothing and tearing at non-existent shapes in the air in front of her, not acknowledging her in the slightest. Amy watched as the woman continued out of the room and into the next hallway, and she could hear her friend, Maria, gasp in horror as Mrs. Coldwater passed by her, too.

Finally, she broke from her spot, scared to death by the bizarre behavior, but wanting to check on Maria, to see if she was alright. She found her friend standing in the drawing room, a hand at her mouth, with a look of shock similar to her own. Mrs. Coldwater was just leaving the room, continuing on her path through the house, screaming and yelling. Amy stood next to Maria; she said her friend was so terrified, she wanted to cry. She suggested to Maria that they go outside for a moment to get fresh air, and the two of them walked back into the hallway, the opposite of the way Mrs. Coldwater had gone, not wanting to run into her again.

The door to the outside was mid-way down the hall that ran back to Candace's room. Lining the hall on one side were windows that faced east, usually making this section of the house a bright, cheery space during the daytime. At the opposite end of the hallway they saw movement; a dark mist was coming toward them, roiling like fog, moving rapidly, absorbing the sunlight as it went.

Amy told me she felt a chill race down her spine at the sight: fog, inside the house?

Considering the sequence of bizarre events that had just occurred, she didn't stop to wonder why it was there, or why it was barreling toward them, cutting off the doorway that led to the courtyard. Instead, Amy grabbed Maria and pulled her back to the drawing room, choosing instead to exit the way Mrs. Coldwater had gone, deeper into the house. There was a back door through the kitchen that they could use, provided Mrs. Coldwater wasn't there.

Although she could hear the matron yelling and screaming as they hurried, Amy found the route clear and soon they were both standing on the cement of the driveway at the side of the house, taking deep breaths. They could both still smell it, the rancid odor somehow leaching out from the house, but the forest air helped dissipate the stench.

Maria pointed to one of the windows on the second story above them, and Amy looked up. It was completely black, as though the glass panes had been painted over. They watched as other windows that appeared normal, exposing curtains hanging just inside, slowly turned opaque and eventually darkened.

Amy said it looked like a deadly disease spreading through the house, and Maria agreed.

They decided that neither of them would go back into the house that day. Amy scribbled a quick note explaining their need to go home due to an emergency, which she left on a counter in the kitchen entryway, and grabbed her and Maria's coat that hung from pegs just inside the door. The two left the property, watching as more windows darkened.

Due at my home for cribbage, she came straight here, surprising me by being an hour early. Naturally I was at the edge of my seat as she related the events. I forgot to drink the tea as a result, and it became cold before either of us touched it.

I asked if she intended to return to work tomorrow, and she said she wasn't scheduled until Monday, but even then, she wasn't sure if she would or not.

I told her she had every right to resign, even though I knew if she were to do so, I'd lose my spy within the house. She seemed conflicted, saying the pay was excellent and that she'd have to think about it.

Then we both speculated on what might have caused the series of events. Since Mrs. Coldwater came from the direction of Candace's room, we decided something must have happened at that end of the house. Amy agreed, confirming that the fog she saw in the hallway was coming from that direction, consistent with our theory, as was the order of the darkening windows.

I quipped that perhaps the house was now infected by something horrible, and Amy chastised me gently, saying she hopes it isn't true – due to her need of a job – but that it sure seemed like that is exactly what had happened.

Chapter Eighteen

Mrs. Hughes closed the book.

"My father," she said, "knew, of course, about the enmity between our families; it was a dynamic that was unavoidable growing up when he did, and it permeated our entire experience living on the mountain. However, he discovered my grandmother's diary only after she died. According to my mother, when he first read his mother's accounts, he began to gradually change, ultimately becoming obsessed with the Coldwaters. It bothered my mother greatly, because she didn't know about any of this history before she married my father, and just wanted to ignore it all and move on, try to live a normal life.

"However, Jack – my father – couldn't let it go. Having read my grandmother's diary many times myself, I understand why. Not only were the events it describes mysterious and incredible, my grandmother was skilled at instilling a sense of family pride through her writing, a rallying cry to defend our name and stand up for our rights against another usurping family that frequently tried to demean and bulldoze over them. I still feel that way now, myself."

"Not surprising," Ron offered.

"So, as I said, my father was obsessed with the Coldwaters, and as obsessions often do, they ruin the lives of the people around them. When I was still small, his focus drifted from his work and career to studying and analyzing the Coldwaters, trying to learn if my grandmother's conclusions were accurate, and digging into the mysteries she hadn't figured out: what caused the events at the house, the smell, the fog, the windows darkening, Mrs. Coldwater's bizarre ranting. The strange items my grandmother found in the yard. All that."

Ron swallowed, knowing now was the time to speak up. "I found one of them. I think."

Mrs. Hughes, who had been relating the story in a calm, unhurried way, suddenly looked up at him, alarmed. "One of what?"

"That item you read about in your grandmother's diary. The one with the hair along the edges."

"You did?"

"It was inside a dresser I found in the house when I moved in."

"Why didn't you tell me?" Jake asked.

Ron shrugged, not wanting to get into his reasons while Mrs. Hughes was still providing information.

The woman opened the other book, flipping through pages until she found the one she wanted. She turned it to Ron. "Did it look like that?" Her finger reached over the top of the page, pointing to a drawing near the bottom.

"Kinda," Ron replied. "Your grandmother wrote that it was five inches in diameter, but the one I found was much smaller."

"Do you have it?" Mrs. Hughes asked. "Can you show it to me?"

"Uh," Ron replied, wondering how to word his next thought. "Well, no. I mean, I have it, in a way, I suppose. It…uh…"

"Sunk into you?" she asked.

He looked at her, trying to translate what she had said into the experience he remembered from a few days before. "Well, I don't know if that's what you'd call it, exactly. I was holding it…"

"…and it disappeared into you," Mrs. Hughes said, cutting him off.

He felt suddenly guilty, as though he might be perceived as part of the enemy by the woman. "I didn't mean to. It just kind of…happened."

"Don't worry about it," she replied, detecting his alarm. She held up her hand, showing him her palm. "I've had several."

"Pardon me," Jake interjected. "What the fuck are you talking about?"

"Pardon his French," Ron added.

"Swearing doesn't bother me," she replied, lowering her hand and looking at Jake. "Do you know what a nazar is?"

"No idea," Jake replied. "Never heard of it."

"In some cultures, they believe that a curse can be cast by a simple look. You've heard the phrase 'evil eye'?"

Jake nodded.

"Well, some people take it very seriously. They make talismans to ward against it."

"This is a nazar?" Ron asked, pointing to the drawing in the book.

"Not precisely," Mrs. Hughes replied. "Similar in concept, but very different in conception, behavior, and results. Have you seen anything odd since it entered you?"

"Entered you?" Jake asked, turning to Ron.

"Yeah, I was holding it, and it just kind of...dissolved. Into my palm."

"And you didn't tell me about that?"

"There was so much other shit happening," Ron replied, then turned to Mrs. Hughes. "To be honest, there's been so many weird things going on the past few weeks, it's *all* odd to me. It's hard to identify any specific thing."

"Think back. When did you find it? When did it dissolve in your hand?"

"Yesterday. No, day before."

"Go back through what happened since then."

"Ah," Ron replied. "The neighbor. He showed up just after that."

"The neighbor?"

"He said he lives on the other side of the ravine."

"What, the ravine by your house?"

"Yes."

"There's no one living on the other side of that ravine."

"I figured as much," Ron continued, "when he drugged me. Wanted me to have a conversation with something that lives in one of my bedrooms."

"That dark thing!" Jake chimed in. "That thing we saw! You talked to it?"

"He said his name was Ezra," Ron replied.

Mrs. Hughes raised a hand to her forehead, rubbing it gently. Then she dropped it to rub at her face, as though she was waking herself up. "Damn."

"Damn?" Ron repeated. "What?"

"I have no idea who that might be."

Jake interrupted. "Would someone please tell me what the fuck is going on?"

Mrs. Hughes took the book back from Ron, placing it in front of her. "I told you my father became obsessed with the Coldwaters. At first it was mild, but as the obsession grew, he became more bold, seeking information he decided he could only obtain by infiltrating their mansion. How he managed to protect himself from them has always been bewildering to me, but also a source of admiration. Whereas my grandfather thought of them as annoying neighbors, and my grandmother considered them enemies, my father took it further. He felt that their mansion was a source of evil, destined to infect the mountain and destroy everyone on it. He took what had been a series of obnoxious neighbor disputes and escalated them into a full-fledged war, justified by the idea that he was on a righteous mission to cleanse things, to eliminate evil. In light of his perspective, he considered all options to be on the table, including robbery."

She reached for the book and lifted it a few inches from the table. "He stole this from inside the Coldwater house. Although a lot of it reads like a puzzle, it, more than anything, offers an explanation of what had happened there."

She put the book back onto the table. "And before we go any further, I should tell you something important. My father's war with the Coldwaters was long and violent. I said all options were on the table in his mind, and that wound up including everything you can imagine. Amongst the various events that occurred in my father's war, one was particularly devastating. When I was fifteen, our family home – the house that my great grandfather originally built on the mountain, and that had belonged to my grandmother, and of course my father – burned to the ground. It was such a hot fire, nothing was left standing but a pile of ash. We were a family of six, and all escaped except for my youngest brother, Marshall. He was five years old. We found teeth in the ash; the rest of him was incinerated."

"I'm sorry," Ron offered.

"That burning escalated my father's war into a series of events that ended with the brutal murder of Mr. and Mrs. Coldwater. By my father. He was executed for their deaths. It brought an end to the active war my father waged, but didn't cleanse this area of evil."

"Wow," Jake muttered. "He murdered them?"

"Yes."

"What about their daughter?" Ron asked. "Candace?"

"Disappeared."

"How did he do it?" Jake asked. "Kill them?"

"He was found by my mother and the local police in the drawing room of the Coldwater mansion, bathed in blood, the body parts of the Coldwaters strewn around the room where he had tossed them. He protested innocence, but it was obvious that he had done it, and the fact that he seemed delighted with the result didn't help the authorities believe his account. By this point, my father had experienced so many unusual and bizarre things at the hands of the Coldwaters, his unfiltered retelling of the events to the police made him sound like a mad man. A jury thought so, too, but in those days, they weren't so willing to consider mental evaluations, and much quicker to execute. They hanged him in Walla Walla.

"My mother forbade discussion of it. We were allowed to visit him in prison before the hanging, but the subject of the Coldwaters and his war with them was off the table, strictly enforced by her. I was never able to learn from him, directly, what he had gone through.

"I found these two books in the trash one day, discarded by my mother. I saved them and kept them hidden from her. She would have been furious if she'd ever discovered them, but I had great hiding places."

They sat for a moment, each drinking in the story, wondering what it all meant.

"So…" Ron started, unsure what to ask next. "Did your father bring this mobile home in, after the house burned down?"

"He did. He had the foresight to move us over here, on the far side of the mountain. One of the lots we rented out was open, so this is where we landed."

"Oh," Ron replied. "I just assumed your house had been here. Where we are now."

"No," she said. "Our house burned to the ground in the exact spot where your house now stands."

Ron swallowed hard. "My property?"

"My mother sold it off after my father was arrested. We were living over here, and she didn't want to own that land anymore. I think, to her, after she finished her period of grieving, her philosophy was to move on from everything – from my father's war with the Coldwaters, from the death of my brother, all of it. She wanted a fresh start, not looking back. Her goal, she said to me, was to try and arrange things so that the rest of us – those of us who had survived – could be happy. So, she sold it off."

"Huh," Ron replied, feeling numb. For a moment he wondered why a mother would want to lose the land that connected her, in some way, to her lost child. *If I ever lost Robbie,* he thought, *I'd try to hold onto everything about him that still existed. I wouldn't want to lose anything that reminded me of him.* That, apparently, was not the attitude of Mrs. Hughes' mother.

He decided to change the subject slightly. "And then my house got built?"

"Not quite yet," Mrs. Hughes replied. "Another house was built before yours, just after the land was sold. It burned, too, about fifteen years ago. They said it was an electrical problem."

"Wow," Jake said. "What a coincidence."

"Did anyone die in that fire?" Ron asked.

"An old man," she replied. "The couple that owned the place, she moved her father into the house when he became too elderly to live on his own. They had gone into town on an errand; when they returned, the house was completely engulfed with her father still inside. He hadn't been able to escape."

"Fuck," Jake muttered.

Ron was beginning to feel nauseous. It had always seemed odd to him that a twelve-year-old house had so many problems; each of those problems now magnified when combined with the fact that he was living at the site of two horrible deaths. He remembered what Tom had mentioned, about an old woman dying in the house, along with her husband, but wondered if it was just something Tom invented, part of their effort to get him to leave. Mrs. Hughes' version of events felt real and substantial, something he could trust. It rumbled around in his stomach like a sour ball of dread, making him feel sick. "What can I do?" he said quietly, under his breath. "The place I'm living in…it's cursed in some way, isn't it?"

"I don't know," Mrs. Hughes replied. "Maybe. I can't say. When my father was really going at it with the Coldwaters, lots of things happened, back and forth. Were they responsible for the fire? He certainly thought so."

"And this thing with Candace," Ron said, "these things she left in your yard…in my yard…the things your grandmother found? What the fuck are they?"

"I can't say for sure, but I have a theory," Mrs. Hughes offered.

"What?" Ron asked weakly, his body feeling exhausted, but his mind still intrigued, wanting more.

"Like I said," she replied, "they've sunk into me before, too." She raised her hand again, showing them her palm. "They like palms, but one entered me here once, on my arm. I think they reproduce out there in the forest, because every now and again I find another one. They go into you, and for a while, you see weird things. The effect fades after a while. But they're very real, and their effect is real."

"Like mushrooms," Ron offered.

"Kind of like that. I have no idea what happened to Candace, and as far as my father goes, I don't know if he ever found out anything about her, either. My personal theory, however, is that she was forced into something by her parents, some kind of horrible role that she didn't want to take, and when my grandmother saw her that night, naked in the yard, I believe she was..."

She paused.

"Yes?" Ron asked, hoping she would finish.

"Well, I know this sounds a little odd, but I think these things came from her. I think she was planting them, spreading them over the mountain. I don't know if the intent was evil, caused by what was happening to her, but their effect certainly doesn't seem evil to me – they simply allow you to experience weird things, things that seem hidden to most people. I've done it a half dozen times, and it's never resulted in anything bad happening to me. Did you feel anything bad?"

"No," Ron said. "It was kind of like being high."

"See," she continued, "I don't think they're evil, not like the other things. I think they might have been some kind of antidote, something Candace was spreading to counter the terrible things that were happening to her, perhaps something she could use to ultimately save herself from whatever her parents had inflicted upon her. And I think they reproduce and grow on their own, out there in the forest."

"Like she was some kind of Johnny Appleseed?" Jake offered.

"Like that," Mrs. Hughes replied, "hoping that someday what she was planting might be useful, to herself or to people who came after. I don't think the poor girl had many options, and she took the only ones she could."

They sat for a moment. Ron's thoughts were anything but calm; he was bombarded by ideas and speculation and intrigue, taken aback by the history of the mountain he used to think would be a quiet refuge from the city. Alternately confused and anxious, he looked up at Mrs. Hughes. "What do I do? I can't move. I can't sell it. There's no water, the well doesn't produce enough. No one could get a bank loan to buy it from me. I'm stuck."

She slid the book across the table until it rested in front of him. "The Coldwater mansion still stands," she said. "It's about two miles from you, south, toward the back of the mountain. I've looked through this book a thousand times, but very little of it makes any sense to me. The pictures sometimes do, but the writing seems to be a different language. I've never had it examined by anyone to find out what kind of language, but maybe you can. There's a chance that whatever the Coldwaters did to Candace is explained in there. Maybe not. It's a place to start, at least."

Ron touched the book, running his fingers over the worn leather cover. It was dark and spotted, and looked as though it had been stained by spilled liquid. He picked it up and opened it, catching brief glimpses of illustrations and text as the pages flicked by.

"As for your well," she said, "how deep is it?"

"There are two wells," Ron replied. "One is just over a hundred, the other goes down four hundred."

"That first well was ours. A hundred feet worked just fine in those days. However, that land is so screwed up with the curse or whatever the Coldwaters might have done to it in their war with my father, the next house, the one with the elderly man, probably had to extend it to find water. You, my friend, might have to go even deeper. Maybe six, seven hundred feet. That's your solution to selling the place and moving somewhere with a lot less history."

"It's gonna cost a lot of money," Ron replied.

"Well, you could always stay and learn to live with it," she replied. "I've lived with the hauntings of this mountain all my life, and you could do worse, unless boring is what you're after." She rose from the table, a signal that the conversation was drawing to a close. "I'd have your wiring checked by a professional, though."

"Thanks," Ron said. "I appreciate that."

- - -

It was already getting dark as they made their way over the small road from one side of the mountain to the other. As he executed turns, Ron noticed the way the tires made contact with the earth, feeling an irrational, oddly deeper connection than before. He remembered when he first located the house – how impossible it had been to find using GPS – and how he felt an immediate attraction to it, and to the surroundings. How he had lobbied Elenore for it, how everything about it, including all the potential problems, seemed right and correct and the smart thing to do.

Now, taking the turns on dirt roads that interlaced between Mrs. Hughes' current residence and her former home, he felt even more connected to the ground below him, despite it seeming more sinister. Knowledge of the past was anchoring him to the mountain, not frightening him away. It was roping him in – making him feel linked to its history.

I am part of it, he thought. *I* own that property. I am now as much a part of the story Mrs. Hughes told as she is.

The sensation of having become so suddenly surrounded by such a complex past, hidden but yet potent, felt like having jumped into the deep end of an enormous pool and finding himself still under water, waiting to rise to the surface for air.

Somewhere on this mountain is the Coldwater mansion, he thought, *sitting there, with all its disturbing past.* It was becoming, in his mind, a front; the headquarters for the opposing side, the home base of the enemy. And where he was headed – his home – was the other HQ of the war, the focal point of his side, the Hughes side. He was slipping into a role, and he felt as though it should bother him, that he should be resisting.

He wasn't.

In some ways, it seemed to make sense. He'd spent the last few weeks battling something; now he knew what, and accepting the answer seemed like the smart thing to do. If that meant becoming a player in the drama, then he was cast. It was done.

"She's right, it's like some kind of weird language," Jake said from the passenger seat, where he was flipping through the book Mrs. Hughes had lent them. "I'd try typing one of these words into Google and see what language it is, but I go from one bar to no bars every ten seconds."

"Signal will be better at the house."

"The pictures are interesting, though." He closed the book. "You think she was telling the truth about all this?"

"I have no reason to doubt her."

"Maybe she wants you to leave the mountain too, just like the ghosts in your house."

"So, she made up this elaborate story?" Ron asked. "Seems like there might be easier ways to do it."

"I think you're right; she's telling the truth. And if she is, man, you need to give this some serious thought. Do you really want to bring Elenore – or, for god's sake, Robbie – into that house? Knowing what happened there?"

Ron knew before meeting with Mrs. Hughes, his answer would have been a quick "of course!" and he would justify away all the odd concerns as mere coincidence, confirmation bias, faulty logic, or outright superstition. Now, he wasn't so sure. *A five-year-old boy died,* he thought. *Robbie isn't much older. How do I feel about asking my son to live over the ashes of a child who was burned alive?*

"I don't know, Jake. I'm still processing through everything she said."

"You could always burn it down for the insurance money. Third time's the charm."

Ron found himself considering the idea, and it surprised him. "How would you do that and not get caught?"

"There are ways."

"I guess I'd have to calculate if what I'd get back from the insurance is better than just paying the price to deepen the well and selling."

"You'd be saddling someone else with cursed land. At least if you burn it, you're sparing some other family what you've gone through."

"Until they decide to build."

"Yeah. No plan's perfect."

"Forget it, burning the place down is ridiculous. I'd be risking fraud. Arson investigators would figure it out."

"Maybe. If you were smart, you wouldn't be the first person to get away with it."

"Seriously, what smart adjustor is going to look at a house that's burned down three times and not think, 'what are the odds'?"

"Just throwing it out there."

"Last resort, amigo," Ron replied, pulling into the long driveway that led to the house. "I can't believe we're even having this conversation."

"Burning down a haunted house always works in the movies. Like *Poltergeist*."

"You're wrong," Ron said, pulling up to the house. "In *Poltergeist*, the house doesn't burn; it collapses on itself, like it's folding up."

"Oh, that's right, I forgot. It kind of blips out at the end, disappears into oblivion or some other dimension or something." Jake got out of the car and stood for a moment, looking at the facade in the waning light. "Too bad we don't have a black hole handy."

"You heading back to the motel?"

"Yup," Jake replied, walking to his truck. "It looked to me like they had plenty of empty rooms there. Sure you don't want to join me? It'd be a lot safer than sleeping in that thing." He nodded toward the house.

"No. Now that I know a little bit more about what's going on, I'm actually intrigued to see what it might throw at me."

"Are all the smoke detectors working? It looked to me like you opened up a few of them."

"They're all hard-wired, but the backup batteries were chirping in most of them, so I pulled them out. I've got a package of nine volts; I'll replace them all before I go to bed."

"I'd put a ladder up on that upstairs porch off the bedroom," Jake said. "Gotta have an exit route if a fire breaks out. You might get cut off from the stairs."

"Not a bad idea. I've got a rope I can stash, just in case."

"Alright," Jake replied, starting up his truck. "See you in the morning. Keep an eye out for a naked girl walking through your yard." He offered a smirk.

Ron nodded in reply and Jake took off, disappearing quickly down the drive. Turning back to the house, Ron took a second to look at it once more, observing it for the first time with the new-found information in mind.

I can't lie, he thought. *I still really like this place, even with all I know about it now.*

"Alright," he said to himself as he walked to the front door. "Let's see what you have in store for me tonight."

Chapter Nineteen

After he ate a microwaved plate of food, Ron browsed on his phone, sitting in a padded chair in the living room. Occasionally he'd hear a sound coming from another room in the house, and he'd look up. Lights from the room reflected off the glass of the windows, making them appear like mirrors.

More sounds drifted down from upstairs as he tried to read from his phone; a thump and a scuttling of feet, sounding as though it came from the room where he'd met Ezra. His inclination was to get up and investigate. This time, however, he remained where he was, ignoring the sounds. *I'll walk all the way up there,* he thought, *and it'll be nothing. The damn ghosts would keep me running all over the house if I let them.*

He brought up Google Maps on his phone and scanned the little roads that networked over the mountain. Turning on satellite, he tried to make out houses, hoping to see if any of them looked big enough to be the Coldwater mansion. Several times he found himself nodding off.

He was awoken by the sound of his phone hitting the floor. He bent over to retrieve it, noticing the time: 8:30.

Wow, I'm old, he thought. *Sleepy at 8:30.* He knew there was something he intended to do, and was trying to remember what it was.

Oh, yes...the book.

He got up and searched, checking the kitchen counters and the table by the door. The book was gone.

Then he remembered: Jake. He had taken it. It was still in his hands when he got into the truck.

He dialed his friend, but Jake didn't answer, and it went to voice mail. He typed a text message: *Do you have the book? I can't find it.*

He watched his phone for a reply. After a couple of minutes, dots appeared, and a minute later: *Yes. I have it.*

I called you, but you didn't pick up, he replied.

I'm sending pictures. I was right in the middle of sending one when you called, couldn't figure out how to do both. Sorry.

Dick picks? :) Ron typed.

No, pictures of the book.

To who?

To Terrell.

Ron found himself fully awake now. *I'm going to call again, pick up this time damn it.*

He dialed. It rang several times. Just as he was beginning to think his friend would let it go to voice mail again, Jake answered. "What?"

"Terrell? Why?"

"Well, I told you I was going to check with him."

"And?"

"He didn't have anything new, but I told him everything we learned today. And about the book. He asked me to send him some samples of it, so I did."

Ron waited. "That's it?"

"Well, he called back an hour later and asked if I'd send him a picture of every page. The Wi-Fi here at the motel is great, so I said, sure."

"Every page? Why?"

"I didn't ask, but I think he thinks he can translate it. Or, his mentor guy can translate it."

"Oh. Really? Can he?"

"Didn't say he could, but I'm not sending him all these pictures for nothing! He knows I'm expecting some kind of reply. He said he needed all of the pages to have a go at it. I figured, why not? If he can tell us what it says, that's good, right?"

"If he's accurate and not just making shit up."

"Unlikely."

"I thought he couldn't have anything to do with what's happening here. He said he was forbidden to get involved."

"Still is. But he said looking at a book wasn't the same thing as being here, subject to attack. I say we let him see what he can do with it. If nothing, it's no skin off our backs."

"Were you going to run this past me?"

"I was hoping I could show up in the morning with something useful. Figured you wouldn't mind."

Do I mind? Ron wondered. *I feel like I should, but that makes no sense. It's stupid to feel possessive about it; the book isn't mine, it belongs to Mrs. Hughes. Correction – it belonged to the Coldwaters; it was stolen by Mrs. Hughes' father.*

"Nah, I don't mind, I guess. Aside from the pictures, it wasn't of much use to us. As long as we can return it to Mrs. Hughes intact."

"I'm being careful."

"I guess we'll see if Terrell comes up with anything. Not holding my breath."

"I got more to send. See you in the morning."

"'Night."

Ron hung up, turned off the lights and ascended the stairs, readying for bed. Soon he was slipping under the covers, cold and naked, waiting for the comforter to warm him up. He reached to the nightstand, turned off the light, and the darkness surrounded him.

The thump from overhead came immediately, followed by the sound of feet on the stairs. He closed his eyes, intent upon ignoring it.

You're in terrible danger, Mr. Costa...They walk it every night, searching for you. It will get worse. You won't be able to sleep. You won't be able to stand it. Ezra's words played like a lyric to the constant drumbeat of the steps, the every-other-second plod. It was a perfect anxiety-inducing drug.

Rather than give in to the unease it was designed to elicit, he instead took a moment to marvel at it. *It goes on and on, giving the impression that someone is coming up the stairs, and will soon make their way to my bedroom door. But there are far more plods than stairs; it's like a loop, a discomforting sound loop calculated to scare. It never makes it off the stairs, it just keeps climbing, making it seem like it's coming, always coming, always after me.*

Ingenious.

And it's effective on other levels, too. It creates a sense of invasion. A house, dark at night, its residents asleep – it's supposed to be quiet and private. This sound makes me feel like someone has broken in, there's a trespasser in the house, prowling around in the dark. It's only a matter of time before he makes his way to my bedroom – probably while I'm asleep – and attacks while I'm defenseless, leaving a bloody corpse to be found by others.

Or stands by the side of the bed and just stares…waits, and watches, giving me the creeps all night long.

Couldn't be more effective.

He chuckled to himself, appreciating how real the scares would be, had he not dissected their purpose and exposed their agenda. He rolled over, finding a fresh cold spot, the sounds becoming just background, a white-noise machine like waves or wind. He would use them to lull himself to sleep.

The real question, he thought, *is who is behind all this? Is it Tom, with his drugged beer? Or is it Ezra, just down the hall in the bedroom on the other side of the house? They're obviously working together. Or is there something else at work, something that Ezra is just a part of?*

He drifted off, the unending sound of someone climbing the stairs echoing through the house like a heartbeat.

- - -

"It's going to be at least two more weeks after the 17ᵗʰ," Elenore said over the phone.

"Why?" Ron asked, pouring coffee.

"I can't control the speed of this, Ron. Deals have their own fits and starts."

"Well, I'm disappointed." A week ago Ron would have meant it, but this morning he wasn't sure the additional time was a bad thing. It would give him more opportunity to resolve the issues at the house.

"What I'm worried about is Robbie," she replied, sounding hurried. "I don't know if my mom can keep him that long. I need you to call her and resolve it, either she can and he stays there, or you'll have to move him on your own."

"I'll call her today and figure out something." *No way Robbie can come here,* he thought, *not yet. Not going to tell her that, though.*

"Gotta run," she said. "Dinner meeting. Please say hi to Robbie for me when you talk to him."

"I will."

She disconnected, and Ron heard the front door open. Jake walked in, bringing his usual bag of breakfast food. "I figured I don't need to knock anymore."

"Yeah, last thing I need is more knocking."

"Noisy night?"

"They tried. I ignored it."

"You don't look very rested."

"I'm worried about Robbie. Was just talking to Elenore. She's going to be delayed – which is probably a good thing, given what we're dealing with here – but I'm not sure Robbie can stay at his grandmother's that long. Gotta make a few calls."

"The last thing you need is your son in this house," Jake replied. "At least until you clear up some stuff."

"I got an electrical guy coming tomorrow to do a safety inspection."

"Good."

"The idea was for Robbie and Elenore to move here together, once she gets back. If I have to move Robbie before that, I'll need a new plan. Maybe stay with him in your motel."

"How are you going to explain that to Robbie? Or Elenore?"

Ron shook his head. "I don't know. I'll have to give it some thought."

"Good news," Jake said, changing the subject. "Terrell was up all night, looking at the pictures I sent him. He called me an hour ago; he's all amped up, wants to talk to us."

"Alright," Ron replied, digging for a McMuffin in the bag. "You want coffee?"

"Sure," Jake answered, dialing Terrell on his phone.

"You know where it is."

Jake set his phone down on the counter and walked into the kitchen.

"Hello?" came Terrell's voice.

"Terrell? It's Ron. Jake's here too."

"Hello! Boy oh boy, do I have news for you! I was up all night, reviewing those pages! What an incredible find!"

"Find?" Ron repeated, as Jake returned to the room with his coffee.

"Never seen anything like it!"

"What language is it?" Jake asked.

"Language? It's English."

"English?" Jake said. "Didn't look like English to me."

"Ah, well, that's a little tricky to explain. Let me just say that I was able to read certain parts of it, and Abe, well, Abe was able to make out all of it, since he's well versed in almost all..."

"Wait," Ron said, cutting him off. "We looked through that book. None of the words made sense. You say it's English, and you can read it? I have a hard time believing that."

"It's called experiential writing," Terrell explained. "It's in English, but you have to have the context of what it's about in order to understand it. Have you ever read a technical sentence, something filled with references and assumptions and realized you don't understand any of it? It's like that. People with the gift, those of us who have had some experience with the subject it's addressing, can make it out. It's common in our line of work."

"Line of work," Ron muttered to Jake, rolling his eyes.

Jake raised a hand to his friend, signaling to temper the sarcasm. "What does it say, Terrell?"

"Well, Abe is still going through it. I spent the night reading what I could, but more than half was undecipherable to me, so I brought it to Abe this morning. He's churning through it now. He's very excited, won't let me interrupt him while he's reviewing things."

"So, you can't tell us anything? Or can you?"

"I can tell you about the parts I was able to decipher. They were a list of instructions, directives really, establishing a long-term haunting. I think I was able to read those parts because that's something I'm familiar with, hauntings, due to my tour business."

Ron couldn't help rolling his eyes again.

"Establishing a long-term haunting?" Jake repeated, thinking it best to keep Ron out of the conversation. "What does that mean exactly?"

"Well," Terrell continued, "hauntings usually start up because of an event, something that happened in the past that was particularly singular and traumatic, or something with strong emotional resonance that causes someone who's died to become confused. Instead of moving on, which most do, confused spirits get stuck, re-playing events over and over. They become so accustomed to the events that they forget about moving on, and remain in a kind of loop, attached to the place where the events happened. That's a haunting. A typical haunting, the most common."

"Alright," Jake replied.

"This, however, isn't a normal haunting. There was no naturally occurring traumatic event. Everything is manipulated. It's been staged. Spirits didn't arise and become confused. They were sent in, like soldiers, under orders to haunt. It's very unusual."

Ron watched as Jake looked up from the phone, intrigue forcing a huge smile on his friend.

"Go on," Jake prompted.

"So, I spent the night trying to decipher the instructions. They're like orders or commands, establishing the haunting. It's very arcane. I don't understand exactly how they can work, it's not anything I've ever seen work before. I knew Abe is old and gets up way early, so around 5 I took them to his place, and he's busy looking at them now. He seemed very impressed; I think this'll land me a mentorship for sure, so I owe you guys."

"I'm happy for you," Ron said, "but that's not much to go on. Did you read anything about how to reverse it?"

"Reverse it?" Terrell said, as though the idea seemed abhorrent. "Why would you…oh. That's right, you want to get rid of it, in your house. Right. Well, no, off the top of my head, I can't think of how you'd do that, compared to a normal haunting. Something else is driving their behavior, so just correcting some wrong or disrupting their loop probably isn't going to work."

"Maybe Abe has some ideas?" Ron offered.

"He probably will. He won't let me use my phone in his house, he's real paranoid. I'm about a block down the street from his home.

I'll go back there and wait while he works, and let you know once he's finished."

"I'm surprised he's willing to help," Ron said. "I thought he put the kibosh on the whole thing, said it was too dangerous for you to be involved."

"This is just a book," Terrell said. "It's physically being at your property that he won't allow. Let me tell you, though, that book was a real find. Have you discovered any of the nazars? The transitions?"

"If by nazar you mean the little thing with the hairs," Ron said, "yeah, I found one."

"Did you use it?"

"I'd say it was the other way around," Ron replied. "It used me."

"Fascinating. Where did you find it?"

"In a dresser."

"You know, there might be more. Check outside. When happened when you used it?"

Ron turned to Jake. "How much did you tell him?"

"I told him everything we learned at the old lady's trailer."

"Nothing about Ezra?"

"You've never really explained that to me," Jake replied.

Ron turned back to the phone. "Once it dissolved into my palm, I met this guy who claimed to be a neighbor. His name is Tom. He showed up one night with beers, and I had one, but I think they were drugged. His whole thing was introducing me to Ezra, who, by the way, lives in the room you slept in while you were here. He tried scaring me into leaving, which, of course, I'm not going to do."

"Interesting."

"Do you know anything about these nazars? Is it still in me?"

"It might be. Their effect probably fades over time. Could be out of your system by now. I think it's really interesting how these are behaving. It's not normal."

"Behaving?" Ron asked. "What do you mean?"

"Normally a nazar is designed to ward off evil in some way. The one you used actually allowed you to interact with them, with ghosts in the house. I've never seen them work that way. A lot of this is very unusual. The instructions in the book are highly uncommon, a very weird way to go about things. The vibe of the book is very mean-spirited, too. Not good. So, I'd tread lightly until Abe can weigh in. I should probably head back. I'll call you when I know more, alright?"

"Thanks, Terrell," Jake replied.

"Yeah, thanks," Ron added, and the call ended.

"You could be nicer," Jake said. "He's doing us a favor."

"It'll be a favor if it winds up being anything useful," Ron replied. "What Mrs. Hughes told us was a favor. The jury's still out on Terrell."

"Well, OK, but while he's working on it and there's hope of something helpful coming from that, don't snuff him out by being rude."

"Have you paid him anything?"

"See, that's what I mean. The cynicism."

"Have you?"

"Just the money for the bus. And that seems fair, by the way, since he took the time to come all the way down here."

"And his food while he was here."

"Nitpicking."

"Jury's out."

"Fine. In the meantime?"

"I want to find Coldwater mansion. It's here, on the mountain, somewhere. I should have asked Mrs. Hughes for its location yesterday. Thought I might swing by her place and see if she'll give me the address."

"And then what?"

"Check it out."

"Go poking around someone else's property? Didn't you say your neighbors like to call the cops?"

"Yeah, that's what the post office guy told me."

"How about we see what Terrell comes up with first?"

"I don't know; might be a fool's errand. The kid seems barely able to scratch his own ass. I'd rather..." He paused.

"Rather what?"

Ron knew he was still in the dark. He really had no clue what to do next, how to solve things. He was at the mercy of others, either more information from Mrs. Hughes, or whatever options Terrell and Abe might be able to provide.

"I need to call Robbie," Ron said, walking into the other room. "Gotta make arrangements."

"I'll be here with the coffee," Jake replied, reaching into the bag for another McMuffin.

- - -

After a morning of work on the exterior of the house, prepping for painting, Ron decided he wanted to make the trip back to Mrs. Hughes' trailer to see if she'd provide the location of Coldwater mansion. They parked in her driveway, and the dogs tied up in front of her home barked furiously, foaming at the mouth and straining on their chains until she told them to be quiet. As the last syllable of the command left her mouth, the animals went slack and wandered away, completely uninterested. She welcomed them in, and Jake's phone rang. He pulled it from his pocket.

"Fuck, it's Terrell," he said as they sat around Mrs. Hughes' kitchen table. "I don't mean to be rude, but I think I should take this."

Ron expected a sour reaction from Mrs. Hughes, but she just waved her hand. "Go ahead. I've got all day." He wasn't sure if she was being sarcastic or not.

As Jake took the call, rising from the table and turning away in an ineffective attempt to speak privately with Terrell, Ron turned to Mrs. Hughes. "He showed the pages of the book you lent us to a friend of his who thinks he can read it."

Mrs. Hughes looked shocked. "You're kidding!"

"I don't know if he really can or not," Ron replied. "But this friend of his has been showing them to someone else, someone who might be a little more scholarly on the subject. He was going to get back to us with their findings."

Jake turned around. "I think you should hear this."

"Do you mind?" Ron asked Mrs. Hughes. "We can put it on speakerphone. You might as well hear this too, if you're interested. It's your book, after all."

"Go ahead," she replied, straightening her dress again as though someone new was about to visit.

Jake sat at the table and placed the phone in the middle. "OK, Terrell, I've got Ron here, and Mrs. Hughes, she's the woman who gave us the book. Go ahead."

"Mrs. Hughes?" Terrell asked.

"Yes?" she answered.

"Can you tell me, where did you get this book?"

"It was my father's. Well, that's not true. He had it, but I understand he stole it from a mansion nearby."

"So, it came from a particular house?"

"Yes, it's called the Coldwater mansion. It's on the mountain where I live, where your friend Ron's house is located."

"I see. Are you familiar with the book's contents?"

"Other than the pictures, it made no sense to me."

"Alright, just like Ron and Jake. That's fine, that's to be expected. Well, I spoke with Abe. He spent all day with the pages you sent me. He's completely freaking out over it, he called it a huge discovery. Make sure you protect that book, put it somewhere safe. It's extremely valuable."

Mrs. Hughes looked up at them.

"Did you bring it with you from the motel?" Ron asked Jake.

"Yeah, it's in my truck."

"Go on, Terrell," Ron said. "Did Abe discover anything?"

"He did."

"And?"

"He, well…"

"Spit it out, Terrell."

"He wants you to come up here, to meet with him."

"Fuck," Ron muttered.

"Can't you just tell us what he said?" Jake asked. "It's a long ways up to Port Angeles."

"I know, but for some reason – that he wouldn't explain to me – he wants to talk to you directly, Ron. I think he has questions for you. And, if I'm being honest, I think he didn't exactly trust me to relay everything correctly. He's only known me for a few days, I'm not sure at what point he'll start trusting me more."

"Terrell, I'm really pressed for time here," Ron said. "I've got all this work to get done on the house before my wife and child move in, and this thing with the ghosts, it's all…"

Terrell cut him off. "I can almost guarantee he's not going to tell me anymore about it until you show up. He was quite emphatic about it."

There was a long pause. Ron could feel Jake and Mrs. Hughes' eyes upon him, waiting for a decision.

He turned to Jake. "How long to get up there?"

"Three, four hours?" Jake replied.

"What do you think?"

"I think, if this guy knows something that could help, why not? Go up now, see him tonight or tomorrow, be back by tomorrow night at the latest."

Ron turned back to the phone. "Alright, Terrell. We're on our way. Can he meet us tonight, after we get there? Say, 8 or 9?"

"I'll check. Call me when you get into town. If not tonight, first thing in the morning. And with Abe, that could be 5 or 6 AM, if you want. Though, personally, I'd like to sleep in. I was up all night with it. I'm exhausted."

"Sleep now," Ron replied. "We're on our way, and we'll call you when we get there."

Jake hung up.

"Sorry about that," Ron said to Mrs. Hughes. "I came over to see if you could give me directions to the Coldwater mansion. I tried looking for it online last night, but couldn't find anything."

"I will, on one condition," she replied, looking at him with all seriousness. "After you finish with this gentleman in Port Angeles, I want to know what happens. I've lived with the stories of this mountain my entire life; some of them had conclusions, but there are so many dead ends that have just hung there with no answers. I've learned to live with them, but, this one – the Coldwater thing – it's the granddaddy of them all, and if there's something new about it, I want to know. Promise me."

Ron raised his hand as though he was swearing on a bible. "I promise I'll share everything I find out," he replied, hoping that whatever Abe might have to tell him, it didn't come on a condition of secrecy.

"Alright," she said, rising from the table and searching for a pad and pen. "I'm going to jot down these instructions while I tell you, because it's complicated. The place has become a little cut off over the years." She returned to the table and sat, uncapping the pen. "Let's see, originally you'd get there off Red Curve Road, but the problem is, that road was blocked off years ago, and I think you have to take Crestridge now, and turn onto a little dirt path that isn't marked. It'll be after the sign for eggs at the McKinston farm, but before the split tree that's just before the power lines. You know the place?"

Ron shook his head, already confused. "I have no idea."

"Don't worry, I'm writing it down," she continued, jotting furiously while she spoke, even squiggling a tiny map. "The dirt road will connect back up with Offerson Road, which is where you were headed if you could have stayed on Red Curve Road. Offerson is blocked too, after about a mile, so you have to take another dirt road, it's called Yate's Court, and that's because the end of it is the driveway to Greg Yate's place. You go about fifty feet down Yate's Court and there'll be a small road to the left, it looks like an old logging road. Might be overgrown. Anyway, you take that, because if you miss the turn you'll wind up in Yate's yard and will have to make a turn around. Greg won't mind, but if he's not home and it's just Janet, she'll let the dogs loose, and they love to jump at cars and scratch your paint."

"Fuck," Jake muttered.

"Go down that old logging road until it ends, and you'll be at Barlow Road. That's the road Offerson used to connect to, but doesn't anymore. It's wider, but it'll be overgrown probably too, since it's been cut off at both ends for years now. Go left, and a hundred yards down you'll come to the house. Can't miss it." She slid the paper to him.

"Christ," Ron replied, looking at the tiny map she'd drawn. "I'll need a search party for when I get lost."

"Quite easy to do, get lost," she said. "Happens to people all the time up here, thinking they can use their phones to get around. None of the GPS directions are right. Hell, even the printed maps I've seen are wrong, they never kept up with the road closures. That," she said, pointing to the paper, "will work. Trust me. You going to go up there?"

"Maybe," Ron said. "After Port Angeles."

"When was the last time you saw the place?" Jake asked. "Can you tell us anything about what we should expect?"

"Well, it's been vacant for a long time," Mrs. Hughes replied. "I haven't seen it since way before Offerson got blocked, at least ten years ago. Don't want to be like my father; he was obsessed with it, and that didn't end well, as I told you. So, I try to put most of it behind me and not dwell on the past. The last time I saw the house itself, it looked run down. That happens to an abandoned house, as I expect you know, Ron. A house has to be cared for, just like a horse, or a farm, or things go bad. No one would buy the Coldwater place after the murders, even though they tried to sell it. Eventually they gave up and since then, it just sits, slowly rotting. I think a niece of Mr. Coldwater owns the property now, but no one I know has ever heard from her, or seen her; don't have any idea where she lives, could be Timbuktu for all I know. I remember hearing from Jane Patterson – she lives over that way – that they were worried about vandals, so years ago a huge chain link fence was put up, all around the house. Probably all overgrown with blackberries now. I'd take a trimmer with you, but don't take anything that'll make noise. Maybe a machete. Yeah, take a machete, to hack your way through."

"And wire cutters?" Jake offered. "For the chain link fence?"

"Yeah," she replied. "Good idea."

"Any chance we'd be seen?" Ron asked. "People on this mountain like to call the sheriff on trespassers."

"You're referring to the Sables," she answered. "Yes, they're on their phone to the cops all day long. They're over by your place, but they're far from this route I'm giving you. Where you'll need to be careful is at the Yates place. If you can get past that driveway without her alerting her dogs, I doubt anyone will have any idea you're there. Now, as for getting into the house itself, provided you can make it through the bramble and past the fence...you'll have to play that by ear. There were several entrances to the mansion, as I recall; I would expect they'd all be locked up, but you'll have to look for a weakness." She paused.

"What?" Ron asked.

"Well, then there's the other little creepy things about the mansion. You'll see, soon enough."

"Some advance warning would be nice," Jake said.

"Well, little things. Some of them might just be stories about the place, made up, or exaggerated. I'd hate to mislead you."

"Mislead us!" Jake said. "I'd like to know what we'll be walking into!"

"Well, there's the windows," she replied. "Do you remember when I was reading from my grandmother's diary? That part about how her friend, Amy, went outside and saw the window panes slowly turning black, as the fog moved through the house?"

"Yes," Jake answered.

"They say they're still black, and they can't be cleaned. When they tried to sell the house, one of the problems was that, after they scrubbed all the windows, they'd turn black again. They brought in maids almost every day, but it didn't matter how many times they wiped them, the black always returned, blocking out the light."

"Whoa," Jake said, leaning back in his chair. "That *is* creepy."

"According to a person I know who was friends with a realtor that worked on the sale, strange things happened to people who toured the place, when it was on the market. The longer they were in the house, the more anxious they would become, and if they spent too long, sometimes they'd turn frantic, wanting to leave. Of course, I thought immediately of Mrs. Coldwater, ranting and raving through the halls. Anyway, one woman who looked at the place hanged herself in her own home the next day. Used a necktie that belonged to her husband. A couple of people reported changes in their hair after they'd been there; hair falling out, turning white, that kind of thing. Just when it seemed as if a potential buyer was warming up to the place, a terrible stink would develop, like rotten meat, or eggs, and it would drive people from room to room in an attempt to escape it. All the realtors were afraid to touch the windows because of the blackening problem, so no air got in to flush it out. It didn't take long for any would-be buyer to lose interest. Naturally they wanted to keep all these things quiet, worried about ruining the chances for selling it, but one of the realtors was pretty gossipy, which is how we learned all these things. Didn't matter anyway, it was never going to sell. No one in their right mind would want to live there, especially with all that, and especially the sightings of...her."

"Mrs. Coldwater?" Ron asked.

"Over the years there were reports of her ghost running from room to room, in different places, all over the mansion," Mrs. Hughes continued. "One realtor who stayed to close it up after an open house said she was chased out of the building by the ghost of a woman. It followed her through the halls, its arms outstretched, like it was trying to grab her. She said it was screaming loud, nonsensical things. Poor woman was terrified. She quit the next day, never went back. The idea of her still there, her ghost moving through the halls like that, well...it's a terrifying image that's kept me up many nights."

She stopped, looking up at them. "Still want to go?"

Chapter Twenty

Ron looked down the street, then in the side mirror of Jake's truck, checking for Terrell. They were parked at the address the kid gave them, but he was late.

"Maybe we should just go in and see this Abe ourselves," Ron said. "That's who I'm here to see anyway, not Terrell."

"Why not?" Jake replied. "I hate it when people are late."

They left the truck and walked to an arching arbor, densely covered in green. Ron tried the large, wrought iron handle on the door, but it wouldn't move.

Jake pointed to an intercom buried under leaves. "Probably have to get buzzed in."

"Yeah," Ron agreed. "Terrell did say he was paranoid." He pushed the small black button on the intercom and waited.

"Yes?" came a tinny voice through the speaker, padded by the soft sounds of classical music playing in the background.

"Abe? This is Ron. Terrell said you wanted to speak to me directly."

"Ron? I don't know any Ron. Where is Terrell?"

"He was supposed to be here ten minutes ago, I think he's late."

"Come back when you have Terrell." The speaker clicked off, abruptly ending the music.

"Welcome to Port Angeles, too," Jake said.

Ron looked up and down the street; there was no sign of Terrell. "I guess we wait."

As they walked back to the truck, Jake's phone rang. "Terrell?" he said, answering it. "We're here, in front of Abe's. You're late."

Ron waited while his friend finished the call. The sky was dark and the temperature a little chilly; although he'd thrown a few clothes into an overnight bag, he neglected to bring a coat, and was regretting it.

Jake slipped his phone into his pocket. "He got hung up with one of his tours, something about a group that wouldn't move on. He's on his way now. Said it'd be five minutes."

"Well, three hours up here, what's another five minutes," Ron replied, getting into the truck. "I shoulda brought a jacket. It's getting cold."

"I didn't bring one, either," Jake replied, starting up the truck and cranking the heater.

Exactly five minutes later they saw Terrell approaching on a bike. He stopped and leaned it against the arbor, waving for them to get out of the truck and join him. By the time they reached him, he already had the gate open.

"Sorry about that," Terrell replied. "They just wouldn't leave. I finally had to kind of shoo them out, which I hate to do, 'cause I want them to buy souvenirs, but I don't think they were going to buy any anyway."

They walked through a heavily overgrown garden, bending a little to get under several drooping trees. "We tried to get in ourselves," Jake said, "but Abe wouldn't let us."

"I could have told you he wouldn't," Terrell replied. "He made me stand out there for hours before he let me in the first time." When they reached the front door to the house, Terrell stopped and reached down to a metal bucket, from which he removed two long necklaces. He handed one to each of them. "Here, put these on."

Ron took the necklace; it was made of dried cloves, strung together with twine. "Garlic?" he asked, holding it up.

"What, over our heads?" Jake asked.

"Yeah, put it around your neck," Terrell answered.

"You've got to be kidding," Ron said. "What are we, vampires?"

Terrell sighed. "He won't let you in if you're not wearing it." Terrell reached into the bucket and removed another, slipping it over his head. "I have to wear one, too. He's made me wear it every time I've come here. I'm not sure why. I told you he's paranoid; I think he's got a thing for vampires in particular."

"Ridiculous," Ron muttered, donning the crunchy necklace. The cloves looked long dried, but still smelled a little.

Terrell opened the door and led them inside.

The place was cluttered, but in an organized sort of way. Stacks of papers and books were everywhere, neatly arranged, as though their owner knew exactly where each of them were but simply ran out of proper storage. Terrell led them through a rabbit trail until they reached a small room that held enough chairs for them to sit. In one of the chairs was an old, short man.

"Abe?" Terrell said. "This is Ron. And Jake."

Abe peered at them over his glasses. "Why two?"

"It's my house that's haunted," Ron said. "Jake has been helping me."

"Whose book is it?" Abe asked.

"Well, neither of ours, really," Ron answered. "It was loaned to us. It was Jake who sent Terrell the pictures."

"Did you bring it?" Abe asked. "The book?" He looked anxious, and Ron could swear the old man appeared to be drooling a little.

"Yes," Jake replied, digging it out of his backpack and handing it to Abe.

Abe looked delighted, but didn't reach for it. "I wonder if you might bring it with you," he said, rising from his chair and leading Jake into the next room.

Jake followed him, and Ron and Terrell were right behind.

Abe led him to a table that was piled high with books and papers. Tucked into the middle was a small chest the size of a miniature steamer trunk. Abe lifted the lid; it was lined with a yellow pinstriped paper, faded in spots. "Place it inside, if you would."

Jake set the book into the chest, and Abe closed the lid.

"Can't be too careful," Abe replied. "There's plenty of trouble that would like to ride in here on the soles of shoes, so I have to be vigilant." While he spoke, he extracted a pair of gloves from under a stack of paper, causing the stack to wobble. Ron was about to step up and brace the tall piles of papers, but Abe slipped on the gloves and rebalanced it before anything slid off. He stretched his fingers within the gloves, spreading them in demonstration to the others, as if he was a magician about to perform a trick.

"Silk," Terrell whispered to Ron, behind him.

Abe opened the chest and carefully removed the book, holding it as though it might explode if he jostled it. "Let's go back to the drawing room; it's more comfortable in there." As he walked, he held it out in front of him, carefully taking each step until he was seated in his chair.

"Terrell, the bookstand, please," Abe said, motioning with his hand to a piece of furniture across the room.

Terrell grabbed a wooden box and wheeled it across the floor until it was in front of Abe, its one angled side positioned right in front of him.

Abe placed the book carefully on the stand, letting it slide down to a small wooden lip. He gently lifted the cover as though he was examining a rare artifact. "Tell me again where you got this."

"I thought Terrell already explained all that," Ron said.

"I'd like to hear a first-hand account," Abe replied, not taking his eyes from the pages he was turning.

Ron recounted a little about what had happened at his home, and more about their meeting with Mrs. Hughes. Abe asked a few questions as he progressed, until finally he'd related most of the tale.

"The picture comes together," Abe muttered, still browsing pages. "Or substantial parts of it, at least."

"Terrell said you wanted to speak to me directly," Ron replied. "Can you tell me what's in that book that's so important?"

Abe stopped looking at it and raised his gaze to Ron. "What is it you want, exactly?" he asked, ignoring Ron's question.

"What I want?" Ron repeated, a little surprised.

"Clarity, please," Abe replied insistently.

"I want my house to be free of whatever is making it impossible to live there."

"Why?" Abe asked. "You've got a wonderful example playing out right in front of you, and you want it to end?"

"I don't consider it wonderful."

"But I do. This is very dark, using methods most people would never employ. I'd love to study it more, if it wasn't so virulent to those of us with the gift. It's a shame."

Ron wasn't sure if the old man was for real or not. "I just want my house. Look, it was a long drive up here. If you have something that can help, I'd appreciate it. Otherwise, I have a ton of work to do."

"We both have work to do," Abe replied. "It's not like I'm in the habit of sublimating my normal routines for a random skeptic off the street. If I'm right, what you're dealing with is extraordinary. Not one hundred percent unique, but rare nonetheless. Extremes rarely employed have been employed here! Quite special. You need to appreciate that."

Ron sighed. "Some specifics would be nice."

"I'm going to carefully meter what I tell you until I decide if I'm in agreement with your desire to clean your place," Abe replied. "When you find something exceptional and exquisite, you don't just chop it into pieces like a brute. With that in mind, I will share with you a little about this book so that you can develop a better understanding of what you're living with."

"That would be appreciated," Ron replied.

"The book is both a set of instructions – a plan – and an execution of a plan, a kind of backup of the steps, to ensure they remain in effect. There are no reasons or strategies here, those are all assumed, I guess. This is just a design."

"Alright," Ron replied.

"The designers of this plan, do they have a name?" Abe asked.

"I assume it's the Coldwaters," Ron answered. "Mrs. Hughes said her father stole this book from them – or, rather, from their house."

"OK," Abe said, retuning his gaze to the book, "the Coldwaters then. Highly committed people. It takes a relentless focus to go through steps like these. They must have really, really hated the other party, who were they?"

"The Hughes family," Ron replied.

"They were dabbling in things extremely dark, very potent and virulent. It's a good thing you left when you did, Terrell. This would have consumed you. It would have consumed anyone with the gift, turning their abilities against themselves and draining their strength for its own purposes."

"That sounds a little like gobbledygook to me," Ron said.

"It's all here," Abe replied, turning the pages. "Many dark rites. No doubt the houses that burned suffered attacks similar to the one you're experiencing now; terror at its worst. Am I right? You have seen things, have you not?"

"All kinds of bizarre things," Jake offered.

"My family needs to move in soon," Ron replied. "How do I stop it? I need this to end before they come. Does that book offer a way for me to shut it all down?"

"I beg you to reconsider," Abe said. "This needs to be studied. It's unusual to find one of these, operational, functioning, and it really needs to be properly investigated and researched, so that…"

Ron cut him off. "You're suggesting I just live with it? The previous two houses burned down, probably at the hands of the Coldwaters, and with people inside them. People who died!"

"Just move out," Abe replied cavalierly. "Donate the house. I know several organizations that would be happy to receive it, to…"

Ron cut him off again. "Are you out of your mind? I can't afford to donate the house! I don't have that kind of money!"

"Really?" Abe asked. "You don't have a benefactor who might step in?"

"Benefactor?" Ron turned to Terrell. "Who the fuck is this guy?"

Terrell tried to formulate a reply, but Abe jumped in before he could. "Fine, fine. It's a shame, though. A real loss."

Ron reached the end of his patience. "Can you tell me how to fix it or not? I'm not going to turn it into a lab experiment or a museum. I've decided to fight this thing, and I intend to win. That house belongs to me, not the Coldwaters, not the former owners, not the ghosts or whatever the fuck they are. I want them out. I'll do whatever I have to."

Abe looked at him; a smile slowly spread across his face. "Good...good. That's what I wanted to know." He flipped through the book. "It's not easy. You'll need to maintain that fortitude. Let's hope it isn't just hot air, this little emphatic demonstration of yours."

"Just tell me how," Ron said, taking a deep breath.

"And you'll have to do it yourself." Abe looked up at Jake. "Are you gifted? Even a little?"

"Gifted?" Jake replied. "I don't think so."

"Good, then you can help him. It would be unwise for Terrell or myself to set foot anywhere near that mountain, and god knows your friend is going to need some assistance. We'll do what we can from here, but you two will have to do the grunt work."

"That's what I normally do," Jake replied, giving Ron a smile.

"I think I have a plan," Abe said, turning back to Ron. "But I'm afraid it's dangerous and fairly gruesome. So, step one, before we go through with it, I want you to verify that what I think is happening is really what is happening."

"Just tell me what to do," Ron said. "We'll do it."

"Within reason," Jake added.

"You'll need to go down to the basement," Abe said, "and check out a few things."

"Basement?" Ron asked. "What, here?"

"No, not here!" Abe replied. "At your place."

"There's no basement," Ron replied. "There's a crawlspace, but it's not more than three or four feet tall."

Abe smiled. "There is a basement. And I suspect it's the focal point, the spot your enemies chose to set up shop. You'll need to go down into it, and check to see if..."

"Wait, wait..." Ron said, cutting him off. "I don't think you understand. There is no basement."

Abe smiled patiently. "There is. It is there. You can't see it, but it is there, it was part of one of the earlier houses at that spot. It might have been filled in before your current house was built. If I'm right, it's a busy place, and the source of most of your troubles. I need you to go down into it, and check it out."

Ron was beginning to think the trip to Port Angeles was a bad idea, that Abe might be making things up. "How do you expect me to enter a place I can't see?"

"If it were Terrell or I," Abe continued, "it wouldn't present much of a challenge. But that isn't possible; in this case, the same gift that would allow us to enter your basement prohibits us from doing so. You, on the other hand, are a simple skeptic, an unenlightened naif. You aren't subject to the danger that Terrell or I would face, since you have absolutely no gift whatsoever."

"Thank you," Ron said. "I think."

"You're welcome. As you cannot naturally cross the transition into the basement, you'll have to do it artificially, with the help of some items. If we're lucky, they'll be compatible with you; seems like there's already been some success along these lines."

"Oh," Ron replied. "You mean, like that nazar? The one I found that sunk into my palm?"

"Precisely," Abe replied. "I can't just give you one, you'll need one that's designed for that land. Based on what Terrell has told me, it sounds as if they're growing in the forest." He rose from his chair and walked to a shelf, where he removed a large book. "Harvest a few of them, and then we'll combine it with this." He opened the book; it was hollow, filled with small bottles secured in foam. He removed two small ones and handed them to Ron.

Ron took them and held one up to the light; it was tiny, not more than half an inch tall, and capped with a small cork stopper. The glass was dark brown, and it was half full of liquid.

"It will be the combination of the nazar with what I just gave you," Abe continued, "that will allow you to cross the transition and enter the basement. You're not gifted, so things are going to seem very fuzzy to you, and you may be confused and unable to think straight. You'll need to summon your resolve and push on, find the transition, pass through, and observe. Note everything."

"What am I looking for?" Ron asked, still staring at the bottle.

"There could be any number of intrigues there," Abe replied. "The stuff in that bottle only lasts a little while. It's different for every person; it might last thirty seconds, or it might last a couple of minutes. Regardless, it's a very short period of time, so I suggest you make sure you are doing it right: don't get distracted. Find the basement, go into it, and memorize everything you see. After you're done, give Terrell a call. Depending on what you report, it will inform the rest of my plan."

"Two bottles?" Ron replied. "Take the second one if the first one doesn't work?"

"The first one will work," Abe replied. "Save the second one for later. If I'm right, you're going to need it down the road."

Ron was completely unsure how to locate a basement he didn't believe existed, despite suggesting to Abe that he was up to it. Somehow, Abe's certainty that it was there carried him along. He wanted to hear whatever the man's theory was, regardless of how ludicrous he thought it might be. As Abe finished, Ron sighed, then said, "Alright. I think I can do that."

"Good," Abe replied. "One word of warning. The entity might be there. In fact, there's a very good chance he's there. You ingested your ghostly friend's beer just before your conversation with this Ezra, did you not?" Abe asked.

"I did. He left a six pack at my place. Four cans left."

"Good. I suspect that means an agent in the beer was needed – along with the nazar, of course – for you to interact with the entity. Do not, under any circumstances, have any more of that beer before you go into the basement. In fact, I think it might be a wise idea for you to protect yourself. Terrell, when we're done here, will you instruct him on the Heraclitean invocation, since I think that's where things are headed."

"But he's not gifted," Terrell objected. "How would it..."

"He'll have the nazar in his system," Abe replied. "It won't be comprehensive, but if he's quick and silent, it might be enough to shield him from detection. That's all we're trying to accomplish, that and whatever he sees with his eyes. It's the simplest way, and simple is best when dealing with the ungifted."

Ron raised a hand to his forehead, rubbing at it in an attempt to forestall what felt like an impending headache. The rational part of his brain, still running at full speed under the layers of bizarre, weird, and outright lunacy that had piled up on top of it the past few weeks, was screaming for him to throw on the brakes, make a speech about how ridiculous it all was, and walk out. By running his fingers along his brow, feeling the wrinkles there and the hardness of his skull under the skin, he was able to temper the impulse. *Just let this play out,* he thought. *You drove all the way up here. Just take in what he's saying. Don't freak out, don't insult him by calling it all bullshit, like you want to.*

Breathe.

Breathe.

"OK," Terrell said. "I'll show him how to do it."

"Good," Abe replied, turning back to Ron. "Alright, got it? Go in, observe, and come back out. Don't stay long, try to be quiet and unobserved. Call me once you find out what's down there."

"And then?" Ron asked, still rubbing his forehead.

"If I'm right, and I usually am, we'll take the next steps. I can see you're already overloaded, so I don't want to confuse you with a lot more information that may not be relevant. That'll come if and when the basement plays out as expected."

"I'd rather know," Ron replied, lowering his hand, attempting to appear more confident. "Tell me now."

"I don't think so," Abe replied, smiling. "I may be old, but my age has allowed me to intuit a thing or two about people. You, my friend, are a baseless skeptic. That's fine; the world needs doubters and cynics. They're very entertaining. However, it has been my experience that skeptics often miss important details when the chips are down. They let their tendency for sensible thinking get in the way of other things, and their brains twist the truth of what they've seen to comport with the norms of rational thought. You say you're dedicated to solving your problem, but I'm not so sure you're ready for the gruesome work that's ahead of you. Let's see how you do with the basement. We'll go from there."

"I feel like I'd be flying blind," Ron said. "If you know what's going on – or, rather, if you suspect you know – you should tell me what it is. I can handle it."

"No, you cannot," Abe said, rising from his chair and leading them to the door. "You've been flying blind for quite a while now. Another day won't change things." He turned to Terrell. "Make sure he knows the invocation."

"Will do," Terrell replied, opening the door.

"Give Terrell a call when you're finished," Abe said as they walked out. "He'll bring that infernal gadget over, and we'll all have another talk." Abe stopped, giving him a good, long look. "I wish I could say I'm confident you'll succeed. The look on your face makes me think you have reservations."

"It's just..." Ron began, then stopped. He took a breath, unable to resist any longer. "It's all just so insane. Crazy. These things you're asking me to do. They're..."

"Irrational?" Abe offered.

"I was going to say ridiculous."

Abe stood close to Ron. "Your house is full of problems, my friend. Paranormal problems. Not rats or termites or bad wiring, not normal problems. *Para*normal. You're going to have to do a few non-normal things if you want to combat it. Irrational things. Things that might seem ridiculous. Feel free to consider them preposterous, if you like, but keep in mind that the forces aligned against you couldn't be further from that. They're deadly serious. You'll want to figure that out and step up, or you'll be bringing a pea shooter to a war." He stepped back inside. "Half the people I send off to do things like this I never see again, so I'll wish you au revoir!"

The door closed. Ron almost felt as though he'd been kicked out; insulted first, dressed down, then kicked out. He looked at Jake, and then at Terrell.

"That's Abe," Terrell said, shrugging. "He knows what he's talking about. I promise."

"Right," Ron replied, realizing it sounded more sarcastic than he intended. "I guess you're going to show me something? This invocation he mentioned?"

"Yeah," Terrell replied, leading them through the garden toward the arbor. "Let's go back to my place. I can write it down for you."

- - -

"So, I shouldn't drink these beers?" Jake yelled from the kitchen.

"The ones with the purple labels?" Ron called back. "No, don't touch them."

Jake walked into the living room carrying a different beer. "Good thing I thought to ask. You think they're all laced, or just the one he offered you?"

"I have no idea," Ron replied, looking at the little pile of nazars resting on the coffee table in front of him. Abe suggested checking the underside of ferns, and it hadn't taken him and Jake more than a half hour of looking before they found a handful, collecting them with gloves. Sitting next to the pile were the tiny bottles Abe had given to him.

"So, beer plus one of those things, you'd see the devil upstairs again?" Jake asked, dropping onto the sofa.

"That's the way it worked last time."

"But no beer this time," Jake said. "Just the stuff Abe gave you."

"Right." Ron looked up at his friend. "Does this seem completely crazy to you?"

Jake belched from his beer. "It's seemed crazy since the first day. This is just more crazy."

"I mean, how can there be a basement? You've seen that crawlspace."

"I don't know if they fully excavated the older foundation," Jake replied, "but it wouldn't take much to fill the whole thing in with a bulldozer. In fact, I think they brought in more dirt and re-leveled it all anyway. The new foundation was probably built on top of that. If Abe's right."

"He called it a transition," Ron replied, picking up one of the nazars with his fingers, careful not to let it settle in his palm. "A transition between what?"

"I would guess Freedom would say it's a transition between this time and an earlier time," Jake offered. "Something like that."

"I'm going back in time?"

"No, you're not time travelling, you're going to check out something that existed physically long ago, but now exists in a different way. Like a ghost. Used to be real and alive, now it's dead, but still around."

"Your explanation is even more fucked up than time traveling," Ron replied, placing the nazar firmly in his palm. "You want to see this? I'm gonna do it now."

Jake stood and approached him, then bent over to look at Ron's hand.

The object just sat on Ron's palm, unmoving.

"How long did it take, last time?" Jake asked.

"I wasn't really focusing on it," Ron answered, looking up at him. "It just kind of happened."

"Ah, look!"

Ron glanced back down at his hand; the last edges of the nazar still showed above his skin, but a second later it completely disappeared into his palm, leaving a ring of red dots.

"I guess a watched pot never boils," Jake replied, sitting back down.

"Huh," Ron said. "Last time it hurt like a son of a bitch. This time it just went right in, no questions asked."

"Maybe it likes you."

Ron reached for the vial and uncorked it. "You gonna keep an eye on me, right?"

"Right. Too bad I can't go with you."

"There's plenty of nazars here if you'd rather be the one."

"No, that's OK, you've had more experience with it. I might do it wrong."

"Fine. Just make sure I don't walk off the roof or impale myself on a piece of rebar."

"I'll watch you every second. And don't forget, you don't know how much time you have. Don't stop until you find it, then get out."

Ron looked once more at the vial, made up his mind, and tipped it into his mouth, swallowing it down with one gulp. "Huh," he said. "Tastes like cherries." He put the vial down, but before he could lean back in his chair, he felt lightheaded. His eyes closed.

"Looks like it's got a kick," he heard Jake say, sounding as though he was talking through an echo chamber many miles away.

When he opened his eyes, he was shocked to see two figures in the room standing near them, still and unmoving. Their expressions were zombie-like, dead and mindless, and their skin was a dull, sterile white – so white it was almost blue. They were watching and listening.

They've been in the room the whole time! Ron realized, suddenly terrified.

Are there more?

He turned to look toward the kitchen. Another figure was standing near the counter, staring down at the tiled floor. It was silent and still, as though it was glued to the spot.

Suddenly he wanted to know how many more were in the house, and where. He stood, feeling curiously light; normally his left knee would complain when he rose, but this time his knee felt fine. In fact, everything felt fine. No aches or pains, no sense of joints creaking, no balking muscles. He stopped, sidetracked by the sensation. *Lack of sensation,* he corrected himself, turning. He could see his body, eyes closed, sitting in the chair.

Fuck. I'm hallucinating.

He moved closer to himself, observing his face. He was sitting still, breathing slowly. His eyes didn't register anything.

Am I out here? he wondered. *Or am I in there, imagining this?*

"Ron?" he heard from the tunnel, far away and echoing. He turned to his friend, sitting across from him; Jake was watching his body intently, not seeing where he actually was, a couple of feet away. "You gone, Ron? Good luck, buddy."

Thanks, he replied, but he knew the word didn't really form, wasn't expressed as real sound that his friend could hear.

A shuffling noise to his right made him turn toward the ghostly figures in the room. Both of them were staring at him now, as though they were aware something had changed, some new consciousness was now present.

They realize they're not hidden, Ron thought, beginning to grasp what was happening to him. *They realize I can see.*

The disorientation he felt was suddenly replaced by anxiety, as he remembered that there was a time limit to the stuff Abe had given him. *What was I supposed to do?* he wondered. The memory of his task felt elusive, just at the edge of his ability to focus, and that if he reached for it, it might slip farther away. He tried to eliminate all of the new stimuli, and concentrate.

Basement. Basement. I'm supposed to find a basement.

He walked, but found his feet didn't carry weight, and they didn't seem to touch the floor. He moved into the dining room, but moved wasn't the right word...more like drifted. Another figure was there, a woman with beautiful, long hair that reached to her shoulders. She stood in one corner, staring intently at the dining table as though she was a paid sentry assigned to monitor it. He walked toward her, wanting a closer look. As he crossed her line of sight, she seemed to register his presence, and her eyes broke from the table, lifting to look at him.

The woman was dressed in clothes from another generation. A strand of pearls circled her neck, and her nails looked freshly painted a faint, dull red color that contrasted against the sterile blue emanating from her skin. The wrinkles on her face seemed more from decay than old age; she still had her features, although her pasty blue-white skin made her look sick. When their eyes met, Ron was worried how she might respond.

She looks confused, he thought. *She doesn't understand. She's never seen this before, whatever I am right now. I probably looked confused, too.*

Basement, the back of his mind signaled. *The clock is ticking.*

He looked down, seeing only the floor. *How do I find it?*

As he moved from room to room, he encountered more ghostly figures, all standing perfectly still, arranged like a bizarre art installation. They seemed to realize he was there, but they didn't move from their spots. They just appeared addled, as though they weren't sure how to respond to what they were sensing.

Nothing on the ground floor looked like anything resembling an entrance to a basement, and he realized he needed to concentrate, and stop becoming distracted by the figures that were all over the house. *Basements are below the ground floor,* he thought. *What's below now?*

The crawlspace.

He moved to the front door, sliding across the floor. When he reached for the handle, he felt his hand pass through it, unable to grasp the metal surface. Momentum from his movement carried him forward, and his hand passed through the door, disappearing behind the wood.

Fuck me! he thought.

He easily passed through the door and wound up standing on the front porch. It was early evening, still light, and he made his way around the front of the bay windows, realizing he couldn't feel the temperature. On the far side of the porch he saw the hatch, cut into the planks. He reached out to lift it up, surprised when his fingers passed through the composite boards.

If I can't lift it, how do I get down there?

Ah, he realized. *Like the door; just pass through. Through the deck. Just go down.*

He intended to go down, but nothing happened. Accustomed to motion by the use of his legs, he didn't understand how to initiate the unusual direction he wanted, and his mind rebelled at the idea of throwing himself on the floor. He tried moving his legs again, finding this only carried him along the porch laterally.

Confused, he tried kneeling. *My hand went through the door when I reached for it,* he thought. *Maybe it can...*

He extended his hand toward the decking, surprised as it passed through to the space beyond. He kept pushing, extending his forearm, bending over as more and more of his arm passed through. Then he added the other arm, and decided if it would allow him to keep bending, he could just dive down. He tipped his head and pressed it against the boards of the patio, feeling no resistance.

A moment later, he was hovering inside the crawlspace, drifting to the wet ground. He twisted himself, trying to orient his feet downward, hoping he didn't continue falling right into the earth itself.

Winding up in China, he thought, laughing to himself at the insanity of what he was experiencing. *I am surely high. I am sitting back in the living room, high as a kite.*

The ground seemed to offer something to right himself on, so he stood, finding there was about four feet available. When he was fully upright, his head rose above the decking and he could see the front porch. When he bent, he remained under it, the dark dampness enveloping his senses.

He'd ventured here once before, and he had a rough idea of the honeycomb of areas, almost like little rooms under the house. He moved through each one, scanning the ground for something that looked like a basement, or the entrance to one. Instead, all he saw was dirt and pooled water. Occasionally a section of insulation had fallen, hanging in the air from the floor above, and he made a note to come back down with a staple gun.

Nearly ready to give up and try ascending to the floor above, he reached the back corner of the house, where it looked as though raccoons might have lived; small items scattered about, torn and shredded. He was grateful that his sense of smell seemed to not work, grateful that he couldn't detect the odor of their defecation. *This needs to get cleaned up,* he thought, making another mental note.

As he turned to leave, a horizontal line appeared to his right, just inside the exterior wall of the foundation. He approached it, surprised at how odd it looked; he wasn't sure what he had expected, but he knew this wasn't it. It wasn't glowing, or pulsing, or emanating anything that would give away its nature; it simply sat in the air six inches off the ground, hanging like a surface-less, unreflecting rod, black and ominous and unlike anything he had ever seen.

The transition?

He approached it, wondering if it was safe. *Abe said to go into the basement,* he thought. *I've got to try, regardless.*

He reached out, letting his fingers touch the rod. They disappeared into it; he felt nothing beyond.

Goddamn, he thought. *Am I really going to do this?*

More of his hand slipped into the void. He knew if he let himself stop and rationally consider what was happening, he'd freak out and the whole thing would be over. He'd return to himself up in the living room, look at Jake, and have nothing to show for it.

He forced his mind to let go, to relax, and stood up. His head accidentally rose above the crawlspace, and he could see into the kitchen, three inches above the tiles on the floor. He lowered himself, and the crawlspace came back. The rod was still there, hanging in the air.

Why not, he thought, stepping forward, letting a foot disappear into the transition. *I've been on all the rides up here.*

Down he went, having the sensation of steps under his feet. He had the distinct urge to hold his breath as his head passed through the bar.

The basement was about twenty feet square, lined with old wooden cabinetry. Something glowed faintly from within the wood; he wasn't able to study much of it before the figures in the room came into focus, sending a chill down his spine. At least forty or fifty of the entities were here, crammed into the space, milling about mindlessly in the center of the room like caged zombies. Something dark moved among them, a figure that didn't look like the others. It passed between the shambling ghosts as though it was checking on them, inspecting them.

Ezra! Ron thought, suddenly terrified as he realized he'd completely forgotten to perform Terrell's invocation. The dark entity was moving slowly, its head turned away, drifting over the ground.

Time to leave, he thought, and turned. A set of wooden stairs was before him, apparently how he'd entered. He began to make his way up, hoping he hadn't been detected. He was tempted to stop and look back, wondering if the entity might have seen him. *The ghosts upstairs picked up on my presence,* he thought. *Did any of the ones down here?* He resisted the temptation and didn't turn. The sensation of running without moving crept through him as he tried to ascend; it was like a dream where traction was slight and progress was much slower than intended. At the top of the stairs only darkness appeared; he trusted they'd lead back through the transition, and kept pushing, kept trying to rise.

As his head slowly passed into the crawlspace, he felt dizzy and disoriented, as though he'd had too much to drink. He wanted to lie down, to press his head against a pillow and sleep it off, knowing his mind wasn't far from shutting down.

He finished ascending, and the rest of his form cleared the horizontal bar that hung in the air. *I won't make it back to the living room before I pass out,* he thought. For a moment he considered drifting directly up and into the kitchen, but quickly rejected the idea, fearful the effect would wear off while he was mid-way through, and he'd become trapped, cut in half by the floor.

He started the trek back through the rooms of the crawlspace, each step feeling heavy, every movement requiring tremendous effort. *I'll have to pass up through the decking anyway,* he thought. *That's how I came down, drifting through the boards. I could get trapped there, too.*

He stumbled forward, expecting to feel the cold ground as his face hit the dirt. Instead the images from the crawlspace receded, quickly replaced by a darkness that shut down his vision.

Moments later, he opened his eyes. Jake was sitting on the couch across from him, looking at his phone. Ron tried moving a toe, grateful to feel it scrape inside his shoe. Pushing down on his thighs, he stood. His left knee popped and sent a brief shot of pain down his leg.

I'm back! he thought. *Thank god.* "Good thing I didn't need your help," he said. "I'd hate to tear you away from Facebook."

"I was watching!" Jake replied, slipping his phone into his pocket. "I can do more than one thing at a time, you know. Well?"

"First off," Ron answered, "there's two ghoulish pieces of shit in this room with us right now. One was standing there, and the other was by you, there."

"You're kidding," Jake replied, his face suddenly serious, sliding on the couch in the opposite direction from where Ron was pointing. "Tell me you're fucking with me."

"No, not fucking with you. They're here, no shit. There's one or two in every room of the house."

"Every room?"

"They just stand there, looking around. Like sentinels."

"Fuck. That's fucked up, man."

"And in the basement, there's dozens. Maybe fifty or so, all crammed together like sardines. And why didn't you remind me to do that damned invocation thing? The Terrell thing?"

"You mean before you drank the stuff? I just figured you'd do it once you were in there."

"I think I was supposed to do it before."

"Were you seen? By whatever's in the basement?"

"I don't know. There was something else with them; might have been Ezra."

"What did he look like?"

"I couldn't see any features. All these ghouls were standing there, kind of shuffling around. Ezra was a little taller and darker than the others, moving around between them. When I realized I forgot the invocation, I just turned tail and ran. And then passed out."

"So, you don't know if you were seen or not?"

"I don't think so. I moved fast, but I have no way of knowing for sure." A wave of nausea hit him, along with a headache that felt like a chisel pounding into his left temple. He ran to the kitchen, arriving at the sink just in time to throw up.

Jake was at his side a moment later. "You OK, buddy? You don't look so good."

"I feel like shit. Let's call Abe and get it over with...I need to sleep."

Chapter Twenty-One

Ron sat holding his head as Jake dialed Port Orchard. Once it began to ring, Jake placed his phone on the coffee table between them. After a few moments, Terrell's voice came on.

"Terrell," Jake said, "it's Jake and Ron. He went to the basement."

"Hold on, I'm at Abe's...let me go get him," Terrell replied, and the phone became muffled for a moment. Soon Terrell's voice returned. "Alright, Abe's here. Go ahead."

"Tell me what you saw," Abe added.

Ron leaned forward to speak. His head was pounding and he wanted to lie down, but knew he needed to soldier through and finish with Abe first. "I found the transition; it was in the crawlspace like you guessed. Went down into it. There were forty or fifty things in there, they..."

"Things?" Abe said, cutting him off. "Be more specific."

"I don't know, ghosts. Ghouls. They were shuffling around like zombies, pacing like they had nothing to do."

"Like animals in a cage?"

"Kinda like that. Drugged up animals."

"OK, go on."

"They all looked the same; faintly glowing, bluish, a little translucent…"

"So, like ghosts?" Abe asked.

"I guess," Ron answered, feeling frustrated. "What the fuck do ghosts look like, exactly? I don't know."

"Did they look like the entities you've seen before, the ones you saw outside the house at night?"

Ron thought back. "Yeah. They did. They almost look like a projection, like there's a movie projector somewhere, making them appear. But there's no screen."

"Ghosts," Abe confirmed. "Continue."

"Anyway, there was something moving between them. It was dark, like a shadow. Blocked the light. Couldn't make out features, but I think it might have been Ezra."

"The thing you saw in the bedroom the night Terrell was there?"

"Yes, exactly like that."

"OK, think…was there anything else?"

Ron replayed his visit downstairs in his mind. The pain in his head made it unpleasant; requiring his brain to function in a specific way was at odds with what his mind currently wanted to do. "I don't know, it was all so weird…"

"Did you see anything else in the room?" Abe prompted. "Was there anything unusual about the space?"

"Yeah, there were wood cabinets along the wall," Ron replied, the image of them returning momentarily. "They were glowing too, but it was different."

"How, different?"

"They weren't the cold blue of the ghosts…it was warmer, yellow, or orange."

"The cabinets were glowing?"

"No, not the cabinets themselves…it was something in them, in the wood. Some kind of writing."

"Symbols?"

"Might have been. But it seemed more like cursive writing, complete words. I don't remember what any of them said."

"You probably wouldn't have been able to read them, anyway. That's good enough, Ron. I think it confirms a few things."

Ron leaned back in his chair. The movement made his head pound more.

"Great," Jake spoke up. "Confirms what, exactly?"

"Well, I have constructed several theories about what might be happening," Abe replied. "You could have seen any number of things in that basement. Based on what you're telling me, it leads me to consider one of my theories as the most likely explanation. It was the one I suspected would be the case, but we had to be sure."

"Which is?" Jake asked, looking up at Ron, who had his eyes closed.

"I think you're dealing with a tactic of war," Abe replied. "Or, more precisely, the remnants of a tactic."

"War?" Jake repeated. "What war?"

"A war between that other family on your mountain, what were their names?"

"Coldwater," Ron offered. "And the Hugheses."

"Yes," Abe continued. "From the stories you told me, they had quite a dispute years ago. It seems likely to me that a war was launched between the two, and one of the weapons deployed by the Coldwaters is still active and working, kind of like an old, undetonated World War II bomb. People found many of them in fields, you know, years after the war ended. Very dangerous."

"A bomb?" Ron repeated, sounding a little confused. "The things in the basement are a bomb?"

"Not a bomb exactly," Abe answered. "They're a remnant, like a left over bomb. They're still working, performing their function…to scare away anyone living there. Even though the house they originally inhabited is gone, they're still there, protected in that basement, which is where I suspect they were originally staged. They're able to emerge from there and continue their work, and return to it for safety. The dark figure you saw, the one you said is named Ezra, he's in charge of them. He's like the captain, tending them, keeping them in line and ready to work."

"Ron said he saw a lot of them," Jake offered. "Where did they come from?"

"Well, they can't be manufactured out of whole cloth," Abe replied. "They had to be recruited from somewhere. Is there a graveyard nearby?"

"Mount Soltis cemetery," Ron said, "on the other side of the hill. Oldest cemetery in the McLean area. Hundreds of graves."

"That could be it," Abe replied.

"So, Ezra collected them?" Jake asked. "What, he just went to the graveyard and conjured them up?"

"Well," Abe said, "here's where my theory is going to get a little tricky. I suspect that Ezra was created by the Coldwaters for the purpose of keeping that collection of ghosts marshaled and focused with the sole purpose of haunting your property. I suspect he's been there for years, continuing this mission. I think he's a Volger, or a type of one."

"Volger," Jake repeated. "What's a Volger?"

"Think of it as an entity capable of controlling ghosts, directing them to do its bidding," Abe answered. "They are very powerful. Most ghosts are individual entities, caught in a loop of their own making, or the result of some extreme experience, like a murder or some other kind of strong, emotional death. They operate within that experience, forever reliving it, haunting the area where it occurred because of the energy generated by the nature of their death. However, the ghosts on your property aren't there because of any such thing; they were resurrected, in a way, and brought there with the intent of haunting you, of haunting the people who used to live there, to scare them away, drive them crazy, that type of thing. Keeping that many ghosts corralled and organized requires not only the energy to resurrect and maintain them, it also requires energy to keep them focused on the mission they've been resurrected to accomplish. In this case, the Volger is fulfilling that role. They're very suited for such a purpose, and I've read cases of them being used in this manner to great effect."

Ron leaned back in his chair. Although the pounding in his head continued, he felt as though he'd heard the first solid idea that might lead to solving things. It gave him hope. *It's a totally insane idea,* he thought, *but at least it's an answer.*

If *Abe's right.*

"Are you sure?" Ron asked. "I mean, Terrell thought it was all kinds of things."

"Terrell isn't very experienced," Abe replied. "I can't say my theory is correct for sure, but I think it's highly likely, particularly since you've confirmed the first part of it with your sojourn into the basement. And if it is, the good news is that there is something you can do about it."

Ron sat up, lowering his hands from his head, looking at the phone. "What?"

"Well, as I said, a great deal of energy is required to keep this all going," Abe replied. "The Volger is supplying the energy to the ghosts, no doubt, but the Volger itself requires energy to continue its work. Volgers are implemented in several ways, but the most common method is a type of separation tension. If your Volger has been created this way, it's relatively easy to end it. Once you end it, its energy will dissipate, and it will be unable to control the ghosts. They will disband and make their way back to the cemetery."

"How?" Ron asked. "How do we end it?"

"Separation tension is created by splitting an entity in two," Abe replied. "The dark entity you see in the basement, the one you've met and talked to, is half of the whole. The other half is somewhere else. The separation of the two halves is what causes the energy; if you reunite them in some way, the tension is relieved and the energy goes away."

"I can guess where the other half is," Jake offered. "Coldwater mansion."

"A very good supposition," Abe replied. "That's where I'd look."

"Are you saying we have to move one of these halves to the other?" Ron asked. "Like, get the one in the basement to go back to Coldwater mansion?"

"No, there is a simpler way to shut down the separation," Abe replied. "The half in your basement is not a physical entity, but the other half, wherever it is, will definitely be physical. Make sure you take a sharp knife with you, and pull out an eye. Cut its stalk, and bring it back to your basement. When the physical Volger sees its non-physical half, the tension will start to unravel. As long as your half can't find the physical half, it will lose control and die off."

Ron began to shake his head a little. "That's crazy."

"What if it finds the physical half?" Jake asked.

"How far away is it?" Abe asked.

"Two miles as the crow flies, maybe more," Jake answered.

"It will never travel that far," Abe replied. "It may search a few hundred feet, but if it's not right there, it won't have the energy to travel."

"Listen to yourself," Ron said. "It'll see itself through a severed eye? Seriously? This sounds like bullshit, Abe."

"It will work," Abe replied. "Well, at least that's what I've read. No tension will exist if it realizes its other half. The energy is created by that lack of knowledge, the mental separation. Once the Volger is reunited in this way, the energy ends and the entity in your basement will die off. The basement will return to normal, which means the ghosts currently under its control will be free to leave. None of them want to be there, I assure you. Well, most, I would expect. There might be one or two laggards who've grown accustomed to the place, but Terrell can help you get rid of those. With the Volger gone, the threat to those of us with the gift will be gone, too. You will have diffused the bomb, so to speak."

"So, that's your theory?" Ron asked. "We need to find the other half of this entity, cut out its eye, and bring it back to the basement? Then it'll be over?"

"That's my best guess," Abe replied. "And with the ghosts gone, your family can move in and not receive a scare every night. Unless you'd like to reconsider and just live with the scares. I can't guarantee they're completely benign, though; could frighten you into walking off a balcony or stabbing someone by mistake."

"No," Jake replied. "We've already seen something along those lines. Too risky."

"Listen," Ron said, still trying to wrap his brain around Abe's insane idea. "I have a hard time imagining this thing is going to just sit there while we cut out its eye."

"Oh, right!" Abe replied. "You are absolutely correct; I forgot to tell you this part. The physical half may, indeed, fight back. The good news is that it's easy to mesmerize. One of you will need a strobe, a portable one, one that you can carry with you. Use the strobe on it until it seems frozen. Let it sit like this for a full minute; it'll slowly become more and more entranced, and once its fully mesmerized, you can do just about anything you want to it. Pull out an eye and cut it off. When you douse the strobe, it'll take a few seconds for the Volger to regain its senses. Make sure you're gone by then."

Ron paused for a moment and looked up at Jake. His friend was nodding, seemingly satisfied with Abe's diagnosis. Ron wasn't at all sure of his own feelings about it; his headache was making analytical thinking painful. "OK, Abe," he finally said. "I guess we go to the mansion and find this thing."

"Take a supply of the nazars with you," Abe offered. "They will be required for you to see and interact with what you find. Don't use the bottle I gave you while you're there, though. You need to save that for your final confrontation in the basement."

"Alright," Jake replied. "Anything else?"

"Good luck!" Abe offered, "and let me know how it goes. Or, rather, call Terrell and let him know."

The line went dead. Silence filled the room for a few moments as the two men considered what they'd been told. Ron ran it over in his mind; each step that Abe described was becoming more and more ludicrous the more he thought about it.

He glanced at his friend. "This is totally batshit crazy, you know that?"

Jake smiled. "I know. But we're gonna do it, right?"

Ron didn't respond. His head hurt too much to think about it.

"Right?" Jake asked again.

"You sound like you want to."

"Well, this thing is fucking up your life, so, yeah, isn't that what we've been trying to do? Get rid of it?"

"By breaking and entering, mesmerizing some kind of creature, cutting out its eye, and bringing it back here. That sound logical to you?"

"Uhh..." Jake replied, "...well, when you say it that way, no, but what else are we going to do?"

He stood up, shuffling toward the stairs. "I'm going to sleep. Ask me again in the morning."

- - -

As he waited for Grace to pick up, Ron wondered why he felt desperate.

Is this like those scenes in movies, where the hero says goodbye to all his loved ones before he goes off to slay the dragon? In case he doesn't survive?

He already tried to reach Elenore, but the call went to voice mail. He left her a message, just saying hello, no emergency, just wanting to hear her voice. It was unlikely she'd return the call until later, probably that night.

He knew Jake was waiting for him downstairs, but he needed time for just one more call.

"Hello, Grace? Hi, it's Ron. Just wondering if Robbie is around. Sure."

He waited while Grace took the phone down to the basement room where his son was staying, wondering how far he should go: *Do I tell him I'm about to do something stupid? That I may never see him again?*

"Hey, son! How are you, bud?...uh huh...she said that? Then you should probably do it, she's in charge until you come up here to the new house...soon, buddy, real soon. You want to come?...good, I think you'll like it here....listen, I wanted to..." He paused.

What exactly did you want to accomplish with this call? he wondered.

"...I just wanted to see how you are, see if everything's OK....sounds like it is...it sure is good to hear your voice."

Don't scare the kid. Don't make him think something is wrong, don't cause him to worry.

"OK...yes, soon...it sounds like everything is fine...yeah, soon, buddy. The house is almost ready for you...just keep minding Grandma and I'll be up there to bring you down, OK? Schoolwork first, right?...good, good...I love you, son."

His son's reply was a quick, cursory "I love you" that signaled the end of the call. He wanted it to be more; he wanted it to represent the deep connection he felt toward the child, and the fear he had of losing that connection. *You can't expect more than that,* he thought. *You only wanted to hear his voice, and to say the words, so that if something bad happens, at least he heard them from you. That's all.*

The phone on the other end was handed off to Grace and Ron gave her a quick update, then hung up.

He sat on the edge of the bed, feeling a little hollow. The words had been said, but, aside from Jake, he felt alone in what he was about to do. Elenore was too busy to return his call; he wouldn't hear from her until after he and Jake were done with the task. And Robbie, well, his son sounded fine, although he clearly wanted to come to the house. Neither of them was the slightest bit aware of the insane things he was about to do.

Or how frightened he felt.

He stood up and slipped the phone into his pocket, then headed downstairs where Jake was waiting.

- - -

"I don't see the house or the dogs," Ron said, rising in his seat, trying to peer ahead. There was a slight hill in Yate's Court, obscuring whatever was beyond.

"And I don't see any left turn," Jake replied, looking out the driver side window as he slowly inched his truck forward. "Dogs that live in quiet areas like this pick up on sounds easily. They're gonna hear the tires on the gravel."

"Just go slow," Ron said, still inches off the passenger seat, trying to see beyond the rise in the road. "It's got to be there. Might look overgrown. Wait...wait, there it is, twenty feet up." He pointed.

Jake moved the truck forward slowly, taking care to not rev the engine or make more noise than necessary. Tension inside the cab was already high, and they hadn't even reached the Coldwater mansion yet. Both of them were on alert, their senses sharp.

As the truck inched forward, Ron strained his ears, listening for barking. "So far so good," he said.

"I really do not want my paint scratched," Jake said.

"I'm more concerned about anyone knowing we are here."

A sign appeared on the right, partly hidden by vines and overgrowth. "No Trespa" appeared on the left half of it, the right obscured, and under that "Private Pr".

"If they really cared about people not coming down their driveway," Jake said, "they'd make sure that sign wasn't covered up."

"Maybe they're just lazy."

"I'll sue if those dogs scratch it. I just had it done last year."

The small turn to the left was a narrow road, scattered with blackberry vines that stuck out from the sides, crisscrossing the path. "Fuck!" Jake said, as he turned the truck. "More shit to scratch at my paint job!"

"It's just blackberries," Ron replied, realizing his friend was as amped up as he'd ever seen him.

The truck started down the constricted path. Plants scraped against the side of the vehicle, and Ron watched as his friend winced and complained.

"They've got *huge* thorns!" Jake said, his face tightening and contorting in response to the slaps and scrapes along the side of the truck.

"They catch on clothes but I doubt they can hurt paint," Ron replied, not entirely sure he was right.

The uneven road made the truck bounce left and right as they slowly crawled down it. Ron turned to look out the back window, to see if dogs were on their trail. He watched as the long blackberry branches snapped back into place as they cleared the truck, swinging obnoxiously in the air. He'd been on the receiving end of swinging stalks; he knew how they could sink into skin and lodge their thorns, producing a nasty cut when they pulled free.

"No dogs," he said. "I think we've cleared the Yates place without being detected."

"Fuck!" Jake spat as a loud scrape worked its way down the left side of the truck. "If I get out and this paint job is all fucked up, I am going to be *sooo* pissed."

"It'll be fine," Ron said, turning back to look out the front windshield.

"Logging road my ass. You couldn't get a logging truck down this thing if you wanted to."

"Abandoned logging road. Probably wider years ago."

It took a couple of minutes fighting against the blackberries before the road emerged onto a slightly more open path that ran left and right. Slight ruts and the absence of trees were the only indication that it was even a road, and green moss growing in the ruts gave the impression that it was rarely used.

"This must be Barlow," Ron said.

"Not much of a road."

"Turn left."

Jake maneuvered the truck off the old logging route, bouncing through a ditch and climbing up to the wider road's surface. "Thank god," he said. "No blackberries. And all that bouncing around was making me sick. And claustrophobic."

"She said a hundred yards, couldn't miss it," Ron replied, looking down at the note Mrs. Hughes had provided. He realized the scrawled map didn't have any orientation or landmarks, making it almost useless.

After a minute had gone by, Jake said, "A hundred yards...sure seems like we've past the length of a football field."

"Yeah, it does…go a little farther."

Jake slowly rolled down the level road, but no house appeared.

"There was something that looked like a turn back there on the right," Ron said, looking in the mirror. "Based on her instructions I thought we'd see the house from this road, but maybe she forgot a turn."

Jake put the truck into reverse and slowly backed up. "She is old."

"And everything seems overgrown."

Ron zeroed in on a faint path that ran between two large trees. "Doesn't look like much, but there is a culvert. This might be it. It's the only thing even close to a hundred yards."

"Great," Jake said, shifting into drive and turning to the right. "More blackberries."

They forced the truck through the overgrowth. The forest became thick on either side, with new growth – hundreds of narrow tree trunks – blocking the view in any direction other than forward. More long blackberry stalks reached out into the path, forcing Jake to push past them, their sharp barbs ringing down the sides of the vehicle as they progressed. Some seemed capable of making louder noises than others, and Jake's entire body contorted in response, as though he personally felt each one.

Ron watched out the front, hoping to see some sign of a house ahead. The last thing he wanted was to wind up lost.

Then, in the same way his home suddenly appeared at the end of his driveway, the Coldwater mansion came into view, revealed in the distance as they passed the last of the overgrowth and entered a clearing. Ron felt a tingle at the back of his neck as the structure he'd heard so much about was now before his eyes. It slowly morphed into dread.

"Fuck," Jake muttered. "It's huge."

A three plank wooden fence marked the edge of what had once been a large grass yard. While some boards had rotted and fallen from their posts, it was mostly intact, effectively stopping the truck at a gate which was kept closed by a thick chain, padlocked.

"The wire cutters we brought aren't going to cut through that," Jake said, stopping the vehicle.

"No problem," Ron replied. "We walk from here."

They got out, and while Jake inspected the paint on the side of his truck, Ron opened the backpack they brought, double-checking its contents: a large pair of shrub shears with sixteen inch blades, a set of wire cutters, a rubber-handled machete they picked up earlier that morning at a hardware store in McLean, two flashlights, and a hand-held strobe that worked on batteries. He closed it up; the blades of the shears, too long to fit completely in the pack, poked out the top.

He slung it over his shoulder and joined Jake, who was running his fingers over a faint line on the driver's side door.

"See, no damage," Ron said. "They're sharp and do a number on skin, but they're too soft to damage paint."

"This mark wasn't here before," Jake worried, pointing at the indistinct line.

Ron licked a finger and rubbed it against the mark; it faded and disappeared. "And it's not there now. Just a smudge."

"Humpf," Jake snorted. He licked a finger too, and rubbed at the line just to confirm; it came off after a moment. "Fine."

They walked to the right of the gate, where a fallen top board made it easy to scale the wooden fence. Jake went over first; Ron handed him the backpack, then followed. Beyond, the grass was three feet high, as high as the species could grow before turning to seed. The road past the gate was overgrown with weeds that filled in all available space, almost making it disappear.

Ahead, the Coldwater mansion rested in the morning sun, hulking against a green forest backdrop. Nonnative deciduous trees, planted in front of the house at intervals, had all died. At one point in time they might have shaded the house, but now their grey, leafless arms reached up, branching in all directions like withered hands, obscuring little. The front facade was dramatic, with a large two-story window above the front double doors.

They walked toward the house, stepping carefully through the tall grass. "Are those windows black?" Jake asked. "I can't really tell with the sun at this angle."

"Hard to say," Ron replied. "Have to get closer."

A chain link fence had been erected ten feet in front of the house. Green ivy and more blackberries had taken over large sections of it, causing it to lean in a couple of places, giving the impression the plants wanted to tear it down. As they approached the fence, Ron saw that it ran to the left and curved; there were more buildings in that direction, all behind the protection of the chain link. Mrs. Hughes hadn't mentioned them, but seeing their shape in the distance, he guessed there might be a garage, or a shed.

"Got those wire cutters?" Jake asked.

Ron sat the backpack on the ground, and his friend opened it to retrieve the tool. It didn't take him long to make two dozen snips into the section of fence in front of them, and Jake pulled it back so Ron could pass under. Once Ron was through, Jake pushed the fence forward, and Ron grabbed it from the inside, lifting to return the favor.

They turned to look at the facade once again. "Does it seem like it suddenly got a lot bigger?" Jake asked. "Like, from outside the fence, to here?"

"Yeah," Ron agreed. He took a few more steps and found himself in the shade of the structure, making it much easier to examine.

"Definitely black," Jake said, joining him. "The windows."

A six pane window, right of the main doors and straight ahead of where they were standing, looked completely dark. Ron walked up to it, pushing through a dead shrub until he was able to reach out and touch the glass. He ran his fingers down it, then examined them. Although they came back with a film of dirt, it didn't account for how dark the windows appeared to be. "It's like they were painted from the inside," he said, showing Jake his fingers.

A thump made him jump, and he turned to look back at the window, as though he might be able to see through the dark panes and determine what caused the noise. "Did you hear that?"

"I did," Jake replied. "Came from inside."

"Well," Ron said, stepping back from the windows, "whoever is in there, they know we're here."

"If it's a who," Jake replied.

Ron walked to the steps of the front porch and approached the doors. He grabbed the large wrought iron handle, pressed down on the latch, and pulled on the door. When it didn't open, he grabbed harder and began to tug back and forth, making the double doors shake inside their frames, but failing to budge.

"You didn't really expect that to open, did you?" Jake asked.

"No, just seemed stupid not to give it a shot. Can you imagine walking all around this thing looking for a way in when we might have just waltzed in the front door?"

Another thump came from inside; this one sounded as though it was just on the other side of the door.

"Hello?" Ron called out. "Is anyone home?"

The doors suddenly began to shake, in imitation of the tugging Ron had just performed. They jostled back and forth, increasing in intensity until they were moving with even more force than he'd used on them, rumbling and vibrating as though they might come apart.

Both Ron and Jake stepped back on the porch, putting space between themselves and the doors, unsure if they might suddenly blow open.

"Fuck!" Jake exclaimed. "What the fuck did you do?"

"You saw what I did."

"Did it cause that?"

The doors continued to shake, as though something angry was on the other side, tugging on the handle, moments from breaking them down.

Then, just as suddenly, it stopped.

"Hello?" Ron said again, stepping forward to approach the door.

"Don't call to it!" Jake said, pulling him back.

Ron shrugged off his friend. "Hey, you, inside! Open up! We're coming in!"

"Don't tell it what we're going to do!" Jake implored, cringing.

Ron turned to his friend. "I think it already knows."

"Don't antagonize it, then. Don't get it all worked up!"

"*It?*" Ron asked. "What is *it*, Jake?"

"Whatever is shaking those goddamn doors!"

While the shaking doors seemed to have spooked Jake, they invigorated Ron. "I have no intention of letting this thing kowtow me, or scare me, or whatever its tactics are. Shaking the door like that, just after I did? It's an intimidation tactic. Get your game face on, buddy!"

Ron walked up to the front door, stopping an inch from the wood. "You hear me in there? I'm coming in!" He turned and walked across the porch and down the steps, then turned to look at Jake. "You coming?"

Jake pinched his eyes closed for a moment, as though he was trying to decide if he really wanted to go through with it. Finally they popped open, and Ron watched as he gave him a smile. "Against my better judgment."

"God, you've been whining all morning. Last night you couldn't wait to get started."

"Don't get all worked up, I'm coming."

Ron headed for the west end of the house, Jake following. He tried to look in windows as he went; they were all blackened over, concealing whatever was inside. Although the house had been painted white years ago, only flecks remained, peeled up from the greyish wood like tiny feathers. The facade was flat and long, interrupted by low shrubs that were dried and dead, while others were still green, surviving off rain.

At the corner, Ron turned and found that along this edge, the bramble had made its way to the siding. Using the machete, he hacked at the thorned branches that were attempting to climb the structure. There were fewer windows on this side, and most of them were on the second floor. Soon a door appeared, and Ron reached for the handle. It was locked.

"We could kick it in," Jake said.

"I was thinking we'd give them all a try, first. See if one opens. If that doesn't work, maybe a window."

"Just considering options," Jake replied, still following behind.

At the back of the house, the wings and courtyard came into view; two long structures extended from the front section of the mansion with a garden area nestled between the wings. A large stone fountain was in the center of the garden, now completely overgrown.

"Christ, she was right, this place is huge," Jake said. "What are we talking, twenty thousand square feet? Thirty?"

"At least," Ron replied, heading for a door at the end of the west wing. He reached for the handle and turned the knob; it was locked solid. Glass in the upper half of the door was opaque, black like all the others, blocking any view inside. He turned and walked toward the garden square, eyeing exterior walls of the west wing that lined the courtyard, looking for a way in. Another potential entrance appeared half way down the wing; it was two double glass doors, the panes of which were coated on the inside with the black film. The handle to the doors was smeared with a dark substance, and Ron reached out to try it, but stopped himself when his fingers were inches from the goo. "Maybe not," he said, trying to determine what the substance was before he touched it.

"I'll try," Jake offered, grabbing the handle and giving it a twist. It, too, was locked. He pulled his hand away and sniffed at it. "Whatever it is, it doesn't smell, thank god."

"This might be a good option for breaking in," Ron said, "if we can't find something easier. Just smash one of these panes of glass, reach in, and open the door from the inside."

"Should work," Jake agreed, wiping his hand on his jeans. "Nice and simple."

They continued around the house, scanning each section of exterior wall, looking for doors. There were many more; two in the center, and two more along the east wing. All were secure.

They rounded the back corner of the east wing, finally able to see some of the other structures on the property. A long, single story building sat in the distance, as well as two smaller buildings next to it. Between the buildings and where they were standing was a sea of bramble four feet high, making the structures seem inaccessible.

"I'm guessing that's a barn," Jake observed.

"Mrs. Hughes said something about horses," Ron replied, turning to hack his way through the blackberries that had grown against the east side of the house.

Another door appeared in the middle of this section, and Ron stopped to try it. The handle had received a good amount of direct sunlight and was very hot; he had to grab and twist quickly, then let go and try again. It, too, was locked.

They worked their way around the rest of the east side, winding up at the front once again. Ron was sweating from his work with the machete, and stopped for a moment to rest.

"Well, I say those glass doors," Jake offered. "The first ones we saw. Easiest way in. There was that door on the upper balcony in the back, but I don't feel like scaling the side of the house, do you?"

"I do not," Ron replied, wiping his brow. "The glass doors it is."

They walked around the house again, the process much easier with the path already cut. On the inside of the west wing they located the double glass doors and stood in front of them for a moment, considering the best approach.

"What do you think is behind all that black coating?" Jake asked, looking at the panes that comprised the doors.

"Well, if you believe Mrs. Hughes' grandmother," Ron replied, walking up to the door and using the handle of the machete to smash one of the panes, "it's a physical manifestation of a curse. Or did she call it an infection? I forget. Something like that." He used the tip of the machete to poke at the remaining shards of glass, taking note that the black coating on the back of the pane seemed to have disappeared, as though air from the outside had blown it away. The film on the inside of the unbroken surrounding panes, however, was still there.

When he finished, they both stared at the opening for a moment, neither one moving.

"You gonna reach in?" Jake asked.

"One of us will have to," Ron replied. He stooped to peer through the broken pane; the sunlight was too bright, making it impossible to see anything inside. He removed a flashlight from the backpack and pointed it through the hole, moving closer to it, trying to determine what was beyond. After unsuccessfully pointing it at various angles, he said, "Fuck it," and slipped his left hand inside, reaching to the right, where he assumed the lock would be.

His fingers landed on flat wood, and he moved them a little, searching. The longer he held his hand through the hole, the more he sensed something was there, on the other side, watching. With his fingertips he felt for metal shaped like a handle, probing for a smooth, cold texture, but the hair on the back of his hand was on high alert. It was such a vulnerable part of the body, with its veins and thin, tight skin. Its hairs were primed, ready to detect any faint wind or disturbance of air that might signal the approach of someone…ready to pull his hand out if he had to, if anything came close to touching him.

His fingertips hit something large, and he wrapped them around it, knowing he'd found the handle. He felt for the end, hoping it would be a simple lock he could turn to release the door. The raised ridge of cold metal told him he was on the right track; he pinched his thumb and finger together to grasp the ridge, making the top of his hand rise up a little, exposing its skin and hair and veins to whatever was standing on the other side, waiting, watching.

Does it understand what I'm doing? he thought. *It must. I told it I was coming in.*

He turned the ridge at the same time he felt something brush the back of his hand; it was something organic, but hard; he didn't know why, but cartilage came to mind. The lock snapped into a new position, and he pulled his hand out of the hole as quickly as he could.

"Careful," Jake said. "You cut yourself."

Ron looked at the back of his hand. The small red streaks running across his knuckles and tendons looked like tiny ridges, and felt very cold.

"That's not my blood," he replied. "Something touched me."

Jake bent to look through the hole. "You gotta be shitting me. You cut yourself on the glass."

"No," Ron said, rubbing at the marks until they came off, showing his friend. "Not my blood. It felt hard, but alive."

"Aww, fuck!" Jake replied, turning away. "Maybe this is a bad fucking idea, Ron. Are you sure?"

Ron reached for the door handle and twisted. This time it spun in his hand, and he pushed...the door opened and he let go, allowing it to swing inside until it stopped, hitting the wall.

For a moment, Ron thought he heard a whoosh of air, as though the mansion had been starved for oxygen and was taking a huge breath. Realizing he felt no motion, no rush of air around him, he wondered if his brain, heightened into a state of anxiety, was embellishing things, creating a sense of drama where none really existed. *It's just an empty old house*, he thought. *It doesn't breathe.*

But something touched me. The house may not be alive, but something inside definitely is.

Light spilled in from the outside, and he stepped up to the doorway, looking inside, wondering if the person – or thing – that touched him was close by. Dark carpet covered the floor, and dust swirled through the air. An unpleasant odor blew out, like stale cloth, sheets that had sat unused for too long. There was a wall ahead, and Ron lifted the flashlight; a square outline darkened the wallpaper, framing the spot where a picture had once hung. Two screws emerged in the center, each secured with a heavy sink.

No one was there.

Ron stepped in.

"Stinks," Jake observed, following closely behind.

The hallway they were in led to the left and the right; left appeared to continue to the end of the wing, while he assumed right would lead deeper into the house. Ron turned right and walked, using his flashlight to scan the walls; most artwork had been removed, but some furniture still remained; a set of columns that had once held planters, a small loveseat placed under an exterior window. The glass above it was dark and black, fighting to block the sunlight outside.

The hallway soon opened into a larger room. Recessions in the carpet showed where the legs of heavier furniture had once been placed. An intricate pattern of wallpaper still clung to the walls, seams beginning to show in some spots. Ron wondered exactly how long the house had been vacant.

Moving into the next area, they came upon a short tiled hallway with open doors; inside each was a small room with a closet and no furniture. A bathroom was next, followed by another large, open area with carpeting. There was a large stain near the center of the room.

"Wonder what caused that?" Jake said, his flashlight pointing at the stain. His voice sounded muffled, suppressed; Ron assumed it was due to the carpeting.

He turned his flashlight up to the ceiling. No markings appeared on the smooth paint, nothing that would indicate a drip. "Not water damage," he mumbled back, his words sounding as if he'd spoken them into a pillow.

Jake moved around the room, examining the walls with his flashlight. "Abe suggested we get in and out, fast," he said. "This place is so big, we need to pick up the pace."

Ron walked on. "And there's still a second floor to check out."

After encountering more hallways and rooms, they reached the front section of the house. A door on a double hinge led to the kitchen, where white tiled counters rimmed every wall. Above each counter were cabinets with glass doors, but the glass had been shattered, leaving only jagged edges imbedded in the frames.

"Look," Ron said. "They were all smashed."

"Vandals?"

"No glass on the floor, though," Jake replied. "It was cleaned up."

Along one side of the kitchen Ron found a door, the one they had tried while circling the west side of the house. A large piece of plywood had been nailed over it, secured by several two-by-fours. Ron examined the boards; thick screws held them to the molding.

"I don't think we'd have made it through there," Jake said, looking over his shoulder, "even if we had tried to kick it in."

"Probably not."

The kitchen bent in an L shape, and after passing through it, they came to another large room that held a long table.

"Dining room," Ron said, walking around it. "No chairs."

"That thing looks heavy," Jake replied. "I wouldn't have wanted to move it, either."

A muffled thump came from overhead; it sounded as though something had fallen over and hit the floor above. Both Ron and Jake jumped, and looked up.

"That wasn't just the house creaking," Jake said. "Something's up there."

A series of lighter thumps followed, like steps running away from the original thump, becoming softer and softer until they disappeared.

"You still got that machete?" Jake asked.

"It's in the pack."

"Give it to me."

Ron lowered the pack from his back and removed the blade, handing it to Jake. "So, listen, you look a little wired up."

"A little?" Jake replied, brandishing the machete in the air in front of him.

"I'd appreciate it if you didn't mistake me for something else and accidentally take off one of my arms."

"Of course not," Jake replied, glancing at him, then swirling the blade in the air, producing swishing sounds. "If this house has been abandoned as long as it has, who knows what we might run into in here. All kinds of ghosts and shit."

"You do realize, traditionally, a machete isn't going to work on a ghost. As far as I know."

"I don't expect it to," Jake replied. "There might be physical threats. Dogs, or raccoons. Might be rabid. Or squatters. Squatters with guns."

"Uh huh," Ron replied, swinging the pack onto his back. "Just keep that blade away from me." He looked into the next room. "You first. I'm not standing in front of you with that thing in your hands."

Jake took the lead and they moved on. Whereas the wallpaper in other areas bore the outlines of artwork that had previously hung there, the outlines in this room framed taller structures.

"There used to be bookcases in here," Ron observed as they moved through the room. "A library, maybe."

Jake, brandishing the machete in front of him, pressed on, entering a large, two story entryway. To their left was the front door of the mansion. They eyed it with suspicion, looking at the handle. Ron knew they were both thinking the same thing: *who shook the doors?*

Behind them the entryway continued, halls leading to the left and right wings. At the end, large glass windows looked out upon the garden court, and to their right, another hallway.

They left the front door and walked through the entryway, toward the large windows. Ron realized it wasn't a hallway down by the windows, but a wide staircase leading up. Once they reached it, he saw that it, too, was lined with windows all along on the left side, and on the right were nails and wire where more frames had once hung. He imagined that when the sun was at mid-day, this area must have been very pleasant and airy; sunlight streaming in, the garden outside on full display. *A great design,* he thought. *Strolling up the stairs must have been enjoyable.*

Now, however, all of the windows were blacked out; faint lines of light eked in around each pane, not enough to illuminate, just enough to highlight the outline of the glass. With both of their flashlights shining up the stairs, the landing at the top was barely visible. Ron guessed the stairs must crest into an open area, because no wall was visible beyond.

Another faint thump in the distance reached their ears. Ron thought it came from upstairs, but his friend was looking the other way, back down the entryway.

"You heard that?" Jake asked.

"Of course I did. Sounded like it came from upstairs again. Maybe that same spot we heard before."

"I thought it came from there," Jake replied, nodding toward the front door. "Like it was outside."

"No, it was definitely up there," Ron said, his flashlight still illuminating the stairs.

They paused, listening, the only sound their breathing. After a moment, Ron said, "Nothing. I don't hear anything more."

"Me either."

"Are we going up?" Jake asked.

"Haven't finished the other side of the house," Ron said. "My OCD says we should finish this floor first, then go up."

"My desire to not run into whatever is up there agrees with you," Jake replied.

They turned, taking the hallway that led into the eastern wing of the mansion.

"You haven't used one of the nazars yet, have you?" Jake asked, as they passed empty room after empty room.

"No."

"Well, since you have to use one of them to see shit, maybe you should. Maybe we passed the thing we're looking for already, back there in the kitchen or the rooms on the other side, and didn't realize."

"I don't think so, but I'll use one if you want." Ron stopped walking and opened the backpack. He'd stored a handful of the small, round objects in a plastic container, which he opened, removing one and sealing up the others.

"This isn't going to incapacitate you, is it?" Jake asked. "I don't want to have to carry you around."

"I don't think so. It didn't the first time I used one; I was still able to walk just fine. It was when I drank that stuff Abe gave me that I left my body."

"And we're saving that for later."

"Yeah."

They both stared at Ron's outstretched hand, waiting for it to dissolve.

"Don't watch it," Ron said, as Jake raised his face to look him in the eyes. "It doesn't do its thing if you're watching it directly, remember. You have to look away, become distracted."

"Oh, yeah, right," Jake replied, then looked down again.

It was gone. A circle of little red dots on Ron's palm was rapidly fading.

"Little fucker works fast," Jake said. "Did you feel it go in?"

"No. Didn't feel anything. Didn't the last time, either."

"Is it working? Do you see anything?"

Ron looked around the hallway they were standing in, glancing into the two open doors before them.

"No," he replied. "Nothing. Come on, let's keep going."

The rest of the east wing's downstairs rooms were non-eventful, empty and quiet, without any indication of something odd or unusual. At the very end of the wing was a staircase leading up; it wasn't as wide as the one in the main part of the house, but it, too, was built with one side lined by windows that would have looked out over the yard, had they not been covered over with blackness.

They ascended. Whereas the central staircase had been carpeted, this one was not, and each step seemed to produce creaks and reverberations, as though the wood didn't appreciate their weight. As Ron was mid-way up, one step felt springy under him, and he wondered if it might give way; he decided to warn Jake about it.

"Careful of this one, it's a little…hey, how'd I let you get behind me with that blade? I can just see myself falling and impaling on it."

"Don't be so dramatic," Jake replied. "Not going to happen."

"You seem to forget that morning with the gun."

"I was dreaming then."

"We might both be dreaming now," Ron mused, continuing up. "Kinda feels like a dream."

"It's that thing in your system. I assure you, I feel very much alive and alert."

"Just don't get all freaked out with that thing in your hand."

"Jesus Christ, will you stop? I'm not going to cut you with it!"

They reached the top of the stairs. It was yet another open space, with a hallway leading away, down the upper floor of the wing. Ron stopped for a moment, thinking the light from his beam had caught movement in the distance; he focused his eyes, trying to make out whatever had caused it.

"You see something?" Jake whispered.

"There," Ron replied, whispering back. "Down this hallway. Can't tell if it's at the very end or not, too far away, but it's standing there."

"It's?"

"Looks like a person."

Jake squinted, his light joining Ron's. "I don't see anything."

"It's standing there, right in the middle, looking our way." He felt himself involuntarily shiver with the willies. "Damn, it's creeping me the fuck out."

Jake kept searching. "I can't see it. Must be the nazar. You can see it, I can't."

"Consider yourself lucky," Ron replied.

The figure down the hallway began to move, slowly coming toward them, and Ron felt the hair on the back of his neck stand in response. The light from their flashlights didn't seem to bother it in the slightest; it kept gliding over the floor, getting closer with each second. Ron could make out features on its face, and its eyes. Another chill went down his spine as he realized they were focused on him.

"It's a man," he said. "He's seen us. He's coming our way."

"Fuck!" Jake said, starting to sound panicked. "What do we do?"

"Just wait," Ron replied. "Maybe he'll stop."

But the figure didn't stop. It kept moving, coming their direction, its eyes fixed on them. When it was ten feet from the end of the hallway, Ron took an involuntary step back. Jake noticed, and raised the machete.

"Hello?" Ron called, unsure of what else to do. "Hello? Are you…"

The figure froze.

"What?" Jake whispered. "What's it doing?"

"He stopped," Ron replied.

The head on the man twisted slightly, then righted. Ron thought he looked confused.

"I think he's surprised that I can see him," Ron whispered to Jake. "That I spoke to him."

Without turning, the figure began to drift to the right until it reached the wall of the hallway. Ron kept watching as the man's shoulder entered the wall and disappeared; within seconds the rest of its body had passed through, gone.

"Fuck," Ron said. "It slid through that wall."

"Slid?"

"Just kind of drifted. Eerie as fuck."

"So, it went into that room?" Jake asked, pointing his flashlight at the first doorway down the hall.

"I guess so."

"What's it doing in there?"

"I don't know, Jake, I can't see through walls."

"Well, fuck, Ron," Jake said, his voice rising, holding out the machete. "Do we go down that hall? What do we do?"

Everything in Ron's rational mind told him that it was time to run, to abandon the effort. Entering the old house had bothered him a little, not because of what might be inside, but because of the guilt he felt at trespassing, at breaking in. The shaking, the thumps…they were all physical things, things his mind insisted must have a rational explanation; reminding himself of that had somehow kept his thinking focused on the goal, undeterred.

The ghostly figure of the man in the hallway, sliding through the wall…that was a different matter.

Now, suddenly, he felt like he'd wandered into the lion's den, the two of them potentially surrounded by any number of disturbing figures like the one he'd just seen. *The house could be full of them, like my house,* he thought. *Are they dangerous? Can they hurt us?* His thoughts left him feeling overwhelmed and outnumbered. Watching Jake wield his machete seemed pathetic; it might have worked to hack through the physical obstructions outside the house, but he suspected it would have no effect here, inside; it wasn't going to be a defense against an entity that could pass through walls.

"I don't know," he eventually replied to Jake, realizing that he sounded unsure, shaken. "I don't know what to do."

You weren't scared like this before the nazar, he thought. *You broke right in and walked through half the house without a care. It's suddenly witnessing these things that's affecting you. They were already here, you're just now able to see them, that's all. Pull your shit together. It's just more information than before. Same house, same goal. Just more information.*

He took a deep breath. "I guess we just push on."

Even though he preferred to have his friend in front of him, keeping the blade from behind his back, he stepped forward, feeling the need to lead. *You're the reason he's scared now,* he thought. *You're seeing things he's not meant to see. There's no need to tell him everything, to blow his mind like this. Edit yourself.*

He walked down the hallway to the first door on the right. If the entity he saw hadn't simply disappeared, but passed through the wall, it would be inside.

Stepping into the room, he felt Jake right behind him, and he took an extra step to make sure he was clear of his friend's blade. Then he looked around.

It was in the corner, looking at him, but it was different; in fact, it was so different, he wasn't sure it was the same creature. What he'd seen in the hall looked like a man – a regular, proportioned man – but the thing in the corner was distorted. Its face was longer – much longer. It looked as though its jaw had been stretched, forcing its mouth open. There were no teeth, just a large, gaping hole that stretched downward a foot or more. The features above it had stretched too; the eyes were shaped like eggs. The pupils inside were alive, though, very much alive: moving, focusing, looking at him.

"Well?" Jake asked. "Is it here?"

"No," he said, still staring at the corner, finding it hard to tear his eyes away from the bizarre apparition.

"You're lying. It's there, in that corner, isn't it?"

"You can see it?"

"I can see you're freaked out by something over there."

"OK, it's there."

"Why'd you say it wasn't?"

"Because it looks even more fucked up than before, and I'm trying not to freak you out."

"I'm fine," Jake said, standing up straight, lowering the machete a little. "You don't need to worry about me. I can handle myself."

"It's different now," Ron said. "It's shifted, it's…"

He stopped. The entity in the corner was slowly morphing as he spoke, its long distended jaw reeling upwards, its face regaining its former shape. The man's eyes were still centered on him, staring. When it finished, it looked just like it did in the hallway, its face normal.

Somehow, normal was even more disturbing than how it looked stretched.

How do I know this isn't the nazar? he wondered. *Maybe it always looks stretched, maybe the nazar is changing it, adjusting it for my brain. Or maybe it looks like a normal man all the time, but the nazar has twisted it, manipulated what I see.*

Not knowing for sure made him feel even more uneasy. *If I can't trust what I see, how do I...*

More thumps came from places distant in the house, causing both of them to jump. Ron felt as though there was a bubble of panic in his chest that had swollen to a size he wasn't able to manage. He began to feel that he'd made a mistake, that the whole enterprise needed to stop, that he needed to find a way to quickly wind it down. Somehow he let himself become wrapped up in this crazy idea, this absolutely insane, irrational solution of Abe's, and what he really needed to do was get out of this mansion, go home, and finish setting his house in order. Elenore would be back from Europe, and she and Robbie were coming to live there. He needed to get it ready. That was the priority. That was what he should be doing.

To hell with all this ghost bullshit.

Then, the creature in the corner began to fade a little; he could see the wallpaper behind it, through it. It was becoming more translucent by the second, as though it had made up its mind to go somewhere else, and was leaving.

A few seconds more, and it was gone.

"It left," he said.

"Good. Where'd it go?"

"No idea. Just faded away."

Jake turned, heading back to the hallway. *He's soldiering on*, Ron thought. For a second he almost stopped him, wanting to tell his friend it was time to leave and throw in the towel. Instead, he found himself following him out, unsure why he wasn't saying the words.

Because you don't want to sound like a coward, he thought. *The house isn't livable unless you do this. Elenore and Robbie would be in danger, would be scared out of their minds if you don't finish this.*

The hallway was quiet and empty, and they moved down it quickly, sticking their heads in each room, speeding up their inspection. Soon they reached the main section of the house, and turned left.

"How many fucking rooms do you need?" Jake asked. "Seriously?"

"I can't fathom what they put in each one," Ron replied.

"That's a ton of stuff. Can you imagine moving all that crap? What an albatross."

"Rich people don't move their stuff, they have other people move their stuff."

"I hate rich people," Jake muttered.

In the center of the main structure they came upon a large room that had huge windows facing the front of the house, and on the opposite wall, windows that would have looked over the garden courtyard. The black film that had coated every window in the house covered these as well, making the room dark and foreboding.

"The stairs," Jake said, standing at one end of the room, his flashlight aimed down. "Must be the ones we saw earlier, before we entered the east wing."

Ron felt something uneasy in the room. He scanned carefully, trying to detect what he was feeling, needing something visual to confirm the odd sensation of being watched. He approached the windows, examining the black coating that blocked the light; he ran his fingers over it, as he had on the one outside before they entered. The film firmly coated the glass like paint. When he pulled his fingers away, he used the flashlight to see if anything had rubbed off. They were clean; not even a sign of dust or dirt.

He turned around to look at the other end of the room, where the other set of windows faced the front of the house. The moment he did, he felt something shift…a fresh set of eyes were now watching him, focused on him. The sensation was eerie, and was driving him crazy.

What?

What is looking at me?

He quickly turned back to the window pane he'd touched, catching a faint movement, the last steps of something in transition. All of the panes of glass looked dark and smooth, but in that moment as he turned, he'd seen something in his peripheral vision, something shifting. And now, the sensation of being watched was still there, but different, coming from a different direction.

He placed his hand upon the glass window pane again, and quickly turned his neck to look at the opposite window.

It was only a split second, but he saw dozens of shifts in the glass panes across the room. Before he could completely bring his eyes to focus on them, they had reset, still and black and motionless.

That's what I'm feeling, he thought. *Something in the glass.*

He turned back, again detecting a response to his movement as the black covered panes behind him reacted to his turn, resetting themselves.

Then he glanced at the pane he'd placed his hand on. Appearing under his fingers was a face in the glass. It looked old and masculine. Wrinkles were etched in the skin, and a faint mustache grew above the lips. It seemed confused by his fingers upon the pane, and its eyes were centered on his hand, gazing at it intently.

My palm, Ron thought. *The palm where the nazar entered me.*

The face in the glass faded quickly, becoming a solid sheet of black film. Behind him, he felt the eyes of dozens of faces that must be present in the panes of the opposite wall. He knew that when he turned, they'd disappear too.

"What are you looking at?" Jake asked, coming up behind him.

"Faces," Ron replied. "In the glass."

"Faces?"

"Yeah." He turned, feeling the windows now in front of him shift to hide, as the ones behind him engaged, watching. "There's a face in each of those panes. Dozens of them. They shift when I'm not looking. They don't want to be seen."

"How do you know?" Jake asked.

"I can feel them," Ron replied. "The nazar, I think it makes it so you can sense things...not just see, but feel. No, that's not the right word, I can't exactly feel them...it's just...I'm not sure how to phrase it. I can *sense* them. And I caught one of them..." He placed his hand on one of the panes and turned quickly, repeating the steps he'd taken before. "The whole wall of them, they disappear when I'm not looking, but..." He turned back quickly. In the glass, under his hand, the same face appeared; old man, heavy wrinkles, mustache, concern upon his brow, looking at his palm. Then it swiftly faded. "But...I caught one of them, by touching the glass."

"You're telling me there's a face in each of these panes," Jake said, looking up at the giant window, "staring down at us right now?"

"Yeah," Ron confirmed. "Both sides." He pointed to the opposite wall.

"Fuck," Jake mumbled.

"Are you sure you still want me to tell you this shit? I can keep it to myself."

"No, I'd rather know."

Ron repeated the steps again, catching another glimpse of the face. "It's an old man. He's looking at my palm. I get the feeling he's confused too, like the one I saw back there, in the bedroom."

"Great, so they're confused," Jake replied. "We should speed this up, take advantage of their confusion before they figure out why we're here."

Ron removed his hand from the glass. "I think you're right."

They moved out of the room and into a hallway that entered the west wing. Each of the rooms was quiet and unremarkable, and Ron didn't sense or see anything odd, until they approached the last hall at the end of the wing. A set of closed double doors appeared twenty feet ahead, centered in the middle of the hallway. Unlike the doorways to the various rooms they'd searched, it was surrounded by ornate molding.

"Something special in that room, I guess," Jake said.

Ron was about to reply when he heard a scream from inside the room, a high pitched wail that carried throughout the hall, reverberating and echoing. It held, sustained, continuing for what seemed like minutes. Ron placed his hands to his ears, trying to cut the sound.

Jake appeared confused. "You hear something?"

"You don't?" Ron replied, wincing.

Jake paused, tilting his head a little like he was straining to listen. "No."

"High pitched scream. It won't..."

It suddenly ended, the wail quickly dropping in pitch and intensity. Ron lowered his hands.

"It stopped?" Jake asked.

Before Ron could reply, a ghostly figure emerged through the wood doors. It was a tall woman. Her hands were outstretched, reaching into the air as though she was trying to claw at something ahead of her. Her eyes were wild, rolling in their sockets, and the hair piled up on her head was disheveled, with strands hanging down.

Her mouth opened, twisting rapidly, forming words he couldn't hear. She moved quickly, racing toward them.

"Step back!" Ron warned Jake, pulling him to the side and holding him against the wall as the crazed figure rushed past, not stopping to look or acknowledge them. The fingers on her hands grasped at the air in front of her, bending spasmodically; the look on her face was one of pure horror. As she passed, Ron heard the faint sound of odd words, a language he didn't recognize.

"What?" Jake asked, as Ron realized the apparition was only for his eyes, something Jake couldn't see or detect. Nevertheless, he kept Jake pinned against the wall as he watched the woman progress down the hall away from them, her words trailing, her legs carrying her quickly into the depths of the house. After she had disappeared from sight, he released Jake and then bent over, taking in a deep breath.

"What was it?" Jake asked again.

He stood back up. "I think that was Mrs. Coldwater."

"Fuck!" Jake replied. "Did she look as creepy as Mrs. Hughes made her sound?"

Ron looked down the hallway. "Maybe more."

Jake joined him, glancing back the way they'd come, trying to see whatever Ron was seeing. "Goddamn. So it's all true, then."

"It was just like she described. Her hands were out in front of her, clawing or grasping for something. She was saying weird words, almost like a chant."

"Did she see us?"

"I don't think so. She was out of her mind. She looked terrified."

They turned to stare at the doors.

"Terrified by something in there?" Jake asked. "Well, fuck."

Ron looked at his friend. Although he didn't have the numb look of horror he'd seen on the woman's face, Jake looked genuinely scared.

"I guess that means what we're after is in there," Jake said. "You wanna get that strobe out? One of us has to use it while the other does the cutting."

Ron slipped the backpack off and opened the zipper, pulling out the strobe. It was square, made of plastic, and had a silver cone on one end with a plastic lens. He replaced the pack onto his back and fumbled with the device. "Is there a switch?" he asked, realizing Jake had been the one who tested it.

"Here," Jake said, handing him the machete. "I'll work that, you do the cutting. You're all worried about me holding the blade anyway."

Ron passed him the strobe, and Jake had it activated within seconds. The hallway suddenly lit up with flashes, making every movement appear to be slow motion.

"Save it for once we're inside," Ron said, and Jake shut it off. "I'm gonna open the doors, and you get ready to turn it on when I say."

"Alright," Jake replied, positioning the device, standing next to Ron. "Open both doors at the same time?"

"Right," Ron agreed.

They reached for the handles, and pushed.

Chapter Twenty-Two

Corpse of a seal.

San Luis Obispo. As they spent most weekends while his family lived there, Ron was on the beach, running in the wet sand toward the blue waters of the Pacific.

He was very young, and he played all over the bay, within the watch of his parents and their spread blanket. It wasn't unusual on some days to find something washed up, and today a new, mysterious lump was on the beach, partially covered by sand. He approached it and noticed a foul smell. Before he could poke at whatever it was, his father suddenly lifted him into the air and returned him to the blanket, calling the lump a dead seal, and telling him to leave it alone.

He kept that sand-covered lump in his peripheral vision most of the day, wanting to examine it more, but knowing it wasn't allowed. He had learned that disobeying his parents was a quick way to cut the time at the beach short, so he didn't risk it. However, throughout the afternoon, the lump never lost its intrigue. If he could find a way to look at it more closely, he might try.

He decided to head for the water, his young brain completely misjudging the power of the ocean. The first wave he encountered was taller than his small, four-year-old frame, and it knocked him over, rolling him sideways, submerging him.

A moment before the wave hit, he had complete control; now, he had none. The wave had engulfed him. There was no defense against it; it was so overwhelming, his choices were suddenly gone, removed from him. He had no option but to submit to whatever the water had in store.

He attempted to recover by pushing himself up, but the sand under his hands eroded quickly as the wave began to recede, giving him little to push against. The tug of the retreating water pulled at his small body unexpectedly, making him twist in a direction he didn't want to go.

Salt water tried to invade his lungs, but he didn't let it. He'd spent many hours in his grandmother's pool; he knew about holding his breath. It wasn't the water covering him, or even how strong it had been, knocking him down. It was the feeling of not having control, of not being able to stand back up…and knowing another wave was coming. He'd watched the waves from the safety of his parents' blanket, and he knew they were endless, they didn't stop. He needed to move back, toward where his father and mother were lying on the beach, back where it was just sun and sandcastles and the bottled soda his mother always brought in a small, Styrofoam cooler. Getting back there was the issue. He had to find a way before the next wave hit, and the next, and the next. They'd keeping knocking him over until he had no strength left, and he'd die right there on the beach.

He'd be just another sand-covered lump, like the corpse of the seal.

The idea terrified him, so he fought.

He wasn't sure what mental levers he managed to pull, but they seemed to be working; the wave that hit him and knocked his mind sideways when they opened the doors to the room was receding. Instead of finding himself twisting in the tug of the undercurrent, he was standing upright, his mind refocusing on what was in front of him, somehow reaching out mentally to brace against the floor, the walls, the ceiling, forcing his senses to orient and right themselves.

Jake wasn't there. The room was dark, but not because of the black film covering the windows. Heavy drapes had been pulled. He couldn't see what was at the other end, but the area around him was faint, shadowy. There was a sickening smell, something rancid and sweet; to his right was a table with a mirror, covered in small perfume bottles.

He was afraid another wave might come, like the beach. He felt the need to brace himself, so he checked the mental bulwarks he'd constructed: imaginary steel beams of rectitude, bolted to the scene in front of him, strong and able to keep him upright if another blast hit.

A scream in the distance pierced through the darkness, focusing his attention. Slowly, a dim light at the other end of the room grew, faintly illuminating a bed. Another scream was followed by deeper grunts, and Ron began to make out figures on the bed, twisting and interacting.

He turned, again looking for Jake, but aside from the scene at the other end of the room, he was alone.

Another scream made him turn back to face the bed. His eyes were wide, trying to take in the faint information the dim light revealed, but it was still too dark to make out more than shadows.

Yet another scream, bloodcurdling, long, and high-pitched; it caused him to take a step back. *The door,* he thought. *I can turn and open the door, and leave. I don't want to see whatever is down there.*

Then his body began to move away from the door, against his will. He was sliding over the ground, closer and closer to the bed. He tried to stop his legs, but realized it wasn't his legs that were forcing him forward. It felt like the receding wave on the beach, pulling him regardless of how much he wanted to control things. He was powerless to stop it.

Forward, across the dark floor, moving smoothly like a camera in a movie, he found himself positioned along one side of the large bed. A small light on a nightstand next to it had a frilly shade, more decorative than functional; its dim radiance provided just enough light to illuminate the bed's surface.

A young girl was on it, wearing a darkly stained dress. She was face down, her arms tied to the bedposts with rope. She twisted against the bindings frantically.

Straddling the girl at her waist was an older man, also fully dressed. He was bulky and large, with a thick neck. Ron couldn't make out his features; he was facing away.

The girl screamed once again, shuddering in pain and agony. She twisted her head toward him; he could see her eyes, rolled back. When they finally centered, they landed upon him. He saw tears. Then, they slowly focused upon him, widening with hope.

Ron felt terror race up his spine as he realized she could see him; she knew he was there. "Help me!" she screamed, her eyes pleading.

Ron felt frozen. His position by the bed wasn't under his control; when he tried to move his legs, nothing happened. He raised an arm, wondering if he might be able to loosen the bindings, but his arm wouldn't move, either. The only thing he could control was his vision.

She screamed again, pinching her eyes shut in pain, her mouth wide as another bloodcurdling yell reverberated throughout the room. Her mouth stayed open as the scream cut off, and her eyes suddenly opened wide with horror.

"Now, now," came a low voice, from the man on top of her. At first he wondered if the man was sexually abusing her; his position over the girl's waist made it appear that he might be performing intercourse. As the man shifted a little, Ron realized it wasn't intercourse; at least, not of a sexual nature. He had her right foot in his hand, bent at the knee.

"You wanted that horsey," the man said. He raised something in his other hand, placing it on the flat sole of the girl's foot, and slowly slid it along the length of it.

The girl screamed again, a terrible, high-pitched wail that shook Ron to the core. Dark red lines of liquid ran down her leg.

"Ya gotta tend to it," the man said as he positioned his hand again. Ron saw that he was holding a wood plane, gripping it by a large metal ball on top. He pressed it hard against the girl's sole and slid it again, from her toes to the heel.

Another desperate scream erupted from her, followed by frantic wails. She twisted under the man, but the bindings were secure, and his large frame, pinning her waist down, kept her from escaping. He examined the results of his work, holding up long, thin pieces of flesh, and seemed satisfied. Slowly he swung his leg off the girl until he was standing on the side of the bed opposite Ron. "You gotta learn responsibility!"

Now, with the dim light hitting the man's face, Ron recognized the wrinkles and the mustache. It was the face from the mirrors. As he made the connection, the man stood more upright, looking right at him.

"Did he send you?" the man asked.

Ron was dumbfounded by the horror he'd just witnessed. He tried to take a step back, but again his legs wouldn't respond. When he opened his mouth, attempting to speak, nothing came out.

"I figured he'd send someone. Wouldn't want to miss the show. Hope you liked it, you sick fuck."

Clasping several pieces of thin flesh between his bloody fingers, the man let the plane fall to the ground. It hit the carpet and made a loud thump.

Ron recognized the sound immediately. Overhead…he heard it every night in his own home, before the sound of steps on the stairs.

It was the same thump.

It made him feel sick.

The man left the side of the bed and walked through the room. Ron tried to turn, worried that he might come up behind him, but he heard the door close and assumed the man had left. Below him, on the bed, the girl's body heaved as she sobbed, her head pressed into the pillow, muffling her cries.

He wanted to reach out and help, to remove the bindings and lift her from the bed, carry her out of the house, but none of his limbs would respond. If he could speak he'd try to console her, to tell her everything was going to be alright, but the words would not come out. He was in no position to make any kind of promises or to offer any kind of comfort; the receding force of the wave still had control, could still make him move or not move.

The light on the nightstand began to flicker, creating short moments of darkness, not unlike a strobe. Ron felt the rumble of another wave building momentum, churning to create energy and form. As the intensity of the strobe gained strength, the wave hit him full force, and he felt as though he was spinning in the salt water, his hands flailing, his legs trying to locate the ground.

I'm a seal, he thought. *A lump of dead seal, waiting to be covered by sand.*

- - -

"Nothing," Jake muttered to his left, turning off the strobe. Ron turned; his friend was walking toward a closet on the far side of the room. "Just like the rest of the house."

Ron wandered farther in, feeling bewildered and confused. He stopped when he reached a spot where a deep indentation was still pressed into the carpet. Turning, he saw three more. *The bed was here,* he thought. To the side, the vestiges of a stain. He knelt next to it. *The man was standing here. The flesh he cut from her was dripping.* He ran his fingers over it. Someone tried to take the stain out…got most of it. But it was still there.

"So, this is a little weird," Ron said.

"What?" Jake asked, joining him. "Did you find something?"

"I saw something. When we walked in."

"What?"

"It was like a vision. It took me over for a few moments. I saw what happened in this room, years ago. At least, I think it was years ago. There was a bed here. This spot…that was blood."

"OK," Jake replied. "Anything else?"

Ron stood, facing his friend. "It was pretty gruesome."

"I'm an adult, I can handle it."

Ron related what he saw to Jake, trying to explain to him the feelings he was experiencing as it happened, the panic at losing control, the sense of being unable to help. When he told Jake about the planing, his friend began to look sick, as though he was about to throw up.

Before Ron could finish, Jake ran to a corner of the room and began to heave, but nothing came up.

"Sorry, you said you wanted to know."

"That's so fucking sick," Jake said, wiping at his mouth with the back of his hand. "Christ."

"He stood right here," Ron said, next to the stain, "and held up the pieces of skin he'd cut from her foot."

"Fuck, stop!" Jake replied, still bent over in the corner. "I get it!"

The memory of the scene made Ron shiver. It was the kind of thing that would live on in nightmares for the rest of his life, and he knew it.

"That's it for the house," Jake said, standing up. "This is the last room. No Volger. Abe's theory was wrong."

Ron left the spot, walking for the door. "Yeah, I'm ready to leave. Don't want to stay here any longer than I have to."

Using a set of stairs near the end of the west wing, they quickly found themselves at the glass doors where they'd broken in. Ron checked his watch; they'd been inside for an hour.

Seems like weeks, he thought.

They stepped out; the morning sun had been replaced with clouds, giving the courtyard a dull, grey look.

"Gotta say, I'm glad to be out of there," Jake mused, his spirits lifting a little. "I'd be fine never going in again."

"Me either," Ron replied numbly, feeling defeated. They'd come trying to finish something, and the only thing they accomplished was to pry open the mystery a little more.

Jake was leading them around the house; Ron presumed to the truck. As they rounded the end of the west wing, Ron stopped, looking back. The edge of one of the other buildings on the property was sticking out behind the view of the east wing; just a few inches of one of the structures, almost hidden.

Might be the stable, he thought.

"You wanted that horsey!"

He started to turn back, to follow Jake to the truck, but stopped. *"You wanted that horsey!"* The man had clearly said it, as he sliced the skin from her foul. Horsey. Stables.

"Jake," Ron called.

His friend stopped and turned. "Yeah?"

"We didn't check those other buildings."

Jake walked back to where Ron was standing. Ron pointed past the east wing. "You remember? We saw them when we were on the other side."

"Oh, yeah…barn? Stable?"

"I'm guessing."

"You think what we're looking for might be in there?"

"Well, we came all the way here. I'd hate to think we packed it in before we checked everything."

Jake nodded. "Sure." Jake took off, headed toward the other end of the house. Ron followed, trudging through the weeds.

When they reached the east side, they found a path that had once led from the back of the house to the other buildings; it was overgrown, and the machete came back into use. Jake swung at the blackberry branches, slowly cutting his way through.

When they reached the stable, two sliding doors on its front had been chained together, secured by a padlock. Jake led them around the side of the building, clearing a path until they came to a door in the rear of the structure. It, too, was locked.

"No window to break to get in," Jake said.

"Wood looks deteriorated," Ron said. "Think we could kick it in?"

Jake placed the tip of the machete into the door jam and wedged it, sliding the blade down. When he pulled back on its handle for leverage, a piece of the door broke free. He lowered the blade and tried it again; the section with the handle completely fell away, and the door slid open a few inches.

"That was easy," Ron said as they walked in.

Spider webs were everywhere. They moved through the structure, swatting at the webbing, sending dust that had accumulated on the fine threads flying through the air, causing them to sneeze. There were four stalls on each side; Ron looked through one side, while Jake took the other. It didn't take long to scan each one.

"Nothing," Ron said, joining his friend near the middle.

"Me either," Jake replied. "I think this is a bust...wait, maybe..." Jake walked to a door that was tucked between the two middle stalls on one side. He opened it, exposing a short walkway beyond. "There's more."

Ron joined him, and they entered the new space. It only ran fifteen feet, studded with alcoves. There was a door on the left, which Jake walked to. "I'll check this."

"I'll get the rest," Ron replied, walking farther down to the alcoves. He heard a rustling behind him, and then a faint screech that sounded like the wail of a wounded dog. He turned, convinced Jake had found something, and ran back to the door.

Jake was standing just inside, peering into the dark. "You heard that?"

"I did." The small room was dark, and whatever Jake had identified was at the back of it, in the shadows. Jake's flashlight scanned the far wall, illuminating a lump on the ground.

The corpse of a seal.

It did look like a corpse; white bones reflected the light, and it was lying still.

Chains had been secured to the wall behind it, and disappeared into the pile of bones.

They stepped closer. Ron saw that, despite the bones, much of the animal was still there; some kind of head and torso still contained flesh. Its legs were hidden under it.

"Looks dead," Jake said. "That's probably why it smells so bad in here, that thing decomposing, stinking up..."

"I'm not sure it's dead," Ron replied, cutting him off.

"Not dead?"

"I think you should find that strobe."

The head of the creature twitched slightly, as though it was waking up. Jake, his flashlight locked on the creature, seemed frozen by the movement. The head rose from the rest of the body; it was quickly apparent that it wasn't any kind of animal they'd ever seen before.

"Come on, Jake, the strobe," Ron urged. His friend dropped the machete and fumbled with the backpack, unzipping sections, searching.

The neck stretched up a couple of feet, and the head on its end tilted down. It was triangular, almost like a praying mantis, but dark in color, sprouting patches of black hair. Nestled on top were two round, black protrusions.

Eyes, Ron thought.

The strobe suddenly went off, pointed in the wrong direction. Jake gained control of the device and aimed it at the creature. The neck extended a little more, raising the head and moving it toward the flashing light.

"Is it working?" Jake asked.

"I don't know. Abe said to give it at least a minute."

They waited, each second seeming like an eternity. The flashing effect of the strobe made looking at the creature difficult, but Ron stared at it regardless, trying to understand what he was seeing. It looked like a strange blend of animal and insect, but it didn't comport with any animal or insect that he knew. The oddity of its size and shape bewildered him, and he struggled to understand it. A huge shadow version of the nightmarish creature was cast upon the wall behind it, looming over the room, looking as though it could engulf them all.

"Can you test it, see if it's mesmerized?" Jake asked.

"How?"

"I don't know, poke at it? The machete is on the ground."

Ron knelt and reached for it, gaining confidence from how heavy it felt. The creature now seemed frozen, its neck stretched and locked in position, staring at the strobe.

"Walk a little that way," Ron said. "See if it follows you."

Jake took a couple of steps to the right. The neck of the creature swiveled, moving its head, tracking the strobe. "Seems like it," Jake said. "Might be working."

Ron approached the head from the side. It was a little larger than a basketball with flattened edges. While the back two corners seemed to hold the eyes, the third corner looked like a small mouth. Insect-like mandibles extended from its cheeks, wiping over the mouth's surface slowly, like it was preparing to eat something.

"You have to pull one out," Jake said. "Abe said to cut it off by the stalk."

"Move in closer," Ron replied. "Get that thing right in its face."

Jake took a step, inching the device toward the creature.

"Closer," Ron urged. "Get right up on it. I want that thing transfixed before I touch it."

Jake took two more steps, positioning the strobe about a foot from the creature's mouth.

Ron stepped closer and extended his hand; it looked odd in the flashing light, jumping and frozen for a moment, rather than a smooth movement. He reached out but didn't touch the head, stopping when he positioned it over one of the eyes.

"Just do it!" Jake said.

"Fuck," Ron muttered in reply, looking at the odd, foreign shape of the creature's head, wondering if the strobe would really keep it sedate, or if, by touching it, it would react. "How am I supposed to do this?"

"You gotta get your fingers into the eye socket and pull," Jake said. "Pull enough out that you can slice it without cutting the eyeball itself."

The smooth, dark surface of the creature's eye was like a tiny dome rising out of the bony head, no more than two inches in width. He reached toward it, pausing just before his fingertips touched its surface. When they made contact, he was shocked by how cold it felt. Quickly he plunged his fingers down between the eye and the socket, feeling the bone and cartilage of the creature's skull against the back of his hand.

"Fuck!" he yelled, his fingers pressing against the squishy surface of the eye, slipping and sliding, trying to gain purchase underneath. The head shifted slightly and the mouth moved towards him. He pressed harder; he could feel sinews and gunk collecting under his fingernails as they descended below the rim of the socket. Once all five fingers were in place, he lifted, shifting the position of his fingers as he felt the squishy ball between them try to slide one way or the other, resisting his pull.

The head turned even more, and Ron saw the tiny mandibles next to the creature's mouth move rapidly, clicking and extending, swinging out from the sides.

"Keep that strobe on it!" he yelled at Jake.

He tugged on the eye, feeling it give in little half-inch bursts, slowly extricating. He couldn't tell how much he'd managed to pull out without bending a little, and he wasn't going to go anywhere near the mandibles.

"Is that enough?" he yelled to Jake. "Can I cut it now? I can't see how much is out!"

"More," Jake replied. "A couple more inches."

Ron tugged, feeling the eye slide hard to one side, trying to escape the little cage his fingers had made. He tightened his grip and tugged again, hoping he didn't squeeze too hard and rupture it. It gave way in a series of quick lurches, then suddenly slipped completely free, trailing a long strand of nerves and connective tissue.

"You're good!" Jake yelled.

Ron brought up the machete with his left hand and cut at the dangling cord. It resisted, and he had to add pressure until the sharp edge sliced through and the cord fell down upon the creature's head, dripping a light brown liquid. Part of it retracted back into the socket, but most of the severed end remained, seeping.

"Don't turn that thing off until we're out of here," Ron said while backing up, working his way out of the room and through the stable.

Jake backed up too, the strobe still positioned squarely at the creature's head. Even when they'd cleared the corner, he kept it going, just in case it found a way to follow them. "Goodbye, Ezra!" he said. "Or whatever half of Ezra you are!" Once they reached the outside, both men kept walking until they reached a spot thirty feet from the building.

A brown substance was dripping from the tendrils of stalk attached to the eye; Ron held it away from his body, not wanting any to land on him, letting it drip upon the ground. "I'm gonna need that container," he said.

Jake switched off the strobe and slipped it into the backpack, then removed a plastic container and lifted off its lid. He held it out for Ron, who dropped the eye into it, and Jake sealed it over, snapping the lid back in place.

Ron held out one hand, covered in slime, wanting desperately to wash it off. In the other, he was still holding the machete. Some of the dark substance was streaked along the blade.

"You look kinda badass, standing there," Jake said.

"I feel fucking gross. I want this shit off my hand."

Jake turned back to the door of the stable. "Do you think it can move? Will it come after us?"

"It was chained up," he replied, heading for the truck. "But we're not staying to find out if the chains hold."

- - -

Ron placed the tiny bottle on his coffee table. "Stuff tastes horrible!" His hand landed on the plastic container on his lap; the severed eye was inside.

"I thought you said it tasted like cherries," Jake replied.

"The last one did. This one tastes like turpentine. Fucking burns. What I don't understand is how I..."

Before he could finish, he found himself drifting away from his body, coming to rest a few feet from Jake. *What I don't understand is how I can carry this eyeball with me...*he finished and looked down; the eyeball was there, his right hand gripping it by the stalk. He glanced to where his body was sitting, and saw the plastic container in his lap. Its clear sides exposed the contents; it was empty.

Oh, I guess that's how...

Something to ask Abe about, after this is all over.

Feeling bold, he decided to drift diagonally through the floor of the room, angling for the area where he knew the stairwell to the basement resided. As he passed through the inside of the house, he thought back to the first time he'd done this; it was only a day ago, but it seemed like an eternity. *I didn't know what I was doing, then,* he thought. *Now I do.*

Arriving in the crawlspace, he searched for the horizontal bar he'd seen before. It was there, hanging in the air, easy to miss if you didn't know what to look for. He slipped into it, and was soon descending to the basement.

The legs of the ghosts appeared first; they were still meandering about like zombified, caged animals, awaiting release by their keeper, Ezra. He knew the dark figure would be here, somewhere. He raised his hand, aiming the severed eye into the room, hoping it would be simple, that Ezra would be surprised and not even realize he was watching himself, doomed.

Separation tension, Ron thought, taking each step slowly, the entirety of the basement coming into view. *Energy from separation tension. Once it sees itself, Abe said the tension would unravel. As long as...*

He stepped off the stairs, now at the same level as the ghosts. Several were shuffling just inches in front of him. One stopped to look; after pausing, it lowered its head and continued to pace, apparently unimpressed.

Where is he? Ron thought, brandishing the severed eye, pointing it in every direction, searching for Ezra. *He's in here somewhere, he's...*

Suddenly his arm involuntarily extended upward, as though it had been lassoed and pulled up by a rope. He gripped the eye stalk tightly, not wanting to drop it, and tried to lower his arm...but could not.

It felt like the receding wave once again, like the force that had moved him across the floor in the young girl's bedroom. It was something he couldn't control.

"Where is it?" came the voice from behind him.

"Where is what?" he answered, immediately regretting it; something tight wrapped around his neck and began to squeeze, making him feel as if his head was about to pop.

"Tell me," the voice insisted.

He recognized it from weeks before, in Terrell's bedroom. It was Ezra.

Ron tried twisting his wrist. If he could turn the eye around to face Ezra behind him, it might achieve his goal. While he was unable to lower his arm, it did feel as though it moved a tiny bit as he tried to turn it.

"Tell me!" Ezra insisted. Ron felt a coldness at his back, as though a solid sheet of ice was pressed up against him.

If I can just turn it a little more, he thought, focusing all the energy he had into his arm, forcing it to twist, to reorient the way the eyeball was pointing. Whatever was around his neck tightened even more, and he realized he was completely unable to breathe.

But you're not in your body, he thought. *How can that be? Breathing shouldn't matter.*

The sensation of suffocation was overwhelming. He considered ignoring it, on the chance that it was some kind of trick. His physical body was upstairs; whatever had him by the throat, it couldn't really touch him, couldn't really cut off oxygen.

Then why am I about to pass out? he wondered. *Why do I feel as though my lungs are about to burst? That I have to breathe?*

"Where's what?" he croaked weakly.

"My half," Ezra replied. "Where? Last time I was there, they had moved it."

If I tell him, Ron thought, *this eye thing might fail...he'll make his way to it and reunite. Abe said that was the only way it could survive.* He twisted his arm harder, feeling it rotate another half inch, hoping at least the edge of the eye might soon face Ezra, and start the unraveling before Ezra forced or tricked him into revealing the location.

"I don't know where," Ron replied, twisting again, feeling another lurch of movement. *Was it enough?*

"If you don't know where," Ezra replied, "then where did you get what you have in your hand?"

Ron forced his wrist to turn again, sure that he had cleared the halfway point. "I found it on a dog," he said. "A dead dog."

"A dead dog's eye? From where?"

Around him, all of the milling ghosts had stopped their shuffling. They were now facing him, watching intently, as though Ezra had put them on alert and were awaiting some command.

"The road in front of my house," Ron replied, hoping he could keep Ezra distracted long enough to finish twisting his arm.

"An eyeball from a dead dog in front of your house. Interesting. Why would you bring such a thing down here?"

He forced his arm again, feeling it budge and shift a tiny amount. "No reason."

"You're lying," Ezra said, and Ron felt the coldness against his back intensify. "That's my eye you're holding, isn't it? Tell me, where did you get it?"

He felt the hands of the ghosts around him, reaching upward, their fingers clawing at the flesh of his forearm as they tried to grab the eye. He stood on his toes hoping it would keep the eye out of their reach. *Distract him,* Ron thought. *Just a little longer, until you can get it turned completely around.* "Your other half is a rotting carcass," Ron said. "It stinks. I drove a stake through its head."

"You did no such thing," Ezra replied. Ron felt his backside begin to go numb from the cold. "And it wouldn't have mattered if you had. No, you removed my eye for a reason. Tell me where they moved it to... Was it the courtyard? The gazebo? Maybe back up into the little girl's room?"

"He fed her to you," Ron said, still hoping to keep him distracted. "Is that how you were created? Fed the flesh of that girl?"

Ezra laughed. "Grasping at straws! No. But he made sure she was well used. He absolutely saw to that. You don't really understand anything, do you? You're just guessing. I suppose that's good."

Ron twisted again, forcing another fraction of an inch. "Coldwater is the reason you're here, haunting this place?"

"I'm tired of your questions," Ezra replied. "Now, answer mine before I pop your head off your body."

Ron didn't think the constriction around his neck could tighten any more, but it did, making it almost impossible to speak. Feeling as though he was just a single turn from completing his objective, Ron croaked out, "What happens if you see yourself?"

"See myself?" Ezra repeated. "What do you mean?"

Ron felt the resistance in his arm give way as he twisted the severed eye fully around, directly exposing its slimy surface to Ezra.

At first he was afraid it was a failure – that everything Abe had predicted had been wrong. Then, slowly, an inhuman scream arose behind him. It was low and guttural, and rose in pitch and intensity until it was deafening. The cold pulled away from his body, and the constriction around his neck loosened.

He turned around, looking behind him. Ezra was there; his features no longer expressed the confidence he'd displayed at their earlier encounter in the bedroom. Terror now filled his eyes, the same terror he had been so intent upon inflicting on others. Pieces of his figure loosened and lifted in bizarre ways, as though gravity had shifted and was acting upon him from all directions. Chunks of his form began to unravel and disappear, and he twisted with a spasm, intense pain on his face. He looked down to see long strands of himself rip out, twisting up into the air and dissolving as they blew away.

It was what he threatened to do to me, Ron thought. *Annihilation.*

Ron shuddered, but he brandished the eye like a trophy, making sure Ezra could see it with the last of his vision. Moments later, only thin strips of the creature still hung in the air like rope, odd lines that hadn't fully dissolved; they shambled backward as a single form, slowly fading, erasing in front of him.

Ron felt his heart pounding in his chest. He turned; the ghosts around him had dropped their interest, lowering their arms to resume shuffling. He took several deep breaths, and after he felt his pulse drop a little, he ascended the steps and rose through the flooring, finding himself in the kitchen. A few moments more, and he settled into his body, opening his eyes. A massive headache was forming in the front of his skull.

"Well?" Jake asked.

Ron lifted the plastic container and removed the lid. The eyeball inside had deflated, as though the liquid it contained had been sucked out through a syringe. The stalk was beginning to dry out, shriveling up, retracting into the organ. "I think he's gone," Ron replied.

"You showed him the eye?"

"The eye saw him, yes," Ron corrected. "I don't think he realized exactly what I was doing. He knew something was up, and was trying to defend himself, but he didn't seem to understand the threat. He just wanted to know where to find his other half."

"He didn't know where it was?"

"No. Somewhere on the Coldwater property, that's all he knows."

"So, he's unraveling now, right now? While we stand here?"

Ron looked down at the strange severed organ in the plastic container. "That's exactly how I'd describe it."

Chapter Twenty-Three

"Your room, kiddo," Ron said, giving his son encouragement by pressing his back.

Robbie stepped into the room and looked around.

"I realize it doesn't have your posters and stuff yet," Ron said, following him in. "But we'll get all that set up. It does have this, though." He led the child to the window. "Look at that view."

"There's so many trees," Robbie replied. "Can I have a tree house?"

"We'll see," Ron replied, sitting on Robbie's bed. "Maybe after your mother's back from Europe and we're more settled in, we can pick out a tree for that."

"Hooray!" the child shouted, jumping. When he landed on the floor, the thump that reverberated through the house bothered Ron; it reminded him of the thump he'd heard in the Coldwater mansion, the thump he now associated with...

He pushed the memory back in his mind. This was a special moment with his son, as he inspected his new room. He didn't want to ruin it with those kinds of thoughts.

"A bathroom!" Robbie said, pushing open a door. "My own?"

"Now you don't have to share one in the hallway!" Ron said, rising from the bed. "And neither do we."

"This is very cool," Robbie replied, pulling back a shower curtain, inspecting the tub. "I can take a shower here, too?"

"Or a bath. Either."

"Do you know what boxes my stuff is in?"

"They're in the garage. I figured once you got here, you could help me pick them out and we'll move them up together."

"OK. And the PlayStation?"

"I think that's in a box in the TV room."

"You haven't unpacked it yet?" Robbie said, running out of the bedroom and down the stairs.

Ron followed him. "Your old man has been busy, getting the house ready for you and your mom."

He could hear Robbie already in the other room, going through boxes, searching. *You have no idea how busy,* Ron thought, walking down the stairs.

- - -

"No sign of anything?" Jake asked. Ron could tell he was slurping a beer on the other end of the line.

"No," Ron replied, sitting on the couch. "It's been a week, and aside from the regular creaks and groans of a house, there's been nothing. No strange thumping, no scratching on the glass. No ghosts."

"No sign of Ezra?"

"None."

"So, Abe was right."

"Must have been. Have you talked to him? Or Terrell?"

"Terrell called me to find out what was going on. I told him everything. He enjoyed the story."

"What about Freedom? Have you told her?"

"Actually, no. To be honest, I think it would just freak her out. She's all into positive energy and shit, and when I brought it up just after I got back, she shut me down real quick. So, I haven't told her much."

"Just as well. Nothing she could do about it, anyway. I guess I owe Abe some thanks. Terrell, too. I suppose."

"I don't think Terrell expects anything. He seemed real sheepish about it all. He thinks he got everything wrong, that everything he tried to do was kind of fucked up."

"That's stupid," Ron replied. "It worked, didn't it? My house is normal. That's all I wanted."

"I think Terrell is embarrassed that he, himself, couldn't do anything about it, and that it took Abe getting involved. He was even criticizing Abe, too, saying he missed a lot of things."

"What things?"

"I don't know, I don't remember what all he was goin' on about. He was talking about paying a visit, he thinks that with the Volger gone, the place is safe for..." He paused, then suddenly yelled, "No! I'm not watching that shit again, Free! No...fuck it, Free, that's bullshit! We agreed...oh fuck off!"

Ron heard a door slam.

"Sorry about that," Jake said, his voice back to normal. "I get so sick of the goddamn *Bachelor*. Between that and the Kardashians, I feel like blowing my brains out."

"Get another TV."

"My other one broke. We're sharing the big one. Not good, I can tell you."

"How about I get you a new one? Least I can do for all your help."

"Make it a sixty incher, OK? That'll fit perfectly in my man cave. Had a shitty little thirty-six inch piece of shit in there, that's the one that went out, but that room definitely needs bigger. What about Elenore?"

"Extended another week. Now she's supposed to be back next Thursday. We'll see."

"Well, I think given the work we put into the place, she should be pretty happy with it."

"I think all the work is great. Her problem is the place itself. She doesn't really like it; that's what it comes down to."

"Well, shit, why'd you go and buy it, then?"

"Good question." *Doesn't matter,* he thought. *I love the house. Maybe I ignored what she wanted because I have this suspicion in the back of my mind that she's been banging her boss for months.*

Explosions and gunfire raged from the TV room, and Ron stuck his head into it, finding Robbie at the controls. "Ten more minutes, you're done for today. That includes save time."

"Aw, Dad!"

"It sounds as though he's liking it," Jake said.

"As far as I can tell," Ron replied.

They talked for a few minutes more, and after they hung up, Ron wandered into the TV room to watch Robbie play before the day's allotment of video game time ran out. He fell into a recliner next to his son, who didn't look up; his eyes were glued to the screen.

Ron watched as Robbie expertly maneuvered a point of view character down a dark hallway. There was no music, and occasionally a creepy sound came from the surround speakers, making it seem like something was behind them.

"There's one of them around that corner down there," Robbie said, his voice low and quiet, as though the video game character might overhear.

"One of what?" Ron asked.

"They're like these zombie things. But they're different, they don't just wander around, they pop out at you. The one down there is badass."

Ron watched as his son slowly crept down the hallway. A gun raised up in the middle of the screen, centered on the corner at the end of the passageway, and cocked, readying for action. His son made a rush for the corner, and a huge horrific creature, bloated and oozing blood jumped out from behind the wall. Robbie shot at it, but it didn't seem to matter; the creature came closer and dealt blows, quickly draining his son's health.

"Maybe if I use the chainsaw," his son said, quickly switching to a new weapon. He leaned the blade into the creature, and blood flew everywhere. The creature screamed in response.

Ron could only hear the scream of the little girl, lying on the bed, as her father sliced a thin strip of flesh from the bottom of her foot. It made him shiver all over, and he knew he needed to stop watching the horrific spectacle on the screen.

"Ten minutes is up. Save and shut it down." He walked out, leaving Robbie to deal with the electronics.

- - -

"Do you think a house can make you paranoid?" he asked, glancing over at Robbie, who was sitting in the next room with a PS Vita, buds in his ears. He was reasonably sure his son couldn't hear them.

"That's a strange question," Mrs. Hughes replied, setting a pot of tea between them and flattening the front of her dress before sitting at the kitchen table with him. "Why do you ask? Has that house made you paranoid?"

"I think it has," Rob replied. "In Portland, Robbie was old enough to leave alone in the house for an hour while I ran an errand. It didn't happen often, but he'd be so bored in stores, it was easier to leave him at home with his games than drag him along, and I really didn't worry. Then we moved here, where I thought it would be much safer, I haven't been able to let him out of my sight."

"When I was young, our parents let us go wherever we wanted," she replied, taking a sip of her tea. "The school bus stopped at the bottom of the hill, and we'd get out, our bikes right where we left them. Then we'd ride the bikes home, and if we stopped off at someone's house, it was no big deal as long as we were home for supper. The only verboten place was the Coldwater property, but it was out of the way anyway, so we never went there. I don't think we ever locked our house; I guess my parents didn't feel the need to. Nowadays...well, you know. Helicopter parents and all. Can't have enough locks. Your wife joining you soon?"

Rob hesitated before answering, then said, "Not sure."

Her hand extended, landing on his. Her skin was surprisingly warm; Ron thought it might be from holding the mug of tea. "I'm sorry, none of my business."

"I don't mind telling you," Ron replied. "God knows you shared a ton with me." He smiled at her. "I'm not sure she'll ever come to the house. I think she's close to bailing on me, on Robbie, on all of it."

"Surely not!"

"A thousand dollars, she's having an affair with her boss."

"Oh," Mrs. Hughes replied. "Any chance that's just wild paranoia, too?"

"Maybe. I'd hate to be naïve. All the signs are there. I think the house was the final straw for her, something she could seize on and use. She never saw in it what I saw."

"What did you see, exactly?"

Ron paused for a moment. "Hard to put into words. You know when you first see something, and you know you love it, right then and there, and feel like you'd be willing to put up with anything to have it in your life, even if you have to put up with a ton of shit? Pardon my language."

"You sound like you're talking about a person, not a house."

Ron paused. "Yeah, I suppose you're right." He reached into his satchel and removed the book, sliding it across the table to her. "Thank you for that. Helped save the day. I doubt Abe would have figured things out without it."

"You're welcome," she replied. "I don't suppose he had anything more to say when you picked it up?"

"I didn't see him, actually. Terrell shipped it back. I suspect he made copies, though. Hope that's alright."

"Perfectly fine with me." She took another sip. "I'll be honest with you, I found your story about Candace very disturbing. It still bothers me."

"Trust me, I found it disturbing myself. It's the kind of thing you can't un-see, as much as I'd like to."

"And the man that did that horrible thing to her, can you describe him to me?"

"Thick," Ron answered, "stout. About six feet tall. Lots of wrinkles, had a mustache."

"Sounds like him," she replied.

"Mr. Coldwater?"

"Yes." She seemed to be mulling something over, unsure what to say next. "I guess I..." she started, but then stopped.

"What?"

"No, it's nothing. Your house is livable now, that's what matters." Her hand reached out again, patting his. "More tea?"

"Sure. You can tell me, though. What were you going to say?"

"You're already paranoid enough," she replied slyly. "No sense in fostering that."

"Now you've done it. That'll make me wonder what you meant, and I'll assume the worst. Do me a favor and just tell me, so it doesn't fester."

"Well, I guess I still wonder why. Why did he do that? What a horrible thing to do to any child, let alone your own child. It's unfathomable."

"There's lots of sickos in the world," Ron replied. "That's why all the locks, remember?"

"Maybe," she said, nodding a little. "Maybe that was it, he was just sick."

"You don't think it was."

"I've been living with the terrible things that happened between our two families for many decades now, so I have a wider view of it than you do. There's still so…" She paused.

He could see the wheels spinning behind her eyes, and for a brief moment it made him step back and try to examine everything from her perspective. It didn't take him long to realize it wasn't something he wanted to do.

"I appreciate your help," he said. "You didn't have to share what you knew with me, and if you hadn't, I'd still be knee-deep in problems. But…" He paused again, looking down at his mug of tea, watching the steam. "This thing between your families…it isn't my fight. I just wanted my house back. I needed to have a home, a place for my family, something livable and stable. I couldn't bring Robbie into a house filled with threats, and with your help, all that's gone. It's stable now. That's all I wanted. I don't want to get wrapped up in something else, something beyond me. I hope you understand."

"You're right, of course," she said, rising from the table and lifting the book. She marched it over to a bookcase and slid it into a spot on the top shelf. "It's best that this whole Coldwater trouble just sink into the past, where it belongs, and not stir things up. God knows it's been nothing but heartache for me, for my parents, for their parents." She returned to the table and sat. "Sometimes things need to rest."

"We'd like to invite you over to the house for a little get together," Ron offered. "It won't be more than a couple of people, just a housewarming thing. Some food."

"That's very kind of you," she replied. "Thank you, but no. There's no way on God's green earth I'll ever set foot on that property again." She smiled up at him. "I hope you understand, too."

- - -

With Robbie settled into bed and the completion of his evening routines of checking every door, every window, every lock, setting the alarm, and switching off every light, Ron slipped off his clothes and got into bed. The cold sheets made him shiver.

He stared up at the ceiling; the moon was full and shining in the side windows, sending plenty of light into the room. *Need to get drapes,* he thought. *Add it to the list.*

The ceiling had no markings or imperfections; it was a pale, unblemished surface disturbed only by texturing. He stared at the spot where he imagined the thumps had come from, wondering what he'd do if he heard one.

Ever since his final encounter with Ezra, there had been no taps at the pane, no ghostly figures in the yard staring through windows, no sound of steps on the staircase. And especially, no thumps in the attic. He wondered if focusing on it now was a bad idea, if merely thinking about it could somehow give it energy, and wind up triggering something, resulting in thumps he didn't want.

Listen to yourself, he thought. *Energy. What the fuck? Be real.*

But they do say that, don't they? That focusing on something gives it energy, can make it real?

Yeah, idiots say that. Charlatans and hucksters say that. People like Freedom and Terrell.

He instantly felt bad for casting Terrell negatively. The kid tried, and although he hadn't really done anything himself, his connection to Abe certainly helped. There was no reason to badmouth him, or think poorly of him.

I need to be more charitable, or I will become a cranky, unlikable old hermit living alone in the woods.

He turned to look out the window. For a split second he expected to see a ghostly form there, raising a finger to scrape against the pane. The window was empty, and the starry night was beyond. It was both calming and frightening at the same time.

The fright will go away, he thought. *You won't always feel a stab of fear every time you look out a window. You love this house. You've known it from the beginning. Living in it will change things, will drive away whatever fright remains. There's nothing here now, no ghosts, no Ezra, no vestige of a war between two families. This house is clean!* He smiled at the *Poltergeist* reference, imagining the short medium uttering the words in her high-pitched voice; the more he thought about it, the more it made him chuckle. Robbie was asleep in his room down the hall, safe and sound. Here he was, lying in his bed, just as secure, everything in order.

Except, of course, the empty spot in the bed next to him.

She's never going to come here, he thought. *I'll get the call any day now, telling me we're through, she's with Ira. It's been inevitable for a long time, and it's almost here. Don't be a rube, don't be a naïve idiot. Don't be one of those people you've always felt sorry for.*

He closed his eyes.

Well, if she really doesn't want to be here, then it's for the best. If she doesn't love me – and I'm pretty sure she doesn't – then why would I want to prolong it? She won't try to take Robbie, I know she won't. She'll want visitation, but she won't push to have him live with her. He wouldn't want to, either.

Robbie is here, with me. That's as it should be.

And although I won't have her anymore, I have something better that I love just as much…maybe more…

This house.

He opened his eyes to look at the spot on the ceiling, waiting for the thump.

He waited a long time, finally drifting off to sleep.

From The Author

Nothing helps other readers discover my books more than word of mouth, and a review is absolutely the best way to make that happen. If you enjoyed this novel, would you help me out with a quick review? All reviews are valuable and greatly appreciated — more than you know, trust me!

I'm always working on a new title, and I'd like to email you when the next one is ready, so please join my private email list, and I'll send you a free River novella! I promise I won't pester you with emails, and I do NOT share my list with *anyone*, so you don't have to worry about that kind of crap. Visit: michaelrichan.com/ns

Coming soon:

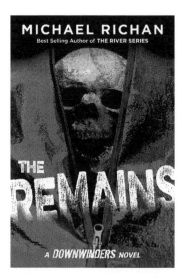

The Downwinders series continues with a new, chilling tale! Deem learns that a mortuary in town is sneaking bodies out a back door under the cover of darkness. Receive an email when this title is released by visiting: michaelrichan.com/ns

I enjoy hearing from my readers, and unless I'm off on vacation, you'll hear back from me. There's a lot of ways to reach me...here are a few:

Michael's website:
michaelrichan.com

Michael's Facebook:
www.facebook.com/michaelrichantheriver

Michael's Twitter:
@michaelrichan

Michael's Instagram:
www.instagram.com/michaelrichan

Michael's email:
michaelrichan@gmail.com

My favorite part of writing the "From The Author" section is where I get to thank my patrons!

Carol Tilson
Joy Steinmiller
Lauren Bingham
Sharon Barbour
Lori Coker
and my other patrons at Patreon.com

Thanks again, you awesome people! Your ongoing support keeps me writing.

I would love it if you'd consider becoming my patron. For as little as $3/month, you'll receive new titles before they're released on Amazon. More goodies at higher levels; cancel any time. I regularly share new ideas, upcoming book covers, and more with my patrons. Check it out at: www.patreon.com/michaelrichan

The Coldwater Haunting was my longest and most ambitious novel to date. I couldn't have published it without the aid and assistance of the following people, who played various roles in helping me cross the finish line:

Kym Miller
Carol Tilson
Joy Steinmiller
Don Gillespie
Jacque Taylor
Sherry Baker
Jessie Dean

My deepest gratitude to each of you, as well as the others who have assisted me on past books. I'm lucky to have people who so generously offer their time. Thank you!

Also, thanks to *you*, dear reader! Thank you for not only reading my book, but for making it this far in the "credits"! I know there's a lot to choose from out there, so I'm grateful you took the time to read my novel, and I hope you enjoyed it. It's always my goal to write something entertaining, and I hope I succeeded in some way.

Keep an eye out for the next one!

Suggested Reading Order
for The River Universe

Although *The Coldwater Haunting* is a stand-alone novel, many of Michael Richan's other books are parts of three series that make up The River Universe: *The River* series, *The Downwinders* series, and *The Dark River* series. It's easy enough to see the order of books in each of these series when browsing online, but since the storylines and characters weave between all three series, this Suggested Reading Order will help maximize your enjoyment. This Suggested Reading Order is updated regularly at the Author's Website (michaelrichan.com) as new titles appear.

You can absolutely read any of the three series on their own, but following the Suggested Reading Order will offer interesting insights between the events and characters.

Three books center on Eliza's early years prior to meeting Steven and Roy. These titles (*The Haunting of Pitmon House, The Haunting of Waverly Hall,* and *A Haunting in Wisconsin*) can all be read stand-alone.

The Coldwater Haunting and *Slaughter, Idaho* touch upon the River universe, where characters appear in other books, but the books truly "stand alone" and no knowledge of another book is needed. For example, Terrell and Abe, characters in *The Coldwater Haunting*, first appear in *The Cycle of the Shen*, although *The Coldwater Haunting* takes place long before the events of that book.

The School of Revenge is also stand-alone, and the only young adult title – so far.

The Suggested Reading Order for the books of The River Universe is:

1. *The Bank of the River* (THE RIVER series, Book 1)

2. *Residual* (THE RIVER series, Book 1a. It's a free novella, available at: michaelrichan.com/residual)

3. *A Haunting in Oregon* (THE RIVER series, Book 2)

4. *Ghosts of Our Fathers* (THE RIVER series, Book 3)

5. *Eximere* (THE RIVER series, Book 4)

6. *The Suicide Forest* (THE RIVER series, Book 5)

7. *Devil's Throat* (THE RIVER series, Book 6)

8. *Blood Oath, Blood River* (THE DOWNWINDERS series, Book 1)

9. *The Diablo Horror* (THE RIVER series, Book 7)

10. *The Impossible Coin* (THE DOWNWINDERS series, Book 2)

11. *The Haunting at Grays Harbor* (THE RIVER series, Book 8)

12. *The Graves of Plague Canyon* (THE DOWNWINDERS series, Book 3)

13. *It Walks At Night* (THE RIVER series, Book 9)

14. *A* (THE DARK RIVER series, Book 1)

15. *The Blackham Mansion Haunting* (THE DOWNWINDERS series, Book 4)

16. *The Cycle of the Shen* (THE RIVER series, Book 10)

17. *The Blood Gardener* (THE DARK RIVER series, Book 2)

18. *A Christmas Haunting at Point No Point* (THE RIVER series, Book 11)

19. *The Massacre Mechanism* (THE DOWNWINDERS series, Book 5)

20. *The Port of Missing Souls* (THE RIVER series, Book 12)

21. *The Nightmares of Quiet Grove* (THE DOWNWINDERS series, Book 6)

22. *Capricorn* (THE DARK RIVER series, Book 3)

23. *The Haunting of Johansen House* (THE RIVER series, Book 13)

24. *Evocation* (THE RIVER series, Book 14)

25. *Descent Into Hell Street* (THE DOWNWINDERS series, Book 7)

26. *The Remains* (THE DOWNWINDERS series, Book 8)

- - -